Review

If a story doesn't exhaust his imagination, Cibrario simply writes another novel to tell us what happens next. He did that with his four novels set in Nepal and does it again with "A Desperate Decision," which follows "Secrets on the Family Farm."

His current novel occurs five years later. The basic plot deals with Adam (now fifteen, not ten) who is in love with Naomi. The problem in the 1956 Midwestern milieu is that he's Catholic and she's Jewish, so the parents take a hard stand against the relationship.

The plot is complicated by an oath Adam took to become a priest, not to mention a mysterious murder, which gets national attention in the news.

As usual, the reader will be intensely anxious to get to the end of the novel to see how this romantic, yet unfortunate set of circumstances works out in southern Wisconsin.

Jim Fisher
Anthropologist
Carleton College

This book is a work of fiction. Although the Wisconsin setting and the location of the family farm are factual, including the historical events on radio broadcasts, the characters and their conversations are products of the author's imagination. Names, characters, and places are used fictitiously. Any resemblances to persons living or dead are coincidental.

ISBN-13: 978-1470191320
ISBN-10: 1470191326

Library of Congress Control Number
201390909036
Publisher: Createspace
North Charleston, SC 29418

Cover design: Kevin Flynn
Minuteman Press
Book Design: Geri Cibrario
Painting for cover: Dominic Cibrario

Dedication

I AM the Soul,

dwelling in all living beings,

O Conqueror of Sleep.

I AM the beginning, the middle

and the end of living beings.

The Bhagavad Gita 10:20

Other Novels

The Pomelo Tree (2004)

The Harvest (2005)

The Shamans (2006)

Secrets on the Family Farm (2008)

Murder in the Mountains (2011)

www.pomelotree.com

Acknowledgments

I am very grateful to my wife, Geri, who spent countless hours reading the manuscript; she offered me helpful suggestions for improving the dialogue of the characters and enhancing the plot. I want to thank John Brosseau for his insightful comments and patience while reading the drafts. I am grateful to Bill DeMark for his proofreading skill with meticulous attention to detail and clarification of ambiguities through research. I would like to thank Joe Sjostrom, a retired journalist from the Chicago Tribune, for his editorial assistance, and suggestions.

I'm grateful to Genevieve Sesto and Briton Road Press for the publication of my first novel and inspiring me to continue writing. I'm also indebted to Heather Bothe and Joe Schackelman for their useful comments during our monthly writer's meetings. I want to thank Doug Bingham for designing and maintaining my website and Jim Fisher for his fine review.

I'm indebted to Ganesh Narayan for his weekly lessons in Sanskrit and his wife, Usha, for introducing me to the *Bhagavad Gita*.

Lastly, I would like to thank the readers of my novels, former students, family, relatives, friends, acquaintances, and total strangers for their interest in my novels.

1

"I haven't seen Naomi
since we got out of school."

"Damn it!" shouted Adam, hurling his sketch pad onto the floor of the porch, which overlooked the orchard in the front yard. The loose pages flapped in the breeze like the wings of an injured bird.

The fifteen-year-old paced back and forth, frustrated by his unsuccessful attempts at capturing the image of Naomi from a photograph that she had given him on the last day of school, just before summer vacation.

Reaching for his sketch pad, Adam made a heroic effort to draw her face once more. A few minutes later he glanced at their dog, growling in the shade of an apple tree.

He was almost done with the sketch when he heard Crispy yelping from being hit by a stone. When another stone whizzed past him, the old mutt rose to his feet and snarled at the intruder coming up the rutted driveway with a slingshot in his hand.

"Neil, why the hell are you slinging stones at my dog?" he gasped as the long haired canine attacked his best friend.

The enraged beast, resembling a tawny lion, leapt at Neil sinking his teeth into his thigh and ripping his jeans.

"Get the fuck off of me!" screamed Neil, kicking the growling dog in the stomach.

Crispy howled, retreating to the shade of a pear tree

while Neil stared at the blood oozing from tooth marks on his leg.

"You should get rid of that vicious mutt. He's blind in one eye and can't see out of the other one," shouted Neil, covering the bite with his hand and limping toward the porch of the farmhouse.

"I'm not getting rid of him just because he's old and crippled. Come up here and sit down. I'll get something to stop the bleeding," said Adam, entering the house and hurrying to the medicine cabinet in the bathroom.

Neil struggled up the front steps, opened the screen door, and sat down on a wicker chair. He glanced around at a half dozen canvases of farm scenes.

Adam returned to the porch to administer first aid by washing Neil's wound and applying iodine.

"What the fuck are you doing? That stuff burns like hell," winced Neil, glaring at a painting of Old Lady Jacobsen's dilapidated barn with an axe and jagged saw hanging from the open door.

"What are you looking at?" asked Adam, putting on the bandage and securing it with adhesive tape.

"Your painting on the floor over there," said Neil. "I wish I had that axe to chop your dog's head off."

"Calm down for Christ's sake. You're not going to die from iodine. It'll stop stinging in a minute."

"Let me see what you're drawing," asked Neil.

Adam handed him the sketchbook with his unfinished drawing of Naomi.

"Wow! That looks just like her. I thought you'd be down at the beach with her, now that your mother isn't around to keep an eye on you."

"I haven't seen Naomi since we got out of school. Every time I call her, Mrs. Rosenberg answers the phone and tells me she's busy," said Adam, annoyed by a horsefly circling his head. He swiped at it with his hand, missing it.

"I've only seen Jennifer a couple of times this summer," said Neil. "How come you're not working in the garden?"

"I got up early to help Grandma with the chores. After breakfast I worked until noon, hoeing the sweet corn and picking four bushels of green beans."

"Where's your brother today?" asked Neil, inserting his slingshot into his back pocket.

"Karl drove Grandma to the Farmers' Market and stayed there until noon," said Adam. "When they finally got home, Grandma wanted me to take a couple hours off from work to sketch," said Adam. "She and Karl are picking strawberries right now."

Neil rose from the chair chewing a wad of bubble gum. He was wearing worn canvas shoes and faded jeans. His shaggy hair needed to be trimmed.

"Where's my transistor?" he asked, glancing toward the orchard, where the dog was sleeping.

"You left it on this side of the driveway," said Adam. "It's over there next to the cherry tree."

"I'll get it," said Neil, dashing down the steps. A few minutes later he returned with the portable radio dangling

11

from his right hand, playing Elvis' hit song, *Jailhouse Rock*. After glancing at his watch, he flicked the dial, pausing to listen to the news.

Good afternoon. This is Bill Schroeder from WLIP in downtown Kenosha with the 2:00 pm news on this sunny Wednesday during the second week of June.

A Roman Catholic priest, Alfredo Boshi, has stated that boxing is sinful and the sport is a violation of the Fifth Commandment, 'Thou shalt not kill.' He claims that professional boxing is immoral and illicit because it produces serious injuries, which can lead to death.

Not only has Boshi been known to attack boxing, but he has been against football and hockey because they cause permanent brain injuries.

"What the fuck is that priest talking about? Everything's a mortal sin these days," said Neil, snapping off his radio. "I'm gonna be a boxer with the Golden Gloves someday."

"My dad used to take my brother and me to see the boxing matches at Spetzman's Tap on Friday nights" said Adam, watching Neil, who was punching the air.

"What the hell's wrong with you? You look like you've just come home from a funeral," asked Neil.

"I'm pissed at my mother for leaving us to go on vacation for two weeks. She took off after Sunday mass on the train with my little sister, Marie, to visit her priest friend, Father Fortmann, in New York City.

"He promised to show them the sites because my mom always wanted to see Times Square, the Empire State

Building, and the Statue of Liberty," said Adam.

"You mean she went to visit that priest from St. George's? He said the requiem mass when your cousin, Kevin, committed suicide." said Neil.

"That's him all right," said Adam, taking a deep breath."That priest caused our family a hell of a lot of trouble five years ago. My father hates the bastard."

Adam told Neil that his father didn't go on vacation with his mother because he had to work at Nash Motors. His dad never said a single word to his mom as he drove them to the North Shore Station.

He didn't even kiss her goodbye or carry her suitcase when she boarded the train with Marie trailing after her. His sister cried the whole time because she wanted to stay home with their father.

"If that was my old man, he would have killed my mother for taking off like that," said Neil.

"Once the train left the station, we headed straight for Spetzman's Tap at the Four Corners. I spent the whole afternoon in the bar watching him get drunk after being sober for five years. My dad cursed my mother all the way home from the bar," said Adam, his fists clenched.

"My drunken father swerved the Plymouth into the opposite lane several times while I prayed to the Virgin Mary to spare our lives. My prayers were answered when we finally got home without crashing the car or going into the ditch," he said.

Adam remembered when he was ten years old during

the summer of 1951. It was when his father crashed their red truck in Old Lady Jacobsen's orchard. His dad nearly bled to death before the ambulance took him to Kenosha Memorial Hospital where he stayed for two weeks with a concussion and a collapsed lung. At that time his mother threatened to divorce him if went back to drinking.

"Why the hell are you staring into space like that?" asked Neil. "You've been acting weird today."

"What did you say?" asked Adam, confessing that his mother had been nagging his father for years. She quarreled with him for going to AA meetings after work at the Alano Club, claiming he wasn't home enough to help with chores.

"After being exhausted from overwork my mother finally called Father Fortmann long distance and told him she was coming to New York for a vacation."

"My Mom tried to leave my dad by seeing a lawyer and filing for a divorce, but her brothers told her that no one from the O'Connor family has ever been divorced," said Neil, pacing up and down on the porch.

"I use to see you with Jennifer every Friday night at the school dances," said Adam, changing the subject.

"Jennifer's a good friend of Naomi. They're always together like Siamese twins," said Neil, pausing to listen to *Don't be Cruel* on the radio.

"Adam, let me see the rest of your paintings. Hey, that's a really nice picture you made of Old Lady Jacobsen's windmill with the horse grazing in the pasture."

"Neil, come with me to the garden. I'm going to bring a

14

pitcher of lemonade to Grandma and Karl," said Adam, feeling thirsty from the heat.

"How can ya drink that shit?"asked Neil.

"It's because we ran out of Kool-Aid," said Adam. "Neil, I thought you disappeared from the face of the earth. I haven't seen you all week. What's happening?"

"I've been helping my old man put a transmission in that fuckin' junk heap of his," he said, setting down the radio on the planks of the porch.

Neil extracted a pack of Lucky Strikes from his shirt pocket and lit a cigarette. It bobbed up and down from his lips while he talked, reminding Adam of Humphrey Bogart smoking in *The African Queen.*

"Don't be chicken. Take one," insisted Neil, offering him the pack.

"Ok," agreed Adam, removing a bent cigarette.

"Hey man, what the fuck are you doing?" said Neil handing him a book of matches. "You've got the end of yours all wet!"

Neil held his cigarette between his index finger and thumb, inhaling deeply and then exhaling a narrow stream of smoke. He laughed at Adam puffing and coughing from the cloud of smoke enshrouding his head.

"You're never going to learn to smoke if you don't practice," criticized Neil, tilting his head back like a rooster drinking water and puffing smoke rings into the air.

After finishing his cigarette, Neil pitched the butt into the lawn, where it smoldered. "Are we gonna hang around here all day or are we going swimming in Kaplin's Pond?"

"Let's go swimming. I'll tell Grandma we're going so she won't worry."

"Don't be an asshole," blurted Neil. "The problem with you is you're too damn honest. Just tell her you're coming to my house to help me work on the car.

"My old man would beat me until I was black and blue with a razor strap if he found out I went swimming this afternoon", said Neil turning the dial back to the news.

Ironically, Khrushchev promotes de-Stalinization within the U.S.S.R because of the brutal massacre of political prisoners...Martin Luther King continues to campaign for desegregation of the south, finding strong support within the Negro churches...Fidel Castro is still struggling to completely overthrow the Batista regime.

"For Christ's sake, turn on some music," said Adam, leaving him on the porch and heading toward the garden. Neil flipped the dial to the medley of Elvis' songs.

16

2

"Let's get the hell out of here," shouted Neil, dashing across the pasture...

Adam charged past the garage and the chicken coop. He opened the garden gate, shouting, "Grandma, I'm going over to Neil's for a while."

Sophia Montanya removed her straw hat, dabbing the perspiration from her wrinkled forehead with a white handkerchief.

"I worry about you keeping company with that Neil O'Connor," she shouted from the strawberry patch.

"What do you mean? He's been my best friend ever since we were in first grade at Whittier School."

"His mother, Marjorie, tells me he gets into trouble because he walks on a-the desks."

"That happened last year when we were in eighth grade. Neil wasn't just walking on them, but jumped from desk to desk like a monkey. He entertained the class until Mrs. Schwartz came back into the room. Suddenly it was so quiet you could hear a pin drop.

"She whacked Neil across the mouth, making him stay inside for recess and write on the chalk board a hundred times, 'I will not jump on the desks,'" said Adam.

"That Neil, he makes me nervous. He don't tell a-the truth to everybody."

"He's not such a bad guy just because he got into

17

trouble at school," said Karl, standing up in the strawberry patch and revealing his bare chest and muscular arms.

"Neil's settled down quite a bit this past year at Lincoln Jr. High. He never used foul language when we had lunch with Jennifer and Naomi," said Adam. "They live next to each other in Allendale."

"Naomi's Jewish," said Karl.

"She invited me to come to the Beth Hillel Temple for the Sabbath with her family," said Adam.

"I went out on a date with Sarah Weisman, a Jewish girl," said Karl. "She tried to talk me into going to college. When I told her I'm planning to go to technical school to become a mechanic, she wouldn't go out with me again."

"Karl, you go to college like that Jew girl tells you," added Grandma. "Adam goes to college to be an artist like Michelangelo."

"What's wrong with being an auto mechanic?" asked Karl scowling. "I get straight A's in math and science without even studying."

"Not everybody has to go to college," said Adam, turning toward Neil shuffling up the driveway with his radio in one hand and sling shot in the other.

"How many pictures did you make today?" asked Grandma, complaining about the heat.

"I did a sketch of Naomi and it turned out OK, but the blue jay needs some work."

"These bugs drive me crazy," said Grandma, slapping a mosquito that landed on the back of her neck.

"Hey, Michelangelo, get us some insect repellent from the medicine cabinet," said Karl. "When you come back you can draw Grandma Moses here, swatting mosquitoes in the strawberry patch."

"I don't like that joke," snapped Grandma, watching Adam disappear into the house. She turned her head when she heard the rooster squawking and running toward the chicken coop with alarmed hens following him.

"Neil! You come over here!" shouted Grandma, angry because he was slinging stones at the chickens.

Neil shoved the sling shot into his back pocket and snapped off the radio. His shirt was unbuttoned and his ripped Levis hung from his hips without a belt. He approached Grandma, who was coming out of the garden with a case of strawberries.

"You take these to your mother, Marjorie," insisted Grandma, handing him a carton overflowing with ripe strawberries. "What's she doing today?"

"She's scrubbing and waxing the floors of some rich bitch...I mean woman, living in a mansion along Lake Michigan," said Neil.

"Your mama, she works too hard," sighed Grandma. "How's your papa doing?"

"My dad's working overtime in the barber shop. He comes home every night mad as a hornet," said Neil, expecting Grandma to scold him for scaring the chickens with his sling shot.

"Next time you come here, you don't shoot my chickens

with stones," said Grandma, noticing his torn jeans and the protruding bandage. "What happened to your leg?"

Neil didn't answer her but pointed to a crow that had landed on a fence post near the cow pasture.

"I'll be damned... I mean darned. If that ain't the biggest crow I've ever seen!"

While he was waiting for more criticism from Grandma, he glanced at Adam coming toward them with the insect repellant, and a tray with glasses of lemonade.

"What are you guys looking at?" asked Adam, heading toward the shade of the maple tree.

"It's a big crow," said Grandma, informing them that when she and Grandpa bought the farm in 1936, there were flocks of crows landing in the cornfield and dozens of pheasants during hunting season.

While his grandmother sipped her lemonade, Adam called his brother to join them from the garden.

Karl came toward them, dripping with sweat. He wiped the perspiration from his brow with his forearm and reached for a glass of lemonade, gulping it down.

After setting his glass on the tray, Karl picked up the mosquito repellent and splashed it on his chest and arms.

Grandma and Adam drank their lemonade, but Neil scowled as if it were poison, refusing the drink.

"I don't care much for lemonade, but these strawberries look real good," he said, removing a stem and popping a strawberry into his mouth.

"You must be hungry," said Grandma, watching Neil

gobble down another berry and reach for more.

"C'mon, Adam," said Neil, "Let's get going or we'll never get my old man's car started."

"I'll come with you," suggested Karl. "I could fix that old Dodge in a half hour."

"Oh, I forgot. My old man drove that jalopy to work this morning," said Neil, averting his eyes from Karl's.

"What are you guys really gonna do this afternoon?" asked Karl, scratching his chest.

"My dad wants me to clean the garage and Adam's gonna help me," insisted Neil.

"Karl, you go now and dig a-the potatoes for the market tomorrow," insisted Grandma, rubbing the repellent on her arms and legs.

"I'll see you later," said Adam, leaving his brother and grandmother standing in the shade of the maple tree.

The two boys hurried down the tree-lined driveway toward the sun-drenched road. Neil continued to devour the strawberries as they headed west down Bentz Road, pitching the empty carton into the ditch. He paused to fill his pockets with gravel from alongside the road.

"What are you doing with those stones?" asked Adam.

"I'm gonna throw them at those fuckin' cows, grazing on the other side of that barbed wire fence, stupid. The fastest way to Kaplin's Pond is to cut through old man Jalinksi's pasture, but his cows are mean sons of bitches."

Ignoring the no trespassing signs, the boys scrambled under the barbed wire fence. They strolled through the

21

pasture where dandelions were still blossoming although most of them had gone to seed.

In the pasture thirty Holstein cows were grazing while another half dozen were lying down chewing their cuds near clumps of wild daisies.

As they approached the herd, Neil wasn't paying attention where he was walking. As he stepped into fresh cow manure, his tennis shoe made a squishing noise.

"Son of a bitch!" he shouted, removing his shoe and wiping it on the grass. "Christ! That cow shit stinks!"

After putting on his shoe, he aimed his slingshot and struck a cow on the back. She jumped and shrugged her coat, glancing toward them.

Neil hurled more stones at the cows, creating a restless movement among the herd. Finally he hit a calf, which bawled loudly. The mother lowered her head, and charged them with her udder swaying like a pendulum.

"Let's get the hell out of here!" shouted Neil, dashing across the pasture with Adam trailing behind him. They just managed to avert the tips of the cow's horns by slithering under the fence.

Safe on the other side, Neil picked up a clod of dirt and hurled it at the agitated cow. He shouted, "Get out of here you fuckin' bitch!"

The clod struck her back and crumbled, leaving the snorting cow pacing behind the fence which separated the pasture from the cornfield. Moments later she returned to the herd, where her calf was waiting to nurse from her swollen udder.

Adam and Neil hurried through the rows of corn with green stalks promising to be knee high by the Fourth of July. They noticed a red-winged black bird, soaring across the corn field into the pasture, where the herd was now grazing quietly.

The teenagers crossed into a newly planted field of soybeans with green leaves protruding from the black earth. Numerous killdeer darted down the cultivated rows warning others with plaintive cries about the arrival of the intruders. In the distance mounds of earth surrounded the pond like reclining camels.

3

"Neil! For Christ's sake! Don't panic! I'll tow you to shore. Grab my hand."

At last Adam and Neil reached the pond, which was half the size of a football field. The branches of the quaking aspen trees stretched toward the water offering shade while their roots clung to the bank among green cattails.

As the boys stripped themselves of their clothing, they noticed the reflections of their nude bodies and the branches of the trees in the rippling water.

Standing naked in front of Adam, Neil asked, "Have you ever fucked a girl?"

"No," said Adam, feeling uneasy. The last time they swam together Neil teased him for wearing his underwear because he was afraid someone might see his dick.

"You ought to try it sometime," advised Neil, glancing at his reflection in the water.

"Have you been having sex with Jennifer?"

"No, Jennifer's parents would kill me if I kissed her in front of them. She's not that kind of girl. Her whole family's very religious. They're the kind of people who wouldn't say shit if they had a mouthful. I've been dating somebody else too," said Neil.

"I've never been out with Naomi alone. Her parents, the Rosenbergs, used to chaperone the dances every Friday night in the gym. They watched us like hawks the whole evening, making sure we didn't sneak out of the building to make out in the park," said Adam.

"You mean you and Naomi haven't ever been on a date alone?" asked Neil. "That's too bad."

"Naomi's parents are real nice. They always gave me a ride home after the dances in their Cadillac convertible. Her family goes to the synagogue every Friday. They want me to join them for the Sabbath sometime at the temple."

"Jennifer's parents invited me to go to Sunday mass with them at St. Mary's two weeks in a row," said Neil.

"Who have you've been seeing behind her back?" asked Adam, shaking his head.

"It's Juanita. She lives with her family in that shack behind the Colonial Inn in the woods," he said.

"They're migrant workers who come to plant cabbage and tomatoes every spring and harvest them in the fall. They go back to Mexico for the winter," said Adam.

"I've been meeting Juanita on Saturday night at Colonial Inn because they show free outdoor movies. I always bring a blanket and buy her popcorn and soda at the concession stand.

"She's already sixteen and doesn't know much English. She can hardly write her name, but she fucks like a mink. You ought to come with me and meet her younger sister, Margarita. She's real pretty."

Adam knew Neil was lying about Juanita. He had been to the outdoor movies with Karl. They saw Neil sitting on the blanket next to Juanita. Her sister and parents sat right behind them throughout the whole show.

"Well, are we gonna talk all afternoon or are we going for a swim?" asked Neil, wading into the shallow water through lily pads.

The mud oozed between his toes and sucked at his feet. When he was knee deep in the water, he turned around to see if Adam was following him.

Adam was standing on the bank mesmerized by the cloud formations in the sky. His muscular body resembled Michelangelo's statue of David.

"Hey, Adam! Come into the water!" shouted Neil. "Are you waiting for an angel to come from heaven with a message for you?"

"You'd better be careful because of that dog bite. You don't want to get an infection," warned Adam.

While swimming toward Neil, he recalled how his parents used to take him and Karl in their Nash to the movies behind the Colonial Inn during the summer when they were kids. That's when his mom and dad were still getting along and his father wasn't going to the bar every night after work and coming home drunk.

The grassy area was packed with cars on Saturday night with parents sitting in their vehicles while their children sat on blankets in front of the big screen.

The free movies were usually in black and white. The children enjoyed films with Abbott and Costello or Roy Rogers and Dale Evans. However their parents preferred, *Dr. Jekyll and Mr. Hyde* or *Casablanca.* Once in a while they'd all watch a colored film like *The Wizard of Oz*.

"Neil, you're lying about having sex with Juanita because Karl used to date her. They made out in the backseat of our car a couple of times until her sister told her parents they were having sex.

"Juanita's father, Pedro, went crazy like an enraged bull. He beat Juanita until she was black and blue for going out with Karl. She had lied to her father about going to her girlfriend's house to study English.

"Pedro Gonzales drove like a maniac to their farm in his rusty truck, carrying a shotgun and shouting in Spanish that his daughter was pregnant. My dad understood everything because Spanish is almost like Italian. Pedro wanted my mom to call a priest to marry them."

While swimming beside Neil, Adam said that his father bribed Pedro to delay the wedding by giving him a gallon of homemade wine. He explained that it would be better to wait for a month rather than jump to a conclusion about Juanita being pregnant.

"Then what happened?" asked Neil, almost out of breath from swimming so fast.

"My dad was mad at Karl for dating Juanita although my brother swore that he never had sex with her. He wouldn't let him go out on any more dates for a month.

"Every morning he dropped Karl off at Bradford High School before he went to work and picked him up after football practice in the evening.

"Pedro came back in a month and told my dad Juanita

wasn't pregnant because she had her period, and the doctor told him that she was still a virgin. He threatened to send her back to Mexico if she ever had sex with anyone before she was married."

As they swam side by side Neil asked, "Did your old man finally let Karl use the car again?"

Adam said his brother could use the car to go out on dates, providing he bought condoms from behind the counter at Bernacchi's Drug Store.

"My mother was furious when she found a condom in Karl's jeans while empting his pockets before doing the laundry. She blamed my father for encouraging Karl to have premarital sex, which is a mortal sin," said Adam.

Neil swam ahead on his back toward the center of the pond. He shouted, "The water's real cool here."

Adam swam toward him, noticing the sudden change of temperature and that he couldn't touch bottom with his feet. In the distance he saw Neil diving underwater, surfacing and then diving again. He was alarmed when he heard him shouting.

"My legs! My legs!" gasped Neil, thrashing with his arms, churning the water, and attempting to swim but scarcely moving.

"What's wrong?" yelled Adam.

"Help me! Help me!" shouted Neil, his arms flailing.

"What's the matter?" asked Adam, gliding toward him.

"Cramps! I've got fuckin' cramps!" he shouted, going under and then surfacing.

"Neil! For Christ's sake! Don't panic! I'll tow you to shore. Grab my hand."

As Adam extended his arm, Neil seized it, lunging forward and dragging him underwater. He clung to Adam with the weight of his body pressing against him as they both surfaced, coughing. Neil's arms were like tentacles wrapped around Adam, pulling them both under. Realizing that Neil was drowning him, Adam punched him in the ribs, but he wouldn't release his grip from around his neck. When they surfaced the second time together gasping, Adam hit Neil in the face with his fist.

Neil fell backward while Adam treaded water choking and spitting out the water. When he finally could breathe normally, Adam noticed that he was no longer in sight.

Adam dove underwater searching for him and located his body suspended in a fetal position near the bottom. Seizing Neil by the hair, he pulled him to the surface. After cupping his hand under his friend's jaw, Adam swam, towing his motionless body to shore.

Adam dragged Neil out of the water onto the muddy bank, and gave him artificial respiration. He crossed Neil's arms, placing them on his chest. Kneeling down, he pressed his rib cage and then lifted the elbows, forcing the water trapped in his lungs to flow from his mouth. He repeated the process several times.

Fear overwhelmed Adam, since there was no sign that Neil was breathing. His own body tensed as he tried to revive him. The tears flowed down Adam's cheeks as he glanced toward the sky, crying out, "Help me, God! Please save Neil!"

Adam sobbed, choking on his salty tears as he hovered over the body of his best friend. He recited the Lord's Prayer, pressing on Neil's chest and lifting his elbows over and over again.

He was terrified that Neil was dead and cried out again, "Help me God. If you save Neil, I'll become a priest!"

Exhausted from his struggle to revive him, Adam was about to give up when he heard a moan. He stared at the rising and falling of his rib cage, indicating Neil was breathing again.

"Thank God. You're alive," blurted Adam, weeping as he lifted Neil. He held him in his arms as if he had just removed the body of Christ from the cross at Golgotha.

Neil's eyes opened slowly; they were distant and vacuous. He shivered from a chill, glancing upward at the aspen leaves wavering in the summer breeze.

"What the fuck are you doing?" he gasped, groaning. "I feel like I've been run over by a truck. Why are you kneeling next to me naked? You ain't queer, are you?"

"No!" blurted Adam, flushing with embarrassment and backing away upon releasing him.

"What happened to me?" gasped Neil, still shaking from the cold. He made a futile attempt to get up.

"You almost drowned, you stupid bastard. You tried to pull me underwater with you."

30

"No shit. My jaw hurts," uttered Neil, shivering. He told Adam that he didn't remember anything about drowning, but recalled going into the pond and swimming toward the middle where the water was cold.

Neil rolled over on his side. "Adam, get me a cigarette. They're next to my radio."

Adam scrambled up the bank and returned with the Lucky Strikes, the radio, and their clothes. He removed two cigarettes, lighting one for Neil and another for himself. Adam once again began coughing from the smoke.

"You ain't never gonna learn to smoke right," said Neil with a sheepish smile. "Why don't you put on some fuckin' clothes? This ain't the Sistine Chapel, Michelangelo."

Adam turned red from shame, putting on his underwear, jeans, and shirt and then handing Neil his clothes.

"Christ! I feel like I swallowed a rock," said Neil, taking a few puffs, coughing, and snuffing out his cigarette.

Propping himself up on his elbow, Neil snapped on the portable radio; he paused to listen to the song, *The Poor People of Paris* and then turned on the news.

Joseph Albers, a teacher, is exhibiting his paintings at Yale University. They are complicated geometrical designs of cubes within squares. Albers studied in Germany and became a teacher at the Bauhaus, where he worked with Kandinsky and Paul Klee. When Hitler shut down the art school, Albers came to America and eventually to Yale.

He encourages his students to focus upon art's basic elements, favoring intellect over emotion...

31

"I don't want to hear about art work," complained Neil, reaching for the radio.

"Don't change the dial. Leave it. It's interesting to me." insisted Adam, continuing to listen to the news.

Bradbury got his ideas about book-burning in his novel "Fahrenheit 451" from Hitler, who ordered the Nazis to burn books by the thousands to control the thinking of his people. Although Germany is free today, the Soviet Union is not...The price of economic progress in the U.S.S.R. is the total suppression of human liberties.

"I've had enough news," said Neil, turning off the radio. "What the fuck. There's a war going on right in my own house between my dad and mom."

"My parents are constantly fighting too. My dad hasn't been the same since he returned from the war," said Adam.

"My old man fought in World War II, but he never talks about it. He keeps it all inside and then when he comes home drunk he's ready to kill us," said Neil.

"I hate the son of a bitch when he comes home with the razor strap from his barber shop and starts swinging at us with it. He's tried to kill my mom a couple of times."

"When my dad was drunk, he tried to kill my mom with a rifle," said Adam.

"My uncle came home shell shocked," said Neil. "He's at the Veterans Hospital in Milwaukee and just sits there all day in a wheelchair staring into space."

After resting for a half hour, Adam helped Neil up from the muddy bank. They put on their shoes and departed,

32

weaving through the fields toward their homes. Their progress was slow because Neil stumbled frequently and had to rest at regular intervals. Eventually they crawled under the final barbed wire fence near Neil's house on the south side of Bentz Road.

"Come over to my place and rest for a while before you go home," said Adam.

"No, I can't! My old man will be home from work in a little while. He always wants us to be in the house for dinner when he walks in the door."

"I'll explain to your mom about you almost drowning in the pond," said Adam.

"No you won't! Don't say a word to anybody about what happened! If my old man found out I almost drowned, he'd kill me!" insisted Neil.

"Look at those doves sitting next to each other on the electric wire between the telephone poles," said Adam, noticing Neil pick up a stone from alongside the road.

Instead of aiming at the birds, Neil gazed at the stone in his right hand and his slingshot in the left. He glanced up at the doves and then dropped the stone to the ground and inserted the slingshot into his back pocket.

"Now I remember having cramps in my legs. I tried to hang onto you, but I pulled us both under water. You hit me in the face, you bastard! My jaw still hurts, but you saved my life," said Neil.

"I didn't save you, it was God who did it," said Adam.

4

"You made a desperate decision under great stress."

During dinner that evening, Adam was quiet. He was disturbed by Neil almost drowning and his promise to become a priest. Staring at his vegetable soup, he sat at the kitchen table with his grandmother, Karl, and his father, Giovanni. They were all in a good mood because his dad had gone through treatment for a week and had quit drinking. He told them that he wanted to attend the evening AA meeting at the Alano Club in downtown Kenosha.

Adam was burdened and depressed, not wanting to betray Neil's confidence by telling his family about what happened at the pond.

"What did Neil's mama say about the strawberries?" asked his grandmother, reaching for the salad bowl.

"I guess she liked them," said Adam. "I really don't know because she was at work."

"I've never see you so quiet," said Giovanni. "Did you and Neil get into a fight?"

"No," said Adam, glancing down at his soup that was already cold. "I...I really don't feel well. Do you mind if I go to my room?"

"You go lay down," said Sophia Montanya. "When you come back, I warm your spaghetti on a- the stove."

Adam rose from the table and left the kitchen, heading

34

for the bedroom that he shared with Karl.

"Giovanni, something happens to Adam today. He looks so pale," said Grandma.

"You're right," said Karl. "He probably went swimming with Neil at Kaplin's Pond. There's a lot of mud on his shoes in the hallway."

"I'm gonna go talk to him," said his father, rising from the table.

"There's something wrong with him," said Grandma.

Giovanni left the kitchen and knocked on the closed door of the bedroom.

"Come in," said Adam, sitting on the side of the bed. He was hunched over with his elbows on his thighs and his hands cupped under his chin.

As soon as his father entered the room, Adam stood up alongside the bed.

"You don't have to get up," said Giovanni, scratching the stubble of his heavy beard. "I better shave before going to my meeting tonight."

Adam sat down on the bed and glanced out the window at the walnut tree. It soared between two huge maples, obscuring the grandeur of the sunset.

"What's the matter, Son?" asked his father, sitting down next to him on the bed. He reached for his cigarettes, but decided not to smoke.

"Neil and I went for a long walk today," he said, hesitant to tell his dad about his friend almost drowning.

"Karl noticed that you had mud on your shoes. He said

you guys went swimming at the pond," said Giovanni, heading toward the window. "I've never seen such a sunset. I bet you could paint one just like it."

"Neil almost drowned in the pond today. He got cramps in his legs. I tried to help him, but he almost dragged me underwater a couple of times. I finally hit him in the jaw, so he'd let go of his grip on me. I didn't realize that I knocked him out," blurted Adam.

He continued telling his father about diving underwater and finding Neil unconscious before towing him to shore.

"I dragged Neil out of the water and gave him artificial respiration, but I couldn't resuscitate him. I tried over and over again, thinking he was dead.

"I prayed to God to save him, promising I'd become a priest, if He spared Neil's life. Sure enough Neil started breathing again," said Adam, his eyes moist with tears.

"I knew something was troubling you," said his father, giving his son a hug.

"If Neil had died, it would've been my fault."

"I'm proud of you for saving Neil's life. You should feel good about that, not depressed."

"Please don't say anything to Grandma or Karl about this," pleaded Adam. "Neil would be very upset if his parents found out he nearly drowned. His father would probably beat him with a razor strap."

"I won't say a word to anybody about Neil, not even his father. Patrick puts in a lot of extra hours at the barber shop. He also mows people's lawns in the summer and plows out their driveways in winter. He never has any time for himself."

"I used to see him regularly at Spetzman's Tap on Sunday morning. That's the only day of the week that Patrick wasn't working so he'd get rip roaring drunk."

"Maybe that's why Neil's afraid of him along with the rest of his family," said Adam

He recalled when his dad came home drunk and tried to kill his mother with a rifle. Instead he accidently shot their cow, Savoya. Adam escaped with his mother, brother, and grandmother in their Plymouth. His father followed them in the truck shooting at them, trying to run them off the road.

"By the way, I got a postcard from your mother and Marie in today's mail. It came all the way from New York," said Giovanni.

"When's she coming home?"

"I'm not sure because I didn't bother to read it," said his father. "I left it on the kitchen table."

"Adam, I'm sure God doesn't expect you to keep your promise to become a priest. You made a desperate decision, under great stress. You were worried that Neil would die, but he didn't."

"God saved his life, not me," insisted Adam. "I'm confused. Nothing's the same anymore. I haven't heard from Naomi since school let out."

"You're changing, Adam. You're not a boy anymore. You're growing into a young man. Come with me to the kitchen and get something to eat."

When they returned to the table, Adam noticed that Grandma was washing the dishes at the sink, and Karl was drying them.

"I warm up the spaghetti and meat balls for you," said Grandma, wiping her hands on her apron and returning to light the gas stove with a wooden match.

"Hurry up and eat, or we'll miss the *Groucho Marx Show*," said Karl.

"I better get going," announced Giovanni, glancing at the rooster clock above the sink and heading toward the door. "It's already 7:30, and my AA meeting starts at 8:00 o'clock sharp."

Adam sat down at the kitchen table waiting for his grandmother to heat his dinner. A few minutes later Karl left to turn on the TV set in the living room.

5

"She dragged his corpse to the orchard and buried him next to the dead horse."

For the next few days Adam got up early to help Grandma milk the cows and feed the animals. After breakfast he weeded and hoed the garden.

His brother Karl drove Grandma to the Farmers' Market each day to sell vegetables at different locations in the city of Kenosha. After helping Grandma unload the truck and set up her stand, Karl went to work at the Mobile Station on Highway 50.

Karl left at noon to pick up Grandma from the market. Upon returning to the farm, he unloaded the truck before going back to work.

After lunch Grandma was so exhausted from selling vegetables at the market, she would take a nap on the couch in the dining room.

While she rested, Adam sketched and painted on the porch until two o'clock before returning to the garden with Grandma to pick vegetables for the next day's market. In the evening they would wash the produce and then load it on the truck.

Neil remained aloof for nearly a week before arriving one afternoon.

"Adam, what the fuck are you painting?" he shouted, sauntering up the driveway wearing Levis without a belt.

"I'm painting Naomi in the pasture," said Adam, standing behind his easel on the porch. "I thought you disappeared from the face of the earth. What have you been doing lately?"

"You always ask the same stupid ass question," said Neil, coming up the steps of the porch. "I've been takin' care of my younger brother and sister all week while my old lady's at work. She finally had a day off. I helped her do the laundry and clean the fuckin' house this morning.

"For Christ's sake, don't you ever get tired of painting Naomi?" asked Neil. "I like her standing between the cow and the calf, but you don't have a rusty hay rake in your pasture. That ain't your barn either.

"I'll be damned. It's Old Lady Jacobsen's place. Let's go over there and have a look at those empty buildings while your grandmother's taking her nap. We haven't been there for five years," insisted Neil.

"I like those gnarled apple trees in her orchard. They remind me of Vincent Van Gogh's paintings," said Adam.

Neil told him that when Old Lady Jacobsen died her son, Fred, who was a sailor at Naval Station Great Lakes in Illinois, came home for the funeral.

"I went to Piasecki Funeral Home to see her with my grandma," said Adam. "Don't you remember? You were there with your mom."

Neil recalled going to pay his respect to the deceased. When he arrived at the funeral home, there wasn't a soul around except for Fred wearing a black suit with a bow tie and his girlfriend in a low cut red dress.

There were no flowers except for a dozen roses in a vase next to the coffin. Old Lady Jacobsen was wrinkled like a prune, but her white hair had been washed and combed. She was wearing a blue velvet dress with a string of pearls. and looked better dead than she ever did alive.

Fred got permission from the county to bury his mother in the apple orchard right next to the dead horse with the broken leg. After the burial Fred boarded up the house and padlocked the doors, but he left the barn and the sheds unlocked.

"There used to be an old broken-down tractor, rusted farm machinery, and all kinds of saws and tools in that barn," said Neil.

"Old Lady Jacobsen came to our house to use our bathtub every fall," said Adam. "She would remind my grandma to come and help her make apple sauce in her basement before the apples rotted in the orchard."

"That old hag always wore clothes made from feed bags and picked lice from her hair, crushing them with her fingernails," added Neil. "She'd stink like a sewer. You could smell her a mile away."

"In the spring she'd come to our house again to use our bathtub," said Adam. "It took us a week to fumigate the bathroom once she left."

"The neighbors used to say her place was haunted," said Neil, watching Adam clean his brushes with turpentine and wipe them with a cloth.

"I'll leave a note for my grandmother in the kitchen," said Adam, turning toward the door to the living room.

"What the fuck's wrong with you? Do you have to tell your grandma every time you take a shit? We'll be back before she wakes up from her nap. Let's get going right now," insisted Neil.

Adam and Neil hurried down the driveway, heading west until they came to the creek where a culvert carried the water under Bentz Road.

They paused to watch leopard frogs plunge into the water and swim toward the bottom, where crayfish scurried out of their way. In the distance a bullfrog surfaced unfurling its tongue to catch mosquitoes.

"Those dragonflies look like miniature helicopters," said Adam, watching them disappear into the cattails.

Neil hurled a stone into the motionless creek, which produced circular waves like yawning mouths.

"Let's get going," he insisted, removing a paperback novel from his back pocket. "No use hanging around here all day."

"What have you been reading?" asked Adam, crossing the road with Neil and approaching Old Lady Jacobsen's property.

"It's *Peyton Place,*" announced Neil, opening the novel. He explained the scandalous story to Adam, pausing to read a few lurid passages, which he had marked by dog-earing the pages.

When they reached the 40 acres of land surrounded by a

barbed wire fence that stretched all the way to Cooper Road, Neil put the novel away to crawl under the fence.

"Son of a bitch!" shouted Neil, angry because he snagged his jeans on the barbed wire. Reaching down, he tore them loose.

After crossing the fence, they jogged through the hay field, not stopping until they came to the orchard, where green apples clung to gnarled branches.

Neil snatched an apple and bit into it. "What the fuck! It's bitter," he gasped, spitting it out.

In the orchard the weeds and grass were so thick that it caused them to stumble as they searched for Old Lady Jacobsen's grave.

"Look over there! It's her tombstone, covered with weeds. It's next to the pit where her old horse was buried," said Adam,

The teenagers headed toward the gravestone and pulled away the weeds. They read the name engraved on the headstone: Beloved Mother, Martha Anne Jacobsen, Born, July 18 1857, Died, Dec. 7, 1954.

There were also rumors that Mrs. Jacobsen had murdered her husband and his parents and left them in the shed all winter. Nobody ever found their corpses. People thought that she buried them somewhere in the orchard in the spring.

"That's what everybody says," agreed Neil, reaching for the crumpled pack of cigarettes in his shirt pocket. He removed two cigarettes and handed one to Adam. "Do you

"Do you wanna hear the real story about the horse?"

"Sure," agreed Adam, not inhaling to avoid coughing. He heard the story before, but each time Neil told it, he added more details.

"Well, Old Lady Jacobsen was getting' up there in years, and she didn't take care of her fuckin' cows and horse any more. Mr. Gascoigne, who lived across the street from her, used to come over and feed and water them for her, until he got pneumonia.

"So nobody came around to help the old bitch out anymore. The cow went dry because she didn't bother to milk her, and the horse nearly starved to death in the barn, over there." said Neil, pointing to the dilapidated building

"It was the coldest winter we ever had in Wisconsin. That was four years ago before she went to the nursing home in Illinois."

"Old Lady Jacobsen came over to Mr. Gascoigne's house and knocked on his door. He answered, wearing his bathrobe because he was still recovering from pneumonia; she told him that her horse and the cow were dying."

Neil informed Adam that Mr. Gascoigne telephoned Koos' Fertilizer to come pick up the starving animals. They sent two men with a truck to get the cow, but they didn't have room for the horse. Somehow the horse survived the winter, but died in the fall of 1951.

Neil said he was raking leaves when Mr. Gascoigne asked him to help bury the horse. The two of them mounted the tractor and rode over to Old Lady Jacobsen's place, where she came hobbling out of the basement and asked them to bury the horse in the orchard next to her husband and his parents.

"The three of us went into the barn, and I nearly puked from the smell of that rotten horse. It was filled with maggots. The horse's carcass had been eaten away by rats and was covered with horse flies.

"Mr. Gascoigne hooked up a chain to the horse's legs and he pulled it out of the barn with the tractor. I nearly broke my back digging the fuckin' grave in the orchard.

"It took me all afternoon because I accidently dug up a skeleton. I sliced the skull right off the neck bones with my shovel and threw it out from the pit. When it rolled toward Mr. Gascoigne, he backed away with his mouth wide open.

"I've been digging too deep," I said, removing the dirt with my bare hands from the skeleton's rib cage, backbone and pelvis.

"It could be Mrs. Jacobsen's husband, Harold. She buried him here in the orchard next to his parents," he said, standing there with his eyes bulging.

"For Christ's sake! I remember her dragging Harold's corpse wrapped in a canvas from her house during the winter. She put it in the shed near the windmill until the snow melted in the spring," said Mr. Gascoigne. "Then she carried it in a wheel barrel and buried him right here.

"Harold died in 1947, a year after Martha Jacobsen's niece, Joyce, moved in with them. His parents, Chester and Phyllis, had died during the Great Depression."

"I was scared shitless that if I kept digging I'd find more skeletons. My hands were trembling when Mr. Gasciogne handed me the skull to put back into the grave. I covered it up and went back to digging."

Neil said once the hole was deep enough Mr. Gascoigne started up the tractor and dragged the dead horse from the barn into the pit. It stunk like hell with flies swarming around the carcass. After helping him unfasten the chain, they stared at the front leg sticking out of the grave.

In the distance they saw Old Lady Jacobsen coming from her basement where she was canning applesauce with Adam's grandmother. She approached them wearing her husband's combat boots from World War I.

She gasped when Mr. Gascoigne lifted the shovel and broke the horse's leg so it would fit into the grave. That's when she put a curse on him by pointing a bony finger and saying the same thing will happen to him.

"Sure enough, during the winter while he was shoveling snow, Mr. Gascoigne slipped on the ice and broke his leg." said Mr. Gascoigne.

"He called me to shovel out his driveway whenever it snowed that year because he was wearing a cast and could hardly get around on crutches. Come on, Adam lets go take a look at that barn where the horse died."

The teenagers walked through the gate and entered the barn through a loose door, where a hatchet and a saw were still hanging from nails like in Adam's painting. The cavernous mouth of the interior seemed to swallow them.

Their eyes adjusted to the darkness, a stark contrast to the sunlight outside.

The smell of moldy hay mingled with the stale odor of horse manure permeated the interior of the barn. A rat scurried past them while pigeons cooed in the hayloft.

"Let's go up to the loft," suggested Neil, scrambling up the ladder with Adam following him.

A few moments later he blurted, "It's hotter than hell up here. We better go back down."

They returned to the ground floor to explore the empty stanchions. Adam found a curry comb for grooming horses on a dusty window sill. On the same wall there were several bridles attached to wooden pegs. A worn leather saddle was slumped over a wooden bench covered with a huge spider web.

"Let's take a look inside the house. Nobody's been around since Old Lady Jacobsen died in 1954 except Fred who hauled away all her new furniture after the funeral," said Neil leading the way.

"Was Fred with her when she died?"

"Hell no," said Neil. "He was on active duty with the navy somewhere. So my mother and your grandma went to stay with Old Lady Jacobsen overnight while she was dying in the nursing home in Waukegan.

"The next day when my dad came back to get my mom and your grandma, I took a peek through the door of her room to see her corpse being washed by a nurse. She was nothing but skin and bones."

"As we were leaving the hospital we saw Fred arrive in his sailor suit to make the funeral arrangements. He was wiping his eyes with a handkerchief because he never got to say goodbye with to his mother.

"My mom didn't sleep for a week after sitting up all night with Old Lady Jacobsen," said Neil.

"My grandma said that Old Lady Jacobsen's ghost kept appearing to her in dreams for about a month," said Adam. "Her soul couldn't rest because her husband and relatives were never given proper burials. It wandered in the morning mist around the apple trees in the orchard with the ghosts of her dead relatives."

6

"There's something floating in this barrel," said Neil, holding the flashlight...

The boys approached the back door and scurried up the creaking steps. The dilapidated front porch facing Cooper Road sagged, and the heavy wooden front door was locked and bolted from the inside. Neil grabbed the knob and pushed against it, but it wouldn't budge.

They meandered past the south side of the house where untrimmed bushes stretched like cat's claws against the unpainted and cracked siding. All the windows were boarded shut with plywood.

"There's the basement door," said Neil, determined to gain entrance to the building.

"Remember how we came here and snooped around after Old Lady Jacobsen was taken to the hospital that summer? Mr. Gascoigne shouted at us that he was going to call the police so we took off like bats from hell."

"Of course I remember," said Neil. "I wonder if those barrels are still in the cellar."

"When you removed the lid on one of them, you were really upset," said Adam.

"It's because it was so fuckin' dark in that cellar. We didn't have a flashlight like we do now," said Neil, removing it from his back pocket.

They headed toward the basement door, passing a pile

49

of charred trash. Empty tin cans were heaped near the springs of a rusted mattress. Pots and pans without handles, broken dishes, empty bottles, a twisted metal picture frame, and a scorched violin case were among the debris that had survived the bonfire. Neil and Adam went down a flight of cement steps overgrown with weeds to the basement door.

"Mr. Gascoigne put a new lock on the fuckin' door," said Neil. He stood back a few feet and kicked the door, loosening the hinges. After a second kick, the door crashed onto the dirt floor of the cellar.

Upon entering the dark and musty basement, Neil flicked on the flashlight so that there were no surprises this time. Dirt and cobwebs smudged the boarded windows, preventing the sunlight from entering. In the center a folded ladder linked the cellar to a tightly closed trap door leading to the living room on the first floor.

"The barrels are still over there," said Neil, proceeding to investigate while Adam pulled the rope dangling from the ladder. It unfolded allowing him to climb the wooden steps leading to the trap door.

"Jesus Christ! It's still here," shouted Neil, the flashlight quivering in his right hand while he held the lid in his left.

"What's the matter?" asked Adam, pausing on the ladder. He hurried down to get a glimpse of the contents in the barrel.

Adam and Neil stood gazing in the barrel with their mouths gaping at the partially submerged hog's head floating in an oily liquid. Its eyes were sealed shut and its snout protruded upward. The mouth was slightly open as if the hog were smiling.

"I thought maybe Old Lady Jacobsen's son might have buried the fuckin' pig!" gasped Neil.

"We never looked in those other barrels the last time we were here," said Adam.

"Then let's go take a look inside them," insisted Neil, slamming the lid down on the barrel with the pig's head.

The two of them investigated the barrels which were filled with oily liquid. They were disappointed when they couldn't find anything inside them except drowned flies.

"There's something floating in this barrel," said Neil, holding the flashlight on the protruding object.

"What is it?" asked Adam.

"I don't know for sure. I'm not putting my hand inside the barrel to find out," said Neil, scanning the basement with his flashlight.

They were both startled by a pair of greasy coveralls hanging on a hook next to a cast iron potbellied stove too heavy to carry out of the basement. On the floor a small shovel was protruding from a bucket of coal.

"Old Lady Jacobsen used to do a lot of canning down here," said Adam, glancing at rows of fruit jars left behind on dusty shelves. "My grandma would come over to help her. She always sent her home with jars of applesauce."

Neil seized the shovel from the coal bucket and went back to the barrel. He began stirring the liquid. "Adam, there's something in here."

"What have you found?" asked Adam.

"I'll hold the fuckin' flashlight so you can fish out whatever's inside with your hands. It's kind of heavy and tied down with a brick so it won't float," said Neil, putting down the shovel.

Using both hands Adam reached into the slimy water pulling up the brick tied with a rope to something heavy.

"For Christ's sake!" he shouted, dropping the human leg onto the dirt floor.

Both Neil and Adam backed away, staring at the foot attached to the leg. The toes were wrinkled, but their nails glistened in the light.

"What the fuck! I wonder if that old witch was making soup out of people and putting them in Ball jars."

"Do you think we should report this to the police?" asked Adam, his voice trembling.

"Hell no!" stammered Neil, grabbing the brick with the leg attached and throwing it back into the barrel.

"That foot belongs to a woman," gasped Adam, his hand trembling while holding the lid.

"I'll be damned," said Neil, illuminating the lid with his flashlight. "There's a label carved on the inside cover. 'In Memory of Joyce Ann Jacobsen, Beloved Cousin: Born, May 6, 1917, Died, February 7, 1952.'"

"You don't think Old Lady Jacobsen murdered her cousin, do you?" asked Adam. "My grandma told me that she didn't get along with Joyce. She treated her like a household slave. Joyce did the laundry, cooking, and

52

baking, which caught the eye of her husband."

Neil said that the whole neighborhood knew that Martha was jealous of Joyce and suspected her of having a love affair with her husband Harold. In fact, Old Lady Jacobsen told anybody who would listen to her that she saw them go into the barn together when she was sick with pneumonia. A year later Harold died during winter and was kept in the shed until spring before he was buried.

Adam stated that Old Lady Jacobsen told his grandma that after Harold died, Joyce used to stand on the porch wearing a low cut blue dress and visit with Ray Wilson, the mailman, every day for ten to fifteen minutes.

When no one was around, they'd go for a walk in the corn field or a romp in the hay. After Joyce disappeared in 1952, everybody thought she eloped to Iron Mountain, Michigan with the mailman because nobody ever saw either one of them again.

"Someone murdered Joyce and stuffed her leg in the barrel. Give me that flash light. I'll take a look in the other barrels," said Adam.

"Here take the fuckin' flashlight. I'm going upstairs. This basement gives me the creeps," said Neil.

"There are only two barrels left," said Adam, lifting the lid on the next barrel. He took the shovel and stirred the oily liquid searching. "There's nothing in this one except some pickled pigs' feet."

"I'm outta here," said Neil, scrambling up the ladder.

"Hey, Neil! There's something in this barrel," shouted

Adam, listening to his footsteps in the living room upstairs.

While shining the flashlight into the barrel, he stirred the slimy liquid with the shovel, noticing another rope with a brick tied to it.

He set the flashlight on the floor and reached into the barrel, pulling up an arm. Adam winced at the sight of a diamond ring on the finger of the left hand. As he dropped the limb back into the liquid, he vomited on the dirt floor.

A few minutes later Adam picked up the lid, noticing another carving with Joyce's birth and death dates. He slammed the lid on the barrel and darted up the ladder and through the trap door. He was trembling as he approached Neil, who was standing near the piano.

"For Christ's sake, Adam! You look like you've seen a ghost!" said Neil.

"This time I…I found Joyce's arm and hand with a diamond ring on her finger," blurted Adam. He scanned the empty room with the flashlight, wondering if her skeleton was lying in a corner.

"No shit!" said Neil, opening the lid of the piano.

"I wonder if Old Lady Jacobsen was insane and killed Joyce for fooling around with her husband?" said Adam, his hand shaking.

"I don't care to find out," said Neil, reaching for the flashlight. "How about playing something on the piano?"

Adam stood in front of the upright piano, noticing the keys glowing in the light like white teeth. After plucking a few chords, he said, "This piano really needs tuning."

"Don't just stand there. Play something," insisted Neil, pacing up and down on the wooden floor.

"Sure," agreed Adam, playing *Old Man River* from *Show Boat* while Neil scanned the dark room with the flashlight.

"That sounds great except for the sour notes coming from those broken keys," said Neil. "Let's go up to the attic. We haven't been there in years.

"Old Lady Jacobsen told my mom that Jesus used to appear to her in the upper bedroom. She'd always have a pitcher of water and a basin to wash His feet," said Neil, leading the way to the stairs.

Adam added that Mrs. Jacobsen told his grandma that she saw her relatives' ghosts in the morning mist, circling their graves in the orchard. They pleaded with her to bring a minister to put their souls to rest by praying for them, but she wouldn't do it because she believed they all deserved to be punished for their sinful ways.

"There's light up here," shouted Neil, waiting for Adam at the top of the stairs.

Upon arriving upstairs, Adam was amazed by the light streaming through the smudged windows, illuminating the deserted rooms with a dusty haze.

Adam and Neil went into the vacant bedroom where an upholstered chair had been left in front of the window with a view of the windmill and the apple orchard.

Neil plopped down into the chair. "Hey, Adam, do you really believe that Jesus appeared to Old Lady Jacobsen when she sat in this chair?"

"I...I'm not sure. If God wanted it to happen, Jesus could appear to anyone," said Adam, surprised by Neil's sincere tone of voice.

"Do you think God loves everybody?" asked Neil. "If God's anything like my old man when he's rip roaring drunk, I don't want to have anything to do with Him."

"I believe God loves everybody," said Adam, recalling how his father also became like Dr. Jekyll and Mr. Hyde when he was drunk.

"How about really rotten people like Hitler, Mussolini, and Stalin, who massacred millions during World War II?" asked Neil.

"I'm not sure about those guys, but I remember reading that when a group of men wanted to stone a prostitute to death, Jesus stopped them by saying, 'He who is without sin should cast the first stone,'" said Adam.

"Those guys who wanted to stone that whore were probably fuckin' her...I mean committing adultery."

"I learned in catechism class that God loves everyone equally and forgives even the worst sinners. He forgave St. Paul for massacring Christians before his conversion," commented Adam.

"I read that St. Paul was struck down by God from his horse and became blind," said Neil.

"I didn't know you read the Bible," said Adam.

"I've been reading it every day since you saved me from drowning in the pond. It belongs to my mother, who got it

56

for a wedding present. Let's get the fuck outta here...I mean let's get going. Jennifer gets mad at me when I use foul language. I'm trying hard to break the habit, but I'm not making much progress."

As they left the house and pulled the cellar door shut, it fell back into the basement. The boys searched the barn and sheds, eventually returning with a screwdriver to fasten the screws back into the hinges of the door.

7

"Adam, I'm so glad you called. I thought you were mad at me," said Naomi.

The Month of June passed slowly. Karl took Grandma to the Farmers' Market every day. On Wednesday and Saturday, Adam went along to sell vegetables at Columbus Park, where most of the customers were Italians and members of Our Lady of Mount Carmel Church.

Adam was able to give Grandma some relief from her routine of dealing with customers by encouraging her to join her friends from the parish for coffee at Mary's Restaurant across the street while he sold the vegetables.

When they returned to the farm early in the afternoon Adam continued his routine of having lunch and sketching on the porch. He glanced up when Crispy began growling in the orchard.

"Neil, how have things been going?" he asked, setting down his brushes. "I haven't seen you for two weeks."

"I've been busy watching my brother and sister all day long because my mother's been working," said Neil. "I get sick and tired of changing their fuckin…I mean their messy diapers. After I put them down for their naps, I've been calling Jennifer."

"How's she doing?" asked Adam, glancing at his painting of Naomi. She reminded him of Esther Williams with her beautiful body and friendly smile.

"Every time I try to talk to Jennifer, someone from the party line listens to our conversation. It's annoying as hell. There's no fuckin'…I mean there's no real privacy in this neighborhood."

Neil informed him that Jennifer's parents, the O'Reillys, had invited him to join them for mass on Sunday morning at St. Mary's Parish. They even came to pick him up in their new Ford. After mass he had lunch with them at their home in Allendale. Throughout the afternoon they played croquet on their expansive lawn. Later in the evening they went swimming at Southport Beach. It was after 9:00 pm when they finally brought him home.

"I'll tell you, Adam; I've never had such a good time in my whole life. Jennifer's the most beautiful girl I've ever met. I swear she looks just like Debbie Reynolds. Her parents are so nice and polite. They even pray before they eat. They want me to come back again next Sunday and spend the day with them."

Adam noticed that Neil wasn't the same anymore. He was undergoing a metamorphosis like a caterpillar into a butterfly. He was trying hard to stop using vulgar language due to Jennifer's influence. Neil no longer carried a slingshot, his shaggy hair had been neatly trimmed, and he wore a new belt to hold up his jeans.

"Jennifer told me that Naomi wants you to call her because she misses you," said Neil, pausing to look at her painting. "You really know how to paint, Adam. I've gotta go now. Jennifer's gonna call me at home at 3:00 o'clock."

As soon as Neil departed, Adam became listless and depressed. While Grandma was snoring on the couch in the dining room, he went to the telephone hanging from the wall in the kitchen and called Naomi. Her phone kept ringing, but no one answered. He was about to hang up when someone answered.

"Hello, this is Adam Montanya. How are you, Mrs. Rosenberg? May I please speak with Naomi?" he asked. "Of course, I can wait."

"Adam, I'm so glad you called. I thought you were mad at me," said Naomi. "I was practicing the piano and didn't hear the phone ring right away."

"Why would I be mad at you? I've been busy here on the farm," said Adam, his heart pounding so loudly he thought that she could hear it through the telephone.

"It's been almost a month since I heard from you," she said. "How's your family?"

"We had a problem with my father drinking right after my mother left with my sister to go to New York on vacation. He's better now."

"I'm sorry to hear about that," she said. "I remember you telling me that he ended up in the hospital some years ago after crashing the truck. I didn't even know you then."

"This time my dad went to rehab for a whole week. He's back to work and going to AA meetings again. How are your mom and dad doing?"

"They argue a lot because my dad's never home. He has his regular medical practice all week and then works at the emergency room on weekends," said Naomi. "My mom says he never has time for the family.

"Will you join us for the Sabbath this Saturday at the synagogue and a picnic lunch afterwards at the beach? Be sure to bring your bathing suit."

"I'm not sure I can make it. I usually help Grandma at the Farmers' Market on Saturday," said Adam. "I'll call you back after I talk this over with my dad. I don't know if he can give me a ride to the Beth Hillel Temple."

"We'll pick you up about 8:20 on Saturday morning for the nine o'clock service. I wanted to talk to you about Jennifer. She's madly in love with Neil and wants to ride her bicycle out to his place and help him babysit on Friday afternoon while his parents are working."

"If you come with her, I'll meet you at Neil's place," said Adam.

"I'd love to join you, but I've got to watch my sister, Lorna. I have to help her get ready for summer camp. Please call me back tomorrow. My mom's home for lunch, and she wants to use the phone before going back to work at the hospital. I love you, Adam. Goodbye."

"I love you too, Naomi," he said, feeling elated for having talked with her. He went back to the porch and sketched Naomi on a new canvas and then mixed several colors on his palette.

For the next hour he applied different shades of flesh tones to her face, neck, and arms until Naomi gradually came to life once again on his canvas.

When Grandma got up from her nap, she entered the porch to tell him that it was time to go pick strawberries in the garden.

"Who's that pretty girl you make in that picture this time?" asked Grandma, her mouth gaping.

"It's my girlfriend, Naomi Rosenberg," said Adam.

"She's got blue eyes like a-the the sky," said Grandma. "What kind of name is that? She's not Italian because she don't go to my church."

"She's Jewish," said Adam.

"You mean, she's a Jew?" asked Grandma.

"Her father's Doctor Rosenberg. You met him at the hospital when Dad had his accident."

"Oh, that doctor. He's a good man. He's not like those other Jews that only want my money."

"You have a stereotype of Jews," said Adam,

"What do you mean by that word?" she asked.

"It's like saying all Italians belong to the Mafia," explained Adam. "People put labels on others to feel superior to them."

Grandma admitted that she put labels on people, although she believed most of the time she was right about them. A few minutes later they left for the garden, with the oil painting drying on the porch.

While picking strawberries, Adam imagined that Naomi was there working beside him. Enchanted by her beauty, he couldn't stop thinking about her the entire afternoon.

Around 4:30 Giovanni returned from work in the '51

Plymouth. After changing his clothes, he wasted no time carrying bushel baskets of beans, beets, and carrots to be washed at the spigot alongside the house.

Grandma carried cartons of strawberries out of the garden while Adam helped his father scrub the vegetables in the stationary tub beneath the kitchen window. As they worked together Giovanni noticed that his son was restless and troubled.

"What's the matter, Adam?" he asked. "Are you still worried about Neil almost drowning in the pond?"

"It's not that. I haven't seen Naomi Rosenberg since we got out of school. She invited me to attend the Sabbath with her family on Saturday morning at the synagogue. After the service they want me to go with them on a picnic.

"I told Naomi on the phone that I always help Grandma on Saturday at the Farmers' Market and didn't know if I could join them until I talked to you."

Giovanni said, "If you want to go with them, I'll take Grandma to the market and help her out. What time do you have to be there?"

"The service starts at 9:00 o'clock. You don't have to drive me to the temple. Naomi's parents will pick me up."

"I know her father, David Rosenberg. We went to high school together. He's the best surgeon in Kenosha. If it wasn't for him, I'd be dead," said Giovanni, peeling off his shirt. His large jaw, hairy chest, and muscular arms resembled Anthony Quinn's.

"Multo grazie, Papa," said Adam, beaming. "I'll call

63

Naomi after supper and tell her that I'll see them on Saturday morning."

"Here comes Karl," said Adam, glancing up at the red truck swerving around the bend with the brakes squealing.

His brother got out and slammed the door. He was wearing greasy coveralls from working all day at the Mobile Station.

"I stopped to pick up the mail," said Karl, sorting through a stack of bills. "Here's a postcard from Mom and Marie at the Statue of Liberty. She says they're having a great time and will be back for the Fourth of July."

"That's only a week and a half from now. The Fourth of July's on a Wednesday this year," said Giovanni. "Did your mother say what time she's coming home?"

"No," said Karl, walking down the sidewalk to the back door. "Mom says she'll write again and let us know when she's arriving at the North Shore Station. I'm going to get cleaned up. I've got a date tonight with Marsha."

Grandma came from the garden carrying the rest of the strawberries layered in a crate. After setting them down near the truck, she shuffled toward the screen door, announcing "It's time for me to turn on a-the news."

Adam and his father heard the screen door slam and her footsteps thundering up the stairs leading to the kitchen. A few minutes later the radio was blaring.

Good evening. This is Bill Schroeder at WLIP in downtown Kenosha with the 6:00pm news. *For six months now the Negroes, led by Martin Luther King, have been boycotting the buses in Montgomery, Alabama, causing the bus companies to lose thousands of dollars.*

In Cuba, a journalist accused Ernest Hemingway of being dishonest for breaking a promise to give a fisherman a new boat as payment for the story about him that he used in his novel, "The Old Man and the Sea." The accusation proved to be false after further investigation.

And now for the local news. *A police car was sent to the abandoned Jacobsen farm on Cooper Road because two teenagers were seen breaking into the basement of the farmhouse by a neighbor, Mr. Clifford Gascoigne. He gave the officers the names of the boys who kicked in the basement door, although they attempted to repair it.*

A few days later, a forensic anthropologist returned to the farm with police officers and found body parts of a woman in the basement. Mr. Gascoigne took the officers to the apple orchard, where they dug up four skeletons near the tombstone of Martha Jacobsen.

Some years ago at different time periods Clifford Gascoigne saw Mrs. Jacobsen dragging corpses wrapped in canvas bags from her house and storing them for the winter in a shed. He admitted that he never saw Martha actually bury the dead bodies in the orchard.

The unidentified skeletons, possibly the relatives of Mrs. Jacobsen, were transported to the laboratory for examination, although they left the coffin with the remains of Martha Jacobsen in the orchard.

Grandma snapped off the radio and pressed her head

against the screened window. She called, "We're gonna eat in a few minutes. Come inside and wash your hands."

While sitting at the kitchen table Adam was silent during supper, not knowing if he should tell his father about breaking into Mrs. Jacobsen's basement with Neil and finding Joyce Jacobsen's arm and leg preserved in barrels. He was fearful the police would come to their house and cause some real trouble for him and his family.

"Do you hear the news?" asked Grandma. "They find a-the bones of Martha's relatives in a-the orchard."

"I never liked Old Lady Jacobsen coming here because she had lice and would stink up the whole house when she came to use our bathtub," said Karl.

"Adam, did you and Neil go over to Mrs. Jacobsen's place to look around again?" asked Giovanni, reaching for the salad bowl.

"Ah...we were only there for little while. Neil kicked in the basement door, but we fixed it before we left."

"You're lucky the police didn't arrest you," said Karl. "You guys could have been slammed in jail for breaking and entering. There are 'No Trespassing' signs all over that rundown place."

"Neil told me that when he helped Mr. Gascoigne dig the pit to bury the dead horse, he dug up a skeleton. I...I didn't believe him at the time."

"The police dug up four skeletons in the orchard," said Giovanni, shaking his head.

"Martha's cousin, Joyce, was such a pretty girl," said

Grandma, standing at the stove, where she ladled bowls of steaming vegetable soup for everyone.

"I help Martha make applesauce when they bury that horse. She don't like Joyce, because Mr. Gascoigne got his eyes on her all the time."

"Joyce was beautiful. She had flaming red hair and green eyes," said Karl. "She was always flirting with the mailman, Ray Wilson. Everybody thought she eloped with him after his wife died of cancer."

"Adam, you better stay away from that place. I don't want you and Neil getting into trouble. The police were patrolling Cooper Road when I came home from work. I'm surprised Mr. Gascoigne told them your names," said Giovanni.

"I'll never go there again," said Adam, sprinkling grated Parmesan cheese on his vegetable soup.

"Grandma makes the best soup," said Karl, reaching for a slice of Italian bread from Paielli's Bakery.

"We eat soup every day when I live in Italy, where your father is born," said Grandma. "In my village we get nine meters of snow in a-the winter time."

"Our village is north of Torino in the Alps," said Giovanni. "I don't remember much about it."

"You are just a baby when we come to this country added Grandma. "Now you got two big sons and a pretty little daughter."

"Sometimes I miss Mom and Marie," said Adam, reaching for a slice of Italian bread.

"I told Margo Brown I'd pick her up at 7:30. Dad, I hope I can use the Plymouth tonight. We're going to the Keno Outdoor Theater to see *Picnic* with Kim Novak, and Rosalind Russell."

"You go take a bath with hot water," said Grandma, rising to turn off the whistling tea kettle on the stove.

"I took a bath when I got home," said Karl.

"One of these days I'm going to surprise your mother and buy a hot water heater," said Giovanni. "But first I must replace the pump. We bought it before the Japanese bombed Pearl Harbor."

"I never forget that war because your father goes to fight in Italy," said Grandma. "At that time your mama works in a-the factory to make airplanes."

8

We weren't doing anything wrong. I was only resting my head on Adam's shoulder...

On Saturday morning Adam woke up early to help Grandma milk the cows, feed the poultry, and cut lettuce for the market. Karl took the Plymouth to work at the Mobile Station while his father drove Grandma in the red truck to Columbus Park where he helped her set up the vegetable stand.

After doing his chores and taking a bath. Adam glanced in the mirror to comb his hair, followed by an application of Old Spice aftershave lotion. Returning to the bedroom, he got dressed in navy blue pants, a white shirt, and brown shoes. He entered the kitchen carrying his bathing suit wrapped in a clean towel.

Glancing at the rooster clock over the sink, he turned on the radio, remembering Naomi's family would pick him up by 8:20.

Adam nervously paced the floor, listening to the morning news. *Floyd Patterson, age 21, fought Tommy Jackson, 24, at Madison Square Garden. In spite of seven rounds of intense competition, Patterson gained momentum during the final three rounds and became the victor.*

Last Friday President Dwight Eisenhower experienced abdominal pains. This time the discomfort began after a dinner party at the White House where the comedian, Bob

69

Hope, and the singer, Pearl Bailey, were present to entertain the guests. Eisenhower was admitted to Walter Reed Hospital, where several surgeons performed a bypass surgery due to an infection of his small intestine. The president has recovered from the surgery and is resuming his duties.

Adam turned off the radio, heading down the stairs and out the back door. He sat on a wooden bench under the maple tree, watching the cows grazing in the pasture, feeling nervous about going with the Rosenbergs.

He strolled down the driveway toward the orchard where Crispy was sleeping. The dog opened an eye to acknowledge his presence, watching him wander in the shade of the trees. He also thought about how Adam and Eve ate the forbidden fruit in the Garden of Eden and wondered if he would be committing a sin by going to the to the synagogue.

Adam remembered Sister Anna wearing a starched white habit with a black veil. She was skinny as a rail and towered over the students like Popeye's girlfriend, Olive Oyl. The nun was always angry because she had to teach public school children catechism on Saturday morning to prepare them for the sacrament of Confirmation.

"You must memorize the entire *Baltimore Catechism* before you're confirmed. Your parents have been informed to drill you during the week. Some of you students should be attending St. Mary's School because we now have a bus that picks up students in the county.

"If your parents can afford to send you to a Catholic School but refuse, they are committing a mortal sin," she insisted. "As you know, there are several kinds of sin. There's mortal sin, venial sin, actual sin, and the infamous Original Sin, committed by Adam and Eve."

"My parents are going to a wedding next week at Trinity Lutheran Church in Racine. My cousin, George, is a fallen away Catholic and is marrying a Lutheran," blurted Tommy, his voice trembling.

"Catholics are forbidden to go to Protestant services. They are not to attend weddings of mixed marriages. Martin Luther is probably in Hell for breaking away from the Catholic Church and forming his own religion."

"My mother went to the Passover last year at the Jewish synagogue," said Billy. "I'm going to tell her that she committed a mortal sin."

"That's right. She should know better. The Jews were once the Chosen People but they aren't anymore because they rebelled against God and worshipped idols. That's why they became slaves in Egypt," said the nun. "Now who can tell me what I taught you about Jews?"

"Jews believe in a punishing God from the Old Testament while Catholics worship the loving God of the New Testament," informed Brian.

"That's right, Brian. You're so smart. You won't have trouble memorizing the catechism."

Adam raised his hand, waiting for her to acknowledge him. "What is your question this time, Adam?"

"If God is so loving why does He condemn Catholics to Hell for all eternity for committing a single mortal sin," challenged Adam.

"It's because God is not only loving but just," informed Sister Anna. "Unless the sinner makes a sincere Act of Contrition and goes to Confession, he will be punished in Hell for all eternity."

Adam returned to the porch where he sat down on a wicker chair across from his second painting of Naomi, which was propped on the easel. He admired her beautiful figure even though the picture wasn't finished.

David Rosenberg arrived ten minutes late, swerving his Cadillac into the driveway. He came to a halt at the end of the orchard near the front porch where Adam was pensively waiting. Upon hearing the car screech to a halt, Crispy woke from a nap beneath an apple tree and began barking loudly.

"Settle down," yelled Adam, hurrying down the steps, carrying his bathing suit wrapped in a towel. He petted the growling dog, quieting him before approaching the yellow convertible.

"Adam, we're so pleased you could join us to celebrate the Sabbath. What a charming bungalow," said Rachel, sitting next to her husband David in the front seat.

"Just look at those maple trees lining the driveway. They're so tall and stately. This is the first time I've seen your house in daylight. It was always dark when I gave you a ride home from the dances," said Rachel.

"Come sit next to me," said Naomi, smiling at Adam. She patted the leather seat with a white glove as he opened the back door. "I'm so glad you didn't forget your bathing suit because we're going on a picnic along Lake Michigan after the service."

"Thank you so much for inviting me to spend the day with you," said Adam to her parents as he entered the convertible.

"Where's your sister?" asked Adam, sitting in the back seat next to Naomi.

"Lorna's at summer camp," she said, reaching for Adam's hand and kissing him on the check.

Adam flushed with embarrassment, not expecting Naomi to place her head on his shoulder.

"We're pleased that you could join us," said David, glancing at them through the rear-view mirror and scowling. "I finally got a day off from work at the Emergency Room."

"The Sabbath is supposed to be a day of rest," sighed Rachel, noticing her husband frowning as he gazed again into the mirror. She turned around to see what was going on in the back seat.

Upon seeing her mother's raised eyebrows, Naomi sat up straight and smiled at her. "We weren't doing anything wrong. I was only resting my head on Adam's shoulder for a minute. After all, the Sabbath is a day of rest."

Adam cleared his throat, feeling trapped sitting next to Naomi, aware that her parents disapproved of her displays of affection.

"I haven't been to the Sabbath since we came back to Kenosha four years ago from Skokie," added David, putting the car in reverse.

"We never missed attending the service when we lived there," said Rachel.

"Dad, the driveway goes around in a circle. You can go straight ahead rather than backing out."

David Rosenberg drove the convertible up the rutted driveway toward the garage, where he slammed on the brakes to avoid hitting a squawking rooster leading a flock of panic-stricken hens to the chicken coop.

Rachel said, "David you'd better slow down. You almost ran over those chickens. Adam, what a huge garden you have! It stretches for miles."

"We only have fifteen acres here. My grandparents bought this place in 1936 during the Depression."

"Hitler was already in power at that time. He had the support of the Germans because he promised to lead them out of poverty by providing a chicken for every pot and a Volkswagen for every family," said David, honking the horn at the geese as he circled the driveway.

"Look at those charming cows grazing in the pasture," added Rachel, avoiding a conversation about the war.

"There were six million Jews exterminated and countless Poles," added David. "Of course after the war Stalin took over Poland, creating more problems for them."

"What are the names of your cows?" asked Naomi,

ignoring her father's comments about the war. She clung tightly to Adam's hand.

"Sylvia, Betsy, and Daisy," said Adam. "We also have two pigs over there in that pen behind the corn crib."

"I understand your father agreed to go to the Farmers' Market this morning with your grandmother," said Rachel. "Your lovely farm reminds me of my grandparents' place in the Ukraine."

David's brow was wrinkled since no one wanted to talk about the Holocaust. He swerved the convertible onto Bentz Road and proceeded east, crossing Cooper Road. He was silent all the way to 39th Avenue, where he turned left, heading north.

Adam asked Naomi to tell him about the Sabbath since he had never been to a synagogue. She said that the Sabbath began on Friday just before sunset and ended on Saturday evening. It was a day of rest, prayer, and celebration for Jews because in Genesis God created the world in six days and on the seventh, He rested, commanding His people to do the same.

"Last night I lit two candles at home just before sunset," said Rachel. "Our menorah in the temple has seven candles, representing the seven days of creation."

"It's strictly the woman's job to light the candles every Friday evening," interrupted David.

"For many centuries the Jewish women stayed home to clean, bake, and prepare for the Sabbath while the men studied the Torah. Women weren't allowed to read. That's changed, especially among the Reform Jews."

"I've been studying Hebrew," commented Naomi. "I'm going to have my Bat Mitzvah after Passover. Adam, I'll send your family an invitation to celebrate it with us."

"Thanks, but don't forget to include my grandma."

"Your father came to my Bar Mitzvah," said David. "After we graduated from Bradford, he was hired at Nash Motors, and I went on to Marquette University and then medical school."

"My dad was working on the assembly line before he was drafted in 1941. He returned there to work after the war," said Adam. "When he first came home my brother and I didn't even recognize him because he had been gone for almost four years.

"He remembers how you took good care of him after he crashed the truck," said Adam, feeling embarrassed by the incident because his father was drunk.

"Giovanni told me all about fighting the Nazis and the Fascists in Italy when he was in the hospital," said David. "I believe he's still stressed from the war. I don't think our soldiers ever get over the trauma."

"War does that to families," said Rachel, biting her lip.

"The Jews have a long history of tribal warfare before becoming Israel," said David.

He informed them that during the Sabbath the Jews remember Moses receiving the Ten Commandments and leading the Israelites out of Egypt to the Promised Land after 400 years of slavery.

Some years later there was the destruction of the temple in Jerusalem and then the Babylonian Exile. Since the Jews no longer had the temple for worship, they celebrated the Sabbath privately in their homes even though they were slaves in Babylon.

"David, this conversation is depressing," said Rachel.

"Sorry, I only wanted to inform Adam that we have a history of persecution," said her husband.

David came to a halt at the Four Corners and turned right onto 75th Street.

"Adam, how's your mother doing?" asked Rachel, changing the subject.

"She's in New York on vacation with my sister, Marie," said Adam, squirming in his seat.

"David and I went to New York on our honeymoon," said Rachel. "We got married after I got my nursing degree and he finished medical school."

"Mom works at St. Catherine's Hospital as head nurse on the pediatrics floor," said Naomi. "Dad's a surgeon at Kenosha Memorial. They want me to go St. Mary's High School this fall."

"Oh, I thought you were going to Bradford," said Adam, glancing into Naomi's sad eyes.

"We're almost to the temple," said David, driving past St. James Cemetery and Baker's Park on Sheridan Road.

"My grandma goes to the Farmers' Market there every Thursday," said Adam, glancing at the vacant park.

"I always stop and buy lettuce and spinach from her. I

77

love talking with her about Italy," said Rachel.

"Here we are at the temple," said David, parking the car in front of the Kenosha Public Library. "We'll have to walk about a block."

Adam held the door open for Naomi as she left the convertible. She took him by the arm and strolled beside him, with her parents leading the way to the synagogue.

"I'm so happy that you could join us," said Naomi, squeezing his hand.

"I'm a little nervous about going into a synagogue," admitted Adam. "Does the rabbi sacrifice animals at the altar in your temple?"

"Not for several centuries," laughed Naomi. "I'm a vegetarian myself, which annoys my parents. They're always worried that I'm not getting enough protein."

"For many generations humans were vegetarians. After the Great Flood, God gave Noah and his family permission to eat meat providing they drained the blood," said David.

"That was the beginning of our dietary laws known as *kosher*," added Rachel "The rules are very precise so that the animals being slaughtered don't have to suffer."

"I've had to help my grandmother kill chickens, ducks, and geese on our farm," said Adam. "I hold the animals by their feet with their head down so that the blood will drain from them."

"Maybe a rabbi taught her how to butcher when she lived in Italy," said Rachel. "There are lots of Jews living there now. The synagogue in Florence is just huge."

"Hurry up, you slow pokes, or we're not going to get a seat," said David. "Naomi, I hope you're not trying to convert Adam to vegetarianism."

"I don't believe anyone has the right to force their beliefs on anyone," said Naomi, entering the synagogue with Adam.

David led them up the aisle, where they sat on the left side close to the Rabbi's podium. On a table in front of them were two unlighted candles.

Adam noticed red vigil lights burning on both sides of the tabernacle, with bronze doors in the center of the sanctuary similar to those in the Catholic churches.

Naomi whispered in his ear, "The Torah scrolls are kept inside the tabernacle and will be removed and carried in procession around the temple during the service."

When the rabbi entered, the service began with the lighting of the candles and the recitation of the prayer,

"Blessed are You, Lord Our God,
King of the Universe, who made us holy
Through His commandments,
And commanded us to light the Sabbath light."

After the lighting of the candles, the congregation sang a hymn, followed by the recitation of psalms.

Naomi whispered to Adam, "The next few prayers deal with the Shekinah, the feminine side of Adonai, who's found in nature. I like to compare Her to Mother Earth.

"My father's prejudiced and doesn't believe that God could possibly be female," added Naomi.

Adam was confused by the idea that God could be masculine and feminine at the same time. He thought about his history teacher mentioning the union of opposites while teaching the class about Yin and Yang from Taoism.

The rabbi began with the prayer which he recited twice,

"Come, my Beloved, to greet the bride;
Let us welcome the Sabbath."
"Come, my Beloved, to greet the bride;
Let us welcome the Sabbath."
"Observe and Remember in one act of speech,
The One and Only God made us hear.
The Lord is One and His name is One,
For renown, for splendor, and for praise."
"Come my beloved to greet the bride;
Let us welcome the Sabbath."

The service continued with readings from the Torah, the first five books of the scriptures, followed by the removal of the scrolls from the tabernacle and a procession of the Torah down the aisles.

Naomi mentioned to Adam that the tabernacle was once a tent containing The Ark of the Covenant with The Ten Commandments.

The service ended with a concluding hymn, followed by the blessing of the Bread and Wine, which reminded Adam of communion at the Catholic mass.

The congregation gathered for refreshments in a side room where everyone socialized before departing from the synagogue.

"I can't wait to change into my swim suit," said Naomi, holding Adam's hand as they left the synagogue and returned to the Cadillac.

"I've got mine right here," said Adam, pointing to his swimsuit wrapped in a towel in the back seat.

"My suit probably won't fit," said David. "I have to admit I've put on weight since I left Skokie."

"It's because you don't get enough exercise," said Rachel. "David would rather have pizza for lunch than a low calorie salad."

"Dad, you've got to go on a diet," insisted Naomi.

"That's right," said David, glancing down at his paunch as he entered the convertible and turned on the radio. "I haven't heard the news all week."

Good afternoon this is Bill Schroeder from WLIP in Kenosha with the afternoon news on Saturday, June, 23, 1956. *Lieutenant Colonel Nasser was swarmed by crowds of people in Cairo as he stood in the spotlight to celebrate the withdrawal of the British occupation after 74 years of ruling Egypt. With Nassar at the helm, the Egyptians had overthrown a corrupt monarchy, destroyed the greedy feudal aristocracy, driven out the fanatical Moslem Brotherhood, and ended the control of the imperialists.*

"Wow! That's some news," asserted David. "Let's listen to the rest of it: *The Israeli Prime Minister, David Ben-Gurion, fired the Foreign Minister and replaced him with Golda Meir from Milwaukee, Wisconsin. The issue dealt with Israel's retaliation against the Arabs, who attacked*

81

and murdered Jewish schoolchildren.

"It's about time women got recognition," interrupted Rachel. "We've been second class citizens long enough. One of these days we'll to be marching for equal rights just like the Negroes in Montgomery, Alabama."

David was silent about women's rights as he drove past the courthouse and Bradford High School while everyone listened to the local news.

Martha Jacobsen's cousin, Joyce, disappeared in 1952. Everyone thought she had eloped with the mailman, Ray Wilson, to Iron Mountain, Michigan. The detectives located him and discovered that Joyce was not there.

The police believe Joyce was murdered and buried in the orchard near Martha's husband, Harold, and his parents, although Martha's son, Fred, had no knowledge of the multiple graves.

Fred obtained permission from the county clerk to bury his mother in the orchard in 1954. She was the only family member with a coffin and tombstone on the property.

"Those skeletons have been getting a lot of attention lately," said David, snapping off the radio. "I hope they discover the truth about what happened on that farm."

"I heard that they found Joyce's body parts in the basement of Mrs. Jacobsen's old house," said Rachel. "Her farm gives me the creeps every time we drive past it."

"Here we are at Pennoyer Park" said David, parking the convertible near Kaiser's Tap.

9

"I told you not to buy a two piece bathing suit. Who do you think you are, Marilyn Monroe?"

Everyone was eager to go for a swim but forgot that there was no place to change into bathing suits in the park. David and Rachel were wearing their suits, but Naomi and Adam were not. Adam decided to go into Kaiser's Bar and change in the restroom, recalling that his father used to take him and Karl there on Friday night. They always played shuffleboard while he watched the boxing match on TV.

Rachel covered all the windows of the convertible with towels so that Naomi could change into her bathing suit in the back seat. David had already stripped off his clothes and left them in the trunk of the car before leaving with the picnic basket and army blankets.

He had gone down the cement steps and up the hill leading to the tennis courts, where he sat down on a park bench to watch the match.

Adam came out of the tavern wearing a blue bathing suit and carrying his towel, clothes, and shoes. His upper body was tan from working in the garden without a shirt, although his legs and feet were pale.

"You can put your clothes in the trunk next to ours," said Rachel, wearing sunglasses and a lavender bathing suit. She glanced toward Adam approaching her from the bar.

"Where did you get those biceps? You look like Charles

Atlas. You must be working out at the YMCA."

"I get a lot of exercise working on the farm," he said. "I also earn money baling hay every summer."

"No wonder you're so muscular," said Rachel. "I wish David would work out regularly. He used to go to the gym everyday when we lived in Skokie."

Adam's mouth opened wide at the sight of Naomi emerging from the car wearing a stunning white two piece bathing suit, decorated with cherries surrounded by green leaves. She carried a towel drooping over her arm.

"You look gorgeous in your new bathing suit," said Adam, embarrassed by a stirring in his groin. "Let me help you with those towels."

"How did you know it's new?" asked Rachel, scowling. She picked up the cooler on the sidewalk.

"She mentioned it while we were talking in the car. I can carry that cooler for you, Mrs. Rosenberg," he said, feeling uneasy by her tone of voice.

After handing Adam the cooler, she removed the towels from the car windows and headed down the steps leading to the tennis court.

"I'm so glad you like my bathing suit," said Naomi, kissing Adam on the cheek.

"You're so beautiful," he said, smiling at her.

"You really look great too," she gasped

Rachel turned around and shouted, "Naomi, your father's waiting for us at the tennis court."

"Do you want me to bring the tennis rackets and balls

from the trunk?" asked Naomi.

"No, just leave them there for now," said her mother. "Don't forget the paper bag on the sidewalk."

Naomi headed down the steps with her hips swaying, carrying the grocery bag.

Adam followed her with the cooler, enchanted by her figure and blonde hair cascading down her shoulders.

Upon ascending the hill, they joined her father, who rose from the park bench. He stretched, revealing a hairy chest and protruding stomach.

Adam put the cooler down on the sidewalk and wiped the perspiration from his brow with his forearm.

"You're certainly looking fit," said David, noticing his daughter's magnetic attraction for Adam.

Naomi couldn't stop looking at his muscular figure. Her roving eyes traveled from his face down to his bare feet and then upward again.

"How about going for a swim," said Rachel, agitated by her daughter's interest in Adam. "Naomi, go back and get the canvas chairs from the trunk."

"I'll get them for you," volunteered Adam.

"We can get them together," said Naomi.

"No, you stay here and help your mother. I'll go with Adam. We need to have a little chat," said David, removing his car keys from his swimsuit pocket.

"Mother, I hope Dad isn't going to make a fool of himself. There's nothing going on between us that you have to worry about," said Naomi, watching her father go down the steps, with Adam following him.

"I told you not to buy a two piece bathing suit. Who do you think you are, Marilyn Monroe?"

"All my friends have them," insisted Naomi, glancing toward the steps. She wondered what her father was saying to Adam.

"I'm not going to argue with you, but you better stop flirting with Adam. It's so obvious that you like him. He's an attractive young man. I don't blame you for wanting to date him, but you're not going steady. Is that clear?"

"Of course," uttered Naomi, glancing up the hill at the street where the Cadillac was parked. She saw Adam standing next to her father, removing the lawn chairs from the trunk.

"I found out that Adam's older brother Karl works at the Mobile Station," said Rachel. "I don't think he has any plans about going on to college."

"That's not true," defended Naomi. "He's a terrific baseball and football player. Karl might get a sport's scholarship. He's been checking out different colleges and universities."

"I suppose he'll become a coach, who teaches history," said Rachel. "That's what they usually do."

"Did you tell Adam you're going to St. Mary's High School in the fall?"

"Of course," said Naomi, biting her lip because she wouldn't be seeing him regularly.

"You'll need at least two years of Latin to get into

nursing school at Mount Mary," said Rachel.

"Mom, I don't want to be a nurse. I was thinking about becoming an elementary teacher."

"Don't be ridiculous. Your father and I expect you and your sister to become nurses or maybe doctors. There's a shortage of female gynecologists. It wasn't easy for me to get my master's degree while raising you two."

"We spent a lot of time with babysitters. You were never home. On weekends you had to study for tests and type your papers," sighed Naomi. "You never had time for Lorna or me. We had to spend our weekends alone."

"You were such martyrs," uttered Rachel. "You forgot that I hired someone to clean the house so you could go to the movies. What was that woman's name?"

"Marjorie O'Connor, Neil's mom," said Naomi. "She lives near Adam's farm."

"Adam hasn't said a word about going to college," commented Rachel. "He'll probably follow in his father's footsteps and end up in the factory."

"Adam's father teaches him Italian. He told me he's going take it next year at Bradford. He wants to be an artist and study for a semester in Florence."

"An artist?" asked Rachel. "There's no future in that field. There are very few Michelangelo's in this world. He should think about studying engineering at Marquette."

"Adam won first place in the art contest at school last year for his oil paintings about his family farm."

"You won't be seeing him once school starts," said

Rachel. "You'll be busy studying Latin. You're also required to take religion. On weekends you'll be studying Hebrew at the temple to prepare for your Bat Mitzvah. Oh, here comes Adam and David."

"That sun is scorching," said David, out of breath from carrying lawn chairs with wooden frames.

"There's not a cloud in the sky. Just look at those huge waves," said Adam, holding two chairs.

"They're so turbulent," sighed Rachel. "It might be too dangerous to go swimming. Let's go down to the beach. You can put the chairs under those oak trees."

"That a good spot," agreed David, leading the way down the hill.

"Don't forget the cooler," said Rachel. "Look over there at the seagulls."

About two hundred seagulls were hovering together on the sand while dozens were diving into the waves and surfacing with small fish in their beaks.

Adam placed his chairs on top of the cooler and followed the family down the hill to the sandy beach.

"My feet hurt," yelled Naomi, aware that Adam was avoiding her since his talk with her father.

"The sand's wet and cool near the water," mentioned Adam, gazing into her sad blue eyes.

"What have you been painting lately," asked Naomi. "I love your farm paintings."

"I understand you got first place," said Rachel. "Did you get anything besides a blue ribbon?"

"I had a chance to spend the day at Layton School of Art in Milwaukee and have dinner with their teachers at Karl Ratzsch before coming back on the train," said Adam.

"Adam paints every day on his porch for a couple hours after lunch," said Naomi. "It would be nice if you got a scholarship to study art."

"This sand is burning my feet. It feels as if we have been walking through the desert," said Rachel.

"The Promised Land's under those oak trees," said David, leading the way.

Naomi followed him, putting down the paper bag to help her mother stretch out the army blanket in the shade.

After David and Adam set up the lawn chairs next to the picnic basket and cooler, they hurried toward the lake, complaining the whole way about the scorching sand.

Everyone paused, cooling their feet on the wet sand a few yards from the gigantic waves, crashing before lapping the shore.

"We'd better be careful," said Rachel, who entered the lake and was knocked down by a huge wave. She got up quickly with her hair and bathing suit drenched.

"The water's cold!" she shouted, shivering and darting toward the shore.

The others waded in the shallow water and leapt over the waves as they unfurled on the beach.

"Maybe it wasn't such a good idea to come out here today because of the waves," said David, going out further and almost being pulled under by a huge wave. He surfaced and returned to the shore.

Adam heroically dived into an unfurling six foot wave, and surfaced on the other side. He swam a few strokes and took a deep breath before diving into the next one.

"Adam! Adam! Be careful!" screamed Naomi as a wave knocked her down. She struggled under water, coming up for air and gasping for breath. Her father seized her by the arm and dragged her out of the water.

When Adam glanced toward the shore, he saw Naomi sobbing on the beach, which reminded him of Neil almost drowning at the pond. He rode the next wave back to the shore and stumbled onto the beach.

"Naomi! Are you all right?" he asked, noticing that her blonde hair was tangled. He could see her firm breasts and nipples through the clinging halter of her wet bathing suit.

"I'm not all right," she said shivering. "I didn't realize the waves were so dangerous."

"Let's have some lemonade before lunch," suggested David. "There's no lifeguard at this beach and the tide is too strong for swimming."

"David, you should have listened to the weather report before we came here," said Rachel, noticing that there were very few people on the beach.

"After going through the desert, we've had to face the Red Sea," said her father. "Where's Moses when you need him to part the waves."

"Adam, let's go for a stroll down the beach," said Naomi, reaching for his hand.

"We'll have lunch first," insisted David, heading back to the oak trees.

Upon reaching their shaded haven, Rachel wrapped a dry towel around her shivering daughter. After everyone dried themselves and shook the sand from their feet, they sat down on the army blanket.

David poured lemonade into their glasses while Rachel unpacked the chicken sandwiches, potato salad, grapes, almonds, and apples.

"Adam, you're the only one who didn't get knocked down by the waves," said Rachel. "Where did you learn to swim so well?"

"My mom taught my brother and me how to swim. She used take my brother and me to visit Grandma Mueller every Tuesday after the Farmers' Market at Union Park. We'd always come down to the beach with a picnic lunch.

"Your mother is so talented. She always performed in the school plays at Bradford," said Rachel. Gertrude reminds me of Vivian Leigh."

"Her father, Frank Mueller, was a prosperous criminal lawyer in town," said David. "I also knew your mother's brother, Pete."

"Your Uncle Pete was married to Clara Solinsky. Her mother came here from Poland. She had been in a concentration camp during the war. I see her regularly at the synagogue," said Rachel.

"Grandma Solinsky's such a sweet lady. I met her during Passover when we came back to Kenosha in 1951.

She told me all about the tragic death of her grandson, Kevin.

Adam was suddenly alarmed by the memory of Kevin attacking him in the barn.

"Kevin wasn't their real son. He was adopted," said Adam, his voice quivering. "My Aunt Clara had a nervous breakdown after Kevin's death. She's never recovered."

"We sometimes give Grandma Solinsky a ride home from the temple. She lives on 46th Street near St. George's parish," said David.

"That's where they held Kevin's funeral after he murdered Father Furstenberg and then killed himself with his father's shotgun," said Rachel.

"I understand your Aunt Clara converted to Catholicism and is now a nun at the convent," said David.

"She's not there anymore. Uncle Pete brought her to the Mendota Mental Hospital."

"These sandwiches are delicious," said Naomi, trying to change the subject. She deliberately let the towel slip from her shoulders, revealing her wet halter clinging to her breasts while she reached for an apple.

Adam averted his eyes from staring at her cleavage, trying to forget about Kevin attacking him in the barn. He also felt disturbed about Doctor Rosenberg's advice while going after the chairs.

Mr. Rosenberg insisted that he didn't want Naomi going steady with anyone because she was only fifteen years old. He expected his daughter to concentrate on her studies in the fall at St. Mary's High School and prepare herself for a career in medicine.

"Dad, I want to go for a walk with Adam on the beach now," asserted Naomi.

"Not until you've changed back into your clothes," insisted Rachel, scowling at her.

"Oh, Mom, my swimsuit will dry in the wind as we go down the beach," insisted Naomi.

"You heard your mother. You're to change into your clothes before walking on the beach," said David, handing the car keys to Adam.

"But I'll have to put these wet towels over the windows so no one will see me naked," said Naomi, pouting.

"I'll help you put them up," said Adam. "Then I'll change in the restroom of the tavern."

"We'll go back to the car together," said Naomi.

"No, you won't," insisted Rachel. "Adam can change first. When he comes back, you go change."

Adam departed carrying the wet towels. He felt overburdened and disturbed by memories of the past. Upon reaching the car, he rolled down the windows to fasten the wet towels so that Naomi would have privacy while changing, before opening the trunk with the keys.

Adam grabbed his clothes and entered Kaiser's Tap, waving to the bartender, who was smoking a cigar like Edward G. Robinson. A haze of smoke filled the entire bar in spite of overhead fans with whirling blades. The interior was dark and gloomy, a contrast to the clear blue sky outside. Adam also saw his own image reflected in the mirror behind the mahogany bar.

He hurried past the customers sitting on stools, gulping foamy tap beers and shots of whiskey while a few female companions sipped cocktails in frosted glasses. All eyes were on the reruns of boxing matches from Madison Square Garden.

Adam got a glimpse of several children at the shuffle board, munching peanuts and throwing the shells onto the tiled floor.

He opened the door to the restroom, repulsed by the acrid odor from the urinal. Upon entering the toilet stall, he locked the door. While he was changing into his clothes, a drunk stumbled into the room from the bar and vomited in the sink.

"I've got to take a shit," slurred the drunken man with enormous hands. He gripped the top of the stall door, trying to rip it from the hinges.

The unshaven man was surprised when Adam suddenly opened the toilet door and darted out of the bathroom. He hurried down the aisle between the bar and the shuffle board, bolting out of the tavern.

10

"I won't settle down. I don't want my daughter getting pregnant out of wedlock."

Within five minutes Adam had returned to the shade of the oak tree, where David was stretched out on the blanket, glancing through a *Time Magazine*. His wife was sitting in a lawn chair next to him, reading Han Su Yin's *The Devastation of Chungking*, a novel about the Japanese invasion of China in 1938.

"Hey Rachel, listen to this obituary," said David, reading to her. *"Hiram Bingham died at the age of 80 after a long illness. He was a famous explorer-author known for his book, "Lost City of the Incas." When he wasn't teaching history at Yale, Harvard, or Princeton, Bingham was exploring the Andes in Peru, where he accidentally discovered the famous ruins of Machu Picchu built centuries ago by Incan Indians."*

"I remember meeting him at a medical convention that we attended in Harvard. I'm going to order a copy of his book," said David, noticing that Naomi's swimsuit was almost dry. She was still reclining on her back to get a tan.

David was annoyed with Adam for removing his shirt, shoes, and socks and lying down next to his daughter.

"Naomi, are you sleeping?" asked Adam.

"I'm so glad you're back. I had the worst argument with my parents while you were gone," she whispered.

"Naomi you can go change now," insisted her mother, peering over her book.

I covered the windows of the car with the towels so that you can have some privacy," said Adam.

"I'll be back in a few minutes," said Naomi, removing her sunglasses and struggling to get up.

Adam leapt from the blanket and offered her his hand, pulling her toward his muscular chest and staring into her sad blue eyes. He wanted to kiss her, but Rachel was watching like an eagle protecting her fledgling in the nest.

"Here are the keys to the car," he said, handing them to Naomi. He felt uneasy because her mother was staring at him with roving eyes.

Naomi seized the keys and darted through the scorching sand up the hill toward the tennis courts.

Adam sat alone on the blanket observing the receding waves in the distance which were no longer threatening. He saw a playful couple splashing in the surf and leaping over the waves. His anxiety dissolved as he gazed into the blue sky where seagulls were soaring and diving for fish.

He glanced over at David, sprawled out on the army blanket, snoring, and Rachel absorbed in her novel. On top of the hill he saw Naomi entering the convertible. He started to feel aroused thinking about her changing clothes in the back seat.

"Mrs. Rosenberg, is it expensive to go to St. Mary's?" asked Adam, sitting down on the blanket. He was fearful he'd never see Naomi again once school started.

"The tuition is reasonable. It's only a hundred twenty dollars a year. We thought of sending Naomi to Prairie School in Racine, but it's too far to drive from Kenosha, said Rachel, removing her sunglasses and hungrily glancing at him.

"David and I decided to send Naomi to St. Mary's, even though the high school is located in the basement of the grade school. Of course, she will have to buy her own uniforms and books from her babysitting money," said Rachel, picking up her novel.

A few minutes later Naomi arrived, wearing a magenta blouse, blue shorts and sandals. She had combed her blonde hair and applied lipstick.

Adam leapt from the army blanket, putting on his shirt although he didn't button it.

"Let's take a walk along the beach," said Naomi. "We can pick up some shells and stones.

"I don't want you two out of my sight," said Rachel, peering over her sunglasses.

"Oh Mother," sighed Naomi. "We're not children. We don't need to be watched every minute."

Adam reached for Naomi's arm and hurried with her across the hot sand until they reached the lake. They paused to listen to the waves unfurling on the shore. Naomi removed her sandals and waded in the surf with Adam, holding her hand the entire time.

"We'd better not go too far out. I'm sorry the day isn't turning out very well," apologized Naomi. "I can't stand my mother planning my future. She's sending me to St. Mary's to keep us apart. When I finish high school she wants me go to college to become a nurse. I'm so angry with her that I don't know what to do."

"I want to go to St. Mary's this fall," said Adam. "That way I can see you every day. I have enough money saved to pay for my tuition and books."

"Oh Adam, that's wonderful. I love you. We can have lunch together every day," whispered Naomi, kissing him on the cheek.

"Your mother's spying on us," said Adam, glancing over his shoulder at Rachel looking at them through her binoculars.

"Let's walk down the beach far enough so that she can't see us," said Naomi. "I hope my father wasn't rude to you."

"He doesn't want us going steady," said Adam.

"My dad's such a jerk. He never takes my mother out to dinner anymore because he's too busy working," said Naomi, holding Adam's hand tightly.

"I'm worried about my mother coming home from New York with Marie before the Fourth of July. Her priest friend sent her money to pay for the train tickets. I didn't expect her to be gone so long."

"My parents argue all the time," confessed Naomi. "They're both stressed out from working overtime. They should go on a cruise without me and my sister along this time. They need to have some time together alone."

"Look at that couple making out in their bathing suits

on that blanket. I know that girl," said Naomi. "It's Cathy Anderson! She was in all my classes at Lincoln last year."

"Her boyfriend's Jim Hayes, a senior at Bradford. He's on my brother's baseball team," said Adam, continuing down the beach.

"There's a clump of trees over there," said Naomi. "It's getting awfully hot in the sun."

Adam led Naomi into the shade of the oak trees, quite a distance from her parents.

"I was amazed when I saw you swimming. You were so courageous to dive into the waves," said Naomi.

Adam removed his shirt, throwing it onto the sand. He reached for Naomi, embracing her with his muscular arms and kissing her on the lips.

"You're so strong from working on the farm," she whispered, caressing his chest with her fingers.

Adam glanced down at her polished nails, noticing they matched her pink lipstick. Gazing into her blue eyes, he held her tightly, enchanted by her perfume.

"Kiss me again," she whispered, her eyes meeting his with anticipation. A few minutes later she guided him to lie down with her on the grass between the trunks and protruding roots of the oak trees.

Adam reclined beside Naomi kissing her intensely on the lips. She received his prolonged kisses and then suddenly broke away from him.

"Just hold me in your arms for a few minutes," she sighed, placing her head on his chest.

Adam held her tightly, his heart beating wildly and feeling aroused. "I love you, Naomi,"

"I love you too, Adam," said Naomi, fearful of his passion for her. She was shivering with excitement as he stroked her blonde hair, with his body pressing hard against hers in the grass.

They stopped kissing when they heard a couple in the distance shouting at someone on the beach. Adam quickly pulled away from Naomi, reaching for his shirt to cover his bulging erection.

Naomi's eyes were wide with terror. "That sounds like my father. I wonder who they're yelling at this time."

"We better get up now," said Adam, rising from the grass. "Your parents will be angry with us for being gone so long. I don't want to cause you any more trouble."

"I wish we could stay here forever," she said, running her hand through her disheveled blonde hair and straightening out her wrinkled blouse.

"I've almost done with another painting of you," he said, putting on his shirt and buttoning it.

"Not another painting from that ugly photograph that I gave you? My hair's so short and I looked so pale."

"You're beautiful. I want to frame all my paintings of you and put them up in our living room," said Adam

Glancing over his shoulder, he saw her parents hurrying toward them, leaving footprints in the wet sand. A few minutes later they met in the shade of the trees.

"We've been looking high and low for you. You've

been gone for over twenty minutes. I was worried that something might have happened to you," said Rachel, glancing at her watch.

"There's not a single lifeguard on duty today," said David. "I suspected you might be hiding from us in that clump of trees."

"I couldn't believe my eyes," shouted Rachel. "We saw a couple having sex under a blanket!"

"When I shouted at them that I was going to call the police, they grabbed their belongings and ran naked up the hill toward the tennis courts," said David.

"We did see a police car parked behind our convertible. I'm sure they were looking for that couple," said Rachel, glancing up the hill through her binoculars.

Naomi informed her parents that she knew the girl from school who was dating the young man and that they were only making out when she and Adam walked past them ten minutes ago.

"What do you mean "only" making out?" asked Rachel. "Making out leads to having sex!"

"Now, Rachel, just settle down," said David, taking his wife by the arm. "There's no use getting so upset."

"I won't settle down. I don't want my daughter getting pregnant out of wedlock. That's the whole problem. I see unwed mothers at least twice a month at the hospital."

Rachel mentioned that working-class parents usually want to put the babies up for adoption, but their underage daughters insist on keeping the infants. However, affluent parents send their pregnant daughters to study abroad for a year, while the middle-class transfers them to private facilities for unwed mothers in California.

"I can't understand why they don't teach birth control to prevent unwanted pregnancies and venereal diseases in the high schools," said David. "It's such a taboo subject."

"What are you saying?" asked Rachel. "That will only encourage young people to have sex as soon as they reach puberty."

"Having birth control might stop abortions in this community," said David.

"What do you mean? This town's more Catholic than the Pope in Rome," said Rachel.

"I treat women and teenage girls who come to the Emergency Room hemorrhaging after having self-induced abortions," said David,

"There's a woman who sells ducks and chickens at the Farmers' Market," said Adam. "Nobody talks about this openly, but everyone knows she performs abortions in her farm house in Somers."

"It's shocking what goes on these days behind closed doors on those farms," said Rachel, scowling.

"There are half a dozen houses in Kenosha where women go to have illegal abortions," said David.

"Maybe we should go for a swim to cool off, now that the waves have calmed down," suggested Naomi, reaching for Adam's hand. "Let's go get our swimsuits from the trunk of the car."

"How about playing a game of tennis instead? It looks like the courts are empty," suggested David, removing his car keys from his pocket.

"I'll get the rackets from the trunk," said Adam, reaching for the keys.

"I'll go with you," insisted Naomi.

"Adam's capable of getting the rackets without you clinging to him. I hope the police picked up that couple for indecent exposure," said Rachel, glancing through her binoculars toward the parked cars on Sheridan Road.

Naomi was angry with her mother for lecturing her while they walked together to the tennis courts. She was relieved when Adam arrived with the rackets. After playing several games of tennis, they returned to the army blankets. David stretched out reading the Saturday newspaper while Rachel returned to her novel.

Adam and Naomi leisurely strolled along the beach, picking up seashells and stopping to make castles in the wet sand. This time they stayed close enough so her mother could see them through her binoculars.

11

"I'd marry Naomi tomorrow,
but her parents wouldn't approve."

Toward evening the Rosenberg family left the beach to take Adam back to the farm. David drove through downtown Kenosha, turning west onto 60th Street. Upon reaching Roosevelt Road, he turned on the radio to listen to the evening news.

Vice President Richard Nixon has been tight-lipped about whether President Dwight Eisenhower is fit to run for a second term due to his abdominal bypass and heart problems. Nixon said, "The man who knows best about his own condition is the President of the United States and he can surely speak for himself."

"I don't want to hear about politics," announced Rachel, snapping off the radio. There was a tense silence except for Naomi whispering to Adam in the back seat until they reached Hwy 50.

As they drove past the Hawkeye Turkey Farm, the trailer park, and the Mobile Station, Adam mentioned to the Rosenbergs that his brother was employed part time at the filling station and had decided not to be a mechanic but to attend college to become a math teacher.

"Karl should go to Marquette and become an engineer," advised David, as he turned onto Cooper Road.

"If he's good in math, he might get a scholarship,"

added Rachel. "There's a need for engineers."

"He's been offered a sports scholarship at the University of Wisconsin at La Crosse. They want him to play varsity football and baseball," informed Adam.

"That's wonderful," said Naomi, placing her head on Adam's shoulder. She ignored her parents, who were annoyed by her display of affection.

David turned onto Bentz Road and continued west. A few minutes later he swerved into the rutted driveway, coming to a halt near the front porch, where Grandma was crocheting in her rocking chair. The family dog rose from sleeping in the orchard and began barking.

Adam left the convertible quickly to calm Crispy, leading him by the collar to be chained at the doghouse beneath the dining room windows.

Upon returning to the front yard, Adam noticed that Grandma was busy talking to Naomi's parents. She had invited them to see Adam's paintings on the porch.

David led the way up the steps, followed by Rachel. Grandma departed for a few minutes, returning with a pitcher of lemonade and glasses filled with ice cubes.

Instead of joining them on the porch, Adam and Naomi took a stroll through the orchard, pausing to watch the grandeur of the sunset. They were in awe of the scarlet and lavender clouds suspended above the radiant burst of the setting sun.

Rachel opened the screen door on the porch. She gasped at the sight of the teenagers kissing at the corner of the orchard near the fence separating the lawn from the neighbor's cornfield.

"What's wrong?" asked David, setting down his glass of lemonade on the window sill.

"Nothing," said Rachel, heading down the steps and hurrying across the lawn toward the couple.

"Adam!" shouted his grandmother, trying to warn them. "Come and get some lemonade!"

Upon hearing his grandmother's voice, Adam stopped kissing Naomi. When he opened his eyes, he saw Rachel Rosenberg charging toward them.

"What's going on here?" she yelled.

"Nothing, Mother, we were just admiring the sunset," said Naomi, defiantly holding Adam's hand.

"I thought you wanted to see Adam's paintings on the porch," shouted her mother.

"That's just where we're going," said Naomi.

"Did you like my paintings, Mrs. Rosenberg?" asked Adam, trying to quell her anger.

"Of course, they're just beautiful. I didn't know that you could paint so well," said Rachel, momentarily forgetting her anger.

"Let's get going," whispered Naomi, hurrying toward the porch with Adam. She glanced over her shoulder at her bewildered mother.

"Wait a minute. There's something I want to say to you," shouted Rachel, her mouth gaping as she stood under the pear tree with her hands on her hips.

"We can talk later in the car," yelled Naomi, going up the steps onto the porch.

"Adam, those are fine paintings," said David Rosenberg, finishing his lemonade. "I'm impressed by your talent. You should go to Florence for a couple of years to study art. I really like Botticelli's paintings at the Uffizi Gallery, especially *The Birth of Venus*."

"My favorite is *Prima Vera,* with the Three Graces and Zephyrs in the background," said Adam.

"When did you go to Florence?" asked David. "I was under the impression that you couldn't afford…I mean that you didn't have an opportunity to travel."

"I've never been to Italy, but I've checked out books about art from the public library," said Adam.

"My grandson, he wants to be an artist someday," said Grandma. "But first he goes to college and then to Italy."

"We better be going because it's getting late and we have to work tomorrow," said David, annoyed by Naomi clinging to Adam while admiring his paintings of her. He left the porch and hurried down the sidewalk toward the parked car.

"Grandma, I finally get to meet you," said Naomi, giving her a hug and a kiss on the cheek.

"Dio mio! Naomi, you look just like that face in the pictures my grandson makes. How do you like going to the Jewish church today, Adam?" asked his grandmother.

"It's not a church. It's a synagogue," said Adam.

"We call it the Beth Hillel Temple," said Naomi.

107

"You're such a cute girl. Just like your pictures. I don't know if I can say that word syn-a-goggle."

All heads turned toward the driveway upon hearing the car door slam. Rachel was arguing with David, who was smoking a cigarette in the convertible.

"Adam, I better get going before my mother kills me," said Naomi, giving Grandma a hug and Adam a kiss on the cheek. "This has been the happiest day of my life."

"Naomi! Come to the car right now!" shouted her mother. "Your father and I have something to say to you."

"Coming, Mother," she said, pleading with Adam to come with her.

Adam accompanied her to the car, opened the back seat door, and waited for Naomi to enter.

"Mr. and Mrs. Rosenberg, thank you for inviting me to attend the Sabbath with you and for the wonderful afternoon at the beach," he said, closing the door.

"We enjoyed your company," said David. "Say hello to your father for us."

"And your mother when she gets back from New York with your sister," said Rachel. "I hope she has a good time with that priest friend of hers."

David started the convertible and drove forward, circling the driveway, leaving a cloud of dust drifting toward the pasture. Naomi waved to Adam as they came around the bend just before reaching the road.

Adam watched the Cadillac disappear down Bentz Road before returning to the porch.

"I like the doctor, but I don't know about that wife of his." said Grandma, carrying the tray with the pitcher and empty glasses into the house.

Adam stayed on the porch until dark gazing at his paintings of Naomi, wishing she were standing next to him. He paced the floor worried that she would be punished for kissing him in the orchard.

Grandma returned to the porch wearing her pink night gown. "What's the matter with you, Adam? It's getting late now. You've gotta get up early tomorrow."

"I don't know what's wrong with me, Grandma," said Adam. "I'm worried about Naomi. I'm afraid I'll never see her again."

"You say the rosary to the Blessed Mother," said Grandma. "She tells you what to do."

"Naomi's parents don't want us going steady," said Adam, shaking his head.

"That Rachel don't want you to kiss her daughter like you do in a-the back yard," said Grandma.

"I shouldn't have done it," said Adam, feeling ashamed.

"It's natural for you to want to kiss that beautiful girl," said Grandma, her brow wrinkled.

"I'd marry Naomi tomorrow, but her parents wouldn't approve," said Adam.

"You're too young to think about marriage. You've got to go to college and get a-the master's degree."

"I'm going to be a sophomore this fall. It will take three years before I graduate. Then I've got four years of college and another year or two before getting my master's degree. You mean I have to wait eight or nine years before I can marry Naomi?"

"You've got to ask God what He wants you to do. I don't know what's going on in this crazy country."

Adam also thought about his promise to become a priest, which made him feel more tense and depressed.

Grandma informed him that she only went to school until the fifth grade in Italy because she had to work in a factory in France to support her family after her father died.

She was twenty-six-years old and his grandfather was forty when they were married in a little church in the Italian Alps before coming to America.

"I don't want to wait until I'm forty to get married," said Adam, shaking his head and pacing the floor.

"Dio Mio! Adam, turn the light off on the porch and go to bed now," said Grandma.

"Buona nocte, Nona," he said, wishing her goodnight and following her into the house.

"Buona nocte," she responded, kissing him on the cheek and entering her bedroom.

Bewildered and confused by everything that happened that day, Adam walked across the blue carpet in the living room. He glanced at the maroon sofa and the empty space on the wall, thinking he would hang Naomi's paintings there after getting them framed.

12

"Now I know what the Nazi Concentration Camps are like."

On Sunday morning Giovanni took Grandma to Our Lady of Mount Carmel Church across from Columbus Park on 22nd Avenue. Adam and Karl accompanied her to mass while his father went to Mary's Restaurant to read the newspaper over coffee until the service was over. On their way home from church, they dropped Karl off at work at the Mobile Station.

Adam was depressed the entire morning, worrying about Naomi being punished by her parents. After lunch he helped his grandmother and father pick strawberries and harvest vegetables for the next day's market.

"What's the matter, Adam?" asked his father. "Didn't you have a good time with the Rosenbergs yesterday?"

"I liked the Sabbath service," said Adam, his brow furrowed. "Naomi told me that our mass is based on the Jewish Passover."

"They have their bread and wine after the service rather than during it," said Giovanni. "You like Naomi a lot, don't you, Son."

"Dad, I'm in love with her, but her parents don't want us going steady," said Adam.

"You're both only fifteen," said his father. "They're worried you'll get into trouble."

111

"Her mom and dad watched us like a hawk when we were at Pennoyer Park. They didn't want us being alone together for even a minute," said Adam, commenting about the lecture he received from David Rosenberg, and Rachel spying on them with her binoculars.

After talking to his father about the pitfalls of going steady, Adam felt relief for the rest of the day. In the evening after supper, he was distracted by watching the NBC special on TV with Bob Hope interviewing his guests: Jane Russell, Betty Grable, Steve Allen, Marilyn Maxwell, and George Sanders.

Grandma got so sleepy that she went to bed early, asking Adam to turn down the volume so she wouldn't wake up. He stayed up late watching TV, finally going to bed around midnight.

Adam got up early on Monday morning to help with the chores. After breakfast he went directly into the garden to hoe the rows of sweet corn and potatoes while Karl drove Grandma to the Farmers' Market at Roosevelt Park.

His brother set up the stand, leaving her there until noon. During his lunch hour, Karl drove grandma home, unloaded the truck and returned to the filling station.

Grandma thundered up the stairs to the kitchen carrying the cash box from the market. She set it down on the table, where Adam was yawning while glancing at the movie section of yesterday's newspaper.

"What's wrong with you today? You must be worried about that Jew girl again," she said. "It looks like you don't sleep last night."

"I spent the whole night tossing and turning, thinking about Naomi. I want to be with her all the time, but maybe God doesn't want us together. Maybe He's angry with me."

"Why should God get angry with you? You only kissed Naomi a little bit. Oh, now I understand. Dio mio! You want to marry that Jew girl because she's gonna have-a your baby. That's why you go with her parents to the syn-a-goggle in town."

"No, Grandma, I've never been on a date with her alone. I used to dance with Naomi every Friday night at Lincoln School in the gym. Mrs. Rosenberg was always there chaperoning and then gave me a ride home.

"I think God's angry with me because I promised Him I'd become a priest. I don't want to break my promise."

"Why do you do such a crazy thing?" asked Grandma. "The priest's life is Via Dolorosa (The Way of the Cross) because the Pope, he don't want them to get married to a woman. Those priests have to stay with men all the time."

Adam explained to Grandma about saving Neil from drowning at the pond and his promise to God that he would become a priest if Neil's life was spared.

She paced the kitchen with her footsteps thudding on the worn linoleum. "Dio Mio! The only way out of this mess is to find God's will for you."

Adam reflected on the words of the Lord's Prayer. *Our Father, who art in heaven, hallowed be Thy name. Thy kingdom come, Thy will be done on earth as it is in heaven.*

"Grandma, how do I know what God's will is for me?"

"Io non cognosco, I don't know. You pray every day and then listen to God for the answer."

Adam was startled by the ringing of the telephone. He leapt from the table and answered it.

"Yes, this is Adam Montanya. Hello, Mrs. Rosenberg... I'm so sorry to hear that Naomi's not feeling well...Yes, I'd like to talk to her."

"Hi Naomi," said Adam. "How are you? I'm sorry you're not well...What?...You mean you're leaving for California after the Fourth of July!...I can't believe you'll be gone for the summer and you won't be back until Labor Day...Of course you can write to me...Sure, I'll call you later... Your mom wants to talk to me again...That's fine...I love you, Naomi."

"Yes, Mrs. Rosenberg...no...I understand...I'm happy that Naomi will be working at the hospital in California... Yes, I understand...She'll start training tomorrow at St. Catherine's Hospital... Oh...she'll live with her aunt in Los Angeles... Yes...thank you for taking me with you to the temple and the beach...I had a good time...Bye now," said Adam.

"That woman, she don't want you to go out with her daughter no more," said Grandma, washing the dishes at the sink. She advised Adam to store his paintings of Naomi in the attic so he wouldn't feel bad by looking at them.

"I can't believe it. They really don't want me seeing her anymore. Grandma, we never did anything wrong. We only

114

kissed. That's all we ever did."

"I believe you, Adam. Maybe it's God's will that you don't go out with that Jew girl. Those people don't pray to Jesus and Mary, only Moses."

"They don't pray to Moses. Jews pray to God. They believe that Moses and Jesus were prophets."

"They don't make a-the sign of the cross like we do," said Grandma, frowning.

"I want to go to St. Mary's High School this fall. I have enough money saved to pay for my tuition and books."

"You talk to your papa about this. I don't know about that school. I'm tired. I go lay down on the couch now," said Grandma, leaving the kitchen.

When the phone rang a second time, Adam picked it up.

"Adam, if my mom knew I was calling you, she'd kill me. She went to fill the car with gas. She'll be back in a few minutes to take me with her to the hospital for training to be a Candy Striper. It's volunteer work.

"My parents yelled at me all the way home from your farm for kissing you in the orchard. I never told them that we kissed on the beach. She was just furious because I defied her. She slapped me across the face because I wouldn't promise her that I won't go steady with you."

"I'm sorry to hear about that," said Adam.

"She's grounded me for the week and doesn't want me talking to you on the phone. My father was angry with me for walking alone with you on the beach. They're sending me to live with my aunt in California so I won't become attached to you. I'll write to you every day. I promise."

"I'm so sorry. It's my fault. I shouldn't have taken you for a walk in the orchard to see the sunset. By the way, I'm planning to go to St. Mary's this fall so I can be with you. I'll sign up for Latin, biology, and geometry. Maybe we'll be in the same classes. Please don't say a word about this to anyone. I love you, Naomi."

"I love you too Adam. Here comes my mom up the driveway in her new Pontiac. I've got to leave now. I'll try to call you tonight after she's gone to bed," she said, hanging up.

"Who is it that you talk to on the phone?" asked Grandma, shouting from the couch in the dining room.

"It was Naomi," gasped Adam, feeling guilty because she was going to California to live with her aunt.

"I thought maybe it was Neil. That boy has changed. He looks so much better now," said Grandma.

"It's because he spends a lot of time with Jennifer and her parents on weekends. I'm going to paint for a while," said Adam, unable to hold back the tears.

Upon returning to the porch, he closed the door to the living room tightly and stood in front of Naomi's portrait, before removing it from the easel.

Adam mixed the colors and painted turbulent waves crashing on the beach while a young couple held hands and gazed at the seagulls soaring above the tide, diving for fish. The sky was dark with storm clouds hovering over Lake Michigan.

He was almost done with the composition when he heard the radio blasting in the kitchen. He knew it was two o'clock and Grandma had gotten up from her nap to listen to the news.

Good afternoon at WLIP in downtown Kenosha. This is Bill Schroeder with the international news: *The U.S. Air Force Chief of Staff, Nathan F. Twining, flew to Moscow to consult with Nikita Khrushchev about their latest developments. Khrushchev gave numerous toasts to peace and friendship between the countries including salutes to Eisenhower for a speedy recovery from his surgery.*

"What are you listening to on the radio?" asked Adam, entering the kitchen to get a glass of water.

"The news," said Grandma, standing near the radio, located on the counter beneath a cupboard. "Just listen. Maybe you'll learn something," said Grandma.

In northern Italy the stockbrokers are on strike in Milan and Torino, where wealthy speculators have made fortunes while thousands of smaller investors are suffering from heavy losses.

"Dio Mio!" interrupted Grandma, making the sign of the cross. I hope we don't have another Depression."

In the literary world Colin Wilson, who is only 25, published his controversial novel, "The Outsider," which is an intellectual thriller that redefines the image of the 20th century man.

"Wow!" said Adam. "I'd like to get a copy of it."

"Shh," said Grandma, hovering over the radio.

The new motion picture about to be released is "The Great Locomotive Chase," set during the Civil War in 1862. The stars are Fess Parker, known for his role as Davy Crockett, and Jeffery Hunter."

"I'd like to take Naomi to see that movie," said Adam, pacing the worn linoleum.

Now for the local news: *Dr. Gerald Richter, the anthropologist who exhumed the four skeletons from the Jacobsen orchard, got permission from the police to examine the contents of the barrels removed from Mrs. Jacobsen's farm house on Cooper Road. He found a pig's head floating in a liquid and a human arm and a leg.*

The male and female skeletons exhumed from the apple orchard were completely intact. They could be the parents of Mr. Jacobsen, who died a year apart during the winter of 1929 and 1930.

The third skeleton appears to be Harold Jacobsen, Martha's husband, who died in 1946. His skull had been severed from the vertebrae; the ribcage was crushed and the pelvis shattered.

The fourth skeleton was without a skull. The torso had only one arm and a single leg, which matches the arm and leg found in the barrels by Dr. Richter. The anthropologist believes the remains might belong to Joyce Jacobsen, who has been missing for over four years. The head of the mutilated woman still has not been found.

"It's time to go back to work in the garden," said

Grandma, turning off the radio and leading the way down the steps and out the door.

"What kind of person wants to kill Martha Jacobsen's cousin, Joyce?" said Grandma. "Martha was a good woman. I know she's crazy when she tells me she washed Jesus' feet upstairs in her house."

"Maybe Old Lady Jacobsen killed Joyce because she was having a love affair with her husband," said Adam.

"Sometimes people get in trouble because they love somebody else's wife," agreed Grandma. "You go to the garage and bring me cartons for a-the strawberries."

Adam helped his grandmother pick strawberries for an hour before digging the carrots and potatoes.

When Giovanni came home from work, he washed the vegetables. As soon as Karl returned from the filling station they loaded the truck for Tuesday's market before going into the house for supper.

After dinner when everyone was settled watching TV in the living room, Adam tried to phone Naomi. Her phone kept ringing until Rachel answered it, informing him Naomi had gone to bed early with a headache and wasn't available to talk.

Throughout the week Adam maintained his routine of helping with the morning chores, working in the garden, and painting on the porch while Grandma took her nap.

Adam completed another painting of a thunder and lightning storm on Lake Michigan, where the lovers were clinging to the sides of a sail boat. He began a third canvas with the two of them in bathing suits fleeing from a pack of ferocious wolves.

During the rest of the week he tried each night to call Naomi after supper but no one answered. Finally her mother answered telling him to never call her again.

On Sunday night, June 30th, Adam heard the telephone ringing in the kitchen. It was around 11:00 pm. He was lying on the bed in his underwear unable to sleep while Karl snored loudly in his twin bed across the room.

Adam darted into the dark kitchen and picked up the phone. "Naomi, I'm so glad to hear your voice."

"I'm sorry my parents have been so rude to you. I've missed you terribly," said Naomi. "I'm so miserable, I just want to die. I don't know what to do. I hate my job at the hospital. My mother's always checking up on me."

"Naomi, I miss you terribly. I've tried calling you every night after supper."

"Each time you called, I was sitting at the kitchen table. It breaks my heart to hear my mother lying to you that I'm not available to talk. I want to run away with you and never come back."

"I rode my bicycle to St. Mary's today and paid my tuition for next fall."

"I'm so glad you'll be coming to St. Mary's. I'll have a chance to see you during my lunch hour," she said.

"I told Sister Georgia that you were a friend of mine. She smiled and checked the schedule. I'm in three out five of your classes."

120

"I'm so relieved," sobbed Naomi. "I can't go on like this. I don't know what to do. I'm a prisoner in my own house. Now I know what the Nazi concentration camps were like.

"My mother grounded me until I leave for Los Angeles next week after the fireworks. I love you, Adam. I wish I could see you."

"I love you too. I think about you all day long and dream about you at night. I must see you before you leave," said Adam.

"The Fourth of July is next week Wednesday, but I heard on the radio that the fireworks won't be held at Simmons Island until Saturday, July 7th," informed Naomi. "It's because the City Council didn't order the fireworks on time. They won't be delivered until Friday night."

"What day are you leaving for California?" he asked.

"My parents are driving me to O'Hare on Sunday afternoon, July 8th. I wish you were coming with me. Maybe you could take a bus to Los Angeles, and we could elope to Mexico."

"I've already spent all of my savings on tuition for next year," stated Adam. "What time are you going to the fireworks at Simmons Island on Saturday night?"

"My parents promised to take me if I stopped threatening to run away from home," said Naomi.

"I'll meet you at the Beach House on Simmons Island when it gets dark, a few minutes before the fireworks start," said Adam.

"We always go to Simmons Island early to get a good seat on the hill," said Naomi. "I'll tell my parents that I need to use the rest room just before the fireworks start so I can meet you for a few minutes to say goodbye."

"I can't wait to see you on Saturday night," said Adam, hearing the thunderous footsteps of his grandmother coming through the dining room into the kitchen. "I have to hang up now. I love you."

"I'll call you again before we meet," said Naomi. "I love you too."

"Who's on the telephone so late?" asked Grandma.

Adam told his grandma about Naomi's parents sending her to California and his intention to take the bus to visit her later in the summer and elope with her.

"You must be crazy," said Grandma, pacing the kitchen floor. "You're too young to get married!"

Adam explained that her parents were sending Naomi to stay with her aunt until school starts after Labor Day because they didn't want her going steady with him.

"Those parents don't know nothing," said Grandma. "Nobody keeps Romeo away from Juliet."

"I can raise money baling hay to pay for my bus trip to California," said Adam.

"You don't go away now. I get a telephone call from your Uncle Pete. He tells me your mother and Marie come home next Wednesday on the Fourth of July.

"Your father's not happy to hear this. He goes outside to smoke a cigarette because that priest in New York likes women too much," said Grandma.

"Dad was so angry that he wanted to kill Father Fortmann after Mom left with Marie," said Adam.

"Your papa causes lots of trouble when he gets drunk." said Grandma. "He's moves out of here before your mother comes home with Marie."

"I didn't know that," said Adam. "He and Mom haven't gotten along since Marie was born."

"It's because of that no good priest. She shouldn't go to visit him in New York," said Grandma.

13

"Once you move out, we'll never see you again."

Adam was getting ready for church a week later when the telephone rang. He hurried to the kitchen, wearing a towel around his waist, hoping it was Naomi.

"It's not your girlfriend this time," said Grandma, handing him the phone. "It's the Jew farmer with lots of land. He wants you to work for him today."

"Hello, Mr. Klein," said Adam.

"I'd like you and Karl to help me bale hay? Your grandmother said you'll be home from church around 10:00 o'clock."

"I can work for you, but Karl's got a job at the filling station. Maybe Neil could take his place. He lives four houses down from here on Bentz Road," said Adam, giving him Neil's phone number.

"Thanks. I'll call him right away," said Joshua. "I'll pick you guys up in a couple of hours."

Giovanni drove Grandma and his sons to the 8:00 am mass at Our Lady of Mount Carmel Church. Instead of going to the bar, he went to the Alano Club for an AA meeting. He left early to pick up his family leaving, Karl at the Mobile Station.

Grandma prayed her rosary while Adam talked with his father as they continued down Highway 50.

"Dad, did you know Mom and Marie are coming home on Wednesday?" asked Adam.

"That's why I'm moving out," said Giovanni, gripping the steering wheel. "I've rented the upstairs apartment at Mrs. Solinsky's house on 46th Street."

"That's where Uncle Pete and Aunt Clara used to live with Kevin," said Adam.

"It's not a good place for you to stay," said Grandma, pausing from praying her rosary.

"Don't worry about me staying there," said Giovanni, turning onto Cooper Road.

"I'll never forget Uncle Pete going into a rage and beating Kevin so badly that he ended up in the hospital with a broken arm and leg, " said Adam.

"The police arrested Pete and kept him overnight in jail," said Giovanni. "The judge refused to let Kevin go back home. When he finally got out of the hospital, he lived downstairs with Mrs. Solinsky."

"That woman's a Jew. She comes to this country from Poland only five years ago," said Grandma, fingering her rosary beads.

"Mrs. Rosenberg gives her a ride home after the Sabbath almost every week," said Adam. "Mrs. Solinsky told her Kevin murdered Father Furstenberg and then committed suicide in her downstairs bedroom."

"Don't think about them," said Grandma, noticing the anger in Adam's voice.

Giovanni asserted that the two priests at St. George's

125

parish caused everyone a lot trouble, especially Uncle Pete, who invited Father Furstenberg to Sunday dinner with him and Aunt Clara. After the meal the priest took Kevin fishing at Petrified Springs and for a stroll in the woods. When Kevin got older they went to Milwaukee to the Downer Theater to see foreign films. Afterwards the priest took him to the rectory to play chess.

"Pete blames himself for trusting Father Furstenberg. He'll never forgive him for molesting Kevin, starting when the boy was five years old."

"Dad, are you moving in with Uncle Pete?" asked Adam, squirming in the front seat with his fists clenched. He still hated Kevin even though he prayed to God to help him forgive the dirty bastard.

"Pete moved out a couple of years ago but left his furniture in the apartment. He's living with his girlfriend. Mrs. Solinsky's renting me his place for $40 a month."

"How's Aunt Clara doing at a-the hospital?" asked Grandma. "That poor woman's crazy."

"Pete goes to see her once a month at Mendota, but she doesn't recognize him. Clara hasn't been the same since Kevin's funeral," said Giovanni.

"Dad, I know that you and Mom don't get along, but maybe you could go with her for counseling instead of moving out. We need your help on the farm," said Adam.

"I asked your mother to go to counseling with me several times. She always gets angry with me, saying 'I'm the one with the drinking problem, not her.'"

"When you were drunk after she left on the train, you said a lot of bad things about her," said Adam.

"I don't remember anything. I must have been in a black-out," said Giovanni, shaking his head.

"You called her a whore," said Adam, feeling burdened by his father's rage before he went to the hospital to detox.

"I've made a lot of mistakes when I was drinking," said Giovanni. "I must make amends to Gertrude, but I'm not ready to do it right now."

"Once you move out, we'll never see you again," said Adam, worried about his father abandoning the family.

"I'll stop in after work to help you get ready for the market," said Giovanni. "But I'll have to leave to attend my evening AA meeting."

"My sponsor suggested I get my own apartment because being around your mother isn't good for me. She's always trying to pick a fight. I need to protect my sobriety."

"You used to take off for the bar and then come home drunk," said Adam. "Mom was always furious with you."

"Most of the time I just took her verbal abuse, but after a while her nagging started to get to me. That's when I felt like I needed a drink," said Giovanni.

"Maybe her vacation settled her down. She told me that Father Fortmann had arranged for her to go on retreat while she was in New York," said Adam.

"I doubt that very much" said Giovanni. "Your mother doesn't always tell the truth. There I go again, criticizing her. I used to blame her for my alcoholism, but I brought on my own troubles because I stopped going to the meetings and calling my sponsor.

"I started drinking heavily after coming home from the war. Your mother told me that I had changed so much that she didn't know me anymore."

"The war does bad things to people," said Grandma, glancing out the window at Martha Jacobsen's abandoned farm across from Mr. Gascoigne's bungalow.

"What happened during the war to change you?" asked Adam as they turned onto Bentz Road.

"I fought at the Battle of Monte Cassino in Italy for months. That's where thousands of soldiers were killed," said his father, clinging tightly to the steering wheel.

"Maybe you can talk to your sponsor about the war," suggested Adam.

"That's a good idea. I'll talk to him after the meeting tonight. I've been carrying that burden for too many years now. I've got to face the past and stop running from it. I've never dealt with my feelings. I've always drowned them out with alcohol."

Giovanni slowed down as he passed the creek, swerving right into the rutted driveway and halting in front the garage. Crispy struggled to get up from under the maple tree, letting out feeble yelps while trotting toward the car.

"Mr. Klein will be here any minute," said Adam, petting the old dog, who was whimpering for affection.

"Giovanni, you pray to St. Francis. He helps you forgive your wife and that good for nothing priest," said Grandma.

"Laudato, si mi Seniore, per quelli che perdonano, per lo tuo amore."

"'Praise be to you, Oh' Lord, for those who forgive for the love of Thee.' Mama you taught me that prayer when I was a boy. I haven't recited it for many years," said Giovanni, his eyes clouded with tears.

"Adam, I said some mean things to your mother when I was drinking because I was angry and jealous of her friendship with Father Fortmann," he said, pausing.

"Dad, I can't talk now," said Adam. "I've got to go change my clothes before Mr. Klein gets here."

"Giovanni, I pray every day for you," said Grandma, heading to the back door. She glanced over her shoulder at him smoking a cigarette in the shade of the maple tree with Crispy lying at his feet in the grass.

After changing his clothes, Adam returned to the kitchen. He glanced up at the rooster clock above the sink. It was almost 10:00 o'clock when the phone rang.

"Naomi! Where are you?" he asked.

"I'm here working at the hospital. I'm calling from the nurses' station. I know I shouldn't be using the phone for personal calls, but the nurse on duty is with a patient."

"It's so good to hear from you. I miss you so much."

"I miss you too. I can't stand living at home anymore," said Naomi. "I just hate my parents for separating us. I don't want to leave Kenosha."

"I'll come to Los Angeles to visit you later in the summer. I'm going to be baling hay this week," said Adam.

129

"Mr. Klein's outside honking the horn of his pickup truck."

"I'll see you on Saturday night at the beach house on Simmons Island. I love you," said Naomi.

"My mom and sister are coming home on Wednesday," said Adam, glancing out the window at Joshua Klein, who was talking to his father in front of the garage with the dog standing between them. "My ride's here. I've got to go now. Naomi, I love you."

Adam hung up the phone and hurried out of the house, almost running into Mr. Klein.

"Didn't you hear me tooting the horn?" he asked.

"I'm sorry. I was talking on the phone," said Adam.

"I saw you at the temple for the Sabbath with the Rosenbergs last week," said Joshua.

"It was a real nice service," said Adam "Naomi invited me to spend the day with her family at the beach."

"She's even more beautiful than her mother, Rachel," said Mr. Klein, entering the pickup truck. "We're gonna stop and pick up Neil."

"He told me he would be going to mass this morning with his girlfriend, Jennifer," said Adam.

"I hope we don't have to wait for him to change his clothes," said Joshua, turning west onto Bentz Road.

There was Neil, standing at the end of his driveway. He talked about Jennifer and her family all the way to Mr. Klein's farm. Adam decided not to say anything about the Rosenbergs' decision to send Naomi to California.

Upon reaching the farm, they walked to the hay baler

parked in front of the barn near the silo, soaring like a gray rocket toward the blue sky. Joshua informed the boys that he would drive the John Deere tractor with the baler and wagon linked to it.

They rode to the field and then worked for the next hour loading the bales. Once the wagon was filled, Joshua drove them back to the barn and parked alongside of the elevator, which stretched to the third storey window of the barn.

Mr. Klein said, "Adam, you'll be stacking the bales inside the barn while Neil stays on the wagon and feeds the bales onto the elevator."

Adam gripped the sides of the elevator and crawled up to the window. Upon entering the oppressive barn, he gasped from the suffocating heat and lack of ventilation. The sweat dripped from his forehead as he dragged the bales and stacked them.

When the wagon was finally unloaded, Mr. Klein rang the iron dinner bell, summoning them to come to lunch in the farm house.

After dinner they returned to the field to continue the baling and loading of the wagon in the scorching sun. Upon coming back to the barn, Adam and Neil exchanged places with Adam throwing the bales onto the elevator while Neil worked in the upper storey of the barn.

Once the wagon was unloaded, Charlotte, Joshua's daughter, arrived with a pitcher of Kool-Aid and frosted glasses tingling with ice cubes. She placed them on a picnic table in the shade of a maple tree near the farmhouse.

"Enjoy your drinks, boys," said Charlotte, wearing a low cut red halter and white shorts. She turned around and headed back to the kitchen with her hips swaying.

"Wow! Is she beautiful," said Neil, his mouth gaping.

"Did you see her diamond ring?' asked Adam, thinking about meeting Naomi at the fireworks on Saturday night.

The young men paused to listen to the radio broadcast through the open window of the kitchen.

The Chinese Premier Chou En-lai spoke at the People's Congress in Peking about negotiating with Chiang Kai-shek about having him peacefully surrender Taiwan, to Red China. Chou promised that the military and civilians could return to the mainland to visit whenever they like, offering amnesty, and permanent jobs to them.

And now for the national news: *A report from the U.S. Office of Education indicated that delinquency in the public schools has increased over the past ten years. Nearly 43% of the teachers reported that more students disregarded doing homework, and one in three students were involved in vandalism, stealing, and profanity. In the slum areas of the country there was an increase in violence against teachers.*

"That's some news about our schools," said Adam, hesitating about telling Neil that he had signed up at St. Mary's so he could be with Naomi.

"I can't wait to see Jennifer again next week," said Neil. "Her parents are real nice. They never argue or even raise their voice. The only problem is that they won't leave

132

Jennifer alone with me for even a minute. We're always being chaperoned by her father or mother.

"Once in a while they have her younger brother keep an eye on us. We never have any privacy. I really like her family, but they're getting on my nerves."

Adam finally told him about spending the day with the Rosenbergs and eventually strolling with Naomi on the beach, where he kissed her several times while lying on the grass beneath an oak tree.

"Wow! I'm surprised her parents let you guys be alone together," said Neil, envious of Adam.

"They were angry with us for being gone for twenty minutes," said Adam, explaining how her mother grounded Naomi when she saw them kissing in the orchard of his front yard after bringing him home in the evening.

"Her parents won't let Naomi talk to me on the telephone anymore and they're planning to send her to California after the Fourth of July to stay with her aunt until school starts," said Adam, his voice strained.

"Jesus Christ, not California!" gasped Neil. "That's where parents send their loose daughters. Naomi's not pregnant, is she?"

"Hell no," said Adam, finally telling him Naomi would be attending St. Mary's this fall and that he was also going there instead of Bradford.

"You must be in love with Naomi to change schools," said Neil. "You and I have been friends since first grade at Whittier School. I won't be seeing you much anymore once you start St. Mary's."

"Please don't tell anybody about this," said Adam. "If Naomi's parents find out I'm going to St. Mary's they'd transfer her to St. Catherine's in Racine."

"My mouth's sealed," said Neil. "The only problem is if Naomi tells Jennifer, the whole city will know about it."

"Here comes Mr. Klein," said Adam.

"You boys ready to get back to work?" he asked, heading toward the tractor.

Adam and Neil boarded the wagon behind the baler and went back to the field. They hauled several loads of hay to the barn, working until sunset.

It was almost dark when Mr. Klein dropped off Neil in front of his house. A few minutes later he swerved his truck into Adam's driveway. Joshua waved to Grandma sitting on the front porch in her rocking chair and then departed.

Adam hurried up the steps of the porch where his grandmother told him that she had kept his dinner warm in the oven.

14

"Some Fourth of July this turned out to be! No fireworks and no husband!"

After finishing his morning chores, Adam glanced at his father departing for work at 6:30 in the Plymouth. He was followed by Karl and Grandma leaving in the red truck with vegetables for the market.

Around 9:00 o'clock Joshua Klein arrived to take him to bale hay. They stopped to pick up Neil, who was waiting for him at the end of his driveway.

The two young men worked all day stacking the bales on the wagon and then unloading them in barn. They only took time out for lunch and a few short breaks before returning to the field. After working ten hours, Joshua drove the boys back to their homes.

Adam headed down the sidewalk toward the back door, glancing up at the open window. He was surprised to hear his mother and sister talking in the kitchen. He opened the screen door and hurried up the hallway steps.

"Adam, I missed you so much," squealed Marie, rushing toward her brother with her blonde hair flowing from her shoulders.

"Marie, I'm so happy to see you," said Adam, hugging her and gazing into her tearful blue eyes.

Gertrude also gave him a hug. "I swear you've grown six inches since we've been gone."

"I've been baling hay this week," said Adam. "Mr. Klein's paying me a dollar an hour."

"Your clothes smell from sweat and hay," sighed his mother. "You need a bath."

"But first you eat your dinner. I have polenta and sausage for you inside a-the oven," said Grandma, rising from the table to serve him.

"We had a lot of fun in New York," said Marie. "Father Fortmann took us to see the Statue of Liberty."

"Where's dad?" asked Adam. "I thought he'd be here after picking you up from the train station."

"Your father was angry because the train was three hours late. He took us home, put our luggage into the dining room, and left for his AA meeting.

"It wasn't our fault that there was an accident near Zion that caused the train to be delayed. A deaf old man drove his car from a country road into the engine," she said.

"Did he survive?" asked Adam.

"No, the car was smashed to pieces," said Gertrude. "It was just awful. The passengers left the train to see the wrecked car. I didn't want Marie to look at that bloody mess, so we waited in our seats until the wreckage was cleared."

"Your father waits for the train too long so he don't eat his supper tonight," said Grandma, passing the salad bowl to Adam.

"Giovanni hardly said a word to me, but he talked to Marie all the way home."

"We rode in a carriage around a big park next to the dinosaur museum," said Marie.

"It was the American Museum of Natural History near Central Park," said Gertrude. "It took us forever to get there on the subway."

Grandma went to the stove and removed the steaming tea kettle. "Adam, you go take your bath."

"Is Dad coming home to sleep tonight?" asked Adam, reaching for the kettle.

"No, Giovanni stays at Uncle Pete's apartment. He takes his clothes there yesterday," said Grandma.

"He didn't say a word to me about moving. I was hoping I could talk to him tonight," said Gertrude.

"Dad got drunk after you left," said Adam. "He went to treatment for a week. His sponsor told him to get his own place for a while until he gets more sobriety."

"I'm sure he blames me for his relapse," said Gertrude, her voice strident. "I've got to unpack our suitcases."

"I'll help you," said Marie, putting her crayons back into the box and following her into the bedroom.

Adam picked up the tea kettle and headed into the bathroom between the two bedrooms. He could hear his mother shouting behind the closed door.

"Your father has a lot of nerve, leaving us. Just look at these empty dresser drawers."

"I want my daddy," sobbed Marie.

"Stop that crying right now!" yelled Gertrude. "It's obvious that your father doesn't love either one of us."

137

"Why doesn't he love us, Mommy?" cried Marie, her voice quivering.

"It's because he's a drunk," she shouted."Now help me unpack this suitcase. When we're done, we have to wash the vegetables outside in the dark."

Adam shook his head as he poured the steaming water into the bathtub. While taking his bath, he heard his mother's shrill voice complaining that the sheets were filthy and hadn't been washed for weeks.

She stormed out of the bedroom, carrying the sheets while Marie followed her with an armful of laundry from their suitcase. They brought them to the basement to be washed before hanging them outside on the line.

A few minutes later Adam wrapped a towel around his waist and brought his soiled clothes to the basement where his mother was scrubbing the sheets in a laundry tub.

"Look at all these dirty clothes piled here," shouted Gertrude, sighing with exhaustion from the long trip home.

"Sorry, Mom, we've been too busy to do the laundry while you were gone," said Adam.

He went upstairs to the dining room, where Marie was coloring at the table with Grandma sitting next to her, knitting a sweater.

"Come. Marie, we go now to wash the vegetables outside. Adam, you look so tired. Go and paint on the porch," insisted Grandma.

Feeling weary, he took Grandma's advice and departed for the porch, where he glanced at his picture of Naomi on the easel. He recalled strolling on the beach with her alone while the waves were caressing the shore.

Leaving the porch, he strolled through the orchard, stopping at the fence where he kissed Naomi. Adam yearned to be with her, wandering in the dark among the trees with green apples and pears forming on the branches.

Upon returning to the porch, he heard the phone ringing. By the time he reached the kitchen it had stopped ringing. Glancing out the screened window, he noticed moths circling the flood light that illuminated the back yard. He overheard his mother complaining.

"Adam went to paint, leaving us to do his work," shouted his mother, surveying the crates and bushels of vegetables that needed to be washed.

"Don't bother Adam. He's tired from baling hay all day," said Grandma, sitting on a stool, scrubbing carrots at the tub while Marie rinsed them with fresh water.

"We're also worn out from travelling all day," blurted Gertrude. "Giovanni should have stayed to help us out'.

"I'm coming out to help you," said Adam from the window. He was about to leave when the phone rang again.

"Mom, it's Dad calling. He wants to talk to you."

"Tell him I'm busy doing his chores. Some Fourth of July this turned out to be! No fireworks and no husband!"

"Dad said he's coming after the meeting to help wash the vegetables and load the truck."

"You can tell him I'll load the truck without him. Where in the hell is that truck anyway?"

139

"Karl takes it to the filling station. He's comes home at 10:00 o'clock. I got his dinner in the oven," said Grandma.

Adam informed his father that they could manage without him tonight. Upon hanging up the phone he went outside to help his family.

"Next time tell your dad we don't need his help around here ever again," said Gertrude.

"Uno momento," said Grandma. "We need Giovanni to bring hay from the field to a-the barn."

"I already talked to dad about hiring Mr. Klein to bale our hay for us on Saturday," said Adam.

"That's when we're supposed to go to the fireworks at Simmons Island. Your dad promised to take Marie to the beach that day," sighed Gertrude.

"Mr. Klein will bale the whole field in a couple of hours. I'm going to help him," said Adam.

Adam insisted that his grandmother go to bed since she was falling asleep. She got up and stretched going into the house. Everyone could hear her heavy footsteps thudding on the hallway stairs leading to the kitchen before heading to her bedroom to put on her pink nightgown.

A few minutes later Karl arrived in the truck. He encouraged his mother to take Marie into the house and put her to bed since she had fallen asleep on the sidewalk.

Karl and Adam finished scrubbing the vegetables and loaded the truck in less than an hour. They talked for a few minutes in the kitchen before retiring for the night.

15

"I don't remember Grandpa," said Marie. "Mommy liked him, but she hates Father Fortmann."

On Saturday morning Adam waited at home for Mr. Klein to arrive with his tractor, hay baler, and wagon. Joshua got there by 9:00 o'clock. He drove the tractor while Adam worked behind the baler, retrieving and stacking the bales on the wagon. After four hours of steady work, they had filled the loft with hay. Early in the afternoon Joshua departed from the farm with all of his equipment.

Even though Adam was tired, he helped Karl unload the produce from the truck when his family returned from the market early in the afternoon.

After lunch while everyone rested, Adam returned to the porch to paint. Within a few minutes he fell asleep on the wicker sofa. An hour later he woke up, startled by the harsh noise coming from the living room.

Adam entered the house, hurrying past his mother, who was vacuuming the blue carpet with her new Hoover Upright. He went to the kitchen where Grandma and Marie were making ham sandwiches to take to Simmons Island for the Fourth of July celebration.

"What can I do to help you out?" asked Adam.

141

"You put my baked beans inside a-the basket," said Grandma, wrapping the last sandwich with wax paper.

"Don't forget the pickles," said Marie, handing him the Ball jar. "I can't wait to see the fireworks."

It was late in the afternoon when Giovanni arrived in the Plymouth to take everyone to the beach. Adam helped him pack the trunk.

Gertrude sat across from Giovanni on the passenger's side in the front seat while Adam sat between Grandma and Marie in the back seat.

"Daddy, I'm so happy to see you again. Thanks for taking us to the fireworks," said Marie.

"How was your trip?" asked her father once again.

"I got to ride on the merry-go-round all by myself in a big park. Mommy got scared on the Ferris wheel."

"Father Fortmann took us to Coney Island. I hated that crowded amusement park, but I loved the views from the Empire State Building and Statue of Liberty."

"We went everywhere on the subway," said Marie. "I was scared because it was dark and made lots of noise."

"It's time for the news," said Giovanni, not wanting to hear about their trip. "Grandma doesn't want to miss it."

This is Bill Schroeder wishing you a Happy Fourth of July Celebration from WLIP in Kenosha. *The crowds have been gathering all afternoon along the shore of Lake Michigan at Pennoyer Park, Simmons Island, and South Port Beach for the spectacular display of fireworks this evening. The cannon will start booming when it gets dark.*

Here in Kenosha people are celebrating Independence Day, but there's tension in Pittsburg and Youngstown, Pennsylvania and Gary, Indiana among the union members after 20 years of collective bargaining. In spite of four weeks of negotiating Dave McDonald, representing the union, was given an ultimatum to settle a contract by John Stephens from U.S. Steel. Management insisted on a five year contract instead of the two year pact. Of course there is the possibility of a strike by the workers.

"I hope we don't have a strike at Nash Motors," said Giovanni. "Our union members are angry over our contract and are demanding an increase in wages."

"The customers have been complaining at the market over the price of vegetables," said Gertrude. "We didn't take in much money today because people are worried about another strike."

"I'm sure the steel workers will go on strike in August, during the hottest month," said Giovanni. "They have about 650,000 union members in Pennsylvania and Indiana."

"Here we are at Simmons Island," said Adam, peering through the open window at the families sprawled on the grass with their lawn chairs and picnic baskets. "This place is really crowded."

"It won't be easy to find a parking space," said his father, slowing down to survey Simmons Island.

Gertrude noticed a space being vacated by an angry young couple carrying a paper bag and cooler. Their two sunburned children were crying in their wet bathing suits because they didn't want to miss the fireworks.

In spite of cars honking behind him, Giovanni stopped the Plymouth on the road ignoring the stalled traffic. He helped his family unload the car before leaving to find a parking space on the other side of Simmons Island.

Adam set up the lawn chairs and stretched out the army blanket while his mother unpacked the picnic basket. Grandma, who was weary from missing her nap, plopped into a canvas chair. She closed her eyes, fingering her rosary beads in the shade of an elm tree.

Sitting down on the blanket with his sketch pad, Adam drew a picture of Naomi from memory. Marie sat next to him with her new box of crayons and coloring book.

When Giovanni returned from parking the car, Gertrude distributed paper plates and glasses of Kool-Aid. She passed around the potato salad, ham sandwiches, and dill pickles, before serving Grandma's homemade ravioli.

"I'm so glad to be back in town," said Gertrude. "My parents used to bring my brother and me here for the whole day every Fourth of July. Uncle Pete and I would dive in the waves and swim for hours while they sat under the trees reading all afternoon."

"Years ago I come here with my husband, Frederico, and Giovanni when he is a little boy," said Grandma. "At that time I work in a factory, making stockings on a-the sewing machine."

While eating together on the blanket, everyone listened to Grandma's stories about her life during the Depression before buying the farm in 1936. After finishing their meal, Gertrude served slices of German chocolate cake.

"Mommy, I want to go swimming now," pleaded Marie.

"Marie, it's getting late. It won't be long before the fireworks start," said her mother.

"A lot of families are coming up the hill from the beach. Of course there are couples lingering under those umbrellas near the lake," said Giovanni.

"I miss Frederico," said Grandma. "His family lives in the village next to mine in Italy. Everybody makes houses from stones with a-the fireplace, but no furnace."

"Grandpa never said an unkind word to me," recalled Gertrude. "It's too bad he fell out of the hayloft and died when Karl and Adam were little."

"My father was skilled with his hands. He made shoes from leather and wove baskets from willows."

"I don't remember Grandpa," said Marie. "Mommy liked him a lot, but she hates Father Fortmann. She never wants to see him again."

"Mark told me that he was leaving the priesthood, but he changed his mind," said Gertrude. "He has a lot of male friends in New York who are actors and directors. Some of them don't like women."

"You gotta be careful with those priests. Look what happens to your nephew, Kevin," said Grandma. "He kills that good for nothing priest and then he shoots himself."

"I used to perform in plays when I went to Bradford," said Gertrude, ignoring Grandma's comment. "I had the lead role of Emily in *Our Town*. I also played Stella in *Street Car Named Desire*."

"Mark Fortmann promised to get me a part in one of the shows in New York, but he never even introduced me to a director. After sightseeing with him and Marie for a few days, I realized he had lied to me."

"That man shouldn't be a priest," said Grandma. "He likes women too much."

"He was snobbish and rude," said Gertrude. "Mark had changed since I saw him last. He preferred the company of his male friends instead of me."

"At first Mommy didn't want to come back home again," said Marie. "But she changed her mind."

"After a week in New York, I was ready to pack my bags and come home," said Gertrude.

"I got tired of Mark's critical attitude toward women. He blamed Eve for giving Adam the apple in the Garden of Eden, which got them expelled from Paradise. He wouldn't admit that Adam was also involved in the Original Sin."

"If he was so mean to you, why didn't you come home after the first week?" asked Giovanni.

"Father Fortmann had lots of tickets," said Marie. "He waved them at Mommy."

"We didn't come back because Mark bought us front row seats to several stage plays, including the Broadway musical, *My Fair Lady*. It's the longest running show in the history of the theater."

Gertrude explained that Father Fortmann begged them

146

to stay after she threatened to take the next train home. He finally apologized and started treating her better.

"May I go to the beach now?" asked Marie.

"I'll take you down there for a few minutes before the fireworks start," said Giovanni, rising from his chair.

"Giovanni, please don't go now," said Gertrude. "I need to talk to you for a little while."

"I'll take Marie to the beach," insisted Adam, hoping that he would see Naomi in the crowd before it got dark.

"Adam, you go with your sister," said Grandma. "Your mother and father need to talk now."

Grandma struggled to get out of her chair even with the help of Giovanni. She wandered in the crowd speaking Italian to friends from her church while her son and daughter-in-law sat down on the blanket to talk privately.

Adam held his sister's hand, weaving down the hill toward the beach. They passed dozens of families playing cards, reading novels, or listening to radios.

A few minutes later they reached the beach where Marie splashed in the waves while Adam scanned the area, hoping to see Naomi.

As the sun set, Adam returned with Marie. His father and mother were sitting in lawn chairs drinking Kool-Aid while Grandma sat beside them talking about growing up in northern Italy, where there were three meters of snow in the Alps every winter.

16

Everyone was in awe over the splendor of emeralds, rubies, and diamonds bursting from the sky.

When it was dark, just before the fireworks started, Adam excused himself to go to the restroom, eager to meet Naomi. He wove his way down the crowded hill. Upon reaching the beach house, he nervously waited for Naomi to arrive.

Adam paced up and down, hoping that she didn't forget her promise to meet him. Ten minutes later the fireworks started with loud cannon booms, followed by oohs and aahs from the crowd. The initial burst of shimmering sparks cascaded from the sky.

Adam tried to watch the grand spectacle over the lake, but he couldn't enjoy it because Naomi wasn't with him.

He had almost given up after fifteen minutes and was about to leave to join his family when he saw three people crossing the road toward the beach house. His first thought was that Naomi was accompanied by her watchdog parents.

"Adam, where are you?" asked Naomi, her voice trembling with fright.

He didn't immediately respond thinking that maybe it was a trick. When the next cannon boomed and the sky was illuminated by a radiating bronze spider, he recognized

Naomi hurrying toward him.

"I'm here," blurted Adam, his back against the shaded wall of the beach house.

"I'm with Jennifer and Neil. My parents said we had to be back in ten minutes or they'd come after us," gasped Naomi, running toward him.

"Naomi!" he shouted, pulling her into his arms and kissing her passionately.

They ignored Neil and Jennifer, hurrying past them into the shade. Both couples were hidden from the spectators, who were watching the fireworks on the hill.

"I'm so sorry I'm late," gasped Naomi, trembling in his arms. "My parents wouldn't let me come here alone."

"You don't have to explain," said Adam, holding her against his chest. His heart was throbbing loudly as he kissed her again on the lips.

"Oh, Adam," gasped Naomi, allowing him to kiss her again before breaking away from him. "You've never kissed me like that before."

'I love you, Naomi," said Adam, pressing his body tightly against hers and smothering her with kisses, not expecting to become so aroused.

"Adam, we must stop now," said Naomi, fearful of his desire to be with her.

Neil and Jennifer unexpectedly stepped into the light of the next display of fireworks over the lake. It was a burst of scarlet followed by a blue and white waterfall.

"We've got to go now," said Jennifer, interrupting them.

"I swear that's Naomi's mom coming down the hill."

"You're right. It's Mrs. Rosenberg," said Neil, glancing toward the hill.

Naomi was stunned, not knowing what to do. She pulled away from Adam saying, "I've got to go now. I'm leaving tomorrow for California. I'll write to you every day from my aunt's house."

"I've saved enough money for a bus ticket to Los Angeles," he said, "I love you."

Adam backed into the shade, watching them cross the street. Sure enough, during the next display of fireworks, he saw Rachel Rosenberg standing there with her hands on her hips, waiting for them. She turned around leading the way back up the hill while the crowd oohed and aahed.

Everyone was in awe over the radiant splendor of emeralds, rubies, and diamonds bursting from the sky and dissolving in the water.

Adam felt tense and bewildered, knowing his parents would be worried about him for staying away so long. He hurried around the beach-house and crossed the sand, ignoring the exploding fireworks above the lake. Upon reaching the paved road, he followed it up the hill, finally locating his family.

"Why do you come home so late?" asked Grandma. "I worry about you."

"I met some friends from school and stayed with them watching the fireworks," said Adam, feeling guilty about lying again.

"We missed you, Adam," said Gertrude, sitting next to Giovanni on the blanket, holding hands.

"We still have about fifteen minutes of fireworks left," said his father. "Who did you meet on the hill?"

"I hope it wasn't that Jew girl, Naomi." said Grandma.

"I was with Neil and Jennifer," said Adam.

"Adam, he goes to the syn-a-goggle with your doctor, his wife and their daughter, Naomi," said Grandma.

"I hope you had a good time at the temple celebrating the Sabbath, and the picnic at the park," said Giovanni.

"I liked the service at the temple," said Adam "We had a good time at the beach."

"Rachel used to give you a ride home from the dances on Friday night. I've known her and David for years. They always came to watch my performances at Bradford," said his mother. "I didn't know you were dating Naomi."

"Her parents don't want us to go steady," said Adam, pausing to watch an emerald burst of fireworks. "Her mother's sending her to Los Angeles for the summer."

"Everybody knows that parents send their daughters to California to have babies and put them up for adoption," said Gertrude.

"Naomi's not pregnant. She's coming back to Kenosha in September and will be attending St. Mary's. Her parents don't want her going to Bradford," said Adam.

"Adam goes to St. Mary's too," said Grandma.

"What are you talking about?" asked Gertrude. "What's been going on with this family since I've been gone?"

151

"Gertrude, please sit down," said Giovanni. "Here comes the finale and you're blocking the view."

"Mommy, don't get mad," said Marie, enjoying the final event of the evening.

The canons thundered with dozens of fireworks bursting over the lake like exploding gems from a jewelry store. They poured from the sky, culminating with multiple cascading waterfalls.

When the show was over, the murmuring crowd gathered their belongings and moved slowly toward their parked cars, carrying picnic baskets, blankets, and chairs.

"Giovanni, where is the car parked?" asked Gertrude.

"It's on other side of the park," he said.

"I'm too tired to walk," said Grandma. "My feet hurt and my back too."

"Just stay here and wait. I'll bring the car around," said Giovanni. "It might take 20 minutes with all this traffic."

"Adam, I want you to tell me about what's going?" asked his tense mother.

"There's nothing to tell," said Adam. "Naomi's parents are sending her to California to live with her aunt because they don't want us going steady."

"They must be worried about your interest in her," said Gertrude, shaking her head.

"I'm going to St. Mary's so I can be with Naomi when she comes back for high school," said Adam. "I've already signed up for my classes and paid the tuition."

"You're heading for trouble," she signed.

17

"Grandma, look what I found.
It's a letter from Naomi."

Adam was depressed during the second week of July because he hadn't heard from Naomi. On Friday he got up to do his chores, spending the whole morning helping Grandma in the garden. Early in the afternoon Gertrude returned with Marie from the market at Baker Park. She was in a good mood because she had earned $80.95.

All through lunch Adam didn't say a word to his mother, sister, or grandmother. He left them chatting at the kitchen table to paint on the porch.

His current composition was dark and sinister, based upon a scene from *Fall of the House of Usher* by Edgar Allen Poe. Roderick Usher was standing in front of the coffin of his twin sister, Madeline. He had buried her alive in the basement of their dilapidated Victorian Manor, which was burning and collapsing into the stagnant pond.

After rising from the couch from her afternoon nap, Grandma entered the porch. She gasped at the sight of Adam's gruesome painting.

"Dio Mio! What kind of picture do you make? That man looks like a-the devil!"

"He's not the devil. He's an insane character from a short story," said Adam, wiping his brushes on rag and placing them to soak in kerosene. "I'm going back to work in garden."

"Adam, what's the matter with you?" asked Grandma. "I know it's that girl, Naomi. You miss her too much."

"I don't want to talk about it," he said, leaving her standing on the porch.

After working for several hours, Adam carried the crates of potatoes and carrots from the field to the spigot beneath the kitchen window. Marie was there helping her mother wipe the dirt from the tomatoes with a damp cloth while Grandma was scrubbing bunches of beets.

"I don't understand why Giovanni doesn't want to help us anymore," said Grandma.

"It's because he doesn't want to sleep here," said Gertrude. "We'll have to get along without him."

"Before you come back from New York, Giovanni was here every day to help us. After supper he goes to his meeting downtown and then comes back to sleep."

"Giovanni's more interested in going to AA meetings than helping us. He's busy working with his sponsor at the Alano Club trying to clear the wreckage of his past, whatever that means. What bothers me is that he doesn't care about me or his family," said Gertrude, scowling.

"Daddy doesn't love us anymore," said Marie.

"Mom, if you weren't always finding fault with Dad, maybe he wouldn't have moved out," said Adam, dejected because his father wasn't home, and Naomi was gone for the summer.

"You're blaming me for his alcoholism. I never forced

him to have a drink. It's not my fault he's an alcoholic," blurted Gertrude.

"What's an alcoholic, Mommy?" asked Marie.

"It's someone who doesn't have the will power to control his drinking," said her mother. "Adam, why do you have such a long face?"

"It's because that Jew girl doesn't write to him from California," said Grandma.

"I have to admit that she's beautiful. You did a nice job painting her portraits," said Gertrude.

"I want to take a bus to visit Naomi in Los Angeles."

"My God, you must be crazy! Naomi's parents would have a fit if they found out you were going there. I was just talking to Rachel on the phone last week. She said that she didn't want you writing to Naomi."

"We never did anything wrong. I can't understand why her parents are so mean to us," said Adam.

"I'm depending on you to help us get ready for the market for the rest of the summer. During the next couple of weeks the tomatoes and sweet corn are ripening, and we're having a bumper crop of beans."

"Adam, don't go to California," begged Grandma. "You can't stay in the same house with Naomi."

"I have enough money saved to pay for a hotel room," snapped Adam, pacing in front of the garage.

"Now don't get angry," said Gertrude. "Grandma and I need your help on the farm. You can still paint every day on the porch while she takes her nap."

"That painting with the devil scares me," uttered Grandma. "The house burns with too much fire."

"I'll stay here to help you," said Adam, equivocating about buying a bus ticket once he got Naomi's address.

"I see Karl finally towed away your father's old Nash. That broken-down jalopy was parked in front of the brooder house for years," said his mother.

"He's fixing it at the filling station so he can take it to Bradford this fall so Dad won't have to pick him up from football practice," said Adam.

"Adam, don't you worry," said Grandma. "You can see Naomi when you go to school at St. Mary's."

"That won't be until September, after Labor Day," said Adam, his face crestfallen.

"I'm surprised her parents aren't sending Naomi to St. Catherine's in Racine that's where Rachel went to school," said Gertrude.

"Don't say anything about me going to St. Mary's," said Adam, putting the last crate of potatoes on the truck.

"Don't worry. I won't say a word to her about it," said Gertrude. "It's time to call it a day. Come on, Marie. You need a bath before going to bed."

"I'm going to write a letter to Daddy and tell him to come home," said Marie, following them into the house.

Adam noticed a stack of envelopes on the kitchen counter across from the telephone. He leafed through the bills, finding a letter addressed to him.

"Grandma, look what I found! It's a letter from Naomi.

.Why didn't you tell me it was here?"

"Dio Mio, I bring the mail inside the house, and I forget to look at it."

Adam went into his bedroom, closing the door. He sat on the edge of his bed reading the letter.

Dearest Adam,   *Thursday, July 12, 1956*

I arrived in Los Angeles on Sunday, July 8. My Aunt Loretta picked me up at the airport in a limousine. She's my mother's older sister. Her husband, Uncle Joseph died several years ago in a plane crash shortly after they were married. They don't have any children, but she has a cook and a maid to do the housework. It took us forever to get to her Victorian Mansion due to the traffic.

I hate living here with her. She watches every move I make and constantly asks me questions, giving me advice about dating, men, and marriage. She'd be angry with me if she knew I wrote to you. My aunt belongs to several committees and entertains women friends for lunch every day in her grand dining room with an imported chandelier from Austria that cost a fortune.

Each morning she has a taxi waiting to take me to Mount Sinai Hospital, where I work as a volunteer. I help the nurses empty bed pans, take temperatures, and bring meal trays to the patients, but I find the evenings at my aunt's home boring. Aunt Loretta is always pressuring me to go with her to a concert or a stage play. I have no time to write in my diary.

I miss you terribly and wish you could come and visit

157

me. It was so wonderful meeting with you at the beach during the fireworks last Saturday. My life's empty without you. I love you so much.

My aunt would never let you stay in the same house with me if you come here. She told me that she'd call the police if you'd even set foot in the door. My mother had to tell her about us kissing in your orchard. I never want to speak to her as long as I live.

I wish we could elope and get married in Mexico. We're not that far from the border. I'm sending you my address. It is Naomi Rosenberg, 1877 North Acacia Street, Los Angeles, California.

Please write to me soon. I love you so much. Naomi

Adam paced nervously in the bedroom and then went to the porch where he turned on the light, which illuminated Naomi's portraits. He removed the canvas from the easel, replacing it with her painting. His heart beat wildly as he gazed at her image.

Leaving the porch, he went for a stroll through the dark orchard. He sobbed with guilt and shame, blaming himself for Naomi being sent to California. Upon returning to his room, he spent a restless night tossing and turning.

18

"Not only did you break the law by trespassing, but you also concealed evidence of a murder."

Adam got up at dawn, earlier than his normal routine to write Naomi a letter, informing her that he couldn't sleep the whole night because he loved her and couldn't live without her.

He promised to travel to California by bus, where he intended to stay in a hotel near Mount Sinai Hospital until they eloped to Mexico with the money he earned from baling hay. He also requested that she send him the hospital's address so he could meet her there.

While his mother and Marie were at the Farmers' Market with Grandma at Columbus Park, he called the Greyhound Bus Station to enquire about the cost of a ticket to Los Angeles. After hanging up the phone, he went to his bedroom where he removed cash from a cigar box hidden in the bottom drawer of his dresser.

After breakfast he mounted his bicycle and rode to the downtown bus depot where he bought a one way ticket to California. The clerk behind the counter informed him that the bus would be leaving Kenosha for the Chicago station at 9:00 pm on Friday, July 20th.

Upon arrival in Chicago, he would transfer to another bus, which would depart at 1:00 am on July 21st for California, making stops in several states to pick up passengers. If all went as scheduled his bus would arrive in Los Angeles early on Sunday.

"That's a hell of a long bus ride," said Adam, folding the ticket and putting it into his wallet.

"It's a very scenic trip. There's a two hour layover in Denver, giving you time to walk around the city," he said.

Leaving the bus station, Adam rode his bike to the library, where he located a map of Los Angeles. A librarian helped him find the hospital where Naomi worked and her aunt's house on North Acacia Street. After departing from the library, he cycled to the filling station where Karl was working.

"What're you doing here?" asked Karl, changing a tire inside the dark garage.

"Could you give me a ride to the bus station next Friday night around 8:30?" asked Adam. "I'm meeting some of my friends at the Wisconsin Dells. I'll call you for a ride home when I come back on Sunday evening."

"Sure, I'll bring you there and pick you up," said Karl. "By then I should be driving Dad's old Nash. I've been working on it in my spare time."

"I'll wait for you at the end of the driveway with my suitcase. I'll call you around 8:00 o'clock next Friday evening to remind you to pick me up?"

"That's a good idea. That way I won't forget," said Karl, removing the flat tire from the car suspended on a lift.

Adam rode his bicycle home and parked it in the garage, noticing that the truck was back from the Farmers' Market.

He hurried into the house and bolted up the stairs.

"Where have you been all spruced up in those clothes?" asked his mother, sitting at the kitchen table eating lunch with Marie and Grandma.

"I went to the library to look up some information," said Adam, forgetting that he was wearing his dress pants and a clean shirt.

"Naomi called you long distance all the way from Los Angeles. She wanted you to call her back as soon as you got home. I told her that we couldn't afford to pay for long distance calls."

"Did she leave her telephone number?" asked Adam.

"No, I told her not to bother calling again, but to write you a letter," said Gertrude.

"For Christ's sake," said Adam, feeling angry with his mother for not writing down the number.

"Adam, I wish you wouldn't use that kind of language. You've been hanging around Neil too much."

"I haven't seen him lately," said Adam, heading toward his room to change into a T-shirt and Levis. He returned to the kitchen to join them for lunch.

"Dio Mio! It looks like Adam's mad because he wants to see that Jew girl again," said Grandma.

"You don't know what you're talking about," shouted Adam, getting up from the table and darting through the house to the porch, ignoring his mother's criticism for being rude to his grandmother.

Adam mixed several dark colors and then painted a

tropical storm on the beach with him and Naomi taking shelter beneath a palm tree with the branches and leaves bending in the wind.

Later in the afternoon he continued with his routine of harvesting vegetables and bringing crates of produce from the field to the spigot to be washed.

Upon returning to the kitchen, he found a letter from Naomi, which he anxiously read on the porch in front of her portrait on the easel.

Dearest Adam,   *July 18, 1956*

I'm in real trouble now. I'm writing this letter to you from the hospital during my lunch hour. I'm here in the cafeteria, stressed out. My Aunt Loretta opened your letter and read it over the telephone to my mother. She was furious over your plan to come to Los Angeles and stay in a hotel near the hospital. She accused you of wanting to have premarital sex with me. They were both shocked about us planning to elope to Mexico.

My Aunt informed the hospital that if I received any letters from you, she would call the police in Kenosha and have you arrested for attempting to molest a child. I'm angry because I'm not a child.

I know we're both only fifteen and you won't be 16 until October, and my birthday isn't until December. I feel like I'm living in Nazi Germany during the time of Hitler. I don't know what to do. I want to run away with you to get married but not to Mexico. Maybe we could go Colorado Springs and have our wedding in the Garden of the Gods.

I love you so much. My heart breaks every day because we can't be together. With all my love, Naomi

Adam was disturbed for the next two days,wondering if he should bring back the ticket to the bus station. After deliberating, he decided to go to Los Angeles.

On Friday morning Adam's mother insisted he go to the market to sell vegetables at Baker Park across from St. James Cemetery. He agreed to help her so she could take Mrs. Solinsky to the hospital for an X-ray.

His mother didn't return to the market until around 12:30 pm, informing him Aunt Clara's elderly mother had come down with a severe case of bronchitis.

Adam was the only farmer still at the market in the 90 degree heat. After loading the truck, he sat in the front seat next to his mother. She drove them back to the farm, complaining the whole way about his father.

After lunch Adam packed his suitcase, hiding it under the wicker furniture on the porch. He painted a picture of Naomi holding hands with him. They were wandering in the desert, where a rattlesnake was hiding behind a soaring cactus. He was almost finished with the composition when his mother appeared on the porch.

"I just spoke to Rachael Rosenberg on the telephone. She knows all about your scheme to sneak away on the bus and get a hotel close to the hospital where Naomi works," snapped his mother. "You must be crazy like your father."

"It wasn't right for Naomi's aunt to open my letter," shouted Adam. "I'm leaving this farm and never coming

163

back. I'm moving in with Dad."

"You can't leave us stranded here on the farm," said Gertrude. "You're only 15years old. You're not an adult!"

"I shouldn't have sent that letter to Naomi's aunt's house," said Adam, picking up his paint brush. He added dark cumulus clouds and a lightning bolt striking the cactus, where the coiled snake was ready to attack.

"There's the phone again," said his mother, turning around and heading back toward the kitchen.

"If it's Naomi, I hope you'll let me talk to her," said Adam, returning to his painting. He looked up when he heard the dog barking.

"Hey, Adam, what's going on?" asked Neil, sauntering up the driveway with Crispy growling at him from the orchard, where he had been sleeping under a pear tree.

A few moments later Neil came up the steps and entered the porch. "Wow! I really like that painting!"

"I've ruined everything," said Adam, adding a flicking red tongue to the snake. "I'm so fucking stupid."

"Jesus Christ, Adam. I've never heard you use that word before. What the hell's going on with you?"

Adam explained to him about the chain of events that occurred, leading to his separation from Naomi and his plan to take the bus to California so he could elope with her to Mexico.

"I'm sure Naomi's aunt will call the police on you," said Neil, frowning. "Things aren't going so well with me and Jennifer either. Her parents are mad at me."

"What the hell happened?" asked Adam.

"Her parents caught us making out on their living room sofa when they went to the grocery store. I swear they purposely took off their shoes and crept into the house so we wouldn't hear them.

"We were really getting hot, even though we had our clothes on. I felt so embarrassed when her parents walked in on us because my cock was the size of a cucumber. Jennifer wanted to take her clothes off and go all the way.

"Her parents blamed Jennifer more than me. They told me I must stop seeing her, and I wasn't welcome to go to mass on Sunday with them anymore," said Neil.

"Her father chewed me out all the way home. He said they made a mistake letting me to spend every Sunday with them because they thought I was a decent guy.

"By the way Jennifer told her mother that you were going to St. Mary's this fall. She called Mrs. Rosenberg to tell her all about your paying for your own tuition there."

"Damn it,' said Adam. "We're in real trouble now."

"What do you mean? Is Naomi pregnant?"

"No, we've only been going steady for a few months now. Why is everyone obsessed about sex in this town?"

"It's because it's forbidden. I couldn't use the word sex when I was growing up without getting my mouth washed out with soap," said Neil.

"I'm worried Naomi's parents will yank her out of St. Mary's and send her to St. Catherine's in Racine," said Adam. "Now what the fuck should I do?"

"Forget about it for a few minutes. You need to calm down," said Neil, turning on his portable radio.

This is Bill Schroeder from WLIP with the news in Kenosha on this sunny Friday afternoon on July 20, 1956.

Our nation has recently experienced the fourth major steel strike since World War II, putting 650,000 laborers out of work in Pittsburg, Youngstown, and Gary. All were members of the United Steelworkers of America and belonged to the A.F.L.-C.I.O

And now for the local news. *Two police officers and an anthropologist, Dr. Gerald Richter, arrived in their squad car with a warrant to search the house of Mr. Clifford Gascoigne, who lives in a bungalow east of Mrs. Martha Jacobsen's abandoned farm on Cooper Road. Some weeks ago they found the severed arm and leg of a female, floating in barrels in Mrs. Jacobsen's basement.*

When the officers appeared on the front porch of Mr. Gascoigne's home, he came out with a shotgun, ordering them to leave the premises. The anthropologist, a karate expert, knocked him down and seized his gun.

The officers handcuffed Mr. Gascoigne and searched his house and basement. They found the severed head of a female floating in a barrel, preserved in formaldehyde, and a dead Siamese cat in another barrel.

The Chief of Police contacted Mrs. Jacobsen's son, Fred, who identified the remains. He was shocked to find the head of his cousin, Joyce Jacobsen and her pet cat, Fluffy, floating in the barrels in the basement.

166

Mr. Gascoigne blamed his mentally ill wife, Winifred, for killing the cat and putting it in a barrel in the basement. He had her committed to the Mental Hospital in Mendota afterwards. Clifford said he had no idea that Joyce's head was in his basement. In spite of his denial and protest, the police arrested him on suspicion of murdering her.

"I'll be damned," said Neil, snapping off the radio. "I wonder if Mr. Gascoigne really did it. His wife always sat in the rocking chair on the porch staring into space and humming to a rag doll as if it were her baby."

"It was bad enough finding Joyce's arm and leg in those barrels in Old Lady Jacobsen's basement. We're lucky we didn't get arrested when we broke into her house," said Adam, pausing. "What the hell's going on? It's a police car turning into our driveway."

The teenagers were surprised when two officers stepped out of their car onto the sidewalk in front of the porch.

"Which one of you is Adam Montanya? I'm Officer Flynn and this is Officer Manning," said the younger policeman.

"I'm Adam," he said, opening the porch door for them.

"I know your father, Giovanni," said Manning, coming up the steps. "He crashed the truck in Mrs. Jacobsen's front yard about five years ago."

"This must be your friend, Neil O'Connor," said Flynn, entering the porch.

"Yah, that's my name all right," said Neil, his voice quivering because the police were there.

167

"Dio Mio!" said Grandma, having been awakened from her nap by the noise on the porch. "What you doing here? Does something happen to my son, Giovanni?"

"No, Ma'am, we're here because Mr. Gascoigne gave us the names of Adam and Neil. He told us you guys were trespassing and broke into Mrs. Jacobsen's basement."

"We explored the vacant place," said Neil

"I hope you're aware that breaking and entering is a crime," said the younger officer.

"We...we didn't steal anything. We were only looking around inside the barn and the house," said Adam.

"I understand you kicked in the basement door the first time about five years ago," said Flynn.

"That's right," said Neil. "That's when we found the trap door leading to the upstairs."

"Did you see anything suspicious at that time?" asked Manning, writing everything down on a pad.

"You bet," said Adam. "I found a pig's head floating in a barrel. It was disgusting."

"What else did you find?" asked Flynn.

"We didn't find anything except an overstuffed chair in the attic where Mrs. Jacobsen used to wait for Jesus to appear to her so she could wash his feet," informed Neil.

"We're not interested in her apparitions," said Flynn. "Mr. Gascoigne said you guys were there a couple of weeks ago, looking around again. This time you had the courtesy to replace the hinge with the lock."

"We were there sometime in June," confessed Adam,

his brow furrowed with worry.

"What did you find the second time?" asked Manning.

"We found an arm and a leg in the barrels," said Neil. "It was really scary."

"Why didn't you report it to the police?" asked Flynn. "Not only did you break the law by trespassing, but you also concealed evidence of a murder."

"I...I guess we were afraid we'd be blamed," said Neil.

"Dio Mio," said Grandma, making the sign of the cross. "Are you gonna take my grandson to jail?"

"No, Ma'am," said Manning. "We're here to investigate the murder of Joyce Jacobsen."

"Did you ever see Clifford Gascoigne talking with Joyce?" asked Flynn.

"Yes, I saw him sitting at the kitchen table having coffee with her about a half-dozen times," said Neil. "It was during the winter when I came to shovel out his driveway. It was after he fell down and broke his leg because Old Lady Jacobsen cursed him.

"That's when Joyce Jacobsen started going there regularly to help fix the meals and do the laundry. Mr. Gascoigne's wife, Winifred, was crazy. She never did anything except stare into space and sit in her rocking chair, holding a doll wrapped in a blanket."

"Adam, do you think Mrs. Gascoigne was jealous of Joyce?" asked Flynn, pacing up and down on the porch.

"It's possible. She was crazy all right," he said.

Adam told them that during that winter his grandma

169

made homemade ravioli and asked him to bring it to Mr. Gascoigne because Clifford was laid up with a broken leg for the winter.

When he knocked on the kitchen door, nobody answered. Adam finally peeked inside, where he saw Mrs. Gascoigne peeling apples with a knife for a pie. She had the dough laid out on the table.

"I could hear some giggling coming from the bedroom with the door closed next to the kitchen," said Adam.

"Do you think it was Joyce with Mr. Gascoigne in the bedroom?" asked Ralph.

"I don't know because I never saw them," said Adam. Mrs. Gascoigne was angry. She had stopped peeling the apples and was stabbing them with her knife. I set the ravioli down on the kitchen table and went back to the car where my mom was waiting for me."

"We have enough information for now," said Flynn. "Let's get going."

"You boys might be subpoenaed to appear in court to testify at the trial sometime in the fall," said Manning."

"Is Mr. Gascoigne guilty of murdering Joyce?" asked Adam, feeling tense.

"We don't know for sure. Right now he's our prime suspect. It will be up to the jury to decide whether he is guilty or not," said Manning.

The officers left the porch and entered their squad car, backing out of the driveway. Within a few moments they were out of sight.

"I've gotta go now before my father gets home from work," said Neil, leaving the porch and heading down the driveway. He hurried past Crispy dozing under the pear tree. The dog opened one eye and growled at him.

"Come on, Adam," said Grandma. "We go back to work in the garden now."

19

"Love is a wonderful thing, but it makes people do things they regret later."

Adam followed his grandmother into the garden, where they hoed the sweet corn that was just beginning to tassel. After filling crates with potatoes and picking two bushes of Bermuda onions, he felt restless and irritable because the day seemed to drag on forever.

Once the vegetables were washed and loaded on the truck for the next day's market, Adam went into the house for supper followed by a bath.

Around 8:00 o'clock he telephoned Karl at the filling station to come and pick him up. He nervously entered the dining room, where his mother and grandmother were watching TV.

"Mom, I forgot to tell you that Karl's taking me and Neil to the Roosevelt Theater. He'll bring us back later on."

"Thanks, I won't wait up for you. I'm just exhausted," she said, waking up Grandma who was dozing next to her on the couch.

Gertrude yawned and headed into the bathroom to brush her teeth. She shouted, "Adam, don't forget you're going with me to the market tomorrow."

"Buona nocte," said Grandma, getting up from the couch and leaving for her bedroom.

Adam entered the porch, closing the living room door

172

tightly. He removed his suitcase from under the wicker sofa. When Karl arrived in the Nash, Adam hurried down the front steps to the driveway where he placed his suitcase into the trunk.

Twenty minutes later Karl dropped his brother at the Greyhound Station downtown. He waited for Adam to board the bus before leaving.

"I'll call you when I get back from the Wisconsin Dells on Sunday night," shouted Adam through the open window, waving to him.

As the bus departed from the station, Adam hung his head with shame for being a chronic liar like Huckleberry Finn, whose drunken father attacked his son with a knife, believing he was the Angel of Death.

Adam was haunted by the memory of his own father getting drunk and trying to kill his mother with a rifle. He accidentally killed their cow, Savoya, instead.

Adam fell asleep on the bus before reaching Chicago. When the Greyhound rumbled into the station, he got out and retrieved his luggage. He waited a few hours before boarding the next bus to St. Louis.

Adam reread Naomi's letters, feeling restless and irritable all the way to Kansas. When the bus finally arrived in Topeka, a police car was waiting at the station where he was confronted by an officer.

"Are you Adam Montanya?" asked Officer Holmes, removing a note pad from his shirt pocket.

"Yes," said Adam, waiting to retrieve his luggage.

"When you didn't come home from the movie theater last night, your frantic mother woke up your brother, Karl. He informed her that you took the bus to the Wisconsin Dells for the weekend," said the officer.

"She called the bus station and found out you had purchased a ticket to Los Angeles. Your mother wrote down the itinerary and phoned the police.

"The Kenosha Police Department informed us you are a runaway teenager. You're travelling to meet your girlfriend, Naomi Rosenberg, in California with plans to elope with her to Mexico. We were told that you are underage and must be stopped.

"I want you to call your mother and tell her you're coming home on the next bus. Police officers will meet you at each stop along the way to be sure that you don't try to run away again," said the officer.

The manager of the bus stop dialed his parent's number, handing Adam the telephone.

"Mom, this is Adam. I'm calling you from Kansas. I'll be coming back to Kenosha on the next bus."

"You have a lot of nerve, lying to me about going to the movies with Neil," screamed Gertrude. "I haven't slept a wink all night. You even lied to Karl telling him you were going to the Wisconsin Dells. You're just like your drunken father, a good for nothing liar!"

"I'm sorry, Mom," said Adam, holding the receiver a distance from his ear.

"You're going to be grounded for the next six months,"

she screamed, unaware that an officer was listening to their conversation.

When he finally hung up the phone, Adam offered to pay for the long distance call, but the manager told him not to worry about it.

Feeling depressed and guilty, he purchased his return ticket and waited at the station with his luggage for nearly two hours while Officer Holmes guarded him, reading the newspaper and drinking coffee.

Adam finally boarded the bus to Chicago. The trip home was long and tedious because at each stop a policeman was there to check up on him. When he finally reached Kenosha, he was exhausted from stress. Upon leaving the bus, he was surprised his father was at the Greyhound Station to meet him.

"I took off from work so I could be here," said Giovanni. "I don't know what to say. I feel bad that I haven't been around to talk to you more often. I understand you're in love with Naomi and want to marry her."

"I planned to meet her in Los Angeles and elope with her to Mexico," confessed Adam.

"You're too young to get married. You must really love Naomi," said Giovanni, scratching his head.

"I know I'm only fifteen, but I love Naomi. I think about her all the time. I can't sleep at night because of her."

"Love is a wonderful thing, but it makes people do things they regret later. I hope she's not pregnant," said his father, putting the suitcase in the trunk of the Plymouth.

"We've never had sex. I only kissed her a couple times. Naomi's parents don't want us to go steady," he sighed. "Dad, I want to move in with you. I hate living on the farm with Mom. She's angry all the time and constantly complains about you. I hate being around her."

"I wish you could move in with me, but your mother and grandma need your help with the chores. In a couple of months you'll be getting your driver's license, and then you'll have more freedom to go out with your friends."

"I won't be sixteen until October," said Adam. "Mom threatened to ground me for six months."

"How about having breakfast with me? You must be hungry," said Giovanni, putting his suitcase into the Plymouth.

"Let's stop at Carl's Restaurant next to Bernacchi's Drug Store. I've heard the hamburgers are good there," said Adam.

"We'll have a long talk before I bring you home," said his father, starting the car.

"I'm sorry for causing so much trouble," said Adam.

"You'll have to apologize to your mother. She doesn't forgive very easily," he said, lighting a Lucky Strike.

20

"Meet me where they keep the elephants. They're always the last act in the show."

Adam got through the month of July feeling depressed. He had written several letters to Naomi, using the address of the hospital instead of her aunt's house. While trying to call her long distance, he discovered that Aunt Loretta's telephone number had been changed.

Feeling desperate about the situation, Adam continued sending letters to the hospital. He went to the mailbox each afternoon while his grandma took her nap, hoping to receive a letter from Naomi but without luck. When a letter finally arrived the first week in August, he read it on the porch in front of her portrait on the easel.

Dearest Adam,   *Sunday, August 5, 1956*

    I couldn't understand why you weren't writing to me. I was hurt thinking that you don't love me anymore. I cried myself to sleep every night for the past couple of weeks, waiting to hear from you. I finally discovered that my aunt had changed the telephone number so I couldn't receive calls from you. Every night before going to bed, she disconnected the phone, making it impossible for me to call you with the new number.

    I was so angry with her that I wanted to run away. That's when she threatened to hire a private detective to watch me around the clock. I think she was just bluffing to scare me.

Last Friday while I was working at the hospital, I was standing at the front desk on the ward talking to the cleaning lady, Maria, when the mailman arrived.

He told me that Naomi Rosenberg must be a very popular girl because he had been delivering letters for her every few days. I told him that I am Naomi, but I hadn't received a single letter in several weeks. I then found out from Maria that the head nurse was confiscating my letters and turning them over to my aunt.

My aunt told the staff that I was not allowed to receive mail or use the phone to contact you because you were an underage hoodlum, threatening to come to Los Angeles to elope with me. I'm fed up with my aunt because she believes that we're criminals for wanting to go steady.

I can't wait for the summer to be over so that I can come back to Wisconsin and be with you. I hate to burden you, but my mother called long distance and informed me that she withdrew me from St. Mary's and registered me at St. Catherine's in Racine. She told the principal to call her immediately if you made an appearance at the school.

In spite of everything, I can't thank you enough for your letter dated July 30th. I'm so sorry that your father moved out. It must be difficult living with your mother. It will be so much easier to get in touch with you once I'm back to Kenosha.

I promise you that I will find a way to meet with you. I'll never confide in Jennifer again for telling my mother

178

you were going to St. Mary's. She wrote and told me that she refused to break up with Neil and intended to ride her bike to his place so they can spend time together. Please don't send any more letters to the hospital since they will be handed over to my aunt. I'm so disgusted with the whole situation.

I'll be flying home on August 25. I can't wait to see you again. I might be able to have the cleaning lady smuggle out a letter to you once in a while. She agreed to mail this one for me. There is no return address on it because I don't want her to lose her job.

I love you so much! Naomi

Adam reread the letter, wondering about how he could get in touch with Naomi. He lapsed further into depression, finding relief by composing a turbulent abstract painting on the porch, which horrified his grandmother because of his sinister crows. They were swooping down to attack a pair of lovers, feeding a flock of hens with their chicks.

Even though the month of August was sweltering, Adam worked for hours hoeing and pulling weeds in the garden, trying to release frustration from not being able to contact Naomi. The sweat dripped from his forehead, drenching his muscular chest and arms.

He was angry with Naomi's aunt for holding her hostage in California, and he hated her mother for transferring her to St. Catherine's High in Racine.

Every morning after helping Grandma Adam fed the animals. Three times a week he cleaned the barn, pig pen,

179

and chicken coup. When he wasn't working in the garden, he was painting on the porch. His recent compositions were turbulent storms, volcanoes, or earthquakes, leaving behind devastated towns, farms, and cities always with a couple fleeing from the wreckage.

As the summer came to an end, he thought about transferring back to Bradford High since he didn't know anyone at St. Mary's.

When Neil made an unexpected appearance a few days before Labor Day, they went for a stroll along the creek flowing through the property. They crawled under the barbed wire fence into the pasture and hurried past the grazing cows. Meandering along they noticed a garter snake slithering in the tall grass. As they approached the creek, leopard frogs and turtles plunged into the water to escape from the intruders.

The teenagers followed the creek south, glancing at the three power towers which soared skyward, which separated the pasture from the cornfields and carried electricity from Wisconsin to Illinois.

"Why in the fuck do you want to go to St. Mary's now that Naomi's going to St. Catherine's?" asked Neil, lighting a cigarette.

Adam noticed that Neil had regressed to using vulgar language again since he was forbidden to see Jennifer by her parents.

"I hate to make a big deal out this," said Adam, finally telling Neil that he promised God he'd become a priest because He spared his life when Neil nearly drowned in the pond earlier in the summer.

"What the fuck did you do that for?" asked Neil, who was tense and angry. "I wish I had died in the pond for Christ's sake. I was so fuckin' stupid for making out with Jennifer in her living room."

"Hey, take it easy. We're both in the same boat," said Adam, telling Neil about his letters being confiscated by Naomi's aunt and her threat to hire a detective to watch her around the clock.

"Jesus Christ, Naomi's a prisoner in her aunt's house," said Neil, picking up a stick, knocking down the cattails alongside the creek and stamping on them.

"Hey, what the hell's gotten into you?" said Adam, backing away from Neil, who was scattering the cotton-like seeds of the cattails all around him.

Neil paused when he saw another snake slithering in the grass. He pressed his foot on its tail causing it to coil and hiss at him. Neil seized the snake and snapped it like a whip, breaking its back.

"Stop that!" shouted Adam. "That snake never did anything to hurt you."

Neil slammed the snake onto the ground and crushed its head with his heal. He hurled the dead reptile into the pasture, wiping his bloody shoe on the grass.

"That takes care of that fucker from the Garden of Eden," shouted Neil.

"What the hell's wrong with you?" asked Adam, his

mouth hanging open. I've never seen you so mad."

"Goddamn it! Take a look," he said, stripping off his shirt and throwing it next to the dead snake.

"Jesus Christ! You've got purple welts all over your back. What the hell happened?"

"Jennifer's mother called my old man at the barber shop and told him that they caught us making out on the sofa in the living room. That bitch said that it was my fault for seducing their daughter when they went to the grocery store. They were angry that I betrayed their trust and never wanted to see me again."

"My old man was drunk when he came home from work with a razor strap. The bastard beat the hell out of me in the garage. I never cried out once. I just took it like a man.

"My father kept asking me if I had sex with Jennifer. I never opened my mouth to tell him anything. So he kept beating me even harder.

"I never told him that it was Jennifer's idea that we make out on the couch. We had been playing croquet in the front yard when her parents left to get groceries. I didn't think it was a good idea because their neighbors were outside barbequing and could say something to her parents.

"Jennifer told me not to worry because her parents always went shopping for at least two hours. I have to admit I really wanted to have sex with her, but we never went all the way.

"Thank God we both had our clothes on when her parents came sneaking into the living room," said Neil. "I think they wanted an excuse for us to break up, so they left us alone to see what would happen," said Neil, pausing "Why are you so depressed?"

"Naomi and I were kissing in our orchard after spending the afternoon at the beach. Mrs. Rosenberg spotted us from the porch and came storming toward us," said Adam. "Her mother was mad as hornet because she didn't want us to go steady. I've been miserable ever since they sent her to California. Maybe God's punishing me for not keeping my vow to become a priest."

"What the fuck would God be punishing you for?" asked Neil, scratching his head.

"I should have enrolled at St. Francis Seminary instead of St. Mary's. Maybe God's angry with me for going out with a Jewish girl."

"You should see a priest and talk it over with him. But it better be the right one," said Neil. "Most of them don't understand teenagers."

"A priest?" asked Adam, suddenly feeling tense. "Don't you remember what Father Furstenberg did to Kevin?"

"Everybody knows that bastard was fuckin' your cousin Kevin ever since he was five years old," blurted Neil.

"Kevin finally got even by murdering him," said Adam, staring into space.

"What's wrong with you?" asked Neil, noticing that Adam's fists were clenched.

"I'd like to beat the hell out of Kevin for molesting me kid," said Adam, gazing into the cloudless blue sky. "He raped me in the barn by putting a knife to my throat when I was ten years old."

"For Christ's sake, I didn't know that! Hey, Adam, snap out of it. Kevin's been dead for five years. He committed suicide after he shot Father Furstenberg," said Neil. "It made the front page of the Kenosha News."

"What did you say?" asked Adam.

"I said Kevin's dead," repeated Neil. "Hey, man, you're acting weird because of the heat."

"It's hotter than hell this afternoon," said Adam, glancing at the cloudless sky.

"Let's jump into the creek and cool off," suggested Neil, removing his clothes and plunging naked into the water.

"How's the water?" asked Adam, removing his clothes.

"The water's nice and cool because it's shaded by the willows and cattails," shouted Neil.

When Adam jumped into the creek, Neil splashed water into his face until they both started laughing.

"You were acting strange for a few minutes," said Neil.

"I…I thought that Kevin was still alive," said Adam. "Maybe his ghost came back to haunt me."

"You're crazy! When the hell's Naomi coming home?"

"She came back to Kenosha last Saturday. I tried calling her several times, but her mother always hangs up on me."

"Jennifer came to see me the other day on her bicycle, but she didn't stay long because her mom came by in their station wagon fifteen minutes later to take her home," said Neil. "Mrs. O'Reilly was mad as a hornet."

They both talked for quite a while, sharing their plans about how to meet their girlfriends without their parents finding out.

"I thought you were going to take a bus to California and elope with Naomi. What happened?"

"I was on my way to California," said Adam. "But the cops stopped me in Kansas and sent me home. I'm waiting for Naomi to call me. Summer's almost over, and we'll be starting school on Tuesday after Labor Day.

"What the fuck did you do to Naomi?"

"I kissed her a couple of times! That's all I ever did. We're in love and her parents can't stand it."

"How does your mom feel about it?"

"She's too busy being angry with my father to pay any attention to me. I swear my mother hates my dad and would like to see him dead. I can hardly stand being around her," shouted Adam.

"Hey, man, take it easy. I can't wait to see Jennifer. She's constantly calling me on the telephone behind her parents' back. They'd kill me if they knew we were going steady."

"Did you give her a ring yet?" asked Adam.

"Not yet, I got my eye on a ring that I saw in a jewelry store downtown," said Neil.

"I going to get one for Naomi," said Adam, coming up the mound of the creek and putting on his clothes.

The young men got dressed and headed toward the farm house, deciding they'd buy rings for their girlfriends from the money they earned baling hay.

"I'd better go before my old man gets home," said Neil. "If I'm late, he'll beat the hell out of me again."

"I'll see you soon," said Adam, hearing the phone ringing. He dashed down the sidewalk through the back door into the house.

"Naomi!" he gasped, out of breath. I can't believe it's you. I tried calling you several times."

"Adam, I love you. I'm calling from Jennifer's house where I'm staying for the weekend. My parents are leaving town to pick up my sister, Lorna, at her summer camp in Michigan. They won't get back until Monday night."

"I'll come to Jennifer's place tonight on my bike to meet you," he insisted.

"No, Adam, meet me at the circus on Sunday evening at the 7:00 o'clock show. I'm going there with Jennifer. She wants you to bring Neil.

"Where's the circus being held this year?"asked Adam.

"It's at Lincoln Park," she said. "The only problem is that Jennifer's parents will be chaperoning us."

"We can meet during intermission. Usually it's a half hour, sometimes longer," said Adam.

"Meet me where they keep the elephants. They're always the last act in the show," said Naomi.

"I'll be there. I love you Naomi. I'll see you at the circus during intermission," said Adam, hanging up the phone.

He heard the screen door slam and Grandma coming up the steps. Upon entering the kitchen, she said, "Who do you talk to on-a the phone?"

"It was Neil," lied Adam. "I'm going to ride my bike to the circus with him tomorrow night."

"Maybe your papa gives you a ride," said Grandma.

"What are you two talking about?" asked Gertrude, coming from the basement where she was doing laundry.

"Oh, nothing important," said Adam. "I'm riding my bicycle to the circus on Sunday evening at Lincoln Park."

"That's a long way to ride in the dark," said Gertrude. "You can come with me and Marie on Labor Day."

"I'd rather go on Sunday. Neil's going with me. We'll be back home by 10:00 o'clock."

"I hope you're telling the truth this time. I'm still upset with you for taking the bus to visit Naomi. You lied to me about going to the theater with Neal," reminded his mother.

"I swear I'm going to the circus," said Adam.

"Be sure the headlight is working on your bike," said his mother. "You might have to pump up the tires."

"I'll check them right away," said Adam.

"You can do it after you bring in the tomatoes and corn from the garden. I need your help scrubbing the potatoes for tomorrow's market."

"I go dig the carrots now," said Grandma.

"I'll dig them for you," said Adam, dashing down the steps and out the door. He was thrilled that at last he would be able to meet Naomi even if it was only for a half hour during the intermission at the circus.

187

21

Removing tubes of paint from a box, he mixed warm and cool colors on his pallet.

On Saturday Gertrude drove Adam and Grandma to the Farmers' Market at Columbus Park. She helped them set up the stand and then departed to take Marie to her piano lesson. The crowd was enormous at the park the entire morning with customers buying vegetables, chickens, and ducks for the Labor Day weekend.

When Gertrude arrived around noon she was pleased they had earned $92.00 and were nearly sold out. After loading the truck, they returned to the farm.

Grandma was too exhausted to have lunch. She collapsed on the couch and fell asleep, snoring with her mouth open.

While Adam was having lunch with his mother, the telephone rang. It was Neil, returning his call to Adam about riding to the circus to meet their girlfriends.

"Who were you talking to on the phone?" asked his mother, eating her salad with Italian bread.

"That was Neil," said Adam. We'll be riding our bikes to the circus tomorrow."

"I suppose you're going to meet Naomi and Jennifer there," said Gertrude, raising an eyebrow.

"How did you know?" asked Adam.

"I wasn't born yesterday," said Gertrude, getting up

from the table to rinse her plate at the sink

"I'm going to paint for a while on the porch," he said, leaving the kitchen and hurrying past Grandma, who was sprawled out on the couch like a beached whale.

Upon entering the porch, he placed a new canvas on the easel. Removing tubes of paint from a wooden box, he mixed warm and cool colors with a spatula on his pallet.

Within two hours he had painted Naomi, standing under a sprawling willow tree, gazing at three elephants wading in the lagoon at Lincoln Park. In the background cumulus clouds floated in a cerulean sky above the circus tent and animal cages.

Adam continued painting until his mother came onto the porch, bringing him a glass of lemonade. She sat down to rest on a wicker chair.

'What a marvelous picture of Naomi with the elephants!" she exclaimed. "I don't regret sending you to those painting classes on Saturday mornings when you were in grade school."

"I really liked going to the museum for lessons after catechism class," said Adam.

"I spent a lot of money on those lessons," reminded his mother. "I was so proud when you got that award for your farm paintings.

"I saw Grandma Solinsky on Tuesday at Union Park. She told me that Naomi's parents always give her a ride home after the temple after the Sabbath service."

"Her parents don't want us dating! They've done

everything they can to keep us apart," blurted Adam.

"Grandma Solinsky told the Rosenbergs all about Kevin and Father Furstenberg," sighed Gertrude.

"Mom, I don't want to talk about it," insisted Adam.

Gertrude changed the subject by glancing around the porch at a dozen canvases on the floor.

"Why, Adam, I haven't had time to even look at your paintings," said Gertrude. "What's that strange building in the painting? It reminds me of a haunted castle."

"Mom, it's the Catholic Church."

"Who's that young man lying down on the bank of the river?" she asked, shaking.

"It's Neil after I saved him from almost drowning in Kaplin's Pond earlier in the summer."

"Oh my God! Why didn't you tell me about that?"

"I didn't think you were interested," said Adam.

"I'm interested in everything that you're doing," she said. "I really like your picture of the cows grazing in the pasture with the hay rake."

"I'm going to paint Adam and Eve, nude in the Garden of Eden. They'll be picking apples with a python hanging from the limbs of the tree," said Adam.

"Don't you dare! What would people think if they saw your painting on exhibit at Pollard Gallery?" asked Gertrude. "You should forget about going out with Naomi. There are plenty of decent Catholic girls at St. Mary's."

"Mom, I love Naomi, and I want to marry her."

"Adam, you're only fifteen years old. You're too young

to be thinking about marriage."

"I'll be sixteen in October."

"I know you really wanted to go to California to be with Naomi. It wasn't a good idea because I needed your help on the farm. That's why I called the police. I didn't want you getting into trouble with her."

"I've been angry ever since I came back to Kenosha because I didn't receive any letters from Naomi for days."

"Adam, you grew up too fast after that horrible incident in the barn with Kevin."

"I don't want to talk about it!" asserted Adam.

"Of course you're more mature than most teenagers your age because you've been working on the farm ever since you were knee high to a grasshopper. You could easily pass for an eighteen-year-old because of your height and muscles from baling hay."

"Would you mind leaving me alone so I can finish this painting?" asked Adam.

"I'm sure you're nervous about meeting Naomi tomorrow at the circus. It's too bad her mother pulled her out of St. Mary's and is sending her to St. Catherine's. I'll go with you to the rectory and get a refund for your tuition. Then you can go to Bradford."

"No, Mom. I'm starting classes at St. Mary's right after Labor Day on Tuesday morning," said Adam.

"Grandma told me you were thinking about going into the priesthood," said Gertrude. "Maybe you should talk to Father Bernard about it. He's your religion teacher."

191

"How did you know about Father Bernard?"

"I happened to take a glance at the class schedule on your dresser when I came to change the sheets."

"I wish you wouldn't be snooping around in my room."

"I was shocked when I saw a box of condoms in Karl's drawer. I never have a chance to talk to him anymore. He's either practicing football or working at the filling station. I wish he wouldn't be spending so much time with Larry and the Wilson girls."

"Gertrude, the telephone is for you," shouted Grandma. "It's that no good priest from New York."

"Tell him that I don't care to speak to him," shouted Gertrude, leaving the porch and entering the living room.

"You tell him yourself," said Grandma, holding the telephone and waiting for her to come into the kitchen.

"He has a lot of nerve calling me," said Gertrude.

"That priest wants to talk to you because his mother died," said Grandma, handing her the phone.

"OK," said Gertrude, snatching it from Grandma. "Mark, I'm sorry to hear that your mother died. No...I can't come to New York for her funeral...No, please don't send me money for a plane ticket...Sure, I'll clip out the obituary from the Kenosha News and mail it to you...Yes, I'll say hello to Marie for you...Goodbye."

"That priest wants you to go back to New York to see his mother in the coffin," said Grandma.

"I don't ever want to see him again," said Gertrude. "He wanted to send me money to fly there for the funeral. I only met his mother once years ago when I went up north to their cottage on the Menominee River."

"Dio Mio! That priest likes women too much."

"No, he doesn't. He's too narcissistic to love anyone except himself," said Gertrude.

"I don't know what that word means," said Grandma.

"I don't have time to explain," said Gertrude, hurrying from the kitchen and out the back door.

"Adam, come here," shouted Grandma. "We gotta go outside and get ready for tomorrow's market."

"No, we don't," he shouted. "Tomorrow's Sunday and Monday's Labor Day."

22

The fifty students sat rigidly at their desks, which were linked together and bolted to the floor like railroad tracks.

On Sunday morning Karl took Grandma to Our Lady of Mount Carmel Church in the Nash and stayed with her during the service. However, Gertrude drove Adam in the truck to mass at St. Mary's.

Adam couldn't concentrate since he was preoccupied with meeting Naomi at the circus that evening. He felt restless from tossing and turning most of the night thinking about her.

He was also worried about being cast into hell for all eternity for committing mortal sins involving sexual thoughts, feelings, and actions.

When it came time to go to Communion, he hesitated about leaving his pew since he hadn't been to confession the entire summer. He decided to recite the Act of Contrition, which would at least keep him temporarily out of hell, providing he was sincere.

"Oh my God, I'm heartily sorry for having offended Thee, and I detest all of my sins because I dread the loss of heaven and the pains of hell, but most of all because they offend Thee, My God, Who are all good and deserving of all my love. I firmly resolve with the help of Thy grace to

confess my sins, to do penance, and to amend my life. Amen," said Adam, tormented by his sins and promise to become a priest.

Adam followed the crowd going up the center aisle to the communion rail. He felt uneasy about receiving the Body of Christ since he wasn't sure if God had truly forgiven him even though he recited The Lord's Prayer a half dozen times.

While riding back to the farm, Gertrude spoke to him. "Adam, I'm so proud of you for deciding to go to St. Mary's High School. At least you'll be associating with some of the better families in Kenosha."

"I'm nervous because I don't know anybody there. All my friends are going to Bradford," he said.

"I was surprised that you paid for your own tuition. I thought your father helped you out with it."

"I never asked him for a red cent," said Adam.

"You'll get a better education at St. Mary's," said his mother. "I went to St. George's from kindergarten through eighth grade. The nuns were strict in those days, not like today. They've eased up quite a bit on the students."

"You said that some of them were really mean."

"I'll never forget Sister Evangeline, my kindergarten teacher, because she was angry all the time. I swear she was going through menopause."

Gertrude told Adam the entire class was so quiet they could hear a pin drop when Sister Evangeline entered the room. The fifty students sat rigidly at their desks, bolted to the floor like railroad tracks. No one was allowed to speak unless called upon to recite. However, Gertrude violated the rule by whispering to the girl across from her during roll call.

The teacher ordered her to stand in front of the class with the palms of her hands stretched out. Holding a thick yardstick, the elderly nun raised her right hand to slap the child's palms. The entire class gasped when Gertrude yanked her hands away from the yardstick, causing the angry nun to slap herself on the leg.

Sister Evangeline seized Gertrude by the braids and dragged her over to the radiator. The students all gasped as the teacher struck her knuckles against the radiator.

Gertrude clenched her teeth, but refused to cry in spite of the pain. Even though her hands were bruised, she returned to her desk without shedding a tear.

"That's some story, Mom," said Adam. "What did your parents say when you got home from school?"

"My mother was furious. She called the rectory and threatened a lawsuit for child abuse because my father was an attorney."

"What happened after that?" asked Adam.

"I was kept home from school for a week due to the bruises. When the swelling went down, I returned to kindergarten, but Sister Evangeline was no longer at the convent. She had been transferred to work at a nursing home for retired nuns in Janesville."

"That old nun was frustrated because she had to deal

with so many kids each day," said Adam, listening to his mother complaining about the nuns as she turned onto Benz Road. A few minutes later they were home.

Adam changed his clothes and went to the porch to paint while his mother and Grandma prepared dinner. Marie was busy at the dining room table writing a letter to her father, begging him to come home.

The day seemed like an eternity to Adam. He painted a scene of Mount Vesuvius erupting at Pompeii with molten lava streaming down from the mountain while a dark cloud of ash covered the city. The terrified inhabitants fled to the beach to escape. The focal point of the composition was a young couple climbing into an empty boat.

After having lunch with his family, Adam decided to go for a stroll along the creek, lingering to watch the turtles, frogs, and crayfish swimming in the water.

He stripped off his clothes and plunged nude into the cool water, swimming up the creek and then back. After getting dressed, he fell asleep in the tall grass on the slope, not returning to the farmhouse until late in the afternoon.

"Look what the cat dragged in. Where have you been all day? You'd better get ready to go to the circus," said his mother, who was canning tomatoes with Grandma in the sweltering kitchen.

"It's already 5:30. I've got to get cleaned up,' said Adam, glancing at the rooster clock above the sink before heading into the bathroom.

Adam washed his hair with White Rain Shampoo and

scrubbed his body in the tub with Lava Soap, rinsing in cold water.

Within twenty minutes he returned to the stifling kitchen, wearing a clean blue shirt and a pair of Levis. He glanced at the rows of canned tomatoes on the counter top with more of them boiling in a kettle filled with Ball jars on the stove.

Adam sat at the kitchen table and ate a salami sandwich with potato salad, glancing at the obituary of Emily Jane Fortmann in the newspaper.

"I didn't know that Father Mark Fortmann was a diocesan priest for fifteen years at St. George's Parish. He's sending his mother's coffin to New York, where he'll officiate at the Requiem Mass in St. Patrick's Cathedral in Manhattan. Mom, are you and Marie planning to go to the funeral?" asked Adam.

"I wouldn't go back there for a million dollars. I never want to see him again as long as I live," said Gertrude, pacing the worn linoleum in the kitchen.

"Mommy's still mad at Father Fortmann," said Marie.

"Adam, please mail my letter to Daddy. Mommy, I need a stamp," said Marie.

"I have them here on the window sill," said Gertrude, reaching for a roll of stamps and handing them to her.

Marie placed a stamp onto the envelope and gave it to Adam, who left through the back door carrying the letter.

23

While the band played loudly, eight magnificent Bengal tigers were released from a huge cage.

On Sunday evening Adam and Neil raced at breakneck speed until they came to the Four Corners, where they dropped Marie's letter in a mailbox. They sped down Roosevelt Road, turning north onto 22nd Avenue until they reached Lincoln Park in time for the evening show.

The teenagers parked their bikes in the rack near the pavilion and hurried toward the Big Top in the outfield of the baseball diamond. After buying their tickets, Adam and Neil entered the crowded tent just before the show started.

They scanned the enormous crowd inside the tent hoping to get a glimpse of Naomi and Jennifer, before climbing the stairs to the top row of the bleachers where there were still a few vacant seats.

The band was playing loudly as the ringmaster, dressed in a tuxedo with a top hat, entered the tent and hurried to the center ring. He began chasing a clown holding a shaggy dog. The puppy leapt to the ground while the clumsy clown darted after him, tripping over his shoes to amuse the crowd. Upon catching the yapping dog, the clown mounted a barrel and rolled toward the exit.

The bewildered ringmaster removed his top hat and bowed, revealing his bald head to the applauding audience. A few moments later he approached the microphone.

"Ladies and Gentleman, and children of all ages, welcome to the Ringling Brothers and Barnum and Bailey Circus!" he announced.

"We have come from Baraboo, Wisconsin today to entertain you on this beautiful Sunday with elephants, tigers, and trapeze artists from around the world.

"Let me introduce our vendors. They are here to serve you refreshments," said the ringmaster, pausing as dozens of vendors in blue uniforms poured through the entrance to the bleachers with their trays.

"Now let the show begin! In the first ring I'd like to introduce you to Roberto Romano, our tiger trainer from Italy. Let's give him a nice round of applause."

While the band played, eight magnificent Bengal tigers were released from a huge cage. They followed each other into the ring surrounded by a wire fence.

"Those tigers are huge," said Neil, distracted from searching for Jennifer in the audience.

"I wish we had come here earlier," said Adam, ignoring the performance. He continued looking into the crowd hoping to find Naomi.

As the tigers arrived in the circle, they leapt onto conical shaped platforms, flat at the top. The skilled trainer approached the first tiger and teased him with his whip, which caused him to roar, revealing sharp teeth.

The second tiger jumped down from its platform and pursued Roberto, who challenged the beast, shouting and snapping his whip. After circling the ring, the tiger leapt back onto his platform.

The trainer approached the next tiger, taunting and teasing him by stamping his foot. This tiger growled and chased after the trainer until he whirled around forcing the angry beast back to the platform with his whip.

While the audience cheered, admiring the skill of Roberto, the vendors thudded up the steps into the stands.

"Get your cotton candy here! Get your iced drinks! Get your peanuts and popcorn here!"

The parents reached into their wallets or purses for dollar bills to pass along through the crowd while the vendors handed over the treats to the smiling children.

"That tiger's real ferocious," said Adam, impressed by the trainer wrestling with the beast.

"That man must be crazy!" shouted Neil.

"He's putting his head into the mouth of that tiger!" screamed a little girl. "Mommy! Look! That tiger's going eat him."

The audience clapped as the trainer removed his head from the tiger's mouth and bowed to the audience while the tiger collapsed onto the ground, playing dead.

The trainer continued amusing the audience by creating suspense as the tigers snapped at him with their sharp teeth or swiped at him with their paws, knocking off his hat.

Adam became restless glancing at his watch, wondering if something had happened to Naomi. He continued scanning the crowd with his brow furrowed.

"Stop worrying," said Neil, watching the tigers return to

their cage, followed by the wire being taken down.

The ringmaster returned to introduce the trapeze artists from Argentina, who entered the middle arena wearing gold sequined costumes. The three women dazzled the audience by bowing and throwing kisses before ascending the rope ladders to perform on the swings and aerial wires above the murmuring crowd.

"Those women are really beautiful," gasped Neil.

The trapeze artist mounted unicycles and crossed the high wire, maintaining their balance with guide poles while the audience clapped and whistled below.

They continued to perform on the swings, where a woman hanging by her feet caught her partners by the arms in midair with no net to protect them below.

As soon as the aerial acrobats came down and departed, six women wearing scintillating silver outfits entered the third arena, riding Palominos. The agile women leapt from the backs of the stallions to the ground and then jumped onto them again as the audience cheered.

This act was followed by clowns chasing each other in the rings just prior to the recess. The ringmaster announced to the audience, "Ladies and Gentlemen and children of all ages, we will now have a thirty-five minute intermission.

"There are restrooms available in the building across the street in the Lincoln Park Pavilion. Take time to enjoy the elephant and pony rides. Don't miss the side shows behind the Big Top. Of course there are concession stands and booths with souvenirs for the children."

Adam and Neil pushed their way through the crowd searching for Naomi and Jennifer. They hurried past the fortune teller's tent, the house of mirrors, and a wax museum.

"Where in the hell do they keep the elephants?" asked Neil, glancing at the children waiting to mount the ponies while their parents stood in line to buy their tickets.

They passed a cage with a black panther on exhibit nervously pacing up and down behind the rusted bars, and a tent which contained the largest boa constrictor in the world. The teenagers continued past several painted wagons and an array of refreshment booths.

"The elephants are chained over there in front of that striped tent," shouted Neil. "Jennifer's there with Naomi!"

"They're feeding hay to the elephants," said Adam, running toward them.

"Adam! Adam!" gasped Naomi, rushing toward him. "I missed you so much."

Adam wrapped his arms around her with his heart throbbing. He kissed Naomi on the lips, holding her tightly.

Naomi finally pulled away from him. She pressed her head against his chest, the tears flowing down her cheeks. "I thought I'd never see you again"

"Naomi, I want to marry you," blurted Adam.

"I'm afraid of being separated from you again," she sobbed while Adam tried to console her.

"Let's go for a walk around the lagoon," suggested Neil, taking Jennifer's hand. She was gasping, out of breath from his passionate kisses.

The couples hurried across the street and headed to the bridge over the lagoon, where they paused to kiss for several minutes before crossing to the other side.

"I wish we could run away and never come back," whispered Naomi, aware that Adam was becoming terribly aroused as he pressed his body against hers.

Adam clung to her feeling the blood rushing through his veins and perspiration forming on his forehead.

"Let's stop for a few moments," she said. "Look at those beautiful swans in the water. We must get back to the Big Top before the show starts in a few minutes."

"Where's Neil and Jennifer?" asked Adam, feeling bewildered and confused.

"They're making out behind that oak tree over there," said Naomi. She called them to return with them to the Big Top. They paid no attention to her, but continued kissing while lying in the grass.

"Naomi, let's join the circus! It would be a great adventure," suggested Adam, holding her hands. "Once we're down south we can find a preacher to marry us."

"I'll go with you! We'll get married in Memphis, Elvis' hometown. The circus will be leaving Kenosha after tomorrow night's performance!" said Naomi.

"What are you two planning now?" interrupted Jennifer, hurrying onto the bridge with disheveled hair.

"Oh, nothing," said Naomi.

"I overheard you tell Adam you'd meet him here

tomorrow night. Are you two planning to elope by joining the circus?"

"Why don't we go with them," blurted Neil, tucking his shirt into this Levis.

"Don't be ridiculous," said Jennifer. "We're underage. My parents would kill me if I ran away."

"Jennifer, please don't say a word about this to your mother. She'll call my parents, and they'll try to stop me," pleaded Naomi.

"Let's go with them, Jennifer," insisted Neil. "We'll have the time of our lives travelling with the circus."

"We'll talk to the manager after the show to see if they'll hire us. I've seen *Help Wanted* signs all over the grounds," said Adam.

"It might be fun to go with you guys," giggled Jennifer. "I'll think it over and let you know."

"Let's get back to the show," said Naomi. "Adam, call me tomorrow before my parents come back from summer camp with my sister."

"I'd like to come over to your house after the show tonight," suggested Adam.

"I'm staying at Jennifer's place overnight," said Naomi. "I'll go home tomorrow morning and pack a suitcase. I'll meet you in the alley next to our garage, but call me first so that I'll know what time you'll be there. I could meet you at the circus by taking a taxi."

"I might be able to get a ride to the circus with my mother. She's planning to go to the last performance with my sister. I never thought about taking a taxi," said Adam, agreeing to call her to finalize their plans.

Adam took Naomi by the hand and led her back to the entrance of the Big Top. She and Jennifer hurried toward the area where Mrs. O'Reilly was waiting for them to return to the bleachers.

Adam and Neil returned to their seats close to the entrance as the ringmaster came out followed by two clowns. They knocked off his hat and stole his microphone, speaking nonsense to the crowd as the spectators were being seated for the second half of the show.

"We might be making a mistake joining the circus," said Neil, glancing at Jennifer taking her seat next to her parents.

"I hope Jennifer will keep her mouth shut this time," said Adam. "She's not very good at keeping a secret."

"We talked it over. Jennifer really wants to come with me this time," said Neil.

"Ladies and Gentlemen, and children of all ages, welcome to the Ringling Brothers and Barnum & Bailey Circus. It indeed is The Greatest Show on Earth.

"We are short of help this year. We need laborers to feed and water the animals. If you're looking for work, please contact Giuseppe, our manager, after the show. He will be giving out applications for those interested in travelling with the circus.

"Now, let's begin the second half of our show with the motorcycle races, encased in a steel globe. We have four professional cyclists who will enter one at a time and crisscross each other, risking their own lives every second they speed around the iron bars on their cycles.

"The first cyclist is Pedro from Mexico City. He is now entering the globe and circling with his motorcycle at a terrifying speed. He's being followed by Frederico from Arizona. Let's give them a round of applause."

"I'd like to learn how to do that," said Neil.

"Next we have Luigi and Ricardo from Italy. Let's give them a round of applause as they zoom up and down in the steel cage."

"That act is really dangerous," said Adam.

"It's no more dangerous than us running away from home to join the circus," said Neil.

"This time we won't get caught," said Adam, watching the cyclists bowing to the audience before leaving.

All eyes focused upon the three trapeze artists entering the middle arena followed by the ringmaster. He introduced Lenore, Liza, and Lolita, who bowed to the audience. Everyone watched a male assistant fasten their long hair to individual ropes which lifted them to the top of the tent.

Upon arriving near the top of the tent, they paused to light flaming batons which they juggled while rapidly spinning themselves around by their hair. After numerous rounds of applause, they performed aerial gymnastics. At last they glided to the ground, unfastened their hair from the ropes and left the arena bowing as the band played.

"Our final act this evening will be performed by our

Asian elephants," said the ringmaster. "And here they come! Our largest elephant is Jumbo, the male with huge ivory tusks. Next is his mate, Mumbo. They are the parents of Dumbo, their baby. Their trainer is Ricardo Tripoli from Italy. Let's give them a round of applause!"

The crowd cheered as the elephants stood on their hind legs and greeted the crowd, waving to them with their trunks. Next they mounted large balls while the audience applauded. The crowd was further amused when the trainer ordered the elephants to roll over and take a nap. After many rounds of applause, the elephants rose and departed through the exit.

The ringmaster announced that the circus was brought to Kenosha by a train with 22 cars of equipment, 28 cars of animals, and 19 cars for the staff. He advised everyone to visit the side shows before leaving for the evening.

When the crowd flooded out of the tent, most people headed toward their cars or the city buses. Only a few stayed to visit the side shows and booths.

Adam and Neil stopped to get their applications for employment, taking extras for Naomi and Jennifer. As they rode home on their bicycles, they continued to plan their escape for the following night.

24

The iron hissed like a snake when she propped it to get some ice from the refrigerator.

Adam got up early the next day to help his grandmother with her chores. She noticed that he was irritable while he fed the cows and helped her milk them. When he was carrying the pails back to the house, he refused to tell her why he was angry.

"Something's wrong with you today," said Grandma. "Dio mio! Do you fight with that Jew girl in the circus?"

"Grandma, her name is Naomi. I wish you wouldn't call her that Jew," snapped Adam.

"I'm sorry," she said. "I only go to school to fifth grade in Italy. I don't know how to talk English."

"That's no excuse for being prejudiced against Jews," said Adam, annoyed with her.

"I don't understand that word, prejudice. Why are you so mean today?" asked Grandma.

"I hate living on this farm with Mom. She's always angry with dad. I feel trapped here."

"That's what your mama tells me every day. Dio Mio! When I live in Italy we only have mountains. We have no room to plant a garden like here."

"Grandma, I'm sorry. I didn't mean to snap at you."

"Never mind. You don't hurt my feelings so easy. Your father is such a good boy when he is little. I don't know what happened to him. Giovanni is away for too many years in that war."

"It left deep scars on him. He saw too many soldiers get killed. Mom always says the war changed him. I don't want that to happen to me and Naomi. I'll always love her."

When they reached the sidewalk, he heard his mother calling from the window. "Adam, you have a phone call. I think it's Neil."

"I'll be right there, Mom," said Adam, hurrying up the steps into the kitchen. He set the milk pails down on the table and picked up the phone.

"Adam, it's Neil. I wanted to tell you Jennifer and I won't be coming with you to the circus tonight."

"What happened?" asked Adam.

"Jennifer's mother caught her packing her suitcase this morning. Mrs. O'Reilly was furious when she found out that we were planning to run away with the circus."

"Did Jennifer tell Mrs. Rosenberg about us?" asked Adam, feeling tense.

"No. Jennifer told me she didn't say a word about you guys. Her mother kept probing her, making her swear on the Bible that she was telling the truth. She felt guilty about lying under oath, but she didn't betray Naomi."

"Thanks," said Adam. "Is Naomi still at Jennifer's house? She was staying there overnight because her parents were out of town."

"No, she went home to feed their cats and tropical fish. She was going to pack her suitcase to run away with you and is waiting for your phone call."

"Thanks for reminding me," said Adam, noticing his mother had entered the kitchen to set up the ironing board.

"I overheard you talking with Neil. I hope you two had a good time last night at the circus," said Gertrude. "Marie and I are going to the evening performance."

. "Is Dad going with you tonight?" asked Adam.

"Your father's too busy going to his AA meetings to be bothered with us, slaving here on the farm."

"Then you'll be taking the truck. I'd like to go with you to see the performance again."

"That's fine. We'll load the vegetables tomorrow morning. Tuesday's Market is always good because I know a lot of people on the north side of town.

"You're awfully nervous this morning," continued his mother, sprinkling Adam's shirt before ironing it. "I hope you didn't have a fight with Naomi last night."

"We're getting along fine. I didn't sit with her. We met during intermission. She went to the circus with Jennifer's mother and sister."

"I overheard you say Naomi was staying overnight at Jennifer's house. I suppose her parents were out of town for the Labor Day weekend."

"Don't worry; Jennifer's mother is very strict. She kept an eye on the girls every minute. I came back with Neil around 10:30. You probably didn't hear me come in."

"I know the Rosenbergs don't approve of you dating Naomi, that's why they've pulled her out of St. Mary's."

211

"I'd rather not talk about it," said Adam, recalling how the police stopped him in Topeka, Kansas because of his mother's phone calls. He glanced up at his grandmother, who was straining the milk with a cheese cloth and then pouring it into quart bottles.

"I've got to help Grandma get ready for tomorrow's market," said Adam, feeling uneasy about creeping up the attic steps last night and bringing down a worn suitcase. He had already packed his clothes and hid it under his bed.

He planned to conceal it under a canvas on their truck and remove it during intermission. Adam intended to tell Naomi to take a taxi and meet him near the elephants. He decided to go directly to the manager with their applications before finding a hiding place until the show was over.

"Adam, you need to pick that bumper crop of green beans. I can help you with them later. Excuse me; I need to use the bathroom. I'll be right back," said his mother.

He reached for the phone, dialing Naomi's number. He was alarmed when Mrs. Rosenberg answered.

"Sorry, I've got the wrong number," he said, hanging up the phone.

"Who was that you were calling?" asked Gertrude, returning to the kitchen and continuing her ironing.

"I tried to call Naomi, but I got the wrong number," said Adam, leaving the house, worried about Naomi's parents finding out about their plans.

He was tormented with guilt as he entered the garden,

where he picked several bushels of beans.

The sweat was pouring from his forehead when he came into the house to get a glass of Kool-Aid. His mother was standing at the ironing board, pressing a dress for Marie. The iron hissed like a snake when she propped it up to get him some ice from the refrigerator.

"It's hotter than hell in this house," said Gertrude. "By the way, Rachel Rosenberg called. She recognized your voice on the phone and was wondering why you were calling Naomi.

"I told her the truth about you meeting her at the circus last night. Rachel and David had just returned home from bringing their daughter back from summer camp."

"Oh, I didn't know they were gone," said Adam.

"Rachel told me that she called Jennifer's mom the first thing this morning."

"Why did she do that?" asked Adam, paralyzed with fear and choking on his drink.

"Jennifer's mom caught her packing a suitcase this morning so that she could run off with Neil. They had planned to join the circus."

"I'll be damned," said Adam, heading toward the hallway steps. "Neil didn't say a word to me about that."

"Adam, come back here," said Gertrude. "I have something for you to put away. It's on the couch in the dining room."

"I'll do it latter," said Adam.

"No, you'd better do it now," insisted Gertrude.

"What the hell's going on here?" asked Adam, hurrying from the kitchen into the dining room. He gasped at his open suitcase, stretched out on the couch with his application filled out to work at the circus."

"You're just like your father. You lied to me again! Jennifer confessed to her mother that you and Naomi were planning to join the circus with her and Neil."

"I hate this fucking family," shouted Adam, dashing down the steps. He brushed past Grandma who was heading toward the garden wearing a straw hat.

"Dio mio! Adam! What's wrong with you?" she asked, hurrying after him. You gotta tell me the truth. I hear your mother yell at you inside a-the house."

"I'm leaving this family to marry Naomi!"

"Dio mio! In nomine patris et filii et spiritus sancti!" she uttered, making the sign of the cross. "What about your education?"

"Fuck high school and college!" he shouted, furious because Jennifer had betrayed them again.

"Adam, I never hear you talk like that before," said Grandma, her mouth hanging open.

"Adam," shouted Gertrude from the kitchen window. "It's the telephone for you."

"Who is it?" he asked with his fists clenched.

"It's Rachel Rosenberg," said his mother pressing her face against the screened window.

"Tell her to go fuck herself!" shouted Adam, snatching two empty bushel baskets and charging into the garden.

214

"How dare you use that kind of language," screamed his mother, hanging up the phone and bolting down the steps and out the door. She hurried through the garden gate, putting her hands on her hips. "You're grounded for a month!"

"Dio mio! Leave him alone," said Grandma.

"No son of mine is going to use filthy language," stammered Gertrude. She rushed toward Adam and slapped him across the face.

"You're a bitch! No wonder Dad doesn't want to live here!" he said, glaring at his mother. He hurled the empty bushel baskets into the tomato patch, knocking several tomatoes from the vines.

"You have a lot of nerve talking to me like that," screamed Gertrude.

Flushed with rage Adam charged out of the garden like a rampant bull. He darted into the house with the door slamming behind him.

"Come back here this minute. You're just like your father. That no good bastard's got another woman on the string. Sex, that's all you men ever think about!"

Upon entering the kitchen Adam looked up the number of the Yellow Cab Company in the telephone directory and ordered a taxi, giving the clerk the directions to the farm.

He hurried into the bedroom and removed the cigar box from his lower dresser drawer, taking out the money he earned from baling hay. After washing his face and hands in the bathroom, he changed his clothes. Picking up the phone, he dialed Naomi's number. He was surprised when she answered.

"Naomi! Thank God, it's you. I just called a taxi to pick me up. I'll meet you in the alley at your garage within the hour," he blurted.

"Here comes my mother. I can't talk now," she said, hanging up the phone.

Rushing toward the porch, Adam gathered up his canvases and stored them in the attic along with his paints and art supplies. Returning to the dining room, he picked up his suitcase and departed through the front door.

His heart was pounding wildly as he walked through the orchard, pausing near the fence where he had kissed Naomi. Adam set down the suitcase on the lawn, waiting for the taxi to arrive. Crispy struggled to get up from under the pear tree, stumbling toward Adam and wagging his tail.

He could hear his mother screaming in the garden. She angrily helped Grandma fill the bushel baskets with tomatoes, complaining about Adam being influenced by her husband. Gertrude blamed Giovanni for abandoning her on the farm and leaving her to discipline her sons.

Grandma agreed with her that Giovanni should be home and not living in an apartment. She also blamed the Rosenbergs for inviting Adam to the synagogue and taking him to the beach for the rest of the day.

"Those Jews don't know how to raise children. They only know how to make money," said Grandma, wiping the sweat from her forehead with her hand.

216

"It's not the Rosenbergs' fault that Adam and Naomi want to go steady. I don't blame them for nipping their relationship in the bud. They're too young to be dating without a chaperone. When I was that age, we went everywhere in groups, with an older brother or sister tagging along to keep an eye on us."

"Dio Mio! When I was sixteen, I work in a factory in France because my father died. I send my check back to my mother."

"Gertrude, look in the driveway. What's that taxi doing here? Adam puts his suitcase in the trunk."

"Adam! Adam! Where do you think you're going?" screamed Gertrude with her hands on her hips.

The two women hurried from the garden with their mouths gaping. They watched the taxi swerve around the circular driveway with Adam sitting in the front seat across from the driver. The Yellow Cab turned onto Bentz Road, leaving a cloud of dust drifting into the pasture.

25

"We provide you with room and board, and expect you to put in a ten-hour work-day."

"Where do you want to go?" asked the driver, removing a crumpled pack of cigarettes from his shirt pocket. He lit the Camel, blowing the smoke out the open window.

"I'm going to the circus at Lincoln Park," said Adam, glancing over his shoulder at the cows grazing in the pasture near the willow tree.

"We'll be there in twenty minutes," said the driver, heading east on Bentz Road.

"Would you mind stopping at the Mobile Station on Highway 50?" asked Adam. "I have to talk to my brother."

"I'll take you wherever you want to go. You're paying for the ride," said the driver, turning onto Cooper Road as the meter registered 10 cents.

"That's Old Lady Jacobsen's farm over there," said Adam, glancing at the dilapidated barn, broken windmill, and the sagging house.

"That place has gotten quite a bit of publicity," said the driver. "Mr. Gascoigne's in jail on suspicion of murdering Mrs. Jacobsen's niece, Joyce."

Adam remained silent as the driver talked about how the police found Joyce Jacobsen's arm and leg in barrels there and her head in Mr. Gascoigne's basement.

When the taxi reached Highway 50, the driver turned

right into the Mobile Station, located in front of Ace Hardware and Connelly Jewel, the grocery store.

Adam got out of the taxi and hurried into the garage where his brother was busy changing the oil on a Ford.

"What are you doing in that taxi?" asked Karl, pausing from his work.

"Do me a favor and call Naomi for me? If her mother answers, tell her that you're calling from St. Catherine's and want to speak to her daughter about changing the schedule of her study hall," said Adam.

"What if she doesn't come to the phone?" asked Karl, wiping his greasy hand on a rag and heading toward the pay phone in the office near the restroom.

"Just tell her mother you'll take care of the problem on Tuesday during her homeroom," said Adam, following him. "If Naomi answers the phone, let me talk to her."

Karl inserted a nickel into the pay phone and dialed the number that his brother gave him. Rachel Rosenberg answered and handed the phone to her daughter.

"It's Naomi," said Karl, passing the phone to Adam and returning to the garage through the side door.

"Hi! I'm here at the filling station on Highway 50. I hired a taxi and have my suitcase in the back seat. I had my brother Karl tell your mom you need a schedule change involving your study hall at St. Catherine's.

"Oh," said Naomi. "I understand it's about a schedule change...Excuse me... Mom, I think someone's knocking at the front door. It's probably the mailman with a letter from Aunt Loretta."

"What's that all about?" asked Adam.

"I don't have time to talk. When will you be here?"

"If you still want to come with me, have your suitcase packed. I can pick you up in 15 minutes."

"I'll be waiting for you in the alley in front of my garage. Here comes my mother. No… I really don't mind the afternoon study hall. Thanks so much for calling. Goodbye."

"Don't tell me you're meeting Naomi. Here take a few of these," he said removing two condoms from his wallet. "They'll come in handy."

"Thanks," said Adam, inserting them into his wallet. He paused, reflecting upon a sermon given by a priest during mass at St. Mary's about the sins of the flesh…fornication, adultery, birth control, and masturbation.

They were all mortal sins which could not be forgiven without absolution from a priest during confession, except by making a perfect Act of Contrition.

The priest informed the congregation regularly at mass that if anyone died with mortal sins on his soul, God would cast him into hell for all eternity.

Karl followed his brother to the taxi. "For crying out loud! Where the hell are you going with that suitcase in the back seat?"

Adam informed him that he was moving in with his father at Mrs. Solinsky's upper flat on 46th Street, and Naomi was going to live there with him."

"I'll stop by for a visit when I'm not busy," said Karl. "Mom will miss you helping her out on the farm."

Adam entered the taxi and slammed the door. He handed the driver Naomi's address. As the taxi departed from the filling station, the driver offered Adam a cigarette, which he accepted with a trembling hand.

"You don't smoke very much do you?" he asked lighting it for him.

"Not very often," said Adam, coughing.

"You must be nervous about going to Dr. Rosenberg's house. I give him a ride home from the Emergency Room almost every Sunday night. He took good care of me when I injured my back last winter because my taxi skidded on the ice into a parked car."

"My father was treated by Dr. Rosenberg some years ago," said Adam.

"I saw his daughter's name written on the address that you just handed me."

"Do you know Naomi very well?" asked Adam, the cigarette trembling in his hand.

"Of course, she's a beauty. I've given her a ride home from the Beth Hillel Temple with her mother and younger sisters several times."

"Please don't tell her parents were joining the circus," pleaded Adam. "We want to take a break from school."

"I won't say anything to anybody. I've got to earn my living. It's none of my business what you do."

Within fifteen minutes the taxi pulled up in front of

Rosenbergs' mansion in Allendale, with Greek columns supporting the veranda at the entrance.

"Please drive to the alley. Naomi will be waiting for us in front of their garage."

The driver went down the block, turning into the tree-lined alley before stopping the taxi at the garage. Adam swung his door open and hurried toward Naomi, helping her with the suitcase.

"I suppose you two would like to sit together in the back seat," said the driver, placing Naomi's suitcase next to Adam's in the trunk.

The young lovers embraced, kissing each other as the driver went back to 75th Street, turning onto 22nd Avenue and then continuing north.

"We're here at Lincoln Park," announced the driver," squealing the brakes in front of the pavilion and jerking the car. "I hope you'll enjoy travelling with the circus."

Adam broke away from kissing Naomi. He was flushed with embarrassment as the driver swung open their door. Adam stepped out first with Naomi following him. She smoothed her disheveled hair, straightening her wrinkled blouse. Removing her compact to put on fresh lipstick, she smiled at the driver as he handed them their suitcases.

"That's quite an expensive ruby you're wearing around your neck," said the driver.

"Adam gave me this ring because we're going steady," she said. "We're getting married in Nashville, Tennessee."

"Be sure and visit the Parthenon there. It's the same size

as the one in Athens. I took my wife there when we were on vacation a couple of years ago. They also have replicas of the Elgin Marbles. They're just like the statues in the British Museum in London."

"I can't wait to see them," said Naomi.

"That'll be three dollars and seventy five cents."

Adam handed the driver a $5.00 bill, telling him to keep the change. After the taxi departed, they picked up their luggage and crossed the street, heading toward the ticket booth at the entrance of the Big Top.

"It's too late to be going to the performance," said the dwarf sitting on an elevated stool collecting tickets.

"We'd like to talk to the manager about working for the circus," said Adam, setting down their suitcases.

"I've got applications for you right here. Be sure you read the fine print. We don't want our workers to get into trouble with the law," said the dwarf.

"We already have them filled out," said Adam.

"You have to turn them in to Giuseppe. He's the manager of the circus. His wagon's over there near the tiger cages. He's got a sign over the door."

"Look, Adam, the elephants are getting ready to go to the Big Top for the final act of the show," said Naomi.

There's another performance this evening. You better see Giuseppe before he leaves the wagon to supervise the concession stands," said the dwarf.

"Those elephants are huge," said Adam.

Adam and Naomi crossed the lot toward the manager's

wagon, pausing to admire the three elephants and their female riders as they lumbered past them.

"I'm nervous about running away and joining the circus. I noticed that the fine print on the application said that you must be sixteen years old to apply for a job with the circus. I left that line blank," said Naomi.

"I wrote that I'm sixteen on my application. We'll have a better chance of being hired if we don't tell the truth," said Adam.

Naomi removed the application from her purse to write down her age, feeling uneasy about lying. A few minutes later Adam ascended the steps of the circus manager's wagon, noticing a sign in bold print above the door, *Giuseppe Romano*. Adam knocked while Naomi waited with the suitcases.

"Are you Mr. Giuseppe Romano?" asked Adam, his voice quivering upon meeting the six-foot-eight manager. He opened the door, yawning and scratching his chest.

"Yup! I'm the manager. I've been with this circus for twenty-five years now. I just got up from my nap."

"I read in the paper that you were hiring people to feed and water the animals," said Adam.

"And clean their cages," bellowed Giuseppe. "There's a hell of a lot of work to do around here. Our workers have to set up the tents and manage the booths before and after the shows. You've got to be flexible and willing to do what we ask of you."

"Here's our applications, all filled out," said Naomi.

After the final show you can help the staff take down the tents and pack. We won't leave here until early tomorrow morning. You can sleep on the train. It's a long ride to southern Illinois," said Margo.

After Adam and Naomi dropped off their luggage, they went to a tent, where a makeup artist painted their faces white and mouths and noses red. She also gave them orange wigs, clown suits and large rubber shoes to wear.

Margo returned within a half hour and led them past a row of booths to their stations. Adam was located across from the pony rides where he sold peanuts, popcorn, and soft drinks. Naomi was nearby selling pink cotton candy.

Her stand was across from a snake charmer, wearing an orange turban and a saffron robe. He lured the customers into his tent by playing a flute while a cobra rose from a wicker basket. After the performance the flutist pulled back a curtain revealing a boa constrictor coiled on an elevated platform to startle the audience.

As the crowd flooded out of the main tent after the show, some spectators departed for home, but most of them took their children to the rides, side shows, and concession stands behind the Big Top.

Adam waited on parents with small children standing in line to get refreshments before leaving for the pony rides. Once the rush was over, he strolled over to talk to Naomi. She informed that she had a steady stream of customers buying cotton candy.

"Just look at that long line of kids waiting to ride the

elephant," said Naomi, distracted by a noisy family leaving the nearby Fortune Teller's and others entering the House of Mirrors.

A half hour later, Margo arrived to remove the cash from their registers, putting the bills into a metal box. She informed them about their next assignment, leading them back to their wagons.

After changing their clothes, Adam and Naomi headed toward the elephants staked beneath the trees. They shoveled the dung into wheel barrels, dumping it onto a distant manure pile. This was followed by sprinkling lime on the heap to keep away flies and reduce the pungent odor wafting through the area.

They scrubbed the elephants with long brushes and hosed them down, filling their wooden buckets with fresh drinking water and feeding them bales of hay.

As soon as they finished their chores, Adam and Naomi returned to their quarters to change back into their clown costumes, returning to their booths to meet the crowd arriving prior to the 7:00 pm show.

Adam was worried that his mother and sister might make an appearance before the show and recognize him. He got nervous when two police officers arrived.

26

They didn't notice the manager coming toward them with two angry men.

"Did you happen to see a young couple on the premises this afternoon? Their names are Adam Montanya and Naomi Rosenberg," asked the grey haired officer, wiping his forehead with a handkerchief.

"By the way, I'm Officer Aiello and this is Officer Anderson. What's your name?" he asked.

"Ah...my name's Mike Weber," lied Adam.

"I've got a photograph of the couple here," said Aiello handing it to Adam. "Mrs. Rosenberg gave it to me."

"I saw them when they came here by taxi earlier this afternoon. They were angry with our manager, Giuseppe, for not hiring them to work for the circus because they were only fifteen years old," said Adam, nervous about being recognized in spite of his painted face.

"Are they still here on the grounds?" asked Aiello.

"The blonde girl told her boyfriend to call a taxi from the phone booth at the pavilion to take them to the North Shore Train Station," continued Adam.

"Mike, did you overhear where they were going?" asked Anderson, taking notes on a pad.

"They were going to Milwaukee and then taking a bus to Mexico," said Adam.

"Thanks a lot for the information. Let's go talk to that

woman, pacing up and down in front of the Big Top. What's her name again?" asked Anderson.

"It's Gertrude Montanya. She's with her daughter, Marie. I've never met such an angry woman. She's furious because she thinks Adam and Naomi are hiding somewhere here on the circus grounds," said Aiello.

"We better tell her that we'll call the Greyhound Bus Station in Milwaukee and track them down like we did when her son, Adam, ran away the last time," said Aiello.

"Her son's a real troublemaker. It was only a month or so ago that we traced him to Topeka, Kansas. He was planning to go all the way to Los Angeles to elope with Naomi, who was living there with her aunt."

"Adam's a chronic liar. I remember his father, Giovanni, making the headlines of the Kenosha News when he crashed his truck in Old Lady Jacobsen's front yard," said Officer Anderson. "That guy's an incurable alcoholic."

"Mike, thanks a lot for your help," said Officer Aiello," glancing toward the main entrance. "We need to talk to that boy's mother right away."

"It was nice meeting you," said Adam, watching them hurry past the manager's wagon and go directly to the Big Top to speak with his mother.

While the last show was taking place, Margo returned to collect the money. She said, "I'd like you to clean the tiger cages before coming back to your booths."

A few minutes later Adam and Naomi changed into coveralls and arrived at the row of empty cages. They knew that the trainer had taken the tigers to the first ring of the Big Top where the crowd was clapping during the final opening of the last show in Kenosha.

After cleaning the tiger cages and placing fresh straw on the floors, they changed into their costumes and washed their hands. Upon returning to their booths, they waited upon customers during intermission until the spectators departed for the Big Top to see the rest of the show.

It was about 9:30 pm on Labor Day when the crowd came flooding out of the tent. Since most families had small children starting school the next day, they avoided the concession stands and rides, departing for their parked cars or the city buses.

About a dozen families decided to take their children for a pony or elephant ride after the show, stopping for refreshments along the way.

Adam was alarmed when he saw his mother coming toward his stand with Marie.

"Mommy! I want some peanuts. That clown's selling them over there," cried Marie.

"You've had enough snacks during the show," insisted Gertrude, grabbing Marie by the arm and dragging her away from Adam's booth.

"Mommy! You're hurting my arm," screamed Marie, breaking away from her. She ran to the concession stand where Naomi was busy with a customer.

"I want some cotton candy!" shouted Marie.

Naomi was terrified that she would be recognized. Her

hand was trembling as she handed the cotton candy to Marie, accepting the money from Gertrude.

"Come on, Marie, we've got to go home. Maybe the police have picked up your brother and that good for nothing girlfriend of his at the bus station in Milwaukee."

A few minutes later, Margo returned, instructing Adam and Naomi to remove their makeup and change into work clothes before helping the crew take down the booths and concession stands, including the Big Top.

About three hours later the young couple had rolled up the canvases and frames, tying them with ropes. They kept busy helping the crew load the trucks before the drivers left for the North Shore Station, followed by the circus wagons being pulled by the horses and elephants. It was almost dawn on Tuesday when the circus train left Kenosha, heading for Champaign, Illinois.

Adam rode in a wagon with bachelor clowns, who were wrapped in blankets and sleeping on the floor. He was awake the entire night because of their snoring and the swaying and rumbling of the train on the tracks.

Naomi was also unable to sleep due to exhaustion from helping the trapeze artists take down the dining room tent and pack kitchen utensils, appliances, and folding chairs.

She was annoyed by the complaints of the unmarried women because their wagon was stifling hot, in spite of the open windows and a faint breeze.

Upon arriving in Chicago, they used the restrooms at the station and had breakfast in nearby restaurants. After feeding and watering the animals, they continued south for several hours, finally reaching their destination on Tuesday evening.

During the rest of the week the employees took their time putting up the Big Top, booths, and concession stands at the Champaign County Fairgrounds. The performers and staff worked together anticipating the weekend shows.

Giuseppe expected everyone to participate in the Thursday afternoon Circus Parade through the twin cities of Champaign-Urbana with horses pulling the wagons. The performers, wearing dazzling costumes, sat on the roofs of the animal cages and waved to the crowds lining the streets. After circling the University of Illinois campus they returned to the fair grounds, exhausted from the heat.

The Big Top was packed during the Friday afternoon and evening shows. Adam and Naomi were busy working at the concession stands between shows, followed by cleaning the animal cages.

They didn't notice the manager coming toward them with two angry men. Adam dropped the box of popcorn that he was handing to a mother with her two children.

"Dad! What are you doing here?" said Adam.

"I've come to take you home," said Giovanni, his brow wrinkled. "Your mother's been frantic with worry about you running away with Naomi."

"Adam, you and Naomi told me you were sixteen years old," said Giuseppe. "You shouldn't have lied to me about your age."

"Where's my daughter!" shouted David Rosenberg, waving his fist at Adam. "If you've done anything to harm her, you're going to be in real trouble."

"She's over there selling cotton candy," said Adam, his face flushed.

"If you two are married, I'm going to have it annulled because you're under age," shouted David.

"We're not married," said Adam, stunned by their unexpected arrival.

David Rosenberg rushed over to Naomi's booth, yelling at her in front of the customers. Giuseppe hurried toward them with Margo accompanying him.

"You take over Naomi's stand for her, and I'll take Adam's place," said the manager.

"I'm sorry about this confusion. Your daughter's such a good worker. Maybe she can come back next summer and work for us when she's sixteen," said Giuseppe.

"She needs to go back to school and get her education," shouted her father.

Naomi was sobbing as her father seized her by the arm and dragged her toward the trapeze wagon to get her suitcase. A few minutes later he reappeared carrying her luggage.

Naomi trailed behind him, wiping her eyes with a handkerchief, pausing at the clown wagon where Giovanni was waiting outside for Adam.

"Are you and Adam riding back to Kenosha with us, Giovanni?" asked David, trying to conceal his anger. "We got plenty of room in the backseat for both of you."

"No, thanks. We're going to take the train back. I'm grateful to you for giving me a ride from Kenosha. Would you mind dropping us at the train station in downtown Champaign?" asked Giovanni.

Adam put his luggage into the trunk of the Cadillac and sat in the backseat next to his father. He felt angry with Dr. Rosenberg for being so harsh with Naomi and depressed because their plans to get married in Nashville were once again thwarted.

David got into the driver's seat and slammed the door. He drove out of the parking lot, gripping the steering wheel while Naomi sat rigidly in the front seat across from him. To break the silence he turned on the radio to listen to the evening news.

Last week the German newspapers listed accounts of violence by U. S. troops, including seven G.I.'s who were arrested and charged with the rape of a schoolgirl in Bamberg. The local government called for the removal of all U.S. troops from their city of 76,000 people.

"Naomi, I want you to see a doctor as soon as we get home. I'll be taking you to the hospital for a physical check up," announced her father as he parked at the station.

"What for?" gasped Naomi, sobbing once again.

"Just to be sure everything's all right," blurted her father, getting out of the car and slamming the door. He went to open the trunk.

When Adam removed his suitcase and set it down

above the curb in front of the station, he heard Naomi screaming as she hurried toward him.

"Adam, don't leave me!" she cried, throwing her arms around him.

"What the hell are you doing?" shouted her father. "Naomi! Get back into the car!"

"I don't want to ride home with you. You're mean and cruel, just like Mom!" she sobbed.

"Naomi, I told you to get back into the front seat!" yelled her father, his face red with rage.

Adam took Naomi by the hand and led her to the front seat. She clung to him trembling while he tried to console her by kissing her on the cheek.

"You must go back with your father," insisted Adam, pulling away from her.

"No! I want to go back on the train with you," she cried, disturbed by spectators forming on the sidewalk.

"What's going on here," said a police officer, pushing through the crowd.

"I'm not going to be abused by my father all the way back to Wisconsin," blurted Naomi "He wants me to ride across from him in the front seat."

"Have you been abusive to this young lady?" asked the officer, removing a note pad from his shirt pocket. "Let me see your driver's license."

"I'm Doctor Rosenberg and this is my daughter, Naomi," he said, showing him his driver's license.

"What's the problem?" asked the officer.

"My daughter's angry with me because her boy friend's leaving on the train, and she has to ride to Wisconsin with me instead of with him. I don't approve of her dating that young man over there."

"I don't see anything wrong with letting her ride in the back seat, if that's what she wants to do," said the officer, pausing to break up the crowd listening to them.

"I'd prefer that you sit in the front seat, Naomi. I have a few things to say to you," said her father.

"I'll never speak to you again as long as I live," said Naomi as Adam opened the door of the back seat for her.

"Then ride in the back seat," shouted her father, entering the front seat and snapping on the radio.

Adolf Hitler used to retreat to the Bavarian mountain resort town of Berchtesgaden, where his 60-year-old sister, Paula Wolf, has been living in a rundown flat, writing her memoirs. She's the only survivor of Hitler's immediate family. Paula mentioned that her brother, Adolf, treated her kindly in spite of his persecution of the Jews and Poles.

Now for the local news: *The United States has fewer cases of polio this summer than last year. Since April only 2,295 cases have been reported while a year ago at this time there were 3,613. Unfortunately there recently has been a severe outbreak in Chicago and the surrounding suburbs.*

Here in Champaign/Urbana the Ringling Brothers and Barnum Bailey circus will be performing every afternoon and evening for the next two weeks at our county fairgrounds before moving on to Nashville…

"Who cares about the stupid circus," said David, turning off the radio. He glanced in the rear-view mirror at Naomi still talking to Adam, who was standing alongside of his convertible.

"I love you, Adam," she said, wiping the tears from her eyes. "I'll be waiting to hear from you."

"I love you too, Naomi," said Adam. "Have a good trip back to Kenosha! Next time we'll join a carnival instead of the circus."

Doctor Rosenberg was furious when he overhead Adam's comment. He stepped on the accelerator, gunning the engine as he sped away. Adam waved to Naomi a final time, following his father into the train station.

All the way home Giovanni waited for his son to tell him why he joined the circus with Naomi. He never scolded Adam or threatened him with harsh words trying to make him feel guilty or ashamed.

"It will take you a few days to get used to St. Mary's after missing the first week of classes," said Giovanni.

"I don't know anyone at St. Mary's," said Adam, feeling depressed. "I've made some real mistakes this time."

As the train rumbled along Adam confessed to his father that he was in love with Naomi and planned to marry her in Nashville. He told him that the manager had separated them into different sleeping quarters because they weren't married.

Adam blurted out that he attempted to have sex with

238

Naomi under the circus wagon, but he stopped kissing her when the watchman came by with a flashlight.

Giovanni tried to convince his son that adolescent marriages were no longer acceptable even though they took place among aristocratic families and the ordinary people when Shakespeare wrote *Romeo and Juliet.*

His father encouraged his son to practice birth control if he decided to have sex in the future, informing him about various methods being used to avoid pregnancy.

Giovanni did not advise Adam to become promiscuous by having sex with multiple partners due to venereal diseases such as herpes, syphilis, and gonorrhea.

Adam felt tense and confused, remembering his promise to God to become a priest because he saved Neil's life. He wanted to talk to his father again about his intense desire to be with for Naomi, but he was too upset to continue the conversation. He glanced out the window at the vast cornfields of southern Illinois, stretching to the horizon.

27

Everyone stood up when Father Bernard entered the sacristy with two altar boys.

On Monday Adam got up early to do his chores, feeling depressed over being separated from Naomi. The day was cloudy and overcast with a prediction of rain. He was nervous about going to St. Mary's because he missed the first week of classes, and he didn't know anyone. All his friends were attending Bradford High. He could have gotten a refund and gone with them, but he had promised God he'd become a priest.

While feeding the chickens, Adam watched his mother leave in the truck with Marie. She planned to drop his sister at Whittier School before going to the Farmers' Market at Roosevelt Park

Adam recalled how his father got drunk and accused his mother of having an affair with Father Fortmann. He knew that Marie's blonde hair and blue eyes resembled the priest's, but her facial features looked like his mother's.

After finishing his chores, Adam took a bath. He put on a new pair of Levis and a short sleeve white shirt. Once breakfast was finished, he hurried down the rutted driveway with his backpack to wait for the bus.

The yellow school bus squealed to a halt in front of their mailbox. The double doors flapped open and Adam greeted the driver, heading down the aisle past a half dozen students, who ignored him. They were preoccupied with discussing their homework assignments or the current movies at the theaters in Kenosha.

Adam sat alone in the back of the bus, gazing out the window, thinking about Naomi. He slouched down in his seat, feeling lonely because he hadn't heard from her since he returned from the circus.

When the bus arrived at St. Mary's, he followed the students down the steps into the dungeon-like basement where the high school was located. The upper stories contained the kindergarten and grade school. Adam asked directions to his homeroom, where he was assigned a seat and a locker by Sister Georgia.

Once the bell rang the students flooded out of their homerooms to place their backpacks, books, and lunches into their lockers, followed by a massive evacuation of the entire building.

"Is this a fire drill or an air raid practice?" asked Adam, following a group of girls from his homeroom. They were hurrying through the halls, wearing white blouses and navy blue jumpers.

"You must be new here because you're wearing jeans," giggled Julie, wiggling her hips. She led the way down the hallway to the stairs leading to the exit.

"You'd better wear dress slacks tomorrow or you'll get expelled," said Joe, cutting in front of Adam, with several football players following him.

"You've got a nice tan," smiled Denise, pausing a few

feet before the crowded stairs. "I'll bet you were on the beach all summer."

"I only went swimming a couple of times in Lake Michigan," said Adam, waiting his turn in line.

"Do you work out at the YMCA?" asked Julie, admiring his muscular physique.

"I worked baling hay for a couple of weeks during the summer," said Adam, bewildered by the Exodus.

"I saw you come in on the county bus this morning. You're a whole week late. School started after Labor Day. Most of us take the city buses to school. Where do you live?" asked Fred, following Julie up the stairs to the exit.

"Out on Bentz Road," said Adam.

"So you're a farm boy," said Fred. "No wonder you're late for school. You probably had to stay home to milk the cows and feed the chickens."

"Don't pay any attention to Fred," said Joe. "He's got a weird sense of humor. We could use you on our football team. We practice every day after school."

"I can't stay after school for sports. My family needs me to help them get ready for the Farmers' Market," said Adam. "I might go out for basketball during the winter."

"You'd make a great quarterback," said Joe, bragging that he was captain of the team.

"Where are we going anyway?" asked Adam, confused by the students streaming past them on the sidewalk.

"To church," said Joe, blocking the traffic so everyone had to walk around him.

242

"It looks like it might rain any minute," said Adam, annoyed by students whispering about his jeans.

"Look at the sky," insisted Fred. "Apollo's struggling to come out from behind those clouds with his chariot."

"For crying out loud, why don't you talk like a man instead of a queer," said Joe.

"Shut the fuck up," snapped Fred. "You don't know your ass from a hole in the ground."

"That's better, Fred. We're going to mass at the new church," informed Joe. "We just passed the old church. It's our gym now."

Adam ignored the bickering between Fred and Joe and hurried up the cement steps leading to the main doors of the new church.

The pews in the front of the church were packed with students from kindergarten through eighth grade. After them came the freshman, sophomores, juniors, and finally the seniors at the rear.

Adam followed Joe and Fred into the sophomore section and knelt down in the pew, where he waited for the mass to begin. He glanced at the crucified Christ hanging on the cross above the altar. The marble statue wasn't in agony, but serene like Michelangelo's sculptures in Florence.

For a few moments Adam wasn't thinking about Naomi, but about Neil drowning in the pond and his promise to God to become a priest. After folding his hands, he prayed for knowledge of His will, hoping for an answer that would settle his conflicting thoughts, emotions, and desires.

"Dear Lord, I know You're the Creator of heaven and earth and omnipresent. You're also over there on the altar in the tabernacle. Please reveal to me Your will and give me the power to carry it out.

"I promised you I'd become a priest because you saved Neil's life, but I'm confused because I'm in love with Naomi. I want to marry her, but I'm not old enough. Naomi loves me just as much as I love her. I'm tormented by my desires to be with her day and night. I have a lot of impure thoughts, feelings, and actions that I need to confess to a priest sometime, but I don't trust the priests in this town.

"I'm still angry about what Kevin did to me in the barn when I was ten years old. I get real mad when I think what that no good priest, Father Furstenberg, did to him when he was growing up.

"Please be merciful to Kevin for murdering him with a shotgun and then killing himself. It was wrong for him to break the Fifth Commandment, but Father Furstenberg was rotten to the core. He shouldn't have been molesting Kevin and getting away with it for ten years."

Adam noticed streams of light filtering into the church through the huge glass windows. He preferred stained glass windows depicting scenes from the life of Christ, especially in the older churches in Kenosha that resembled the churches in Europe that he had seen in library books.

He wished he could elope with Naomi to Paris, where Victor Hugo wrote *The Hunchback of Notre Dame.* Adam thought about how the French author got the idea for his novel from a news article about an archeologist finding a female skeleton entwined in the arms of a male skeleton with a deformed shoulder. The human remains were excavated in a street that was being repaired near the Notre Dame Cathedral.

Adam pleaded with God for guidance, disappointed that He didn't answer his prayers immediately through an inner voice or an outward sign. He decided that the Creator wasn't available. He was too busy monitoring the rising and setting of the sun and bringing forth a birth every thirty seconds or causing a death every minute-and-a half.

God also had to listen to the prayers of millions of people who hardly had enough food to survive, especially in India and China.

Everyone stood up when Father Bernard entered the sanctuary with two altar boys. They genuflected before the tabernacle on the altar. The priest made the sign of the cross and prayed in Latin. *"In nomine Patris et Filii et Spiritus Sancti.* In the name of the Father, and of the Son, and of the Holy Spirit."

After the *Gloria* and the *Confiteor,* the crowd paused, striking their chest, when the priest said, *"Mea culpa, mea culpa, mea maxima culpa."*

"May almighty God have mercy upon you, forgive your sins, and bring you to everlasting life," said the priest.

The Latin mass was slow and tedious for Adam. After reading the *Gospel,* the priest broke the monotony by giving a short homily, followed by greeting the students and their teachers and wishing them a successful second week of school.

Following the recitation of *The Lord's Prayer*, the server rang the bells for the transubstantiation. The priest elevated the host and said, *"Hoc Est Enim Corpus Meum,* Take all of you and eat for This is My Body."

This was followed by the consecration of the wine by the priest elevating the chalice and reciting more prayers. *"Hic Est Enim Calix Sanguinis Mei.* For this is the chalice of my blood."

Adam didn't feel worthy to take communion since he hadn't been to confession since Easter. He didn't know if he should remain in the pew or join the crowd heading toward the altar. Not wanting to appear like an outcast in mortal sin, he decided to follow his classmates to the altar.

He recited an *Act of Contrition*, asking God to forgive him for running away with Naomi with the intention of having premarital sex with her and for being deceitful and lying to his parents.

Adam promised God he'd go to confession in the near future, while kneeling at the altar to receive the Body of Christ, present in the Host.

After communion there were further prayers, finally concluding with a blessing from Father Bernard. Adam was relieved when the mass was over and everyone headed back to their classrooms in the basement of the school, which he labeled The *Inferno* after Dante's classic.

28

"They were queers. Just like those freshman boys with hair bleached with peroxide."

Adam's first class of the day was geometry with Sister Mary Catherine. He lied to her about being a week late because of his grandfather's death and funeral. She was sympathetic, offering her condolences and prayers.

After handing him the class rules, she assigned Adam the last seat in the first row. He noticed every seat was filled except for the empty desk across the aisle, which should have been Naomi's.

Sister Mary Catherine stood in front of the class with a piece of chalk, scratching a problem on the board and ordering the class to solve it.

After reading the answer to the problem, she ordered the class to exchange papers and correct their homework. When the papers were collected, she gave them the assignment for the next day.

Once the bell rang and everyone departed, Sister Mary Catherine spoke to Adam. "You may buy a used geometry text at the bookstore after school. They are cheaper than the new copies. If you need help, I'll tutor you after school."

"I've missed five assignments, but I'll try to get caught up tonight," said Adam.

"I want to warn you that we don't allow students to wear jeans. You must wear dress pants."

"I forgot all about the dress code," said Adam, flushed.

"If you come to class wearing jeans tomorrow, you'll be sent to the principal's office. Sister Philomena will send you home to change."

"I won't forget to wear dress pants," said Adam, leaving the room and hurrying down the hallway.

A few minutes later he entered his Latin classroom, filled with freshman except for three sophomores from his homeroom. Adam introduced himself to Sister Regina, a tall incarnation of the Goddess Athena, wearing a white habit and black veil. She assigned him a seat and asked Rebecca to share her textbook with him.

"You will all settle down and open your books to today's assignment," announced Sister Regina as soon as the bell rang.

She paraded up and down the rows with her grade book checking to see that everyone had done their assignment. This was followed by practicing the singular and plural forms of the First Declension and correcting the translation of the *Poet and the Farmer*.

"For tomorrow you are to memorize the vocabulary words from the *Trojan War* and translate the paragraph about Helen eloping with Paris at the end of the chapter," she announced a minute before the bell rang.

As Adam was leaving the classroom, Sister Regina noticed his jeans and called him aside and threatening to give him six demerits if he didn't wear dress pants on Tuesday.

His next class was biology with Mrs. Grant, an overweight lay teacher, wearing a green silk dress. She sat behind her desk most of the period.

When Adam entered the room, she didn't notice his jeans, but she asked Annette Wilson to share her book with him. After reading a few paragraphs from the cumbersome text, Mrs. Grant asked the class questions about the skeletal system of the frog.

While the students studied the next chapter, she wobbled up and down the aisle glancing at their homework and putting checks in her grade book. Their assignment was to memorize the musculature of the frog and compare it to the human body.

Adam sighed with relief when he arrived in English class. Miss Jennifer Casper informed her students she intended to leave teaching and enter the convent the next semester after teaching at St. Mary's for the past ten years. She gave a lecture on the life of Charles Dickens while the students took notes for a quiz the next day.

During lunch Adam joined a group of sophomores from his homeroom in Bell Hall.

"You're new here," said Ralph, noticing Adam's salami sandwich made with Italian bread. "My father's Italian. We go to Milan every summer to visit my relatives."

"That's where Leonardo Da Vinci painted the *Last Supper* in the refectory of *Sancta Maria della Grazie*," said Adam, informing them that his grandparents immigrated to Kenosha from northern Italy.

"My grandparents came from a village near Ludwig's Castle in Germany," said Fred. "Ludwig lived there with Richard Wagner, who spent all his time composing music."

"They were queers. Just like those freshman boys with their hair bleached with peroxide. Give me a pair of scissors, and I'll chop it off of them," said Joe.

"Those guys wear yellow shirts on Thursday like the other fairies in this school," said Fred.

"They hang out together outside the convent, waiting for the nuns to come out so they can carry their books to their classrooms every morning," said Steve.

"Did you guys hear about Willie Williams?" asked Ralph, changing the subject. "He's the Negro who won the 400 meter relay race in Mexico last year."

"He injured his leg playing football while attending the university," said Adam. "His injury ended his career in football, but he started running when he joined the army."

"Willie had stomach trouble at the international track meet in Berlin this year. In spite of his illness, he broke Jessie Owens' world record by one tenth of a second," informed Ralph, surprised by Adam's comment.

"Who is Jessie Owens?" asked Fred, wiping his smudged glasses with a handkerchief.

"He's the Negro who won the world record in the 1936 Olympics in Germany when Hitler attended the games in Munich," said Adam,

"What's your last name?" asked Steve.

"Montanya," said Adam.

"I've heard a lot about you," said Steve. "I'm a friend of Naomi and Jennifer. Ralph and I live along Lake Michigan in Allendale near them. Naomi talks about you all the time. She really likes you."

"She was supposed to be coming here to school, but her parents decided to send her to St. Catherine's instead," said Adam, his ears turning red. "How's Naomi doing? I haven't seen her for a while."

"I only spoke to her for a few minutes when she got home from the circus in Illinois," said Steve. "I guess she was there earning credit from some university. She told me to say hello to you because you were there too, taking the same class and that's why you're coming here a week late."

"She said Jennifer was dating your friend Neil. They're both going to Bradford," said Ralph.

They continued talking through lunch until the bell rang for the afternoon classes. Adam went to his study hall where the supervisor was Mr. Jeffrey Hartman, the physics and chemistry teacher. He corrected papers at the desk while everyone worked on assignments.

After study hall Adam went to Father Bernard's religion class. The bald-headed priest threatened everyone with six demerits if they didn't settle down. He spent the entire period talking about the Seven Deadly Sins, focusing mainly on Lust. There was a lethal silence when the bell rang and the students left the room with flushed faces.

The last academic class of the day was world history with Sister Cecilia. She defined imperialism by writing it on the board and expected the students to memorize it for a quiz the next day.

"Please open your books and read the chapter about Dutch imperialism in South Africa until the bell rings."

Adam hurried out of the classroom without any further comment about his jeans. He left the building to go to his physical education class in the gym of the old church.

Coach Michael Reynolds gathered the sophomore boys in the locker room, informing Adam he could buy his uniform after school at the book store. He reminded him to bring sweat socks, a jock strap, a towel, and tennis shoes to class the next day.

Everyone ran around the gym for twenty minutes while Adam waited on the sideline, reading his geometry text. He removed his shoes and joined them when they did stretch exercises for another fifteen minutes.

While everyone headed for the locker room, the coach approached Adam. He said, "If you expect to get an A in this course, you have to go out for a sport."

"I can't, because I have to help out on the farm after school," said Adam, departing from the gym.

By the time Adam bought all of his books, the county bus had left without him. He departed from the building and strolled south down 39th Avenue past the fenced parking lot.

29

"I'll give you a ride home in my new Chrysler convertible," said Camille.

Adam walked from school, carrying his overloaded backpack to Carl's Restaurant, west of Bernacchi's Drug Store. He sat alone at the counter with his Coca Cola, leafing through his biology textbook.

"Hey, Adam, come and join us," requested a redheaded girl sitting in a booth.

Adam strolled over to the booth where he recognized the familiar face of Annette Wilson from his biology class.

"This is my sister Marlene and our good friend Camille," said Annette. "We've been going to St. Mary's since we were in kindergarten."

"Frankly, I'm fed up with school, especially the nuns and their demerits. "Would you like a cigarette? asked Camille, offering him her pack of Parliaments.

"No thanks," said Adam. "I don't smoke. I missed the school bus because I was buying books. I guess I'll have to walk home. I live on Bentz Road."

"I'll give you a ride in my new Chrysler convertible," said Camille. "It's parked out front. I live on Cooper Road, next to Marlene and Annette. I used to take the bus with them before my father bought me this car. Now we all ride together to school."

"That's a nice looking car," said Adam, glancing out the

window into the parking lot.

"I've seen you at the Farmers' Market. Sometimes I go there with my mom on Saturday mornings," said Camille.

"How's your mom doing now that she's back from New York?" asked Annette. "Your grandmother tells my mother everything about your family when she sees her after mass at Our Lady of Mount Carmel."

"She had a good time with my sister Marie. They were gone for three weeks," said Adam, feeling embarrassed over his mother's friendship with Father Fortmann.

"How's your dad?" asked Marlene. "Your grandma mentioned that he's living in town in an apartment."

"My dad comes home once in a while to help us load the truck," said Adam, squirming in his seat. "I'll try one of those cigarettes."

"You're well built. I bet you can sling bushels of potatoes onto your truck without any effort," said Camille, lighting his cigarette.

"He's strong from working on the farm, just like his brother Karl," said Marlene.

The girls giggled when Adam choked on the smoke, which caused him to put out his cigarette. He patiently waited for them to finish their drinks, listening to their conversation about the injustice of the school system.

As they departed from the restaurant, Camille insisted that Adam sit next to her in the front seat, with Marlene and Annette in the back seat. She drove past the Hawkeye Turkey Farm and the trailer park, stopping for gas at the

Mobile Station to say hello to Karl.

"How are you doing, Camille?" he asked, wiping his greasy hands on a rag and nodding to Adam.

"Just fine," she said, waving a five dollar bill. "Karl, fill the tank with regular and check the oil. You remember the Wilson sisters?"

"Of course, you always come to Bradford's football games with your boyfriends. Where are you taking my brother?" he asked, reaching for the hose to fill the tank with gasoline.

"They're bringing me home because I missed the school bus," said Adam, feeling nervous sitting in the front seat.

"What are you doing on Saturday night, Camille?" asked Karl. "How about going with me to the Keno Outdoor Theater to see *Gone with the Wind* with Vivian Leigh and Clark Gable?"

"I'd love to go with you, but I have a date," said Camille. "Bill's taking me to a wedding reception at the Holiday Inn in Waukegan."

"You've been going steady with Bill for a couple years now," said Karl, noticing the diamond ring hanging from a chain around her neck.

"Just because I wear Bill's ring doesn't mean he owns me. He's stationed at Great Lakes in the navy. I'm going to pick him up and drive him to the reception. We're renting a room at a motel for the night."

"If your parents found out you're staying overnight with Bill, they'd be furious," said Marlene, opening the top button on her blouse and removing a golden chain with a ring attached to it. "Frank asked me to marry him after I graduate. We're going to the Roosevelt Theater tomorrow night to see *Blackboard Jungle*."

"That's a nice ring," said Karl. "Annette, maybe you'd like to go with me to the outdoor theater."

"She glanced up from her novel, *Peyton Place*. "I have a date with Joe. He invited me to see *Tea and Sympathy*, at the Gateway Theater," said Annette.

"You've got a full tank now, and the oil's just fine. I've checked the tires." said Karl, reaching for Camille's $5.00 bill. I'll bring back your change. Have fun at the wedding reception and the movies this weekend."

"Keep the change, darling," said Camille, starting up the car and blowing Karl a kiss. "We'll go out another time."

"Adam, your brother's really handsome. If I weren't engaged to Frank, I'd go out with him," said Marlene, removing her compact from her purse and applying lipstick, since makeup wasn't allowed at St. Mary's.

"Adam, why don't you join us for a few beers before we take you home?" asked Camille.

"I promised Grandma I'd clean the barn and help her with the chores," insisted Adam.

"We have a swimming pool in my back yard. My parents are still at work, and they won't be home until later. The four of us could have a lot a fun for a couple of hours," said Camille, turning onto Cooper Road.

"Maybe next week," said Adam, who changed the

subject. "What's *Tea and Sympathy* about?"

Annette told them she read a review about the movie, involving a teenager named Tom, who was uncertain about his sexual identity. He was teased by his classmates at a male boarding school for playing the part of a woman in the school plays.

"I don't know why there are so many movies that deal with weird men these days," said Marlene.

"*The Shrike* is playing at the Orpheum Theater. June Allyson's married to a psychotic husband, played by Jose Ferrer," said Annette.

"Annette's attracted to strange men," said Marlene. "I like Frank, because he's ordinary. He works at A&P after school and is saving his money for our wedding. We're only going to have two children once we're married."

"I hope you're not using the rhythm method for birth control. It's not safe. Have you thought about using a diaphragm?" asked Camille, turning right onto Bentz Road.

"Frank and I agreed not to have sex until we're married. Having premarital sex is a mortal sin," said Marlene.

"You guys are so old fashioned," said Camille, swerving the car into Adam's rutted driveway and slamming on the brakes in front of the garage.

Adam got out of the car with his backpack and thanked Camille for the ride.

"Don't forget to bring your swimsuit next time," she said. "You can spare a couple of hours before coming home to help your grandmother."

"'I'll meet you at Carl's Restaurant next Friday with my swimsuit," said Adam, waving goodbye to the girls. He watched them speed around the circular driveway, leaving a cloud of dust drifting into the pasture. Adam glanced toward the garden where his mother was carrying a bushel of green beans.

"I'll help you with those," he said, setting down his backpack on the sidewalk near the spigot.

"Go help Grandma with that crate of zucchini," said Gertrude. "Who was the blonde girl driving the Chrysler?"

"I know her. That's Lucile Flynn's daughter. Sometime I see her at a-the market," said Grandma. "I know those girls in the backseat because their mama, Luciana, comes to my church on Sunday. Sometime she brings her daughters with her. Her husband's Sam Wilson. He's a big shot at the factory where Giovanni works."

While carrying the produce in from the garden, Adam explained to them that he met the Wilson girls and Camille at Carl's Restaurant and got a ride home with them because he missed the bus.

"We've got a lot of work to do before we take a break," said his mother, annoyed by the interruption.

Adam changed his clothes and then helped dig the potatoes and pick the sweet corn, carrying the crates and bushels of produce from the garden to the spigot.

"Mom, I've got homework due for tomorrow," insisted Adam."I'm already behind a whole week."

"You go do your homework now," said Grandma. "I

help your mother wash a-the vegetables."

"That's the phone ringing," said Adam, dashing into the house to answer it.

"Adam, I'm so glad you're home from school. I've missed you so much," said Naomi, her voice trembling.

"Naomi, I love you," said Adam. "When can I see you again? I hate being at school without you there."

"I don't know. I'm just overwhelmed with homework. I tried to call you several times when I first got back from Illinois, but no one answered your phone."

"We were probably working in the garden. I've been going crazy without you. I love you so much," said Adam.

"Damn it! Here comes my mother. I can't talk now!" said Naomi, hanging up the receiver.

"For Christ's sake," said Adam, pacing the kitchen floor. "Now what am I supposed to do?"

"Who was that on the phone?" asked his mother, coming up the stairs into the kitchen.

"It was Neil. He said that he likes going to Bradford. He might come over so I can help him with his geometry," said Adam, feeling guilty for lying.

"I wish you wouldn't hang out with Neil. I don't trust him. His father is mean to his mother. Marjorie told me she's wants to file papers for a divorce."

"That's not going to happen because Neil told me that his mother tried to divorce her husband for beating her up, but her brothers wouldn't let her sign the papers because they're staunch Catholics and believe divorce is a sin.

30

Camille backed out of her paved driveway, not bothering to look into the rearview mirror.

Adam was unable to contact Naomi the rest of the week. He called her as soon as he got home from school and again later in the evening. When he was finally able to reach her, they decided to meet at the public library, but their plans didn't materialize due to the vigilance of her parents.

Naomi tried writing letters to Adam by using Jennifer's address until her mother, Mrs. O'Reilly, put a stop to the correspondence.

Adam took the bus each morning to school and back to the farm in the late afternoon. On Friday he once again met with Camille, Marlene, and Annette at Carl's Restaurant. They sat in a booth smoking cigarettes and discussing the current gossip at school while drinking Coca Cola.

"Did you hear about Roxanne?" asked Camille.

"Of course, everyone knows she's pregnant with Alfred's baby. They've been going steady ever since they were freshman," said Annette.

"Roxanne wears a trench coat to her classes to cover her stomach," said Marlene.

"If anyone else wore a coat to class they'd be given four demerits," said Annette.

"Steve got into trouble the other day when Sister Mary

Catherine overheard him gossiping about Roxanne's pregnancy," said Adam. "He should have kept his big mouth shut."

"She gave Steve six demerits for ruining Roxanne's reputation by making slanderous remarks. I was right there when it happened after class," said Annette.

"It's too bad Roxanne's a straight A student, yet she didn't have enough brains to go to the doctor and get fitted with a diaphragm," said Camille, sipping her Coke. "She didn't want Alfred to use condoms because it's a mortal sin. I heard all about her pregnancy when I saw her at the fireworks on Simmons Island."

"Her parents wanted to send her to California to have the baby, but she refused to go. Roxanne plans to marry Alfred during Christmas vacation in the rectory, not in the church. Their baby's not due until the end of January. She asked me to be a bridesmaid," said Marlene "I told her my parents wouldn't approve of me being at the wedding."

"Roxanne told me that she was using the rhythm method when they started having sex last year," said Camille.

"They should have waited until they got married. Premarital sex is a mortal sin and so is practicing birth control," said Marlene.

"I don't believe everything the priests tell us in religion class," said Camille. "What do they know about birth control, dating, and marriage?"

"It's best not to have sex before marriage," said Annette, getting up from the booth to stretch.

"Everyone's invited to my house for a few beers and a swim in the pool," said Camille, leading them out of the restaurant to her parked car.

Adam removed his backpack and entered the front seat, mentioning he brought along his swim suit and a towel. He noticed Annette was reading *The Outsider* in the back seat while Marlene was leafing through a fashion magazine.

Upon reaching Camille's house everyone changed into their bathing suits and dove into the Olympic-size pool. They enjoyed swimming and throwing a beach ball. After an hour of giggling and teasing Adam, they returned to the patio where they opened bottles of Pabst Blue Ribbon on ice in a plastic cooler.

Adam felt relaxed while drinking his beer, noticing how attractive the three girls were in their bathing suits. He wished that Naomi had been invited to join them.

Annette informed them that she had cancelled her date last weekend with Joe because her parents objected to them going to see *Tea and Sympathy* because it was X-rated by The Legion of Decency, which is supported by the Catholic Church.

While chatting over a second round of beers, Adam started to feel intoxicated. He noticed that Camille had switched from drinking beer to Manhattan cocktails.

"I'll have one of those cocktails," said Adam.

Camille seized the bottle of Four Roses, filled her glass and mixed him a cocktail. "How about you girls?"

"We never drink hard liquor," insisted Annette.

"I'll just take a sip of yours," said Marlene

"Let's go skinny dipping to cool off. Come on you guys. Don't be chicken," slurred Camille, mixing herself another drink and gulping it down.

Her friends gasped when she peeled off her halter and tossed it into the pool.

Adam stared at her firm breasts, uttering. "You've really got a nice tan."

"Camille! It's almost 5:00 O'clock," blurted Marlene, glancing at her watch. "Your parents will be home shortly."

"I'm supposed to be helping my grandma get ready for tomorrow's market," said Adam, rising from the wicker chair on the patio. "She'll be mad at me for being so late."

"Adam, are you coming into the pool with me or not," said Camille, diving into the water.

"Your mom and dad will be home from work within ten minutes," shouted Annette, who never finished her first beer. "We better get rid of these empty bottles."

"Oh my God," gasped Camille, climbing out of the pool, holding her halter. "My parents will kill me if they find us here drinking."

"I'm putting the bottles in this paper bag that I found in the kitchen," informed Marlene.

"Come on, everybody, we've got to drive Adam home," announced Camille, hurrying into the house to get dressed. She returned barefoot, wearing jeans and a pink blouse.

"You shouldn't be driving," asserted Marlene, putting the bag into a garbage can.

"Just grab your clothes and get into the car," shouted Camille, weaving her way to the car.

"Adam, still wearing his swimsuit, opened the door to the back seat for Marlene and Annette.

"We're not going with you. We only live a couple of houses away from here," said Annette, watching Adam slam the door and enter the front seat. "We'll walk home."

Camille backed out of her paved driveway, not bothering to look in the rearview mirror.

"Look out for your mail box!" screamed Annette. "You're going to run it over."

The Wilson sisters gasped upon hearing the wooden post cracking and the aluminum mailbox crunching under the back wheels of the Chrysler.

"Oh fuck!" said Camille. "I probably damaged my car."

"You shouldn't have had those cocktails," said Annette, her mouth gaping. "Just look what you've done!"

"Camille, you're drunk," sighed Marlene.

"Let's go home!" said Annette, putting on her backpack. "Camille, you better drink some coffee before you drive Adam home."

The two sisters departed barefoot in their swimsuits, wearing their backpacks and carrying their clothes, shoes, and wet towels.

"For Christ's sake!" said Camille staring at the squashed mailbox and broken post. "Adam, come here and take a look at my fender."

Adam stumbled out of the front seat feeling dizzy.

264

"Your car's scratched and dented."

"Come on! I'll take you home," she said, waiting for him to return to the front seat. "Hurry up. It's getting late."

Camille pulled the convertible away from the wreckage and backed out of the driveway. When she shifted the clutch and slammed her foot on the gas pedal, her car jerked forward, speeding down Cooper Road.

She zoomed past Whittier School and then turned left onto Bentz Road. A few minutes later, the Chrysler was rumbling up the rutted driveway of the farm. It came to a halt near the sidewalk in front of the garage

Adam glanced at his mother and grandmother scrubbing vegetables at the spigot alongside of the house. He swung open the door and stepped out of the car, wearing only his swimming suit. Adam winced because his feet hurt from the gravel as he reached for his backpack.

"Camille, have a nice...nice weekend," muttered Adam, staggering barefoot until he arrived at the sidewalk where Grandma and his mother were working.

He paused, waving to Camille, who honked the horn as she swerved around the circular drive before turning onto Bentz Road.

"What the hell's going on?" said Gertrude, standing at the spigot with her hands on her hips.

"We went swimming at Camille's pool...after school. I'm sorry... I'm so late," slurred Adam.

"Sorry nothing. You've been drinking! I can smell beer and whiskey on your breath. This is a fine how-do-you-do.

Grandma and I have been slaving in the hot sun all afternoon while you were drinking at Camille's house."

"Marlene and Annette Wilson were there too," said Adam, stumbling down the sidewalk toward the door."

"Dio mio! You're just like Giovanni! Why do you come home drunk like that?" asked Grandma, making the sign of the cross.

Adam staggered up the stairs and hurried into the dining room, leaving his backpack on the couch. He went into the bathroom, stripped off his clothes, and climbed into the tub, turning on the cold water and splashing himself until he got over his dizziness.

After drying with a towel, he got dressed, returning to the kitchen where he heated the coffee pot and drank a cup of black coffee. He slouched at the kitchen table and fell asleep. An hour later he woke up with a headache and left the house to help wash the vegetables and load the truck.

"You ought to be ashamed of yourself," blurted his mother, not expecting him to come back to work.

"I'm sorry. I only had two bottles of beer, but they went right to my head," he said, not mentioning the cocktail.

"Why do you go out with that Camille Flynn? What happened to that nice Jew girl?" asked Grandma.

"I'm going to meet Naomi at the Halloween Dance at St. Catherine's in a couple…of weeks," said Adam.

"You're not going to that dance. You're grounded. I'm calling Camille's mother and giving her a piece of my mind about you coming home drunk," said Gertrude, heading toward the back door and up the steps to the kitchen.

Adam crouched down to help Grandma scrub the final crate of potatoes, glancing up at the kitchen window. He could hear his mother talking to Mrs. Flynn on the phone.

"I'm totally disgusted with my son coming home drunk. Your daughter, Camille, drove him home in that new car of hers. I could tell by the way she was driving that she was inebriated."

"Yes…I'm listening…What? What do you mean? Oh, I didn't realize that Camille was in an accident on the way home… I'm sorry to hear about that… Is she all right?

"How terrible…You mean she actually ran into a telephone pole…It was on Cooper Road near Whittier School. How awful. No…don't tell me she totaled the car…I'm terribly sorry to hear that she's in the hospital… Oh, no! Really…Ah…of course…Oh, you're waiting for your husband to call you from the hospital…Sorry…I'll talk to you later."

After hanging up the phone, Gertrude went to the refrigerator and removed a tray of ice and a pitcher of lemonade. A few minutes later she came down the steps carrying glasses of lemonade for Grandma and herself.

Adam stood up, holding a scrub brush. "I'm really sorry for drinking those beers," he said. "I should've come right home from school to help you with the chores."

"Camille's in the hospital," sighed Gertrude, her hand trembling as she sipped her lemonade. "After dropping you off, she crashed her new car on Cooper Road. An

267

ambulance took her to the hospital."

"Is she all right?" asked Adam, feeling guilty.

"Lucile is waiting for her husband John to call her from the hospital. Camille was unconscious when they pulled her from the car and put her on a stretcher."

"Camille drank more than all of us. She had two beers and then switched to cocktails," said Adam.

"Oh, my God," said Gertrude. "She shouldn't have driven you home drunk. You should've called me to pick you up at her house."

"I didn't realize she was so drunk until she backed into her mailbox. She drove like a maniac going 80 miles an hour all the way here. Maybe we can go to the hospital and see how she's doing," said Adam, his brow furrowed.

"We're not going anywhere. Grandma and I are exhausted from doing your chores. If you want to go to the hospital, call your father to take you. He's either at an AA meeting or sitting in some bar in town."

"I've gotta go milk my cows now," said Grandma. "Adam, you come with me to feed the cows. Where's Marie? She promised to feed a-the chickens?"

"Marie's at her piano lesson," said Gertrude. "I have to pick her up shortly. I never have a moment to myself."

"I'll feed the chickens for her," said Adam, stumbling toward the chicken coop to fetch the oat bucket.

"Dio mio, Adam! You walk just like your father when he's drunk," sighed Grandma making the sign of the cross.

31

"Just look at my hands. They're callused from working in the garden like a peasant."

On Monday morning the entire student body and faculty at St. Mary's High School were concerned about Camille's auto accident, having heard about it on the radio or read it in the newspaper.

Her father, John Flynn, was an attorney who denied that his daughter had been driving drunk. He threatened a lawsuit against The Kenosha News if they published slanderous information about Camille.

John told the reporters that his daughter was over-tired from working all night on a term paper prior to the accident. She fell asleep at the wheel after dropping a friend off from school.

In spite of everything, there were photographs in the newspaper of Camille's car wrapped around the telephone pole and a picture of the ambulance at the hospital with her on a stretcher. However, there was no mention of drunk driving in the news.

The rumors about her accident circulated among the students on the bus and at the school. Adam and his friends, Marlene and Annette, made a pact not to tell anyone that they were swimming with Camille at her pool and drinking prior to the accident.

Every morning and evening during October Adam rode

the school bus with the Wilson girls since Camille was no longer able to give them a ride.

After staying in the hospital for two weeks, Camille was too bruised to return to school. Her parents admitted her to Hazelden in Minnesota, a treatment center for alcoholism.

"Camille's father had a lot of nerve telling our parents we were a bad influence on her," said Marlene, sitting next to Adam on the bus.

"Mrs. Flynn blamed her husband for buying Camille a brand new car for her birthday instead of spending time with her on weekends," said Annette.

"Did you know how much she drank the night of the accident? I didn't even finish my second beer, but Camille slammed down three Manhattans after drinking two beers," said Marlene.

"I was high as a kite from two beers and a cocktail," said Adam. "My mother grounded me for coming home drunk. She doesn't want me going to the Halloween Dance at St. Catherine's."

"I didn't even finish my first beer," said Annette. "Camille's parents don't know that she's been going steady with Bill. They'd be furious if they knew she was going with him to motels and practicing birth control.

"Her mother's more Catholic than the pope, but her father fools around with other women," said Marlene.

"Camille told us her mother threatened to divorce her father because of his love affairs. She works in his law office so she can keep an eye on him so he won't flirt with his clients and the secretaries," added Marlene.

"Mrs. Flynn enjoys the status of being the wife of a lawyer, but she won't admit that her marriage is a miserable failure," said Annette.

"Does Naomi still write to you?" asked Marlene.

"She writes at least twice a week during her study hall and mails the letters after school," said Adam.

A few minutes later the bus arrived at St. Mary's, coming to a halt in front of the gym. The students departed, heading into the building.

Adam worked hard on his assignments, but during home room and study hall, he thought about Naomi, wishing she were with him.

The next few weeks passed slowly with the leaves changing colors and falling to the ground. During the third week in October, on Wednesday, Adam returned home from school and waved to his mother and grandmother, who were working in the garden. He went directly into the house and sat down at the dining room table to work on his term paper.

He was typing from the rough draft when he heard the screen door in the hallway slam and footsteps coming up the stairs to the kitchen. Adam got a glimpse of his mother hurrying across the worn linoleum toward the sink.

"It's hotter than hell out there," she said, wiping the sweat from her forehead with his father's red handkerchief.

"That's because it's Indian Summer," uttered Adam, continuing to type his paper about Tibet.

271

Tibet was once an independent theocracy ruled for many centuries by several Dalai Lamas at their headquarters in Lhasa, known as the Patala. The country is 470,000 square miles and located north of India with the Himalayan Mountains as a natural border.

Adam was distracted by his mother running water in the kitchen sink while she removed ice cubes from the refrigerator and emptied them into a glass pitcher.

"Do you want a glass of lemonade?" asked Gertrude.

"No thanks," said Adam, ignoring her intrusion. *The Chinese soldiers forced the monks and nuns to leave their monasteries along with shopkeepers from the villages. The soldiers ordered the hostages to plant rice in the fields along with the peasants instead of their traditional crop of barley.*

Gertrude entered the dining room with her glass of lemonade. "We're breaking our backs in the garden, working like slaves, while you sit here like King Tut on his throne typing."

"Mom, my term paper's due next Friday. I'll help you as soon as I'm done typing."

"Adam, you're as slow as molasses in January when it comes to typing," she said, picking up a copy of Pearl Buck's short story, A *Field of Rice* from the table. "What's this about? I had to read *The Good Earth* when I was in high school."

"In her short story the Chinese communists broke the fingers of a concert pianist, forcing him to plant rice with

272

his bandaged hands," said Adam, taking a deep breath.

"Just look at my hands! They're callused from working in the garden like a peasant. I don't have a single fingernail left," sighed Gertrude.

"Mom, why are you so angry all the time?"

"I never have any time for myself to read or go to the movies. That's all I do is work from morning to night."

"But you went to New York for three weeks with Marie on vacation," said Adam.

"Some vacation that turned out to be!" she snapped. "Adam, we need your help in the garden!"

"For Christ's sake," he said, going into the kitchen. "I'll never get this damn paper done."

"Why do you always write about underprivileged people in Asia?" asked his mother.

"Because I'm interested in that part of the world," he said, bolting down the stairs and out the back door.

Adam almost knocked over Grandma, who was carrying an apron full of green beans to make soup for supper.

"I go now in the house to listen to a-the news," she said. "It's almost six o'clock."

Adam held the door open for Grandma as she trudged up the steps with the beans. He wondered how she always knew the time because she never wore a wristwatch.

A few minutes later Gertrude came outside. She went directly to the aluminum tub to scrub the potatoes. Adam joined her on the other side, overhearing the evening news blaring through the screened window.

Good evening. This is Bill Schroeder from WLIP in downtown Kenosha with the six o'clock news on Thursday, October 18th.

In a few weeks our country will be holding the 1956 election for President. Adlai Stevenson doesn't have a large percent of followers among the Democrats. He seems to lack the confidence to draw crowds due to his inability to deliver a plausible speech, according to reporters from the New York Times.

On the other hand, Dwight Eisenhower is extremely popular after four years in office. He inspires confidence because of his ordinary manner. He's not afraid to take a stand and deliver a good speech.

Recently the captain of the Italian ship, Andrea Doria, testified in a Manhattan courtroom about the sinking of his ship when it crashed into another ship, the Stockholm. The fatal crash took place during a thick fog on July 25 about 3:00 pm, 175 miles from Nantucket.

"Dio Mio," uttered Grandma. "I feel sorry for that captain because his ship goes down. Next time I fly to Italy in a-the airplane to visit my family. I don't want to take a-the boat no more."

"Grandma was planning to go to Italy this year on the Andrea Doria," said Gertrude. "I'm so glad that she's postponed her trip until next summer."

In the world of sports the New York Yankees arrived in Brooklyn for the World Series.

"I don't want to hear about baseball," said Grandma,

turning off the radio.

"Adam, I have a headache. Go get the crates from the garden. We need to get the rest of the vegetables washed before it gets dark," said his mother.

After the truck was loaded for Saturday's market, everyone went into the house for supper. Grandma served them her homemade vegetable soup sprinkled with grated cheese.

Once the table was cleared and the dishes were done, the family watched the *Bob Hope Show* on TV. No one wanted to miss the program by taking a bath, even though the tea kettle was steaming on the stove.

Grandma finally left them glued to the set while she took her time bathing without anyone interrupting her by coming in to use the toilet or brush their teeth.

32

His classmates were murmuring because a policeman had come to take him away.

On Friday the students at St. Mary's attended mass in the new church, led by Father Bernard. The service was long and drawn out with a sermon about the importance of receiving the sacraments on a regular basis.

After delivering the homily, the priest asked someone from the freshmen class to come to the podium to recite *The Ten Commandments*.

Margaret Wren volunteered, rising from her pew and adjusting her glasses. She straightened her wrinkled navy blue uniform, genuflected, and made the sigh of the cross before approaching the microphone.

Taking a deep breath, she recited, "I Am the Lord Thy God, thou shalt not have strange gods before me. Thou shalt not take the name of the Lord..." Margaret continued until she had finished the commandments.

After she departed, Father Bernard requested a sophomore to recite *The Seven Deadly Sins*. Annette Wilson came forward and spoke into the microphone, "Pride, greed, lust, envy, anger, sloth, and gluttony." She genuflected, made the sign of the cross, and returned to her seat next to Adam.

This was followed by a junior reciting *The Beatitudes*, and a senior *The Mysteries of the Rosary*.

The service continued without interruption. Everyone appreciated being able to stretch as they left their pews to go to communion. Father James arrived to assist Father Bernard with the distribution of communion while Father Smith heard confessions at the rear of the church throughout the entire mass.

Adam felt uneasy about going to communion since he was fearful over committing numerous mortal sins. He made a sincere Act of Contrition promising God that he would go to confession after mass with Father Smith. Suddenly he felt tormented, remembering his promise to God to become a priest.

Adam found it difficult not to think about having sex with Naomi. Each time an impure thought entered his mind he recited a Hail Mary. In spite of his effort, the thoughts returned like a flock of crows landing in the cornfield to feast on the ripe ears of corn.

Once the mass was over, the grade school children left for their classes led by the nuns in charge. They were followed by the high school students and their teachers.

Adam stayed behind to pray in the empty church, waiting to go to confession. He suddenly noticed a shadow blocking the sunlight streaming through the window.

"Adam, I have something to say to you," said Father Smith, coming out of the confessional dressed in his black cassock with a white collar. He paused as Tammy Miller, clinging to her rosary, hurried past him, leaving the church.

"What is it?" asked Adam, rising from the pew. "I've

had a lot of temptation lately, but I reject the thoughts just like you told us to do in your sermon the other day."

"Keep up the good work. Don't forget to take cold showers. It always works for taming the savage beast. I wanted to let you know I can't hear your confession after school today. I must go to the nursing home to give extreme unction to a dying man."

"That's too bad," said Adam.

"Your whole class is scheduled to go to confession on Tuesday before All Saints Day. I'll see you at that time."

"No problem," said Adam, watching him hurry down the aisle and disappear into the dark sanctuary.

Adam headed back to his homeroom. When the bell rang, he went directly to Sister Mary Catherine's geometry class, followed by Latin.

Once the attendance was taken, Sister Cecilia asked the students to open their text books.

"I would like Adam to read the Latin and translate the first paragraph of *A City Is Taken By A Horse*."

Adam quickly opened his spiral binder and read to the class. "*Olim filius regis Troiani per Graeciam iter faciebat*…Once the son of a Trojan King was travelling through Greece. He saw the beautiful queen of the Greeks there and immediately fell in love with her. Afterwards he led her across the sea to the city of Troy."

"You did very well. Now tell me, Adam: Who is the stranger from Troy travelling from Greece?"

"The stranger is Paris," said Adam, feeling uneasy about

reciting before the whole class.

"Now tell us the name of the queen, whom Paris took back to Troy," requested Sister Cecilia.

"It's Naomi," shouted his friend Steve. "Everyone knows that Adam and Naomi ran away together to join the circus. That's why he was a week late coming to school."

"Steve, no one asked you to spread scandalous rumors. For your outburst, you will get four demerits! Now, Adam, please answer my question."

"The name of the queen was Helen. She was the wife of King Menelaus," he said, flushed.

"Now class which commandment did Paris violate by running away with another man's wife?" asked the nun.

"The Sixth Commandment...Thou shalt not commit adultery." recited the students.

"That's right, class. If they were unmarried, and ran away together, what sin would the couple commit?"

Sister Cecilia waited for a response, but the class didn't respond. "The sin is called 'fornication.'"

"How many of you have read Homer's *The Odyssey*, dealing with the Trojan War?" asked Sister Cecilia, waiting for a few moments. "I'm surprised that no one has read this famous classic."

"I read it last year for a book report when I was at Lincoln Jr. High," said Adam, his face flushed.

"Adam, please give us a summary of that epic novel," requested Sister Cecilia.

He informed the class that the Greeks sailed to Troy to

get Helen back. Once the fleet left Greece, the war lasted ten years before the they built the Trojan Horse. This ultimately led to the occupation and destruction of the city of Troy by the Greeks.

"Thank you, Adam. For your assignment, class, please translate the next two paragraphs. Excuse me. Someone's at the door," said Sister Cecilia, hurrying toward the exit.

All heads turned toward the door, where a police officer was speaking to their teacher.

"Adam, please gather your things," said Sister Cecilia, returning to her desk. "The officer wants to speak with you in the hallway."

Adam rose from his desk, placing his Latin text into his backpack. As he was leaving the room, he glanced over his shoulder at his classmates. They were murmuring because a policeman had come to take him away.

"I have a subpoena for you to appear in court, Adam. It should have been mailed to you last week, but the secretary from the district attorney's office left town for a funeral and forgot to mail it," said the officer.

"Mr. Gascoigne's trial is scheduled for 11:00 o'clock, and you've been summoned to be there to testify. We already spoke to your principal about excusing you for the rest of the day. Here, take a look at the subpoena."

Adam sighed with relief as he read it, grateful that he wasn't being arrested for running away with a minor.

"I need to go to my locker and get my books," he said.

"Make it snappy," said the officer, glancing at his

watch. "The trial will be starting in a half hour."

"Adam hurried down the hallway, stopping at his locker just as the bell rang. Within seconds the students flooded into the hallway on their way to their next class.

All eyes were on Adam standing at his locker, putting his books into his backpack with the uniformed police officer towering over him.

The students were whispering among themselves about Adam coming to school a week late because he had run away with Naomi. Others were gossiping about him being with Camille the day she crashed her car.

"So you finally got caught for eloping," said Steve.

"I've been subpoenaed to appear at the murder trial of Joyce Jacobsen," said Adam.

"Come on Adam, we don't want to be late," said the officer, leading the way toward the exit.

33

"The evidence will show that he murdered the deceased on February 7, 1952."

Adam was flushed with embarrassment as he headed up the stairs and out the door of the school. When he reached the squad car, the officer opened the door to the back seat. After removing his backpack, Adam entered the vehicle.

"What the hell are you doing here?" asked Adam, surprised that Neil was sitting there.

"I have to appear in court with you, but I never got the letter because that stupid secretary didn't mail it. I was yanked out of my science class at Bradford to testify."

"I'll be damned," said Adam, placing his backpack on the floor next to Neil's.

Since time was limited, the officer drove with the siren blaring to courthouse on the corner of 56th Street and Sheridan Road.

Upon arrival at the Kenosha County Courthouse, Adam and Neil followed the officer up the steps and down the hall to the courtroom. The young men were escorted to the second row and were seated.

They recognized Mr. Gascoigne sitting beside his attorney at a table to the left of the judge's bench. On the opposite side of the room was the district attorney reviewing his notes.

The witnesses in the first row were Mrs. Jacobsen's son,

Fred, wearing his sailor suit and his girlfriend, Elaine, who wore a low cut pink dress.

Adam recognized the mailman, Ray Wilson, sauntering up the aisle and taking his seat next to Fred. Everyone thought that he had eloped with Joyce Jacobsen.

Feeling nervous about testifying, Adam glanced over his shoulder as more people entered the courtroom. He was surprised to see Grandma coming through the double doors with Mrs. O'Connor, Neil's mother. They came up the aisle and sat down beside Fred.

"Dio Mio. We don't get that paper to come here until a- the last minute. The police bring us here in their car, making lots of noise," said Grandma. "It hurts my ears."

"It wasn't a very pleasant trip with the siren on the whole time," said Mrs. O'Connor.

"I didn't expect to be pulled out of my classes to be here," said Neil to his mother.

"They should have notified us sooner," agreed Adam, worrying about his classmates gossiping about him.

All heads turned to the bailiff, facing the jury.

"Here ye! Here ye! All rise," he said, pausing until everyone stood up. "Circuit Court One of Kenosha County is now in session with Judge Eliot Carlson presiding.

The judge entered the courtroom from a side door, approaching his bench wearing his black robe. Facing those present in the room, he said, "All witnesses are to leave the courtroom until their testimony is needed," said Judge Carlson, observing them depart through a side door.

"All be seated. The court is in now in session. The prosecutor and the defense attorney are present to begin the trial of Clifford Gascoigne for the murder of Joyce Ann Jacobsen. We will start with the prosecutor's opening statement," said the judge.

District Attorney Mitchell Evans rose from behind his table. "Ladies and Gentlemen of the Jury, the State of Wisconsin will prove that Mr. Clifford Gascoigne intentionally murdered Joyce Ann Jacobsen. The evidence will show that he was having an affair with Joyce and murdered her on February 7, 1952. He dismembered the corpse and concealed her body parts in several barrels containing chemical preservatives.

"The state will provide witnesses to verify the affair and the discovery of a body part in the basement of Mr. Gascoigne's home. Furthermore, the state will prove that other body parts were found in the basement of Mrs. Martha Jacobsen's house. At that time she was in a nursing home, unaware of the murder of her niece.

"Mr. Gascoigne took the liberty to padlock the entrance to the basement of Mrs. Jacobsen's house and post *No Trespassing* signs on her property to conceal the evidence. He also violently resisted arrest with a weapon when an officer and the anthropologist appeared to investigate his basement."

"Ladies and Gentlemen of the jury, I encourage you to examine the evidence and find Clifford Gascoigne guilty of the murder of Joyce Ann Jacobsen."

The defense attorney, Charles Ryan, rose from the table where Mr. Gascoigne was seated next to him and approached the jury.

"Ladies and Gentlemen of the Jury, I am here today to prove that the evidence will reveal that Mr. Clifford Gascoigne was a good neighbor and loyal friend of Martha Jacobsen for many years. Prior to the death of her husband and his parents, he assisted the Jacobsen family with chores on their farm. Even after their deaths, he took care of the livestock when Mrs. Jacobsen was ill or in the hospital.

"Concerned about Martha Jacobsen's welfare, he visited her in the nursing home every month for two years. Being a kind-hearted neighbor, Clifford assumed the role of caretaker of her property without payment, focusing upon the security of her buildings.

"The defense will show through testimony that persons other than Clifford Gascoigne could well have been involved with the heinous murder and dismemberment of Joyce Jacobsen.

"I request the jury to carefully weigh all the evidence and find Clifford Gascoigne innocent of the crime of which he is accused," said Attorney Ryan, sitting down next to Mr. Gascoigne.

"Are you ready to present your first witness?" asked Judge Carlson.

District Attorney Evans called Ray Wilson to the stand and waited for the bailiff to swear him in by having him put his hand on the Bible.

"Do you promise to tell the truth, the whole truth and nothing but the truth so help you, God?"

"I do," said Ray, whose hand was trembling when he removed it from the Bible. He sat down, fidgeting with his blue tie and glancing down at his polished black shoes.

"I understand, Mr. Wilson, that you were a mailman for many years in Kenosha County. How long did you deliver mail to the Jacobsen family on Cooper Road?"

"I would say about 16 years. I began delivering mail in 1936 during the Great Depression," said Ray, running his hand through his red hair.

"When did you begin delivering mail for Joyce at the Jacobsen address?" asked District Attorney Evans.

"I don't exactly remember. I believe she moved in with her Aunt Martha in 1946, after the war was over."

"Did you speak to Joyce when you were delivering the mail?" asked the attorney.

"Yes, sometimes I'd have a glass of lemonade with Martha and Joyce on the front porch, especially when it was hotter than blazes outside."

"I believe you were married at the time. What year did your wife die of cancer?"

"Rita died in 1950," said Ray, shaking his head.

"Did you date Joyce after the death of your wife?"

"We went out a couple of times," said Ray, blushing. She was kind to me after my wife died."

"When did you leave for your new job in Iron Mountain, Michigan?"

"I left on February 3rd but I didn't start to work until February 10, 1952." said Ray.

"Why did you leave your job in Kenosha to work as a mailman in Iron Mountain?"

"I left to take care of my aging parents. They live in a cottage along the Menominee River near Pembine. My parents knew I was lonely after the death of my wife. They asked me to stay with them since they were getting old and didn't want to go to a nursing home."

"Then you commuted each day from Pembine to Iron Mountain?" asked the district attorney.

"Yes, it's about a 35 mile drive."

"Were you aware that Joyce disappeared during the first week of February of 1952?" asked District Attorney Evans.

"No, I didn't know about it," said Ray, sighing.

"Do you have any knowledge about her murder?"

"I didn't know about it until I received a subpoena to appear in court about two weeks ago," said Ray.

"Thank you for your testimony. No more questions your honor," said the district attorney, returning to his seat.

Attorney Charles Ryan approached the witness stand. "Mr. Wilson, you testified that you only dated Joyce Jacobsen a couple of times. Did you ever bring her to The House of Gerhard Restaurant?"

"Oh, I forgot about that," said Ray, squirming in his chair. "I invited Joyce to be my guest at our annual postmen's banquet during the Christmas Holidays."

"Did you pick her up and take her home that evening?"

"Yes, her Aunt Martha was waiting for us on the porch the evening after the party."

"Did you date Joyce after that?"

"I took her to the movies a couple of times in January before I left to take care of my parents in Pembine."

"Did you take her anywhere else?"

"We used to go to Mable's Bar on Friday night and square dancing at Bloxdorf's Inn on Saturday evening."

"How long did you date Joyce?"

"We dated for about two years after my wife died."

"Did you ever ask Joyce Jacobsen to live with you at the cottage in northern Wisconsin?"

"Yes, I thought she might like living along the river since it's beautiful there year round in Pembine."

"How did Joyce respond to your invitation?"

"Joyce said she's didn't want to leave her Aunt Martha in a nursing home. Besides, she had been taking care of Mrs. Gascoigne while her husband was at work."

"Mr. Wilson, at first you said that you and Joyce only dated a couple of times. A few moments ago you admitted that you were dating Joyce for two years. I would like the jury to know that Ray Wilson is guilty of lying under oath. Therefore, he is a key suspect in this murder trial."

"Objection," shouted the district attorney.

"Sustained."

"I object to this ploy by the defense attorney on the grounds that he is prejudicing the jury," said the district attorney," rising from his chair.

"Sustained," repeated the judge. "The comments of Attorney Ryan are to be stricken from the record and disregarded by the jury. If the defense continues to make such statements, he will be held in contempt."

"After becoming intimate with Joyce for two years, Ray, didn't you ask Joyce to live with you in Pembine?"

"I already told you that she refused to go with me," said Ray, his face flushed.

"When she refused to go with you, did you murder Joyce and conceal her body in barrels?"asked Attorney Charles Ryan.

"No, I did not!" shouted Ray,

"No more questions your honor," said Attorney Ryan.

"I didn't do it," gasped Ray Wilson, stepping down from the witness stand and returning to his seat, trembling.

Those present in the courtroom were murmuring over the unexpected accusation by the defense attorney.

"Do you think that Ray's guilty?" asked Adam, glancing into the courtroom from the door of the waiting room.

"I don't know," said Neil. "It's strange that he left for a new job a few days before Joyce was murdered."

"You boys, get back to your seats," said an officer, opening the door for Grandma to depart to testify.

34

She seized the butcher knife and tried to kill Joyce, but she only stabbed her in the arm.

"I would like to call Mrs. Sophia Montanya to the witness stand," said District Attorney Mitchell Evans.

Adam watched his grandmother approach the stand, wearing a black silk dress with white polka-dots. Her pair of thick-heeled shoes struck the tiled floor, echoing throughout the courtroom. After being sworn in by the bailiff, Grandma sat down.

"Mrs. Montanya, I want you tell the jury about the last time you saw Martha Jacobsen."

"I go see Martha's body at Piasecki Funeral Home in 1954 because I was in the nursing home when she dies. She looks nice in her new dress."

"When was the last time you saw Martha's niece, Joyce Jacobsen?"

"I see Joyce before she runs away with the mailman, four years ago. I don't think Ray killed her. He's a good man. He tells a-the truth."

"Mrs. Montanya, please answer the questions of District Attorney Evans more directly," interrupted Judge Carlson.

"Let's get a few things straight. Joyce Jacobsen did not run away with Ray Wilson. She was brutally murdered and dismembered. Her arm and leg were found in barrels on Mrs. Jacobsen's property and her head in Mr. Gascoigne's basement. The rest of her skeleton was found in the apple orchard with the remains of her husband and relatives," said the district attorney.

"Mrs. Montanya, when did Joyce Jacobsen come to live with her Aunt and Uncle?" asked Attorney Evans.

"She comes to live with Martha and her husband, Harold. Let me see, after the Big War, in 1946."

"How did Mrs. Jacobsen feel about her niece living in the same house with her?"

"Martha's jealous of Joyce because she' so young and pretty. She always plays cards with her husband, Harold, on their porch."

"What kind of woman was Martha Jacobsen?"

"She works hard. I never hear her complain about nobody. When her husband dies in winter, she wraps him in a canvas and puts him in a-the tool shed until spring. Then she buries him under some trees."

"Did you know Harold's parents very well?"

"I don't know them very much. Martha buries her relatives Phyllis and Chester, in a-the orchard because she has no money for funerals."

"Did you ever go into Mrs. Jacobsen's basement?"

"Yes, I go down there every year to help Martha make applesauce. I bring her a bushel of tomatoes for canning from my garden."

"Did you notice anything peculiar in her basement?"

"I go there to help her can, not to look around for something," said Grandma.

"Did you see Mrs. Jacobsen very often?"

"I go there only at Christmas time and Easter to bring her a present. She comes to my house to take a-the bath because she has no bathtub or sink inside her old house with no toilet."

"No more questions," said the district attorney.

The attorney for the defense, Charles Ryan, approached Grandma, who wiped her forehead with a handkerchief.

"Mrs. Montanya, did Martha Jacobsen get along with her husband's parents?"

"Martha complains about them when she comes to take her bath at my house. She tells me Harold's father, Chester, is mean to her. He gets angry if there's no supper on a-the table at 5:30, but his mother, Phyllis, is nice to everybody but she sleeps all the time upstairs."

"How did Martha Jacobsen treat her mother-in-law, Phyllis?" asked Attorney Ryan.

"I feel sorry for Martha; she takes care of her mother-in law because the horse kicks Phyllis and breaks her back. That poor woman stays in bed all the time and takes morphine from a-the drug store."

"How did Chester and Phyllis treat Joyce?"

"When Joyce comes to live with them from California, those parents are dead already," said Grandma.

"Did Martha get angry with her husband's parents?"

"I never see Martha angry. She's a holy woman. She tells me she washes Jesus' feet when He comes to visit her upstairs in her house," said Grandma.

"Tell me about Clifford Gascoigne and his relationship with Martha Jacobsen," said the defense attorney.

"I don't think they make love together if that's what you mean," said Grandma, startled by the laughter.

"Did Martha Jacobsen get along with Mr. Gascoigne?"

"He's a good neighbor. He helps Martha all the time. When Martha gets old, Mr. Gascoigne comes twice a day to milk her cows. After the horse dies, he buries it next to her relatives in one big grave by the apple trees."

"Would you say that Mr. Gascoigne was kind to Martha Jacobsen?" asked Attorney Ryan.

"Of course, he helps her take care of her farm when Martha was old and sick."

"What do you know about Joyce's relationship with Ray Wilson?" asked the defense attorney.

"When Martha comes to take her bath at my house, she tells me Joyce goes out every weekend with Ray Wilson. During the week she takes care of Mr. Gascoigne's wife, Roxanne, because she's crazy."

"Mrs. Montanya, what kind of woman was Roxanne Gascoigne?" asked the defense attorney.

"Everybody knows Roxanne goes away every winter and comes back in summer. She never talks to anybody because the gypsy woman put a curse on her."

"Would you explain that to the jury?"

Grandma informed the jury that Leona Fortunato was a gypsy, who lived on Cooper Road across from the mink ranch. People came to her all the way from Chicago to have their fortune told.

One evening in the fall Grandma was sitting on the porch with Martha Jacobsen after helping can tomatoes in her basement. It was evening when Joyce came from the kitchen with a cake to celebrate Roxanne's birthday. The three women left the porch and crossed Cooper Road together.

When they entered Clifford Gascoigne's house, he was sitting at the kitchen table drinking wine alone. His wife, Roxanne, was in the living room holding her Raggedy Ann doll and staring out the window.

Joyce lit the candles and carried the decorated cake into the living room where everyone sang Happy Birthday to Roxanne. She didn't pay any attention to them, but clung to her doll, refusing to join the guests in the kitchen.

They were seated at the table eating cake when there was a knock on the door. It was Leona Fortunato, wearing a pink dress and carrying a black bag. She had come to tell fortunes because Joyce had invited her to the party.

Grandma refused to stay in the same room with Leona because she was a witch and excommunicated from Our Lady of Mount Carmel Church.

Martha followed Grandma across the street, returning to her porch. After a short time the two women saw a police car arrive at Mr. Gascoigne's house with the siren blasting loud enough to awaken the dead.

"I see the policeman bring Roxanne outside with a-the handcuff. She screams because she wants to take her doll to the hospital, but nobody goes back to get it.

"I find out later that Roxanne gets angry because her husband Clifford sits with Leona and Joyce to eat her birthday cake."

Grandma said that Roxanne was so jealous that she ran into the kitchen screaming. She seized a knife and tried to kill Joyce, but she only stabbed her in the arm. Clifford leapt from the table and grabbed his wife from behind, taking away the knife. He locked Roxanne in the bedroom, bandaged Joyce's arm, and finally called the police.

The gypsy woman, Leona, came outside with her black bag. She was angry because nobody paid her for coming to read the Tarot cards. After the police took his wifeto the hospital, Clifford gave Leona two dollars.

"When did Roxanne try to kill Joyce?"

"It is just before Thanksgiving when Mr. Gascoigne and Neil buries the horse in a-the orchard," said Grandma.

"In December Clifford Gascoigne falls down on the ice, he breaks his leg. That's when Joyce goes over to his house everyday to check up on him. His wife Roxanne comes back from the hospital for Christmas that year."

"No more questions your honor," said Attorney Ryan.

"You may step down now," said the judge. "We will have a recess for lunch. Please return at 1:30 pm."

. "I don't like that man. He asks me so many questions," said Grandma.

"You did a good job on the witness stand," said Adam, approaching her from the waiting room with Neil.

"The only place we can eat is Thompkin's Ice Cream Parlor," said Neil. "They don't serve sandwiches."

"Let's go to the Ben Franklin Store. They have a lunch counter there," said Marjorie O'Connor.

"I don't mind going there," sighed Grandma. "Today, I miss my nap on the couch."

"I'm gonna have a Cherry Coke and a grilled cheese sandwich," said Neil.

"I hope they'll call me to testify after lunch," said Adam, feeling nervous and wishing Naomi was there to reassure him.

35

"She was wearing fuzzy purple slippers, a yellow night gown, and a maroon robe."

After returning from lunch and everyone was seated once again, Judge Carlson entered and resumed the trial with introductory comments. A few minutes later District Attorney Mitchell Evans announced, "I'd like Neil O'Connor to come to the witness stand."

"Good luck," said Adam, feeling restless.

"I'll need it," blurted Neil, heading to the stand, where he placed his hand on the Bible, promising to tell the truth.

"Neil, I would like you to tell us what you know about Mr. Gascoigne."

"Well…ah…he called me on the phone and asked me to help bury Old Lady…I mean Mrs. Jacobsen's dead horse some years ago. He agreed to pay me a dollar an hour for digging a pit in the orchard. That's when I dug up a skull and a skeleton buried there. I guess it was Mrs. Jacobsen's husband, Harold. I didn't know at that time that she had buried his parents, Chester and Phyllis, there.

"After I dug the pit for the dead horse, Mr. Gascoigne arrived on his tractor dragging it behind him on a chain. When he finally pulled the carcass into the grave, one of its legs was sticking out."

"When did this take place?" asked the district attorney.

"It was in the fall of 1951. I remember Grandma

Montanya was there canning applesauce and tomatoes with Old Lady...Mrs. Jacobsen in her basement at the same time we were burying the horse.

"Well, anyway, Mrs. Jacobsen came over wiping her hands on her apron. She was angry when she saw Mr. Gascoigne break the leg of her dead horse with a shovel."

"Then what happened?"

"Mrs. Jacobsen put a curse on Mr. Gascoigne," said Neil. "She pointed a bony finger and told him he'd fall down and break his leg during the winter."

"How did Mr. Gascoigne react?"

"He laughed and told her to go back to her canning."

"How did Mr. Gascoigne treat you?"

"I liked him because he gave me seven bucks for digging the hole and covering the horse with dirt even though I was only there for about four or five hours."

"Did you see Mr. Gascoigne during the winter?"

"I received a phone call the second week in December. It was Joyce Jacobsen. She told me Clifford had fallen down shoveling snow and broke his leg. They wanted me to come over and shovel his driveway .

"Tell the jury what you know about Joyce Jacobsen."

"She was real nice to everybody. I saw her several times that winter after shoveling Mr. Gascoigne's driveway. Joyce was always there taking care of Mrs. Gascoigne."

Neil informed the jury that one night after dark he knocked on the door to get his pay, but no one answered. After opening the door to the kitchen, he saw his two dollars lying on the kitchen table in front of Mrs. Gascoigne. She was sitting there staring into space holding a butcher knife with her rag doll stretched across her lap.

"Where was Mr. Gascoigne?"

"I think he was in the bedroom off the kitchen with Joyce. They were both giggling with the door closed. I felt uneasy because Mrs. Gascoigne was fidgeting with that knife and looking real angry. I snatched up my money from the table and left, closing the door behind me."

"When did this happen?

"It was about a week before Christmas back in 1951, because I could see their tree in the living room all lit up."

"When was the last time you saw Joyce Jacobsen?"

"I saw her for the last time during the first week in February before Valentine's Day in 1952 because I was shoveling snow when Fred put his mother in the nursing home in Waukegan.

"Were you ever in Mr. Gascoigne's basement?"

"I only went down there one time to get a snow shovel," said Neil. "It was next to the coal bin."

"Did you see any wine barrels in his basement?"

"I saw barrels down there, but I didn't bother to look into them," said Neil.

"Did you see a wood burning set there?"

"No, I didn't go down there to snoop around."

"No more questions," said District Attorney Evans.

"When was the last time you saw Joyce at Mr. Gascoigne's house?" asked Attorney Ryan.

"I saw her there the first week in February. The next thing I heard was that she ran away with the mailman, Ray Wilson, over there."

"Do you think Mr. Gascoigne was having a love affair with Joyce Jacobsen?"

"I don't really know. She might have been trying to cheer him up after he broke his leg. I only heard them giggling in the bedroom once. The other times she was in the kitchen fixing dinner for him and Roxanne. I saw all three of them eating at the table a couple of times. Once in a while Mrs. Jacobsen would be there having supper with them too."

"Neil, did you ever break into Mrs. Jacobsen's house?" asked Attorney Charles Ryan.

"Yes, I broke into her house twice with my friend, Adam. The first time was back in 1951 and the second time this summer."

"Tell the jury what you found in the basement."

"I didn't find anything, but my friend Adam found body parts in the barrels. There was a leg and arm."

"No more questions," said the attorney, returning to his seat next to Clifford Gascoigne.

"I'd like to call Adam Montanya to the stand," said District Attorney Evans.

Approaching the witness stand, Adam passed Neil, who didn't look him straight in the eye but glanced down at the floor. His hand was trembling on the Bible while taking the oath to tell the truth.

"Adam, how long have you known Mrs. Jacobsen?"

"I first met her when I was about three years old because she used to come to our house to take a bath."

"Adam, when was the first time you broke into Mrs. Jacobsen's basement with Neil O'Connor?"

"It was in the summer of 1951. Mrs. Jacobsen became sick and had to go to the nursing home for about three months to recover from pneumonia."

"Was the house unoccupied when you broke into it?" asked the prosecuting attorney.

Adam told the jurors that the house was empty because Fred Jacobsen removed all of his mother's old furniture and belongings and heaped them into a huge pile in the yard. Later in the summer he and Neil could see the flames of a huge bonfire all the way from their houses on Bentz Road. When they walked over during the night to see what was going, they saw Fred tending the fire.

"What did you find in the basement once you kicked in the door?"

"I didn't kick in the door," said Adam.

"Then who did it?" asked Attorney Evans.

"My friend Neil kicked in the door. I had a flashlight with me, and we snooped around investigating the fruit cellar filled with jars of applesauce and tomatoes."

"Tell the jurors what you found in the barrels."

"The first time we went there we found a pig's head floating around in a liquid."

"What about the contents of the other barrels?"

"We never bothered to even look inside of them. Neil and I climbed up the ladder leading to the first floor."

"What did you find upstairs?"

"The house was empty at the time. Later in the summer Fred Jacobsen brought a truckload of used furniture and a new stove for his mother when she came back from the nursing home."

"Did you explore the house?"

"Yes, there was only an old piano there that needed tuning in the living room and an armchair upstairs in front of a window, facing the windmill."

"Was that the only time you ever broke into the house?"

"No, we broke into her house again this past summer. This time when we left, Neil repaired the door with a screwdriver."

"What did you find the second time?"

"The same old pig's head was still floating in the barrel, but I found a woman's arm and her leg in separate barrels. I fished the limbs out with a coal shovel because they were heavy and tied to bricks.

"How did you know the limbs belonged to a woman?"

"Because the left hand had a diamond ring on the finger," said Adam, turning pale.

"How did you react to the limbs?"

"I got sick and threw up on the basement floor."

"Did you find information on the lid of the barrels?

"Yes, I saw the name of Joyce Jacobsen carved onto the lids with the dates she was born and died."

The district attorney headed back to his desk and picked up the lid of a barrel, reading it to the jury. *"In Memory of Joyce Jacobsen, Beloved Cousin. Born, May 6, 1917, Died, February 7, 1952."*

"Adam, is this the lid that you saw when you broke into Martha Jacobsen's basement this past summer?"

"Yes, there were two lids with the same information. It looked like someone used my wood burning set to make the letters."

"Adam, did you ever speak to Joyce Jacobsen?"

"Only one time after Mr. Gascoigne broke his leg," said Adam. "It was after Mrs. Jacobsen put a curse on him for breaking the leg of the horse."

"Were you there with your grandmother helping Martha Jacobsen can the tomatoes and applesauce while Neil was digging the pit to bury the dead horse?"

"No, I wasn't there. I was helping my mother at the Farmer's Market at Union Park."

"When did you last see Joyce Jacobsen?"

"I went with my grandmother to bring Joyce and Mrs. Jacobsen Christmas presents. My father dropped us off on his way to a meeting. He agreed to pick us up in a couple of hours."

Adam said that it was dark when they arrived with the presents. Mrs. Jacobsen invited them into her living room where they sat on her new velvet sofa and admired her Persian rug. She made tea for them on her new stove. She told them that her son Fred put up a Christmas tree for her with bulbs, tinsel, and lights. She never had a tree in the house before because her husband Harold and his parents didn't want to waste their money on decorations.

"Was Joyce there with her Aunt Martha?"

"No, she was over at Mr. Gascoigne's house. My grandma told me to bring Joyce's present to her."

Adam informed the jury it was snowing when he trudged across Cooper Road. He saw their lighted tree through the picture window in the living room. Arriving at the back door, Adam knocked several times, but no one answered.

He was about to leave when Joyce turned on the porch light and opened the door. She was wearing fuzzy purple slippers, a yellow night gown, and a maroon robe. Joyce invited him to sit down at the kitchen table while she went into the bedroom to help Mr. Gascoigne put on his robe.

"Where was Roxanne Gascoigne at that time?"

"I could see her from the kitchen, sitting in a rocking chair in front of the Christmas tree holding a rag doll. A few minutes later Mr. Gascoigne came into the kitchen on his crutches. He seemed angry that I had disturbed them by knocking on the kitchen door.

"I stood up at the table eager to leave, but Joyce insisted that I stay until she opened the present from my grandma.

"She poured herself a glass of wine and sat down at the table, removing the pink bow and white tissue paper from the present.

"Joyce was pleased with the scarf my grandmother

knitted for her. She rose from the table and placed the blue scarf over her blonde hair and sang *Jingle Bells.*"

"What did Mr. Gascoigne do at this time?"

"He lit a cigarette and sat at the table smoking. After taking a few puffs, he put it out in the ash tray and asked Joyce to fill his wine glass and bring me one."

"I told him I had to go since my dad was going to pick me and grandma up at Mrs. Jacobsen's place."

"No more questions, your honor," said District Attorney Evans, returning to his table.

Attorney Charles Ryan approached the witness stand and began asking questions

"Adam, did you ever see Joyce after that night?"

"No, the next thing I heard was that she had run away with the mailman, Ray Wilson."

"When did you discover the arm and leg of Joyce Jacobsen in the basement of Martha's house?"

"It was this past summer in June," said Adam.

"When did you sell or lend your wood burning set to anyone?" asked Attorney Ryan.

"Mrs. Jacobsen asked my grandmother if she could borrow my wood burning set when she went there to can applesauce back in 1951. She said that Joyce wanted to teach her how to put names on wooden Christmas ornaments that Mr. Gascoigne made in his basement."

"Did she ever return your wood burning set?"

"No, I was angry with her for not giving it back."

"Were you ever in Mr. Gascoigne's basement?"

"No, I never went down there. My friend, Neil saw barrels down there just like those in Mrs. Jacobsen's basement," said Adam.

"Did he find anything in the barrels?" asked Mr. Ryan.

"He told me that he didn't bother to look into them."

"Why did Neil go into the Mr. Gascoigne's basement?"

"He broke the handle on his snow shovel and went down there to get another one."

"No more questions, your honor," said Attorney Ryan.

Adam headed back to the waiting room, relieved that the attorneys didn't ask him any questions about joining the circus with Naomi and getting caught with her in southern Illinois.

36

"She was telling everyone that she washed Jesus' feet in the bedroom upstairs."

"I would like to call Fred Jacobsen to the witness stand, your honor," said District Attorney Mitchel Evans.

Fred approached the witness stand and swore to tell the truth with his hand on the Bible. After he was seated, the DA began questioning him.

"When did you first meet Joyce Jacobsen?"

"She came on the bus all the way from California to live with us in 1946 because she didn't have any place else to go. She divorced her husband, Jim, after he came home from the war shell shocked and ended up in a mental hospital in San Diego."

"Did you get along with your cousin, Joyce?"

"Of course, I really liked her, but she made my mother angry by playing cards on the porch with my dad instead of helping with the chores. My father died during the winter some months after Joyce arrived."

"Were you aware that your mother wrapped his corpse in a canvas bag and put him in the shed across from the windmill until she buried him in the spring?"

"I didn't know about that until I came home on leave from the navy," said Fred.

"Why did you put your mother in a nursing home during the summer of 1951?"

"When I came home on leave from the Philippines, I was worried about her health because she was coughing. I took her to the doctor, and he said she had pneumonia. He kept her in the hospital for two weeks.

"I didn't want to bring my mother home because her house was such a mess. When she was feeling better, I decided to put her in a nursing home in Waukegan while I cleaned her house and replaced her furniture."

"Fred, what do you know about Clifford Gascoigne?"

"He always was a good neighbor. Mr. Gascoigne used to plow our fields with his tractor and plant the corn for my parents. He also helped my dad during haying season every year. My parents never had any money to pay him so they gave him a third of the crop.

"I asked Cliff to keep an eye on the place while my mother was recovering in the nursing home. He agreed to do it for nothing even though I offered to pay him."

"Were you aware that Adam Montanya and Neil O'Connor broke into the basement of your mother's house during the summer of 1951?"

"Mr. Gascoigne informed me that they had broken into our basement. It happened after I cleaned out the entire house and burned everything that my mother accumulated except for the upright piano and an armchair."

"How did your mother, Martha, treat Mr. Gascoigne?"

"She was worried about Joyce flirting with him since he was a married man. My mother was also annoyed that the mailman, Ray Wilson, was taking Joyce out on weekends."

"Was your mother a religious person?"

"Yes, she always read the Bible, but I was concerned about her when she started having visions of Jesus. She was telling everyone that she washed Jesus' feet in her bedroom upstairs."

"When did she start having the apparitions?"

"They started when she came back from the nursing home after Labor Day in 1951. She loved all the used furniture that I bought her, especially the sofa, the Persian rug, and her kitchen stove."

"Why did you bring your mother back to the nursing home in February of 1952?"

"Well, Mr. Gascoigne broke his leg shortly after burying her horse in the orchard. He had been taking care of her cows, but they stopped producing milk, so he sold them for fertilizer."

Fred said that his mother started arguing with Joyce because she was going out with Ray every weekend and leaving her alone in the house. She complained that Joyce wouldn't help her with the meals and housework, but was spending all her time with Mr. Gascoigne. He had hired her to take care of his wife, Roxanne, when he was at work during the week.

"Was your mother angry with Joyce?"

"My mother was not one to express her feelings. I was worried about her when she started losing weight and becoming senile. I decided it wasn't good for her to be living alone in the house because Joyce wasn't around to keep an eye on her. That's when I brought her back to the nursing home in Waukegan."

"No more questions," said the DA, taking his seat.

Attorney Ryan approached the stand. "Fred, were you attracted to Joyce Jacobsen?"

"Of course, she was very beautiful. That's why my mother was jealous of her. She was always flirting with my father on the porch."

"When did Joyce start paying attention to you?"

"It was after my father died, but I had enough sense not to get involved with her. I was dating a girl in town at the time, but I wasn't going steady with her."

"Why did you join the navy?"

"I wanted to get away from the farm. After I graduated from Kenosha Technical School as a certified mechanic, I enlisted in the navy at Great Lakes."

"Did you leave because of Joyce Jacobsen?"

"How did you know? I…I was feeding the cows when Joyce showed up in the barn to help me. We were both startled when my mother came through the door to get oats to feed the chickens.

"She started screaming at us for making out in the hay. I don't know why she got so crazy because we had our clothes on. My mom charged at us with a pitch fork and tried to kill Joyce, so we took off like bats out of hell.

"After that incident, I joined the navy because I didn't want to stay in the same house with two angry women."

"No more questions, your honor," said Attorney Ryan.

37

She wore a flowing yellow gown with red high heels that echoed throughout the courtroom.

District Attorney Mitchell Evans rose from his chair. He was about to summon another witness but was disrupted by a policeman escorting a stranger into the courtroom.

All heads turned toward the woman, wearing an orange turban and carrying a black bag. She wore a flowing yellow gown with red high heels that echoed throughout the courtroom.

After determining her identity, the district attorney said, "I would like to call Leona Fortunato to the witness stand. She has finally arrived."

Leona approached the witness stand. After swearing to tell the truth with her hand on the Bible, she sat down.

"Mrs. Fortunato, I'm so grateful that you showed up for the trial. Tell us what you know about the disappearance about of Joyce Jacobsen."

"I'm sorry I'm late. I was busy working in my garden when the squad car showed up to take me here. The policeman handed me the subpoena because the secretary never bothered to mail it to me. I had to take a bath and change my clothes because I was filthy dirty."

"We're pleased that you're here. Now tell us what you know about the murder of Joyce."

311

"I went over to Mr. Gascoigne's house one evening because Joyce invited me to tell everybody's fortune. I removed my Tarot cards from this black bag and put them on the kitchen table. I was about to tell Joyce's fortune when Roxanne Gascoigne rushed into the kitchen from the living room and stabbed Joyce with a knife in the arm. She pushed over the kitchen table so that my all my cards were scattered on the floor.

"While Joyce was screaming, Clifford Gascoigne pulled Roxanne away and locked her in the bedroom. He then wrapped a kitchen towel around Joyce's arm and called the police, leaving me to pick up the cards from the floor.

"I didn't expect to run into so much trouble. Roxanne kept pounding on the door, screaming that she wanted to kill Joyce for stealing her husband from her."

"Did you know Mr. Gascoigne very well?"

"No, I only knew what Martha Jacobsen told me about him. Before leaving for the nursing home, she said he was having a love affair with Joyce."

"Were you a good friend of Martha Jacobsen?"

"Yes, I used to visit her regularly when my daughter Magnolia was little. We'd sit on Martha's porch and chat for hours. That was a long time ago.

"In those days Martha got along with Clifford. She said he was a good man because he helped her father-in-law, bring in the hay and plow the fields."

"Did you see Martha before she went to the nursing home during the summer of 1951?"

"Yes, I warned Martha to take care of herself or she'd end up in the hospital, but she didn't pay any attention to my predictions.

"I was worried about her because she had lost weight and was very pale. She was also angry with Joyce for not helping her with the chores.

"Of course Joyce was busy taking care of Roxanne Gascoigne all week and dating the mailman, Ray Wilson, on the weekends. Everybody knew about her love affairs."

"No more questions, your honor," said District Attorney Mitchell Evans, shaking his head and perspiring because he had failed to personally interview her. He was unprepared for her dramatic arrival and unexpected support of Clifford Gascoigne.

Attorney Charles Ryan approached the witness. "Mrs. Fortunato, would you please tell us when Roxanne stabbed Joyce with the knife."

"It happened in the fall of 1951. It was after Martha came back from the nursing home and while she and Sophia Montanya were canning in her basement."

"Mrs. Fortunato, when was the last time that you saw Martha Jacobsen?"

"I saw her before her son took her to the nursing home the second time, where she stayed for two years. Martha brought me down to the basement to give me two Ball jars. One of them had applesauce in it. I have the other one in my black bag. May I show it to you?"

"Of course," said the defense attorney.

Leona removed the sealed Ball jar from her bag, holding it up for the defense attorney to examine.

"It looks like you have carrots in that jar," said Charles Ryan, reaching for it.

"They're not carrots," said Leona Fortunato. They're fingers. There's a ring on one of them. This hand belongs to Joyce Jacobsen!

"Martha gave it to me. She told me that Joyce was angry with Clifford Gascoigne and begged him to divorce his wife and marry her."

"When he refused to divorce Roxanne, she insisted that he give her $2,000 so that she could move to Iron Mountain where she intended to work at the local post office and live with Ray Wilson in a cottage with his parents on the Menominee River," said Leona.

Everyone in the courtroom began murmuring as Attorney Ryan submitted the evidence to the judge handing him the jar with the fingers.

"Leona, why didn't you report this to the police earlier?" asked Attorney Ryan.

"I never looked at the contents of the jars. I put them way back in my cupboard thinking Martha gave me a jar of carrots. That was four years ago. A few minutes before leaving in the squad car, I opened the cupboard and removed the dusty jar. I nearly fainted when I saw the hand inside. I told the policeman about it while riding here in his car with the siren blasting.

"Just a minute! I forgot to tell you that I went to visit

Martha with Mr. Gascoigne the day before she died. We saw Sophia Montanya there with Marjorie O'Connor."

"Why did you go to the hospital with Mr. Gascoigne?"

"Because Marjorie O'Connor phoned him that Martha was dying, and he wanted to say goodbye to her. I happened to be there reading his tarot cards in the kitchen when he asked me to go with him.

"All the way to the hospital, he told me how much he missed Joyce and hoped she was happy living in Pembine with Ray Wilson."

"No more questions, Leona," said Attorney Ryan.

"I would like to call the anthropologist, Doctor Gerald Richter to the stand from the University of Wisconsin at Madison," said Attorney Mitchell Evans.

"Dr Richter, will you tell the court what you found while digging in the Jacobsen Orchard?"

"This past summer we found the remains of a horse with a broken leg, and three human skeletons buried in the orchard at different intervals. They were the remains of Harold Jacobsen and his parents, Phyllis and Chester."

"Did you find any other remains in the orchard?"

"Yes, I found the partial skeleton of a woman, whom I have identified as Joyce Jacobsen. The skeleton was not complete. Her head, left arm, and right leg were missing."

"Doctor Richter, where did you find Joyce Jacobsen's severed arm and leg?"

"They were found in barrels in Martha Jacobsen's basement this past summer," said the anthropologist.

315

"And where did you find her head?"

"I found it in a barrel in Mr. Gascoigne's basement."

"When you examined Joyce's skeleton from the orchard, what did you discover about her right arm?"

"I discovered that the right arm did not have a hand," said the anthropologist.

"With the permission of the court and judge, will you please examine the Ball jar on the desk, presented as evidence by Leona Fortunato," said Attorney Evans handing him the jar.

"This could be the missing hand of Joyce Jacobsen. I would have to examine it further in the lab," said the anthropologist.

"Are you sure that the head you found was Joyce Jacobsen's?"

"Yes, I had Fred Jacobsen and Ray Wilson come to my lab. They identified the severed head as Joyce Jacobsen's."

"When the body parts were examined, did you find any trace of drugs being used by the deceased?"

"Yes, Joyce's body parts were found in the barrels, preserved in formaldehyde and saturated with morphine, which indicates she was given multiple injections of the drug by someone."

"Doctor Richter, please tell us where you and Officer Stanley Martinson found Joyce Jacobsen's head."

"We found her head floating in a barrel in Mr. Gascoigne's basement. We also found Mrs. Gascoigne's mutilated cat in another barrel."

"How did Mr. Gascoigne respond when you came to the door with the police officer," asked the district attorney.

"He stood in the doorway with a shotgun and threatened to kill us if we didn't get off his property. I think he might have been drinking because I could smell wine on his breath," said the anthropologist.

"When Officer Martinson showed him the search warrant Mr. Gascoigne came outside in a rage. That's when I tackled and pinned him to the ground. Officer Martinson immediately handcuffed and placed him under arrest."

"Why do you think Mr. Gascoigne threatened to kill you, Doctor Richter," asked the district attorney.

"It seemed as if he were concealing something."

"Thank you, Doctor Richter. No other questions, your honor," said Attorney Evans, returning to his seat.

"Mr. Ryan, do you wish to cross examine the witness?" asked the judge.

"No, I don't," said Attorney Ryan.

"I would like to call Officer Martinson to the witness stand" said District Attorney Evans."

"I'm sorry, Officer Martinson is no longer with us. He died in 1955 from pneumonia," said the judge.

"Then I will rest my case," said the district attorney, demonstrating his lack of preparation to try the case.

"We will take a 15 minute recess," said Judge Carlson.

38

"I had her committed to the hospital. The psychiatrist diagnosed her as schizophrenic."

"I would like to call Mr. Gascoigne to the witness stand," announced Attorney Charles Ryan, waiting for his client to be sworn in by the bailiff.

"Mr. Gascoigne, how long have you been living in your house on Cooper Road?"

"My wife and I moved there in 1928 before the stock market crashed. We had been living up north on a small farm near Crivitz."

"Did you know the Jacobsen Family?"

"Yes, I became acquainted with them when Martha's husband Harold and his father Chester, asked me to help them bring in the hay and plow their fields with my John Deere tractor. I only helped on weekends because I had a full time job at Cooper's, cutting patterns for underwear.

"At that time my wife, Roxanne, worked at the Ben Franklin Store downtown as a clerk because we didn't have any children to take care of at home."

"Did you get along with the Jacobsen family?"

"Of course. Chester and his wife, Phyllis, always invited us to Sunday dinner after church."

Mr. Gascoigne informed the jury that Harold read passages from the Bible and prayed before they had their meal, but they didn't go to church.

Martha always made sure Phyllis was brought down the stairs and placed in a wheel chair at the dinner table. She was bedridden from a spinal injury after being kicked by the horse. During the week, Martha brought Phyllis her meals to her bedroom upstairs. Since there was no indoor toilet, Phyllis had to use a bedpan, which Martha emptied several times a day.

"Did Phyllis see a doctor regularly?" asked Attorney Charles Ryan.

"The doctor came twice a year to check on Phyllis. He always ordered cases of morphine from Bernacchi's Drug Store to be delivered to their home in the fall and again in the spring.

"It was a relief when Phyllis finally died because Martha was worn out from taking care of her bedridden mother-in-law for so many years."

"Was your wife a good friend of Martha? Jacobsen?" asked the defense attorney.

"Yes, they were friends until my wife got fired from her job at Ben Franklin Store for shoplifting baby clothes after working there for 18 years.

"Roxanne became depressed from being alone all day. She began staring into space and neglecting her chores. It's because she wanted a baby, but she couldn't stay pregnant more than two months without having a miscarriage.

"I wanted to hire Martha Jacobsen to look after my wife, but she was too busy preparing meals and helping with the chores. She didn't even have running water in the house, but used the pump beneath the windmill. Martha recommended that I hire her niece, Joyce, to take care of my wife," said Clifford Gascoigne.

"How long did Joyce work for you?"

"She started taking care of Roxanne in 1948. Joyce kept an eye on my wife all day long and stayed until she went back home to bed at night."

Mr. Gascoigne informed the jury that when he came home from work, Joyce had supper on the table for the three of them. She always invited Martha, but she rarely joined them at the table.

"When did you first send your wife to the mental hospital in Mendota?"

"After Roxanne started getting violent, I had her committed to the hospital. The psychiatrist diagnosed her as being schizophrenic. She remained under surveillance during the fall and winter at the hospital, but she was allowed to come home for the spring and summer."

"Did you get along well with Martha Jacobsen?"

"I always got along with her, but I noticed she was very depressed after her husband died. It seemed strange to me that the drug store kept delivering cases of morphine to her house twice a year for several years.

"I called the doctor's office to cancel the order for Martha, but he had moved to Chicago. The secretary at his old office didn't know anything about morphine being sent to Mrs. Jacobsen's place."

"Did you ever see Martha Jacobsen inject herself with

the morphine?"

"No, but she behaved strangely when she came to my house for dinner. Martha talked constantly about Jesus coming through the second story window of her bedroom to comfort her. She claimed she washed his feet in a basin and dried them with her hair."

"Were you there when Fred Jacobsen took her to the nursing home in the summer of 1951?"

"Of course, I was there helping him clean out her filthy house once she was gone. I was startled when we went into her dusty bedroom and found dozens of rusted needles in the waste basket and a wooden case with empty vials of morphine.

"Fred was very upset at the time. He told me that he took his mother to the hospital because she not only had pneumonia but was addicted to morphine.

"When Fred went back to his post at Great Lakes, I took care of Martha's garden and farm animals for her."

"In the meantime, what happened to Joyce Jacobsen?"

"Well she stayed at my house in the guest room until Fred came back in August with a truckload of used furniture for his mother. Once the rooms were painted and furniture installed, Joyce moved back into her Aunt Martha's house."

"When did Martha Jacobsen return to her home?"

"She returned from the nursing home after Labor Day and was normal for some months."

"When did she start to change again?"

"She started to change when the delivery truck arrived from the pharmacy with a case of morphine in October."

"During all this time how was your wife, Roxanne?"

"My wife was fine for the summer. She got along with Joyce and helped her do laundry in the basement."

"Did you have any barrels in your basement?"

"Yes, I had a half dozen barrels in the basement left over from when I used to make wine."

"What did you find in the barrels?"

"I found my wife's pet cat, Fluffy, floating in one of the barrels in a liquid. I suspected my wife killed the cat so I sent her back to the mental hospital in Mendota."

"Did you find anything else?" asked Attorney Ryan.

"No, I never bothered to look in the other barrels.

"Was your wife ever violent again?"

"Yes, she attacked Joyce with a knife on her birthday. I had her hospitalized for quite a while but she came home for Christmas that year. I didn't send her to Mendota until February of 1952.

"One evening when I came home from work a few weeks before Christmas, Joyce was sitting at the kitchen table with a wood burning set. She was teaching Roxanne how to burn names in the wooden ornaments I made in the basement."

"Were you in the bedroom with Joyce when Adam Montanya came to your house with Christmas presents?"

"Yes, we didn't answer the door right away because Joyce was helping me get dressed. I had broken my leg and it was still in a cast. Joyce had just come from the basement with a basket of clean clothes that had been drying on the clothes line down there.

"Joyce brought me a clean pair of pajamas and a bathrobe. Since it was the day before Christmas Eve, I asked her to pour us each a glass of wine to celebrate. Adam only stayed long enough for Joyce to open her present. It was a scarf, knitted by his grandmother."

"How did Martha Jacobsen feel about Joyce working for you?" asked Attorney Ryan.

"Martha was jealous of Joyce spending so much time at my house. She resented her. I noticed that when Martha came for dinner a few times during the week she was in a stupor from using morphine.

"I tried to call Fred to inform him that his mother was back on morphine. I left messages at Great Lakes, but he never returned my phone calls.

"When Fred finally came home on leave, he decided to put his mother back in the nursing home. He was worried that she was a drug addict. Fred told me he didn't know why the morphine hadn't been cancelled by the doctor.

"After Martha left for the nursing home and Joyce disappeared, my wife became angry because Joyce didn't show up to fix dinner. She went into a rage and started smashing things. I called the police and had Roxanne hospitalized and then transferred back to the mental hospital. She hasn't been home since."

"Why did you come to the door with a shotgun when

Officer Martinson arrived with Doctor Richter?"

"I had too much wine that night because I was lonely and missed Joyce. I got scared over the publicity in the newspaper, especially when I found the decapitated cat in the barrel a few weeks ago. I slammed down the lid and went upstairs to get another glass of wine. I guess I was afraid that I'd be suspected of killing Joyce."

"Did you know that Joyce's head was in one of your barrels?" asked the defense attorney.

"I didn't know anything about it until the next morning. I was handcuffed and taken to jail, where I spent the night," said Clifford, wiping his eyes with a handkerchief.

"No more questions, your honor," said Attorney Ryan.

District Attorney Evans approached the witness stand to question Mr. Gascoigne.

"Clifford would you please tell the court what you know about the deaths of Martha's husband and his parents."

"I was surprised they all died during winter. First it was his mother, Phyllis, in 1929, then his father, Chester, in 1930, and finally her husband, Harold, in 1947, a year after Joyce arrived. After each death, I saw Martha Jacobsen dragging the corpses wrapped in a canvas bag to the shed where they stayed until spring.

"Once the land thawed she buried them in the apple orchard. I don't believe Mrs. Jacobsen reported the deaths to the County Clerk's office."

"You mentioned that the drug store kept delivering cases of morphine to Martha Jacobsen. When was the last case delivered?"

"In in the fall of 1951, a few weeks before Neil and I buried the horse, I had called the drug store at least three times to have them stop delivering the morphine, but I was told that the doctor's office never cancelled the order and the bill was sent to Great Lakes where it was deducted from Fred Jacobsen's monthly salary."

"You testified that Martha encouraged you to hire Joyce to take care of your wife. How did Martha feel about your relationship with Joyce?" asked the district attorney.

"Martha was a jealous woman. First she was angry with Joyce for flirting with her husband and spending time with him playing cards on the porch. After I hired Joyce to look after my wife, Martha was angry with her niece and me."

"Why was Martha angry with you?"

"She was angry with me because I had talked to her son, Fred, who finally called the drug store to cancel her order of morphine. He was unaware it was being deducted from his pay check for years. The delivery man told her that this was the last case of morphine being sent from Bernacchi's Drug Store.

"Do you believe that Martha was a morphine addict?"

"I never saw her inject herself with morphine, but when Fred and I cleaned out her house we found dozens of rusted needles and empty vials of morphine in her room."

"Mr. Gascoigne, why did you come to the door with a shot gun when Officer Stanley Martinson arrived with the anthropologist, Doctor Gerald Richter to question you?"

"I was stressed out because I found my wife's cat, floating in the barrel about two weeks ago. I got angry when they came to the door with a search warrant because I had been drinking wine. I momentarily went crazy. I didn't expect Doctor Richter to tackle me and Officer Martinson to handcuff me."

"Were you told what they found in your basement?"

"I was told in jail the next morning that they found my wife's decapitated cat in a barrel," said Clifford Gascoigne, his voice trembling.

"What else did they find in your basement?"

"They found the head of Joyce Jacobsen, floating in another barrel," gasped Clifford, "I couldn't believe that she was dead."

"Mr. Gascoigne, tell the jury what you know about the heads in your basement," asked the district attorney.

"I knew nothing about them. I was shocked over Joyce's murder," he sobbed. "I was very fond of Joyce."

"Were you in love with her?"

"Yes," whispered Mr. Gascoigne.

"Were you concerned about her dating Mr. Wilson?"

"I didn't know anything about their love affair until Ray testified in the courtroom."

"No more questions, your honor," said Attorney Evans.

Mr. Gascoigne left the witness stand and returned to his seat, wiping his forehead with a white handkerchief.

"I never knew that Old Lady Jacobsen was a drug addict," whispered Adam, listening at the door of the waiting room.

"I thought something was wrong with her because every time my mom came home from visiting her, she had a different story about washing Jesus' feet," said Neil.

"Mrs. Jacobsen told my grandma that Jesus climbed into her bedroom through her second story window to comfort her when she was lonely," said Adam.

"Those lawyers certainly made you feel uncomfortable," said Neil. "You were red as a beet after testifying."

"I was worried that they would ask me questions about running away with Naomi," said Adam.

After a short break the trial resumed with Attorney Ryan rising from his chair.

"I would like to call Mrs. Marjorie O'Connor to the witness stand, your honor."

Neil's mother entered the courtroom, leaving Grandma in the nearby waiting room with her son and Adam listening at the door.

"Mrs. O'Connor, I understand that you were visiting Martha Jacobsen in the nursing home prior to her death."

"Yes, I talked to her the night before she died."

"Tell us what you know about Martha Jacobsen."

"Martha was a kind woman. She took care of her bed-ridden mother-in-law for years before she died."

"Why didn't she contact the authorities after she died?" asked the defense.

"She was too poor to afford a formal burial. She told me that she buried the corpses of all of her relatives in the apple orchard."

"When did Martha start using morphine?"

"It was after the death of her husband, Harold."

"Did Martha talk to you about her morphine addiction?"

"I didn't know anything about it until I visited her in the nursing home before she died."

"What did you find out?"

"Martha was delirious at the time and blamed herself for killing relatives by giving them overdoses of morphine."

"I object to this line of questioning," said Attorney Mitchell Evans. "Martha Jacobsen has been dead for two years. Therefore this evidence is not admissible. I have a continuing objection to this line of questioning."

"Objection overruled. Please continue with your questions, Mr. Ryan."

Marjorie O'Connor told the jury that Martha also confessed that she murdered her niece, and that Roxanne helped her carry Joyce's corpse into her basement

The two women sawed off Joyce's leg and arm and put them into barrels in Mrs. Jacobsen's basement... They also used a wood burning set to write on the lids of the barrels. When they were finished, they carried Joyce's severed head to a barrel in Roxanne's basement.

Later they went to the orchard with a pick and shovel and dug through the frozen soil. It took two hours to dig a grave where they put Joyce's skeletal remains.

"No more questions your honor," said Attorney Ryan.

"Do you have any questions to ask the witness, Mr.

Evans?" asked the judge.

"Mrs. O'Connor, I have a few questions for you. Do you believe Mrs. Jacobsen was a religious person?"

"Yes, she begged Jesus for forgiveness on her death bed for murdering Joyce, her husband, and his parents.

"Just before her death, Martha told me that Jesus was there holding her hand. He was going to take her to the Pearly Gate where St. Peter was waiting for her."

"Did Martha Jacobsen mention Clifford Gascoigne's name prior to her death?" asked Attorney Evans.

"Martha told me that Mr. Gascoigne helped kill her relatives. He also put Phyllis, Chester, and Harold out of their misery by handing her the needles while she gave them injections."

"That's a lie! I never helped with any injections," shouted Clifford Gascoigne, standing up and shouting while everyone gasped and murmured.

"Order! Order in the court! Mr. Ryan, please control your client, or he'll be removed from the court. The reporter will strike Mr. Gascoigne's comment from the record. Do you have any further questions for the witness, Mr. Evans?" asked the judge.

"No your honor, I don't," said the district attorney.

"Do you have any more questions, Mr. Ryan?"

"I have no more questions your honor."

"There will be a fifteen minute recess before the attorneys give their final statements to the jury," said Judge Eliot Carlson.

.39

"He was infuriated because she wanted to elope with Ray Wilson, whom he detested."

Adam rose from his seat in the waiting room and stretched. He talked with Neil while following the others out of the courthouse.

"I know Mr. Gascoigne was having a love affair with Joyce. I swear she was in his bedroom when I knocked on the door to bring Joyce her Christmas present," said Adam, leaving the building and walking across the street to Civic Center Park.

"Joyce shouldn't have been fuckin' Clifford Gascoigne and Ray Wilson at the same time," said Neil, reaching for his Lucky Strikes.

"Do you think he helped Mrs. Jacobsen murder Joyce and her relatives?" asked Adam, standing in front of the statue of Lincoln in the center of the park.

"I don't know what to believe anymore," said Neil, lighting his cigarette.

"I'll have one of those," said Adam, his hand trembling while Neil lighted it. "I thought the district attorney would ask me a lot of questions about my relationship with Naomi."

"Why would he do that? She had nothing to do with the case," said Neil, exhaling a cloud of smoke.

A few minutes later they returned to the courtroom,

taking their seats in the front row. After the judge entered, he requested the attorneys to make their concluding statements to the jury.

District Attorney Mitchell Evans rose from his chair and spoke to the jurors. "Members of the jury, you've just heard the testimony of several witnesses about Clifford Gascoigne's character and his involvement with not only the death of Martha's niece, Joyce, but her husband, Harold, and his parents, Chester and Phyllis.

"It's very clear to those present in this courtroom that Clifford was having a love affair with his housekeeper, Joyce Jacobsen. It's also obvious that she was involved with the mailman, Ray Wilson. Joyce no doubt was an attractive woman, but Mr. Gascoigne was a married man. His wife, Roxanne, was so jealous of the love affair that she attempted to kill Joyce with a knife.

"Although Clifford looked after Martha Jacobsen's estate for her when she was in the nursing home, his involvement with Joyce was an obsession with him.

"According to Martha Jacobsen's death-bed confession, it is quite obvious that Clifford Gascoigne did not want Joyce to leave him. He was infuriated because she wanted to elope with Ray Wilson, whom he detested.

"Mr. Gascoigne's jealousy of Ray Wilson was his motive for assisting Martha Jacobsen with the murder of Joyce by giving her a lethal morphine injection.

"The deranged women, Martha and Roxanne, with the assistance of Clifford Gascoigne, dismembered Joyce's corpse by cutting off her arm and leg and placing them in barrels in Martha's basement. They also removed her left hand and put it in the Bell jar, which is here in this courtroom. In addition they severed Joyce's head and placed it inside a barrel in Clifford Gascoigne's basement.

"All evidence in this courtroom points to Mr. Gascoigne assisting Martha Jacobsen with the murder of Joyce Jacobsen. He no doubt was also involved in the murder of Martha's husband and relatives as well. I'd like the jury to ponder the testimonies of the witnesses carefully and find Mr. Gascoigne guilty of the murder of Joyce Jacobsen," said District Attorney Evans. "That's all, your honor."

Attorney Ryan approached the jury, clearing his throat. "Ladies and Gentlemen of the jury, I would like to thank you for being so patient with the evidence presented during this trial. It is obvious that in spite of her death-bed confession, Martha Jacobsen's testimony is hearsay. Unfortunately, she died in a nursing home two years ago.

"The accused, Mr. Clifford Gascoigne, clearly stated that he helped the Jacobsen family by planting and harvesting the crops. He also looked after Martha's farm animals during the summer of 1951 when she spent three months in the nursing home.

"Clifford was a good neighbor who helped Martha's son, Fred, clean the house. He secured the locks on the doors and put up *No Trespassing* signs. Fred Jacobsen trusted him as the caretaker of his mother's property when she was taken to the nursing home the second time, where

Mrs. Jacobsen remained until she died in 1954.

"Mr. Gascoigne explicitly stated that he saw Martha carrying out the remains of Phyllis during the winter of 1929, Chester in 1930, and Harold in 1947. He also testified that Martha took care of her bed-ridden mother-in-law for several years, giving her morphine injections to relieve the pain.

"Two witnesses testified that Martha Jacobsen claimed that she washed the feet of Jesus. Although she was a religious person who read the Bible, the apparitions were surely induced by her use of morphine.

"Due to the neglect of her health from drug usage, Martha was hospitalized with pneumonia during the summer of 1951, before Fred put her in a nursing home.

"After being restored to health, Martha returned to her home, where she resorted to using morphine again even though Mr. Gascoigne tried to cancel the orders.

"Mr. Gascoigne hired Joyce Jacobsen to take care of his wife, who was diagnosed with schizophrenia. Roxanne in a fit of rage tried to kill Joyce, her caretaker.

"It's quite clear that Martha was also jealous of her niece for spending time with Roxanne instead of taking care of her.

"While Mr. Gascoigne was at work, the evidence indicates that Martha injected Joyce with lethal doses of morphine and with the help of Roxanne dismembered her corpse. The women canned her fingers and placed her limbs and head into barrels in their basements.

"Martha Jacobsen was mentally deranged due to her prolonged use of morphine. There is further evidence that her illness might have caused her to murder her husband and his parents as well."

"While hallucinating on her death bed, Martha tried to shift the blame of her multiple murders onto her loyal neighbor and friend, Mr. Clifford Gascoigne.

"Ladies and Gentleman of the jury, after examining the testimony of the witnesses without bias, I request you to find Clifford Gascoigne innocent of the murder of Joyce Jacobsen. Thank you," said Attorney Ryan, returning to his seat next to his client.

"Ladies and Gentlemen of the Jury, you will now retire to the jury room to discuss the evidence presented and come to a unanimous decision about the guilt or innocence of Mr. Clifford Gascoigne," said the judge.

"You must weigh all the evidence that has been presented and return with a verdict of guilty as charged or not guilty in accordance with the laws of the State of Wisconsin. The bailiff will now escort the jurors to their room for deliberations. Court is recessed until a verdict is reached, said Judge Carlson, hitting his gavel on the bench and leaving the room.

"All rise," said the bailiff, escorting the jury from the courtroom.

"Let's get the hell out of here," said Adam, leading the way to the exit from the waiting room.

"The police said to meet them across the street at the

park. They promised to give us a ride home after the trial," recalled Neil.

"Their squad car is parked over there," said Adam.

"Let's go explore Old Lady Jacobsen's place one last time before it gets dark," suggested Neil.

"You've got to be crazy. I'm never going back there again," said Adam, crossing the street to the police car where an officer was sitting in the driver's seat.

"Wait for us," shouted Grandma, hurrying down the steps of the courthouse with Marjorie O'Connor.

"You can ride with us," shouted Adam, opening the back door of the police car for them.

"Dio Mio! I got such a headache," said Grandma, entering the back seat and sitting next to her neighbor.

"I'm a nervous wreck," said Marjorie, her voice strident.

"The Devil was in Martha's house, not Jesus," said Grandma. "You boys stay away from that place."

"I'm not shoveling snow for Mr. Gascoigne this winter. I don't want my head ending up in his basement," said Neil, sitting beside Adam in the front seat.

"I'm worried about going back to school," said Adam, taking a deep breath.

40

"Make me the scapegoat! Go ahead and blame me. It's all my fault he's an alcoholic…"

Adam returned to school on Monday feeling sad because he hadn't heard from Naomi over the weekend. His friends were curious about why the police took him away on Thursday since information about the trial was on the radio and in the Kenosha News.

His classmates were suspicious when he told them that he knew Martha Jacobsen personally and explored her basement during the summer, where he and his friend, Neil, found the limbs of Joyce Jacobsen.

He also said his friend Neil had dug the grave in the orchard where the horse was buried, and that's where the anthropologist discovered the skeletal remains of Mrs. Jacobsen's relatives, including Joyce's skeleton.

After returning home in the evening on the bus, Adam went straight to the mail box. He was elated because he finally got a letter from Naomi.

Dearest Adam,   *October 19, 1956*

I miss you so much. Here it is Saturday afternoon and I've been listening to the radio about the trial that you attended on Friday. I was wondering if the jury will find Mr. Gascoigne innocent or guilty over the murder of Joyce Jacobsen.

I was horrified when I found out that you had been

subpoenaed to testify. Jennifer told me all about it since Neil went out with her over the weekend without her parents' permission.

I heard that you were real nervous at the trial. Apparently Attorney Ryan knew all about us joining the circus because he's a friend of Jennifer's father, Attorney O'Reilly. My mother was worried that you would mention my name at the trial.

I don't care if the whole world knows about us dating. My mom also threatened to call the police if you make an appearance at the Halloween Party next Friday. That means we've got to find a way to meet at the party by wearing costumes that no one will recognize.

I know you've been confused about the date but you should check the calendar. Halloween's on a Wednesday this year, followed by All Saints Day. Since these are school days, our party will be held this Friday night on October 26th, your birthday. I can't wait to see you in your costume. I still don't know what to wear. Do you have any ideas? We must keep everything a secret. I'll call you.

With love, Naomi

Adam folded the letter and put it in his pocket, hurrying up the driveway covered with maple leaves rustling beneath his feet. After waving to his mother, who was carrying pumpkins from the garden, he hurried into the house to change his clothes.

Upon entering the kitchen he greeted his grandmother, hovering over the radio listening to the news about the trial.

Adam set down his backpack on a dining room chair and went into the bedroom to change. Upon returning to the kitchen, he spoke to Grandma, pacing the worn linoleum.

'What's going on with the jury?" he asked.

"The jury's still out! Maybe they find Mr. Gascoigne guilty tomorrow," she said. "I don't trust that man. He stays with Joyce too much in the bedroom. Dio Mio! That's why Roxanne wants to kill Joyce with a-the butcher knife. I don't like that witch, Leona Fortuanto."

"Grandma, do you think Mr. Gascoigne was guilty?"

"Dio mio! He's the Devil's helper. That's what Martha tells Marjorie O'Connor when she's dying in the nursing home. Martha's a good woman. She's little bit crazy, but she kills nobody."

"Then who committed the murder?"

"That trial makes me mad. Nobody tells the truth. Two days before Martha dies, Leona Fortunato comes with Mr. Gascoigne to visit her in-a-the hospital. I'm there too with my friend, Mrs. O'Connor.

Grandma informed Adam that she and Marjorie left Martha's room to have a cup of coffee in the cafeteria. When it came time to pay for their coffee, they had no money so she returned to the room where she left her purse.

When she walked into the room Mr. Gascoigne was still there with Leona. He was holding something in his hand and wanted to give it to Martha, but he quickly put the object in his pocket so no one could see it.

"For Christ's sake, Grandma!" blurted Adam. "Why the

hell didn't you tell this to the jury when you were on the witness stand?"

"I'm always too nervous. I forget about it. My head's no good anymore. We better go outside. We gotta help your mother get ready for the market tomorrow."

Adam headed down the steps of the hallway and out the back door, wondering if Clifford Gascoigne and Leona Fortunato were intending to murder Mrs. Jacobsen in the nursing home.

The rest of the week seemed an eternity for Adam. He yearned to be with Naomi and thought about her constantly, tossing and turning all night long. She finally telephoned him on Wednesday evening, informing him she decided to wear her clown costume from the circus to the party. Naomi convinced Adam to wear his costume because no one recognized their painted faces when they were with the circus.

When Adam came home from school on Thursday afternoon, he was surprised to see Karl working in the garden. He wondered why he wasn't at football practice. After changing his clothes Adam helped his brother carry the vegetables from the garden to be washed for Friday's market at Baker Park.

Grandma was sitting on the bench under the maple tree, surrounded by bushels of tomatoes. She was wiping the dirt from them with a damp cloth.

Adam and Karl began scrubbing the potatoes in a tub of water beneath the spigot. They glanced up at their mother coming through the garden gate carrying a bushel of sweet corn. She set it down on the sidewalk and wiped her forehead with Giovanni's handkerchief.

"Adam, you promised to rake the leaves and cut the grass in the front yard," she said.

"Mom, I need to work on my term paper as soon as I'm finished washing the potatoes. It's due tomorrow."

"If you don't cut the grass, I won't take you to get your driver's license after school."

"Don't bother. Dad said he'd take me," said Adam.

"For Christ's sake! I'll cut the fucking grass for him," shouted Karl, entering the garage and coming out with the hand mower and rake.

"Karl, watch your mouth. I hate that filthy language. I don't want you doing Adam's chores for him."

"I said I'd cut the grass for him. Leave Adam alone! It will be my birthday present to him," said Karl.

"I forgot his birthday's tomorrow. I suppose I'll have to bake a cake. I don't have enough to do around here," said their mother, scowling.

"You don't have to bake any fucking cake. I'll buy him one at Dober's Bakery," said Karl.

"You boys are defying me just like your father!" shouted Gertrude, with her hands on her hips. "Karl, I suppose you're going out drinking with Larry again tomorrow night."

"No, I have to work at the filling station after the football game on Friday night. The only reason I'm helping

340

you is that the coach dismissed the team early from practice because the quarterback passed out when he was tackled."

"It's probably because Dale was out drinking last night with Larry," said Gertrude, picking up a scrub brush to help Adam with the potatoes.

"Karl, I wish you wouldn't hang around with Larry. He needs to get a job after school," continued his mother.

"Larry doesn't have to work because he inherited a lot of money from his grandfather," said Karl, pushing the lawn mower down the rutted driveway.

"Larry gets drunk every weekend and then sleeps until noon," shouted his mother. "If he keeps drinking, he won't graduate with his class."

"Karl's old enough to choose his friends," said Adam. "Dad would be here with us if you weren't such a bitch."

"Make me the scapegoat! Go ahead and blame me. It's all my fault he's an alcoholic and has to go to those AA meetings every night of the week. It wouldn't surprise me if your father's still seeing Ellie!"

"Mom, she's been dead for the last three years," said Adam, nearly finished with the potatoes. "This water's really filthy."

"Your father's probably got another woman on the string just like your Uncle Pete."

"Mom, knock it off!" said Adam. "That's all you ever do is whine about Dad."

"I'm exhausted. I've been working all afternoon picking vegetables," sighed his mother.

341

"I come to help wash potatoes for Adam. You go now and type your paper," said Grandma, reaching for the stool in front of the lilac bush.

"Thanks, Grandma," said Adam, hurrying toward the back door and entering the house.

"Adam's got a lot of nerve leaving us here to do his work," shouted Gertrude, surveying the crates of potatoes still to be washed.

A half hour later Karl came up the driveway to put the lawn mower away. He glanced at his watch, informing his mother that Larry was going to pick him up because they were going to the library to study for a chemistry test. He dashed into the house to get cleaned up.

Within ten minutes Larry swerved into the driveway coming to a halt in front of their garage in his Buick Roadmaster. Karl entered the spacious white and orange car, carrying his backpack. He waved to his mother and grandmother as they departed around the curved driveway.

Gertrude was angry, refusing to wave to him. She paused when she heard the phone ringing in the kitchen, waiting for Adam to answer it.

"Hello, Dad...Yah...I'm busy working on my term paper...Yah... Mom could use your help...I'd like you to drop it off...We'll see you later then."

Adam pressed his forehead against the screened window. "Dad's coming over to help you wash the vegetables and load the truck for tomorrow's market."

"You can call him back and tell him I don't want him

coming here. I don't need his help!" she shouted.

"You'll have to call him yourself!" shouted Adam. "I've got a paper to write."

"That bastard has a lot of nerve coming here without being invited," said Gertrude, entering the hallway.

"Dad's also coming to bring me a birthday present," said Adam, leaving the kitchen and returning to his typewriter in the dining room. He could hear his mother's footsteps on the stairs as he typed from his notes.

In Tibet prior to the establishment of Buddhism in the Sixth Century, the Tibetans practiced the Bon religion. The shamanistic faith involved worshipping of gods and goddesses along with exorcisms of evil spirits.

These practices from the ancient cult were gradually integrated into Tibetan Buddhism, including the use of prayer flags, sky burial, sacred rocks, and the construction of traps for evil spirits.

Gertrude picked up the phone and called the Alano Club. Since the line was busy, she paced the kitchen floor repeatedly trying to call her husband. She finally slammed the phone down when someone told her that Giovanni had left the club and was coming to the farm.

A few minutes later she heard Grandma yell from the sidewalk that she was going to feed the chickens and then get ready to milk the cows.

41

"She's too much like Eve, offering him forbidden fruit in the Garden of Eden."

Within twenty minutes Adam heard the tires of his father's Plymouth rumbling up the driveway, followed by the screeching of his brakes and the slamming of the car door. He paused at the typewriter, hearing his mother screaming at his father.

"I told you never to come here again!"

"I came here to make amends to you," said Giovanni. "I've made a lot of mistakes over the years."

"Can't you see we're busy," shouted Gertrude, returning to scrubbing the potatoes.

"I was wrong getting involved with Ellie. I shouldn't have done it. Please forgive me."

"I'll never forgive you for betraying me. You told me you were going to AA meetings. The truth was you were having an affair with that barfly!"

"That was over five years ago. How's Marie doing?" asked Giovanni, trying to distract his angry wife.

"She should be home any minute now. Marie's been rehearsing after school for a play with students from her class," said Gertrude, calming down.

"I haven't seen her very much since you've come back from New York. I'm sorry I missed her recital last week. I had to work overtime. I understand she's been taking piano lessons from a teacher at St. Mary's," said Giovanni.

"She was disappointed because you missed the recital," said Gertrude. "Marie's been taking lessons every Saturday afternoon since school started. She played *The Farmer in the Dell* with her friend Lily singing the verses."

"She's got musical talent just like Adam. I came here to drop off his birthday present. I can't believe he'll be sixteen tomorrow," said Giovanni.

"'He's been defiant lately and so has Karl," she said, biting her lip.

"I promised to take Adam to get his driver's license after I come home from the Farmers' Market," sighed Gertrude. "I'm just exhausted."

"You don't have to do that. I'm picking up Adam right after work tomorrow to get his license," said Giovanni.

"I haven't had time to bake a cake for him," she said.

"Let me give you a hand with those potatoes," said Giovanni, picking up a scrub brush. "I have a present for Adam in the car."

Gertrude wiped the perspiration from her forehead, complaining. She reminded Giovanni of Vivian Leigh, playing Scarlett O'Hara after the collapse of her aristocratic life style in *Gone with the Wind*.

"How's Karl doing these days?" asked Giovanni, removing his shirt and exposing his hairy chest.

Gertrude informed her husband about football being cancelled and Karl going to the library with Larry.

"It wouldn't surprise me if they go out drinking

afterwards. Karl came home drunk last Saturday. I wish he wouldn't be hanging around with Larry," she said.

"I agree with you. Larry needs a job. He's been loafing ever since he got that inheritance from his grandfather."

"He's a bad influence on Karl," said Gertrude.

"Where's Adam?"

"He's working on his term paper. I'm worried about him dating Naomi. He wants to meet her at the Halloween Party tomorrow night at St. Catherine's, but I grounded him for being disrespectful.

"He constantly paints pictures of himself with Naomi in their bathing suits," sighed Gertrude, "It's not easy raising two sons by myself on the farm."

"I had a long talk with Adam about going steady when we came back from Illinois on the train," said Giovanni.

"I know he's crazy about Naomi, but mixed marriages don't work," said Gertrude. "Besides, he's too young to think about marriage. She's too much like Eve, offering him forbidden fruit from the Garden of Eden."

"This water's really dirty. It needs to be changed," said Giovanni, emptying the aluminum tub into the lilac bush. He observed the water flowing down the grass toward the front tire of his car.

"Have you heard from Father Fortmann?" asked Giovanni, turning on the spigot to rinse the tub.

"No," snapped Gertrude. "I shouldn't have gone to New York with Marie."

Gertrude paused when she heard a car coming up the

driveway. "That must be Marie. Her teacher agreed to give her a ride home after practice."

"Maybe I should move my car out of the way so she can go around the driveway."

"You don't have to be bothered," said Gertrude, hearing the door slam and the car backing out of the driveway.

"Daddy! Daddy!" yelled five-year-old Marie, running toward him with her blonde hair flowing in the wind. She threw her arms around her father and hugged him.

Marie's blue eyes were filled with tears. "Daddy, I missed you so much. Please come home and live with us."

Giovanni picked her up under the arms and twirled her like he did with his sons when they were little. Marie laughed as he put her gently down on the gravel.

"I've got a Halloween gift for you in the car and a birthday present for Adam. I drove all the way to Racine to get it at Martha Merrell's Bookstore."

Giovanni hurried toward the Plymouth with Marie following him. He removed the presents, handing his daughter her gift.

"Mommy! Mommy! Come see the present Daddy gave me!" shouted Marie, running to the shade of the maple tree where Grandma was resting on the bench.

"What you got there, Marie? Buona sera, Giovanni!"

"Good evening," said her son, kissing her on the cheek.

Gertrude arrived, watching Marie open her present.

"It's a crown and a wand!" shrieked Marie. "How did you know that I'm going to be a princess for Halloween?"

347

Grandma's making my costume because Mommy's too busy to do it. Oh, thank you so much, Daddy!"

Marie put on the tiara and waved the wand, wishing they could all live happily ever after.

"You're like Tinker Bell from TV," said Grandma, smiling. "I like that Walt Disney show with a-the castle."

"When you wish upon a star, makes no difference that you are," sang Marie, circling the maple tree and waving her sparkling wand. *"When you wish upon a star, your dreams come true."*

Giovanni stood there, enchanted by Marie's singing and her spontaneity. He also knew that she was often stubborn and defiant.

For a few moments he recalled *The Scarlet Letter,* when Hester Prynne left the jail carrying her baby named Pearl. She was a social outcast and a criminal for giving birth to a child out of wedlock.

Hester was sentenced to be hung at the scaffold by the Puritans. The pastor, Arthur Dimmesdale, saved her life, concealing that he was the infant's father.

"Giovanni, what are you so busily pondering?" asked Gertrude, annoyed by Marie's playfulness.

"I was just thinking that Marie reminded me of someone from a story I read in high school," he said, turning toward his daughter, who was chasing the squawking chickens with her wand and trying to cast a spell on them.

"Daddy, next Halloween I'm going to be the Wicked Witch from *The Wizard of Oz*!"

348

"Marie, you stop chasing my chickens," yelled Grandma. "I don't know what's wrong with that girl. First she's a princess, then she's a witch, like that no good Leona Fortunato!"

"She may be beautiful, but she's strong willed and disobedient," sighed Gertrude. "Marie, stop that right now or I'm going to ground you."

Giovanni tried to intervene, "Marie, come over here. Please stop chasing those chickens!"

Marie ignored her parents, chasing the chickens into the coop. After a few minutes the panic-stricken rooster rushed out, followed by a dozen Rhode Island Reds, squawking as if they were being attacked by a wolf.

Gertrude entered the dark chicken coop and snatched the wand out of Marie's hand, breaking it into two pieces.

Marie let out a horrific scream as she followed her mother out of the hen house, sobbing.

"Mommy, you broke my magic wand! Look what you did! Daddy! Daddy! Mommy broke my wand!"

"Marie, come over here. I have another present for you in the car. I was going to save it for Christmas."

"Please, Giovanni! Don't give her any more presents. She should be spanked for defying us!"

"Maybe Leona Fortunato cursed Marie with the evil eye," said Grandma.

"Don't be ridiculous," said Gertrude. "Marie's only imitating her brothers. They're always defying me."

"Mommy! You're mean. You don't like Daddy! I want

to go live with him!"

"Marie, you better listen to your mother," said Giovanni. "She's the boss when I'm not around."

"People say Leona put the evil eye on Camille. That's why she has that car accident," said Grandma.

"Don't talk nonsense. That's nothing but superstition," insisted Gertrude. "Camille had the accident because she was driving drunk."

"Giovanni, you stay for supper tonight. I go now and make spaghetti for everybody," said Grandma.

"I've already put a roast in the oven, but you can make the salad," said Gertrude.

"I can't stay. I've got to go as soon as we finish scrubbing the vegetables and loading the truck."

"Marie, you go show your daddy the new earrings I bring for you from Italy," said Grandma.

"I told Grandma that she shouldn't be giving Marie earrings," scowled Gertrude.

42

"Daddy, I love you," cried Marie.
"I hate living here with Mommy."

A few moments later Marie came bolting down the stairs, wearing her sparkling tiara and carrying a felt box with golden earrings.

"Look, Daddy! They're just beautiful! I can't wait to have my ears pierced."

"You're too young to have your ears pierced," snapped her mother, biting her lower lip.

"No, she's not too young. In Italy girls get their ears pierced when they're little," insisted Grandma, carrying a half bushel of tomatoes to the truck.

"We're not living in Italy. This is the United States of America," shouted Gertrude.

Giovanni picked up his shirt and removed a flip top pack of Marlboro from the pocket. He paused, lighting a cigarette with a silver lighter.

"I thought you quit smoking when you were in treatment," said Gertrude. "You're no example to your sons. It wasn't so long ago that Adam came home from Camille's house, drunk."

"Why didn't you tell me about this sooner," said Giovanni, exhaling a cloud of smoke.

Everyone paused when they heard the back door slam as Adam came down the sidewalk to give his father a hug.

"It's time for me to milk my cows. I'm already late. I go now to get the pails in-a-the kitchen."

"We're not keeping those cows much longer," said Gertrude. "We can hardly afford to feed them anymore."

"How you talk, Gertrude. We need cows for milk, butter, and cheese," argued Grandma.

"Oh fine," said Gertrude. "In this family nobody ever listens to what I have to say!"

"Grandma, please show me how to milk the cows," said Marie, following her into the house with her earrings.

"Dad, how can I help?" asked Adam.

"You can load the vegetables on the truck," he said.

"Giovanni, I thought you had a birthday present for Adam," said Gertrude, rising from scrubbing the potatoes.

"It's in the car," said Giovanni, hurrying toward the Plymouth and returning with the gift.

Adam read the card and removed the wrapping on the present. "It's a copy of *Moby Dick*!"

"The movie was just released," said Giovanni. "Gregory Peck's playing Captain Ahab."

"It won't be coming to Kenosha until next summer," sighed Gertrude. "It always takes movies a year to come to this godforsaken town."

"I'd like to see *La Strada* in Italian," said Giovanni. "It takes place in northern Italy with Antony Quinn playing the role of a stunt man at a carnival. It's now in Chicago."

"Dad, everybody says you look just like him," said Adam, leafing through his new novel.

"People say I look like Vivian Leigh. I don't know why they compare me to her," said Gertrude. "I hated her role in *Streetcar Named Desire*, with Marlon Brando."

Everyone heard the door slam when Grandma came out of the house, carrying two aluminum pails. "It's getting late for me to milk a-the cows."

"Be careful in that barn," said Gertrude. "Those cows are mean when it's hot like this."

"Adam, you come and help me with my cows. Then you go feed a-the chickens and ducks," said Grandma.

"OK," he said, setting his book down on the sidewalk.

"Grandma's too old to be milking those cows. One of these days they're going to knock her off the stool and break her back," said Gertrude.

Giovanni carried tomatoes from the maple tree to the truck, pausing when he heard the back door slam.

Marie hurried down the sidewalk wearing faded blue jeans. She rushed past her mother scrubbing potatoes.

"Where are you going like a bat out of hell?" asked Gertrude, scowling.

"Grandma's going to teach me how to milk the cows."

"Marie, I want you to set the table for supper right now," insisted her mother.

"Mommy, I can't do it right now," cried Marie, dashing toward the barn.

"Oh, never mind, I'll set the table myself," she said, wiping her hands on her jeans. She picked up *Moby Dick* from the sidewalk and headed into the house.

After Giovanni loaded the last crate onto the back of the truck, he interrupted Adam, who had returned from the barn with a kettle of oats to feed the chickens.

"How are things going at home?"

"They haven't been the same since you left," said Adam. "Mom's always mad about something."

"I hope you understand, Adam, I left home to protect my sobriety. I can't be stacking up resentments against her if I want to stay sober."

"I understand, Dad. I'm still angry over testifying at Mr. Gascoigne's trial. It's been getting a lot of publicity lately."

"How did it turn out?" asked his father.

"The jury is still out. I wonder if they'll find him not guilty," said Adam.

"Adam, when did you come home drunk?" he asked.

"That was weeks ago. I got high on two beers and a cocktail. Camille was drunk when she drove me home."

"I read about it in the newspaper, but I didn't know you had been drinking with her. How's she doing?"

I went to see her in the hospital a few days after the accident. After some weeks of recovery there, Camille went for treatment at Hazelden in Minnesota," said Adam.

"Are you still drinking?" asked Giovanni.

"Hell no, I only got drunk once. It won't happen again. I feel guilty about Camille smashing her car into a telephone pole. She could have been killed."

"She's lucky to be alive. How do you like going to St. Mary's?" asked his father.

354

"It's all right. I really miss Naomi, but I've made friends with Marlene and Annette. We ride the bus together all the time now. I also eat lunch with some guys every day."

Gertrude pressed her forehead against the screen window of the kitchen. "Giovanni, you're welcome to stay for supper tonight."

"I can't stay. I'm going to my meeting," said Giovanni, heading toward the Plymouth.

"Daddy! Daddy!" yelled Marie, coming out of the barn, carrying a kitten. "Look what I've got!"

"I better go help Grandma," said Adam, noticing she was struggling with two pails of milk.

"Dio Mio! That barn's hot inside tonight like a-the furnace. You go let the cows out now," she said setting down the pails and wiping her forehead.

When Adam released the cows from their stanchions, he noticed that they hurried through the pasture to graze in the shade of the willow tree near the road.

He dashed toward Grandma to help her carry the pails, walking beside her toward the house.

"Why is Marie crying?" asked Adam, pausing at the back door while Grandma went entered the hallway.

"Daddy! Daddy! Please stay and eat supper with us. I miss you so much," she sobbed, clinging to the kitten.

"I can't stay," he uttered, sitting behind the wheel of the Plymouth with the window rolled down.

"Daddy, I love you," cried Marie. "I hate living here with Mommy."

"Marie, don't bother your daddy now," said Grandma, shouting from the dining room window. "You come inside and eat your supper!"

"Dad, don't forget to pick me up to tomorrow so I can get my driver's license," shouted Adam, carrying the milk pails into the house.

"I'll be here right after work tomorrow," shouted his father, going around the circular driveway.

"Daddy! Daddy. Come back!" screamed Marie, chasing after the Plymouth. Upon hearing his daughter's cries, Giovanni slammed on the brakes.

"What is it, Marie?" asked Giovanni. He noticed that the cows had stopped grazing and were looking toward them.

"Come into the house with me," pleaded Marie. "We want to sing Happy Birthday to Adam."

Giovanni got out of the car and took her hand, walking with her toward the house.

"Grandma showed me how to milk Daisy. She swished her tail and knocked me off the stool," said Marie, leading him into the kitchen, where the table was set for dinner.

"I thought you left for your meeting," said Gertrude, hovering over the cast iron stove.

"Mommy, we're going to sing Happy Birthday to Adam. We won't have time to do it tomorrow."

"After we sing, you eat supper with us," said Grandma, filtering the milk with a cheese cloth at the sink and pouring it into glass bottles with a funnel.

Adam stopped typing and went into the living room. He

356

sat at the piano bench waiting for his family to join him. A few minutes later he played Happy Birthday on the upright piano while everyone sang.

When he was finished playing, they all clapped and shouted "Happy Birthday" together.

"Why do you look so sad?" asked Marie.

"I wish Naomi could be here with us," said Adam. "I can't go to the dance tomorrow night because I'm still grounded."

"Adam, you may go to dance. You're no longer grounded. That's my birthday present to you. Promise me you won't do anything foolish," said Gertrude.

"You can drive the car to the dance after you get your license tomorrow," said Giovanni. "I'll walk back to my apartment from the AA meeting."

"Thanks," said Adam, giving his parents each a hug.

"Here's a paper heart I made for you and Naomi," said Marie, handing it to him.

"I got a present for you to give to Naomi," said Grandma, handing him a golden heart-shaped locket. "This is for her to wear at a-the party. Your grandpa Frederico, gives it to me for our wedding. I only wear it one time."

"It's just beautiful," gasped Gertrude.

"Maybe you ought to give it to Mom," said Adam, not expecting such a gift.

"No," said Grandma. "I want your girlfriend to have my necklace. I got something for your mother."

Grandma went into her bedroom and returned with

357

golden earrings in a velvet box. "I wear these earrings at my wedding. Gertrude, I want you to have them."

"Oh, my God!" said Gertrude. "They're just gorgeous."

"When can I wear my earrings?" asked Marie, pouting.

"After you get your ears pierced," said Gertrude.

"I've have to get going now or I'll be late for my meeting," said Giovanni, heading toward the kitchen.

"Before you go, Giovanni, you say the blessing for supper," insisted Grandma.

His family followed Giovanni to the kitchen. They all took their seats at the table with Giovanni sitting at the head of the table near the telephone.

Giovanni made the sign of the cross and prayed, *Bless us, O Lord, and these thy gifts which we are about to receive from Thy Bounty through Christ, our Lord. Amen.*

All heads turned toward him as he hurried down the steps and out the door. The rest of the family sat silently at the table, listening to the back door slam, followed by his footsteps on the sidewalk. They paused as he started the engine of the Plymouth and left the farm.

43

"I'm sure rumors have been spreading around town about me and Father Fortmann."

Gertrude was sullen during the meal while Marie chatted about learning to milk the cow, getting her ears pierced, and wearing her princess costume for the Halloween Party at Whittier School.

"Please pass the mashed potatoes and the salad," said Adam, interrupting Marie. "Maybe I should practice parking a few times with the truck tonight."

"Dio Mio," said Grandma. "The last time you drive the truck, you almost run over my chickens."

"I'll be more careful this time. I finally learned how to look over my shoulder and use the rearview mirror."

"Mommy, I'm mad at you for breaking my wand."

"I'll get you another one at the Ben Franklin Store tomorrow. They have all kinds of masks and costumes there," said Gertrude.

"I don't know if I should go as the Lone Ranger or Bozo, the Clown?"

"If you go as a clown, I'll have to buy you a clown suit and face paint," said Gertrude. "You can reimburse me when I get home."

"That's a great idea, Mom. I'll go as a clown," said Adam, recalling how his mother didn't recognize him and

Naomi when they were dressed as clowns at the circus.

"Mom, I forgot all about the clown suit and the wig I have in my suitcase," said Adam. "Giuseppe, the manager of the circus, gave it to me to wear when I substituted for a clown, who was sick with bronchitis."

"That will save us some money. Let me see the costume," requested his mother.

"I'll get it from my suitcase in the attic," said Adam, returning a few minutes later with the costume.

"I'll wash it tonight and iron it the first thing in the morning," said Gertrude. "I'll rinse the wig in hot water and hang it to dry in the basement."

"I'm done eating," said Marie, wiping her mouth on her napkin. She carried her plate to the sink. "I'm going to practice the piano."

"Can't you wait until I finish my term paper," said Adam "I'll be done typing in an hour."

"You always linger at the typewriter making corrections half the night. We have to walk on eggshells when you're typing," said his mother, leaving for the basement with his costume.

Adam was annoyed by his mother's criticism. He returned to the dining room to work on his paper.

When Gertrude came back to the kitchen to wash the supper dishes, she heard a car drive up. A few minutes later Karl hurried up the steps into the kitchen with his gym bag.

"How was studying at the library?" asked his mother.

"Fine," said Karl, reaching for his plate on the table and

filling it with roast beef and potatoes from the stove.

"I'll warm them for you in the oven," said his mother. "It'll only take me a few minutes."

"Don't bother," said Karl, wolfing down his dinner at the kitchen table.

"Karl, slow down. You'll get indigestion if you swallow your food without chewing it," complained Gertrude.

"Larry's waiting for me in the car. We're going to the Colonial Inn to play pool for an hour."

Gertrude peered out the kitchen window at Larry's new Buick. "Who are those girls laughing in the back seat?"

"Marlene and Annette are coming with us," said Karl. "We met them at the library."

"What?" asked Gertrude. "Don't tell me you're going to bring the Wilson girls to the bar with you to play pool. They're both unde rage and related to Ray, the mailman, accused of running away with Joyce Jacobsen."

"They're not related to him," said Karl. "There are dozens of Wilsons in Kenosha. You don't have to worry about the girls, Mom. They never check ID's. Besides, we're only drinking Coke."

"If their parents find out you took their daughters to a bar on a school night, they'll have a fit," said Gertrude.

"We'll be home by 10:00," said Karl, bolting down the stairs. "I promise we're not drinking tonight."

Gertrude finished the dishes and then sat at the kitchen table on the vacant chair where her husband used to sit every night before he got in the habit of staying at the bar.

After reading the newspaper she was restless and irritable. She began scrubbing the kitchen sink with Old Dutch Cleanser.

"Gertrude, you look tired," said Grandma, coming into the kitchen in her pink night gown. "I dry the dishes for you and put them in the cupboard."

"I'm so depressed. I just want to die!"

"Gertrude, you're too young to die."

"I don't know what's wrong with me," she sobbed, sitting in Giovanni's chair. "I feel so ashamed."

"Maybe Joyce's ghost comes to bother you because nobody buried her in a-the right way."

"What do you mean?" asked Gertrude, wiping the tears from her eyes with a lace handkerchief.

"Maybe Leona Fortunato puts the evil eye on you. That's why you have so much trouble with Giovanni and that no good priest in New York."

"I'm sure rumors have been spreading around town about me and Father Fortmann. I never expected him to be so cold and rude to us. I know Giovanni thinks that Marie is Mark's child, but I swear she's not."

"Dio mio! Why do you tell me this?" said Grandma.

Gertrude put her head down on the table and began sobbing while Grandma tried to console her.

"It's all Leona Fortunato's fault. She makes too much trouble for this family because she's a witch," she said.

44

"That Jesuit makes sense. The protestors need to keep their noses out of people's sex lives."

When Gertrude came home from the Farmers' Market on Friday, she parked the truck in front of the garage. She was singing *Somewhere Over the Rainbow*, recalling how she took her sons to the Orpheum Theater to see *The Wizard of Oz* when they were children.

"Gertrude, what makes you so happy today? You don't sing much anymore," said Grandma, coming out of the garden and carrying a half bushel of acorn squash.

"I sold out at the market and made almost a hundred dollars this morning," she said.

"Dio Mio! That's a lot of money," uttered Grandma.

"I'm just exhausted," said Gertrude, wiping the sweat from her forehead with a handkerchief. She entered the house carrying a paper bag with a new wand for Marie and clown makeup for Adam.

"You go rest now," said Grandma, coming up the hallway stairs into the kitchen.

"I can't. I have to iron Adam's costume," said Gertrude, hurrying to the basement. She removed the clown suit and orange wig from the clothes line. Upon returning to the kitchen, she set up the ironing board.

"I just now bake Adam's birthday cake," said Grandma, sitting down at the kitchen table to catch her breath.

"That's a nice sponge cake," said Gertrude, sprinkling the clown suit and then ironing it. "I bought chocolate frosting and candles at A&P on my way home. I'll put them on the cake later."

Grandma opened the refrigerator and took out a bowl of lettuce, setting it down on the counter. She chopped an onion and some garlic, adding vinegar and oil to the salad.

"It's time to eat lunch," said Grandma, putting the Italian bread and salami on the table. "You must be hungry from all that work."

"I'm starving," said Gertrude, bringing the costume into the dining room and putting it on the oak table.

"It's hotter than Hades inside this house. I wish we had air conditioning," said Gertrude, returning to the kitchen.

"I bring you a fan from my bedroom," said Grandma.

"Don't bother," said Gertrude, sitting down at the table. "There's a breeze coming in from the window."

After lunch Grandma collapsed on the couch for her afternoon nap while Gertrude went to lie down in her bedroom with the door closed.

Later in the afternoon the two women returned to the garden to prepare for Saturday's market.

By the time Adam returned from school on the bus, it was after 3:30. He didn't bother to change his clothes but went into the garden and carried the produce to the spigot to be washed.

His mother and grandmother followed him from the garden into the house where they sat down with him to eat a slice of his birthday cake.

When Giovanni arrived in the Plymouth, he honked the horn, eager to leave with Adam. In the kitchen Gertrude sliced two pieces of cake for her husband, wrapping them in wax paper. She inserted them in a brown paper bag and handed it to Adam.

"I've got to get going," he said, kissing his mother on the cheek. "Thanks for pressing my clown suit. I'll come right home after my driver's test to get dressed for the party. Mom, did you buy the paint for my face?"

"Of course," said Gertrude. "I'll paint your face when you come back with your license."

Giovanni was waiting inside the car. He revved the engine and departed from the farm with his son.

"I brought you some birthday cake," said Adam, setting the bag down on the front seat.

"I'll have it for lunch tomorrow," said his father, turning on the radio.

Some Catholic women from the Chicago Archdiocese led by Monsignor Thomas Fitzgerald have been protesting about explicit sexual material on sale in bookstores. This pressure group demands that proprietors remove all books on the black list of the National Organization for Decent Literature.

Among the authors being criticized for writing about sex are Ernest Hemmingway, William Faulkner, John Dos Passos, and George Orwell.

Coming to the defense of the authors is the moral

theologian, Father John Courtney Murray, a Jesuit priest from Woodstock College. He states, "No minority group has the right to impose its religious or moral views on other groups through the use of force, coercion, or violence" The priest also claims that Catholics involved in such boycotts are doing damage to the faith.

"That Jesuit makes sense. The protestors need to keep their noses out of people's sex lives," said Giovanni. "That's the problem with most priests. They have no business counseling married people about sex. If they themselves were married and had children, they might have some credibility."

"Dad, why's premarital sex a mortal sin?" asked Adam.

"I don't know why the theologians put such an ugly label on it. I suppose they're worried that girls will get pregnant out of wedlock. The problem is that they've made birth control a sin whether you're married or not. It just doesn't make any sense to me."

"Is that why you don't go to church, Dad?"

"I don't want some priest telling me what I should or shouldn't do in my bedroom," said Giovanni. "It's none of his damn business.

"Christ doesn't discuss sex in the Gospels. It was Saint Paul who made a big issue about it. I know for a fact that parish priests were allowed to get married right up until the eighth century," continued his father.

"I didn't know that," said Adam, recalling his promise to become a priest because God saved Neil's life.

366

Giovanni drove Adam to the police station downtown and then waited for him while he took his driver's test. He was pleased that his son passed the test.

"I guess Karl did a good job teaching you how to drive," said Giovanni. "I hope you have a good time at the Halloween dance tonight. Be extra careful if you're driving Naomi home. Remember what I told you about having safe sex when we came back from Illinois on the train."

"I'll be careful, Dad," said Adam, thrilled to be able to drive the car for the first time to the Alano Club, where he dropped his father off before returning to the farm.

Once he got home, Adam's mother painted his face and helped him put on his clown costume and wig. Gertrude laughed as he strutted around the dining room table, flapping his rubber shoes, pretending he was a clown.

"Have a great time at the party tonight," she said, putting the shoes into a large paper bag for him.

After his mother wrote down the directions to St. Catherine's High School, he left the house feeling tense as he drove to Racine, anxious to meet Naomi.

45

"I swear that guy wearing the Frankenstein mask is Adam, and his monster is Neil."

There was very little traffic on Sheridan Road until Adam reached Main Street. He turned left on 16th Street and then right onto Park Avenue. A few minutes later he parked the Plymouth near St. Catherine's High School.

Adam followed students dressed in their costumes to the gym. Across the street several students were dressed as pirates. They were smoking cigarettes except for Captain Hook, who was tying Peter Pan's hands with a rope.

Upon reaching the gym, Adam paid a dollar at the entrance. He received a stamp on the back of his hand from the senior class president, wearing a mask of Abraham Lincoln and a stovepipe hat.

The president was standing next to Sister Therese, a stout Dominican nun. She was inspecting pockets and purses to be sure students weren't bringing pints of liquor or bottles of beer into the gym.

Adam turned his head as the horrified nun shouted at a scantily clad Little Bo Peep, who was stood behind him holding a stuffed lamb.

"You can't go into the gym unless you cover yourself!" insisted the nun, alarmed by the exposure of the girl's cleavage. "Take off that sash from your waist and put it on, otherwise you'll have to leave the premises."

"Are you her date for the evening?" she asked Adam.

"No," he said, glancing at the student wearing a wolf mask behind him. "He must be her date."

"I'm her date all right," growled the wolf, stretching his paw to receive a rubber stamp from Abraham Lincoln.

"You'll need extra tickets for *The Grand March* and the other activities," said Sister Therese "You can get them from the girls behind the table over there.

"All profits go to our missionary sisters in Africa, and scholarships for our poor students. They always need tutoring because they come from public schools."

Adam entered the gym and approached the table where Queen Elizabeth stood between her Ladies in Waiting. Sir Walter Raleigh was standing behind them with his sword in its sheath. They all wore Renaissance costumes.

"I'd like to buy a ticket for *The Grand March*," said Adam, scanning the room, hoping to find Naomi.

"We also have tickets for *Pin the Tail on the Donkey, Bobbing for Apples, Pumpkin Carving, and Fortune Telling*," said the queen. "The tickets are 25 cents each."

Adam reached for his wallet, removing $2.00, which he handed to the queen. She gave him his tickets and change from a cigar box.

All heads turned toward the commotion at the entrance where another couple was the center of attention.

"Oh my God," gasped a Lady in Waiting, removing her silver mask attached to a stick. "Just look at Lila and Roger. They've come as Tarzan and Jane. I'm sure Sister

Therese won't let them into the gym."

"They've been going steady since their sophomore year," announced the queen, wearing a golden half-mask.

"Roger's on the wrestling team. He never loses a match," informed Sir Walter Raleigh. "Just look at him showing off his muscles like Charles Atlas."

"You're not coming into the gym half naked," insisted Sister Therese. "Lincoln, go get the principal right now."

"We bought our tickets in advance," bellowed Roger, barefoot and wearing only a tiger skin loin cloth.

"There's nothing wrong with our costumes," insisted Lila, showing off her leopard skin, two piece bathing suit. She clung to a furry chimpanzee, faded from being washed too many times.

Standing behind the couple, Count Dracula removed his red cape and wrapped it around Tarzan. He bowed, saying, "Roger may now go into the gym."

"What about her?" shrieked Sister Therese, pointing at Lila. "She will have to go home and change!"

"Come on, Lila. Let's get out of here," said Roger, hurling the cape onto the floor. He let out a shrill cry as if he were about to swing on a vine in the jungle.

"I'm giving you each four demerits for creating a disturbance," announced Sister Therese, reaching inside the pocket of her white habit for a pen.

"Come on Sister," said Roger "We weren't trying to cause any trouble. We were just having a little fun."

"Then go home and put on some decent clothes. You're

holding up the line," insisted the nun.

Adam turned toward the girls selling the tickets. "Have you seen Naomi Rosenberg this evening?"

"I saw her go into the *Fortune Teller's* booth about ten minutes ago," said a Lady in Waiting. "She's wearing a clown suit just like yours."

"Are you her boyfriend from Kenosha?" asked Queen Elizabeth, setting her mask on the table.

"I'm her cousin Benjamin from Loyola Academy near Skokie," said Adam. "Naomi invited me so she'd have a companion for the *Grand March*. She broke up with Adam some months ago."

"Oh," said the queen. "We thought you might be her boyfriend. Naomi's mother is over there serving the punch next to the *Pumpkin Carving*, where students are carving pumpkins for the contest.

"If you see Adam you should tell Mrs. Rosenberg. She's giving $25 cash to the person who can identify him at the dance tonight," said another Lady in Waiting.

"He'll probably come dressed like a farmer with a straw hat and bib overalls," laughed Sir Walter Raleigh. "I heard he sells vegetables at the Farmers' Market in Kenosha."

"How quaint," said the queen, removing her mask.

"He might come dressed like Jack the Ripper with a concealed weapon. Adam and his friend Neil appeared in court to testify against Mr. Gascoigne. He was arrested for murdering Joyce Jacobsen," said Sir Walter Raleigh.

"Oh my God!" gasped the queen, fanning herself with

her mask. "The police found Joyce's severed head in a rain barrel in Mr. Gascoigne's basement. That's what I heard from Jennifer O'Reilly, Naomi's friend who dates Neil."

"Those farm boys are real hoodlums. Five years ago they attacked Mrs. Jacobsen's house and broke all of her windows on Halloween," announced Adam. "She drove them away with a shot gun."

"The murder of Joyce has gotten a lot of attention. My father's a lawyer who works in Illinois. He told me he has been following the case in the Chicago Tribune."

"I read about it in the New York Times," said Sir Walter Raleigh. "The police went to their schools and brought Adam and Neil to the courthouse in handcuffs."

"Who's that girl coming out of the *Fortune Teller* tent with my cousin Naomi?" asked Adam.

"That's her best friend, Jennifer," announced Queen Elizabeth. "Her mother has forbidden her to date Neil."

"How strange," said a Lady in Waiting. "Benjamin here is wearing a clown costume that's identical to Naomi's."

"Look over there at the entrance," said Adam. "I swear that guy wearing the Frankenstein mask is Adam, and his Monster is Neil."

"I'm going to tell Mrs. Rosenberg," said Sir Walter Raleigh. "I could use a little extra cash."

"I hope you'll split the twenty-five dollars with me," said Adam, leaving the ticket booth. He wandered around the gym, keeping his eye on Naomi while the band played Elvis Presley's *Don't Be Cruel*.

Adam avoided going directly toward Naomi, who was playing *Pin the Tail on the Donkey*. When she finished the game, Naomi went to the table where her mother was serving the punch. Sir Walter Raleigh was standing there telling Mrs. Rosenberg that Adam and Neil had arrived at the gym, expecting to receive his cash reward.

"That's definitely not Neil," interrupted Jennifer, dressed as Esmeralda. "He called me this morning and said he won't be here because he had bronchitis."

"Are you sure about that?" asked her mother, Jean O'Reilly, who was helping Rachel serve the punch.

"Adam is much taller than Doctor Frankenstein," said Naomi, reaching for two glasses of punch.

"We won't find out until after the *Grand March* when everyone takes off their masks," said Rachel.

"I think that's my cousin Benjamin over there," said Naomi, hurrying toward Adam. He was standing in front of the gate leading into the fenced pumpkin patch. .

Naomi's hand was trembling as she handed Adam a glass of punch. She turned and waved to her mother, who had been watching them.

"I can't live without you," he whispered, giving her a hug. "I love you, Naomi, and want to marry you."

"I love you too," she said, backing away from him and spilling punch on the floor.

"My heart's beating like a drum in my chest," he gasped, taking her by the hand.

"We can't leave the dance. There's a nun guarding

every exit. They even have guards outside the bathrooms. The whole convent's here tonight, chaperoning with dozens of parents," said Naomi.

"Would you like to enter the *Pumpkin Carving Contest* now or later?" asked a Roman Soldier, opening the gate to the pumpkin patch for them.

After handing Julius Caesar their tickets, Adam and Naomi found two large pumpkins, which they carried to a card table with carving knives.

"I don't know how we can escape from the party," said Adam, slicing the top of his pumpkin and removing the lid.

"I'm going to cry, and my tears will ruin my clown makeup. Will you help me cut the top of this pumpkin? I'm not very good at carving."

"As soon as I arrived at the gym, I found out your mother's giving a reward to anyone who can identify me."

"My mother's been a real bitch. I hate her!" said Naomi, glancing at the heads of carvers turning toward her for using foul language.

"I told the girls at the ticket booth that I'm your cousin Benjamin just like we planned," he said, removing handfuls of slimy seeds from his pumpkin.

"I missed you so much," she said. "I'm so glad my cousin agreed to help us out. Ben's almost your exact height and weight. I spoke to him for quite a while on the phone last night about how to escape from the party.

"Ben suggested that I tell my mother that we should leave after the *Grand March* to visit my grandmother in the hospital."

"Now we have to figure out how to escape without drawing a lot of attention to ourselves," said Adam.

"Adam, my mother's suspicious of you because you haven't said hello to her yet. She hasn't seen Ben in four years because he was living in Tel Aviv with my Aunt Sarah and Uncle Joe.

"She keeps looking over this way. You stay here and carve my pumpkin while I go talk to my mom. Be sure and wave to her when I glance back at you, otherwise she'll feel slighted."

Adam began carving their pumpkins while Naomi hurried to the punch stand to speak with her mother.

"Mom, I'm so thrilled that Ben was able to come here all the way from Skokie!"

"Tell Ben I want to see him right after the *Grand March*. He called me on the phone last night when you were decorating the gym to let me know he was taking you to the party and would wear a costume like yours. He said he wanted to leave the dance early to visit grandma in the hospital.

"Oh, I didn't know he called you," said Naomi.

"He told me you asked him to be your date for the Halloween Party. That's why I'm here. I want to keep an eye on things in case Adam shows up," said her mother.

"Ben's a junior at Loyola Academy. He knows his Hebrew from living in Israel, but he's behind in his Latin. He's trying to catch up with the class," said Naomi.

"I loved my Latin classes when I was here at St. Catherine's. Sister Matilda was an excellent teacher, but she favored the girls and hated the boys," said Rachel, waving to her nephew. Adam paused from carving his pumpkin to wave back.

"I hope that boyfriend of yours doesn't show up," said Rachel. "I understand Adam got into trouble for drinking when some girl crashed her car on Cooper Road."

"Her name is Camille Flynn," said Naomi, frowning. "She's coming to St. Catherine's next semester after she gets back from rehab in Minnesota."

"You've been wasting your time with Adam. His family has a history of drinking. His father, Giovanni, is separated from his mother and spends all his spare time at AA meetings," said her mother.

"Adam told me all about it," said Naomi.

"Don't forget Ben is leaving after the *Grand March* to visit Grandmother in the hospital. Your father and I are going to Skokie on Sunday to see her. We want you to come along with us."

"I can't go. I've got a term paper due on Monday. I'll remind Ben to come over and visit with you," said Naomi, departing. "I'll see you later."

When Naomi joined him, Adam stopped carving the pumpkin to discuss her plan to leave the building with her.

"My cousin Ben agreed to call the office here at Catherine's, pretending that he's my Uncle Joe, requesting permission for you to leave the building with me to go to the hospital to visit my sick grandma," said Naomi.

"I will ask my mother if I can go with you to the hospital because grandma wants to see our costumes," said Naomi, her hand trembling.

"That's a great idea," said Adam, finishing Naomi's pumpkin and putting the final touches on his own.

"You go talk with Jennifer for a few minutes while I have my fortune told," said Adam. "Maybe your mother will stop looking this way if we're not together so much."

Naomi picked up her pumpkin, carrying it across the room to show it to her mother and Mrs. O'Reilly.

Before entering the *Fortune Teller's* booth, Adam noticed Sister Therese was no longer standing at the door. She was testing the microphone across from *Bobbing for Apples*, where students were dipping their faces in and out of tubs of water.

46

"They don't want anyone sneaking out of the building to make out in the parked cars."

"We will begin the *Grand March* after the awards are given for the best pumpkins," announced Sister Therese, turning the microphone over to the principal.

"Good evening," said Sister Benedict. "I'm so grateful to the parents and our Dominican Sisters for chaperoning our annual Halloween Party. Let's give them a round of applause for helping us out.

"We all know how important it is to be safe from outsiders from the public schools, invading our dances like barbarians."

Once the clapping and whistling subsided, the principal said, "And now I will present the awards for the best pumpkins. The First Place will go to Naomi Rosenberg. Please step forward with your pumpkin to receive your blue ribbon."

Naomi hurried toward the microphone carrying *Juliet*, with tear drops carved on her cheeks. Adam stood in the distance holding his pumpkin, *Romeo*.

"I have to admit my cousin Benjamin from Skokie did most of the work on my pumpkin. I can't accept the blue ribbon because I didn't really do the carving," said Naomi.

The crowd applauded while the principal returned to the microphone. "That was so honest of you, Naomi. The word

378

for 'truth' comes from Latin, *Veritas*. Because of your honesty, you may give the blue ribbon to your cousin for his pumpkin, *Romeo*. I'm so proud of our students here at St. Catherine's for abiding by the rules and coming to our dances without a trace of liquor on their breaths.

"Let's go on with the awards. The second place winners are Lila and Roger for their pumpkins, *Cain* and *Able*. I'm so glad they decided to go home and change into their costumes of Roy Rogers and Dale Evans. We will forgive them for appearing earlier as Tarzan and Jane."

Everyone in the crowd laughed, applauding them as they stepped forward to receive their red ribbons

Third place was given to Queen Elizabeth and Sir Walter Scott for the severed heads of *Mary Queen of Scots* sand *Ann Boleyn*."

After the applause subsided, the principal announced that the *Grand March* was next. It was the main attraction of the evening with prizes for the best costumes.

While the band played *Some Enchanted Evening*, the couples lined up and marched around the gym three times, with Sister Benedict consulting nuns and parents about who should win the prizes.

Adam and Naomi joined the procession around the gym, nervously passing the table where Rachel Rosenberg and Jean O'Reilly waved to them.

"Oh my God, there's my daughter Jennifer dressed as Esmeralda. She's being escorted by Quasimodo. I hope that hunchback isn't Neil. He was supposed to be home, sick in

379

bed with bronchitis."

"That's the problem. You can't trust this generation. They don't tell the truth," said Rachel.

"I'm so disappointed in Jennifer wanting to go steady with Neil. She should have more sense than to date someone from the county. They don't have the same moral values that we have in the city," said Jean O'Reilly.

"I know exactly what you mean. I can't understand what Naomi sees in Adam. His family has been involved in a lot of scandal in Kenosha. You probably know about Kevin Mueller, who murdered the priest at St. George's."

"Of course, the whole incident made the front page of the Kenosha News a few years ago," said Jean.

"Kevin was Gertrude's nephew. Her brother, Pete, was married to Clara Solinsky. They never had any children so they adopted Kevin. People say he was an orphan from Nazi Germany," commented Rachel.

"I understand that Clara's in the mental hospital in Mendota. She had a nervous breakdown after Kevin shot Father Furstenberg and then committed suicide with his father's gun," said Jean O'Reilly, shaking her head.

"Just look at those costumes. I think that Beauty and the Beast ought to get the first prize," said Rachel, changing the subject.

"Here comes Antony and Cleopatra," gasped Jean. "They've been intimate since they've entered the gym. I watched them kiss a half a dozen times. After that I lost count. I'm surprised they haven't been kicked out."

"Naomi's separated from her cousin Benjamin. She's walking with Count Dracula, and Ben's strolling with Little Bo Peep. I really want to talk with my nephew. He had been living in Israel with my brother and sister-in-law for several years."

"Thank God! Naomi and Benjamin are back together," said Jean. "Just look at that Big Bad Wolf pawing Little Red Riding Hood. I would think one of the nuns would separate them. I guess they're too busy monitoring the bathrooms and exits. They don't want anyone sneaking out of the building to make out in the parked cars."

"It's a shame this generation doesn't have any morals," said Rachel. "It's because of Hollywood Movies. It all started with Marilyn Monroe and Elvis Presley. Most singers and actors are sexually promiscuous because they smoke marijuana, drink, and take tranquilizers."

"And now for the prizes," said Sister Benedict. "This year the award for the best costumes goes to Quasimodo and Esmeralda. Will you please come forward and remove your masks. Congratulations Jennifer O'Reilly and Michael Anderson."

"That's a relief," said Jean. "I thought maybe Neil was hiding behind that mask."

"Second place goes to Anthony and Cleopatra. Please come forward and identify yourselves," announced Sister Benedict, pausing while everyone applauded.

Naomi rushed to the table where her mother was putting ice into the punch bowl.

"Mother, Ben invited me to go with him to visit our grandma in the hospital. He promised to bring me home after a short visit with her. Could you write a note so I may leave the gym with him? Sister Therese is still guarding the exit like a watchdog."

"Where's Ben? I wanted to see him before he leaves," said her mother, scanning the crowd. "I understand Uncle Joe phoned the office to get permission for you to leave with Ben to visit grandma."

"He's already outside, waiting for me."

"Did Ben forget visiting hours are over at 8:00 pm at the hospital in Skokie? You won't be able to see her tonight."

"He made an arrangement with the hospital to be admitted by the security guard to see her later because of the dance tonight," said Naomi.

"What time will Ben bring you back home?" asked Rachel. "It's a long drive to Skokie."

"After midnight," said Naomi, glancing at her watch.

"You can go with him," said Rachel, scribbling a note on a napkin and handing it to Naomi. "Have him call me at home before you start back to Kenosha. The dance is over at 11:00. It's already almost 9:00 o'clock."

"I'll tell him right away. Have you got some extra napkins? I need to wipe off this makeup. I don't want to go to the hospital with my face painted like a clown's. "

"Here" said Rachel, reaching for them on the table. "Take these with you."

"Thanks so much, Mom. I love you. I'll see you later."

As Naomi approached the exit of the gym she could hear the principal speaking at the microphone.

"Now that the prizes have been given out for the best costumes, you may want to go to the *Fortune Telling* booths and participate in the other activities in the gym. Don't forget the *Jitterbug Contest* will begin promptly at 10:00 pm. It's the final activity of the evening."

"I have my mother's permission to leave the gym," said Naomi. "She wrote this note."

"Let me see that note," said Sister Therese, blocking the exit. "Your cousin Benjamin was very rude. It's not my fault that his grandma's in the hospital in Skokie. His father already called the office informing me you were leaving the building."

The angry nun sent a Lady in Waiting to verify the note from Mrs. Rosenberg, giving Naomi permission to leave the dance.

After what seemed an eternity, Naomi left the building. She was delighted to see Adam waiting for her in the streetlight. He was nervously pacing on the sidewalk in front of the gym. Adam immediately embraced Naomi, kissing her on the lips before hurrying with her to the Plymouth parked down the block.

As soon as they entered the car, Adam kissed her passionately. Naomi felt overwhelmed by his desire to make love to her. She broke away from him, trembling in his arms.

All of a sudden they saw a light scanning the parked cars. Naomi gasped, fearful they would be discovered by the night watchman.

"We better get out of here," said Adam, glancing in the rear view mirror at Sister Therese coming toward their car with a flash light.

Adam started the car, revved the engine, and pulled away from the curb. They glanced at the nun scowling with her mouth open, holding the flash light. She was hoping to find couples making out in their cars so she could have them expelled for the rest of the semester.

"Let's go to a filling station and take off our makeup. It's annoying and greasy," said Naomi, rolling down the window to get some fresh air.

A few minutes later Adam turned right onto 16th Street and drove until he came to a Shell Station. They took turns in the restroom, wiping the make up from their faces and washing in the sink.

Upon returning to the car, they began kissing again until they were interrupted by the service station attendant wearing a uniform; he knocked on the steamed window.

"Do you want me to fill your tank with gas?" he asked.

Adam broke away from kissing Naomi, flushed with embarrassment. He headed back to Sheridan Road, going south to Kenosha.

"If your mother finds out that I'm not Benjamin, she'll send you right back to California," said Adam.

"She won't find out. My cousin told the truth about our

grandma being in the hospital, but Ben's at home working on a term paper tonight. He'll call my mother later to tell her we arrived at the hospital."

"You're brilliant," said Adam. "Let's go for a walk along the beach at Pennoyer Park. We're almost there."

"I'd like that," agreed Naomi.

"We can stroll in the moonlight and curl up on a blanket to listen to the waves," said Adam.

"Maybe we could go swimming," suggested Naomi. "But I didn't bring my bathing suit."

"Neither did I," said Adam rolling down the window. "There's a cool breeze coming from Lake Michigan."

"It's too cold to go swimming," said Naomi. "I have so much to tell you. It was such a nightmare living with my aunt in California. I thought things would get better once I got home, but my mother's made my life a living hell ever since I came back from the circus with my dad. He was angry with me all the way home."

"I know what you mean. My dad talked to me on the train about premarital sex. He told me if we decided to have sex I should use a condom, provided you agreed. He suggested we practice some other form of birth control as well," said Adam. "I was surprised my parents weren't opposed to us going out tonight. They just don't want us going steady."

"My parents are obsessed about us having sex," said Naomi. "It only makes me want to do it even more. The truth is I'm scared to death about getting pregnant. It's about the worst thing that could happen to a teenage girl," said Naomi.

"I won't be very good at it even though I'm in love with you. I'm so uptight from being watched the entire evening by my mother. I was scared to death that she'd find out that you weren't Ben," said Naomi.

"I'm kind of scared myself about having sex. My brother Karl gave me a couple of condoms. I have them in my wallet," he said.

"We tried to have sex under that circus wagon around midnight at the County Fair Grounds in Illinois. Our plan was interrupted by the footsteps of the night watchman making the rounds with his flashlight," said Naomi.

"He paused, wearing his gestapo boots right next to our wagon, shining his flashlight into the animal cages. He finally woke up a tiger with her cubs. She growled and paced in her cage to protect her babies," said Adam.

"We got out of there by crawling out from the opposite side of the wagon. I hurried back to my wagon and spent a restless night with the trapeze artists, but I couldn't sleep a wink that night," said Naomi.

"The same thing happened to me. Once I got back to the clown wagon, I lay there awake the whole night, tossing and turning on my cot while the clowns snored," said Adam slowing down. "Here we are at Kaiser's Tap."

47

"What are you doing this time of night?" asked the officer, restraining the German Shepherd.

Adam parked the car on Sheridan road, a block away from Pennoyer Park. After he removed the key from the ignition, he wrapped his arms around Naomi, kissing her tenderly on the lips. The second kiss was more intense. They stopped kissing when a drunken man came out from the bar and stumbled toward them singing.

A few minutes later Adam went to the passenger side and opened the door of the Plymouth, offering Naomi his hand. When she stepped out of the car, he embraced her against his muscular chest, kissing her again.

"You're beautiful in that clown suit," he said, admiring her blue eyes in the street light. He stroked her blonde hair with a calloused hand from baling hay.

"I'm so thrilled to be with you," she said, clinging to him, anticipating his kisses under the street light with the juke box playing *Unchained Melody* in Kaiser's Bar.

Adam removed the blanket from the trunk of the car and tucked it under his arm. They walked together holding hands, pausing in front of the bar to listen to the Juke Box playing *Moonlight in Vermont* by Don Eliot.

While the music faded, they continued down the steps and up the hill toward the deserted tennis court, pausing to gaze at the full moon illuminating Lake Michigan.

"It's so cold here," said Naomi, shivering as they headed toward the beach holding hands.

They removed their shoes and rolled up their pant legs, wading in the surf in spite of the cold, which lapped the shore like tongues of mythical beasts.

The couple strolled in the moonlight hugging and kissing every couple of yards. Upon reaching the cluster of trees where they kissed during the summer, Adam stretched out the blanket on the sand.

Naomi fell to her knees shivering while Adam covered her with half of the blanket. As they lay side by side, they paused for a moment to listen to the waves unfurling on the beach. Adam kissed her hungrily on the mouth which aroused him. He became so wild with passion that Naomi was frightened. She wanted to please him, but she pushed him away from her, gasping for breath.

"Please stop," she cried, fearful that he would tear the clown suit from her body.

"What's wrong?" he blurted, glancing at her stricken face in the moonlight.

"Let's go for a walk along the beach," she suggested, beginning to sob. She pulled away from him and stood up, the tears flowing down her cheeks. "Adam, I'm so sorry that I've ruined the evening. I shouldn't have led you on like I did."

"It's my fault," he said, bewildered. "I should have been more considerate of your feelings."

Naomi hurried toward the water with Adam stumbling

after her through the sand. She splashed cold water into his face until he calmed down.

After a stroll down the beach and more splashing in the waves, they returned to the blanket and curled up once again, holding hands for a long time and talking about how lonely they had been and desperate over being separated from each other for so many months.

After shivering together under the blanket, they took off their costumes, finding warmth from each other's naked bodies, which they explored with their hands and lips. They kissed gently, whispering in each other's ears until Adam became aroused once again.

This time he kissed her gently stroking her breasts and then allowed her hands to guide him past her stomach. When they were both aroused and trembling with desire, Adam entered her for the first time, expressing his love for her with a strong passion that wasn't aggressive but satisfying to both of them.

After repeating how much they loved each other, they kissed numerous times before finally falling asleep in each other's arms. They didn't wake up until they heard a dog barking in the distance and footsteps coming toward them with a flashlight scanning the beach.

"We'd better get going," said Adam alarmed by the dog barking. He rose from the blanket and stepped into his clown suit. Sitting on the blanket, he reached for his shoes while Naomi grabbed her clothes and got dressed behind the tree.

"What are you two doing here at this time of night?" asked the officer, restraining the German Shepherd. He scanned them with his flashlight since the moon had disappeared behind the cumulus clouds.

"We decided to take a walk along the beach," said Adam, feeling awkward in his clown suit.

"You two must have been at a Halloween Party. I saw Giovanni Montanya's Plymouth parked in front of the bar and decided to come down here and take a look around."

"That's my dad's car," said Adam.

"I stopped at Kaiser's to say hello to Giovanni but he wasn't there. I heard he was going to AA Meetings after his wife left him to marry a priest in New York.

"Let me see your driver's license," asked the officer, waiting for Adam to remove it from his wallet. He glanced at the license. "You just got it today on your birthday."

"So you're the driver of your father's car," said the officer. "I graduated with him from Bradford during the Depression. You were just a kid when he crashed his truck in Old Lady Jacobsen's yard a couple years ago.

"Adam, do your parents know that you're down here on the beach with this young lady?"

"They knew that I was going to meet Naomi at the party and was planning to take her home" said Adam, flushing with embarrassment.

"My mother told me that I have to be home by 12:30," said Naomi glancing at her watch as the moon appeared from behind the cloud.

"What time was the party over?" asked the officer, pulling the dog away from sniffing Adam.

"It was over at 11:00. We haven't been here very long," said Adam, lying about leaving the dance early.

"Then you'd better take this young lady home before you get into trouble with her parents. It's already almost midnight."

"Let's get back to the car," said Naomi, reaching for her shoes. "My mom will be worried if I'm late," said Naomi.

Adam shook the sand from the blanket, embarrassed by an unused condom falling onto the sand in the moonlight.

"I see you two have been busy here tonight," said the officer kicking sand with the side of his shoe to cover up the wrapped condom.

"I hear noise coming from those trees over there," said the officer, unfastening the dog from the leash. He departed abruptly, following the German Shepherd barking at teenagers, who had started a bon fire.

"Wow! That was a close call," said Adam, leading the way up the hill toward the parked car.

"I love you, Adam. The next time we have sex, I won't push you away," whispered Naomi.

"I'm sorry I was so rough with you," apologized Adam.

"I really wanted to please you, but I didn't want to get pregnant. I've been working at the hospital as a Candy Striper every Saturday with a nurse. I'll ask her about birth control methods. The nurse told me condoms aren't very safe," said Naomi. "I'll let you know what she says the next time we get together."

"When can we meet again, Naomi?"said Adam, feeling aroused just talking to her about having sex again. "I forgot all about using a condom. It must have fallen out of my pocket when we were getting undressed.

"I'll call you during the week. I've been in love with you ever since you kissed me on the beach last summer. You won't think badly of me if we practice birth control, will you? I know you Catholics believe it's a sin to use birth control, but I don't."

"I really enjoyed being with you tonight," said Adam.

"My mother would kill me if she knew I was with you. She doesn't believe in couples having sex unless they're married."

"I'm worried about your parents finding out that I went out with you tonight," said Adam.

"Don't worry. My cousin won't tell a soul about us being together. He agreed to help us escape to Nashville during Christmas vacation so we can get married."

"That's wonderful! Naomi, I love you," said Adam, halting the car in the alley in front of her parents' garage. They were hidden in spite of the porch light illuminating the entire the back yard.

Once the car was parked, Adam began kissing Naomi.

"I've got to go now," she gasped. "My parents will be furious if they see your car parked here. I love you Adam. Let's meet again next weekend. I'll call you Sunday evening," she said, hurrying from the shade of the garage into the light of her backyard.

Adam wanted to escort her to the door and tell her parents how much he loved Naomi. He hated being deceitful the whole evening, pretending that he was her cousin. His conscience started to bother him as he was driving home.

He knew that lying was only a venial sin. However, he wondered how many mortal sins he had committed that evening by getting aroused while kissing Naomi and then having sex with the intention of using a condom. It addition he was planning to have sex again in the future.

As he drove home alone in the car, he was tormented by guilt and shame. What if he died in the night having committed so many mortal sins? The priests and nuns had told him repeatedly he'd burn in hell for all eternity if he wasn't in the state of grace.

Adam had been tense all evening and finally got relief after having sex with Naomi. He wondered why God hated teenagers for having premarital sex, especially those who practiced birth control.

He was also tormented for breaking his promise to become a priest and planning to run away with Naomi to get married in Nashville. After turning onto Cooper Road, he felt depressed driving down the deserted country road. He drove past Old Lady Jacobsen's desolate place, feeling abandoned by God for committing so many mortal sins.

48

"Dio Mio! Do you want to ruin your life? You're only 16 years old…"

The weekend proved to be difficult for Adam since the principal announced on Friday that all students at St. Mary's were expected to go to confession prior to All Saints Day on Thursday. The students had been informed that the parish priests had cancelled their religion classes to be available to hear confessions.

The Dominican Sisters had encouraged the students to prepare themselves for confession over the weekend by reviewing the Commandments and the Seven Deadly Sins.

On Monday the juniors and seniors went to confession in the afternoon while freshman and sophomores were expected to go on Tuesday, October 30th.

Adam was nervous about going to confession. He could scarcely concentrate during his classes because he was thinking constantly about Naomi. He obsessed about the Halloween Party and being with her at the beach, feeling guilty for committing sins.

When he finally returned home on the bus, he was frustrated because he had to do his chores, finish his homework, and prepare for confession on Tuesday.

After supper he was sitting at the dining room table, memorizing Latin verbs for a quiz the next day when the telephone rang.

"Adam, the phone's for you," called his mother.

"Who is it?" asked Adam, hurrying into the kitchen to pick up the phone.

"It sounds like a young woman's voice," said Gertrude, wiping the dishes and putting them into the cupboards.

"Why, Naomi! How nice to hear from you. How are things going?"

"I can't talk very long," she said. "My mother called Aunt Sarah this afternoon at work. She told her that Ben spent the weekend working on his term paper. He never left the house, not even to visit grandma in the hospital."

"It's all my fault. We shouldn't have left the dance," gasped Adam.

"My mom found my clown suit in the basement with sand on it this morning. She threatened to throw me out of the house if I didn't tell her the truth. I finally told her that you were the other clown at the party, not Benjamin."

"Oh no!" said Adam. "Did she ground you?"

Naomi began sobbing on the phone. "I didn't know what to tell her. She tormented me with her questions."

"I shouldn't have taken you down to the beach," said Adam, overwhelmed by guilt.

"When I told her that we had gone down to the beach, my mother was furious. She slapped my face and told me she's sending me to a Jewish boarding school in California. I'll be leaving from O'Hare this Friday on an evening flight to stay with my aunt."

"No!" gasped Adam. "When will I see you again?"

"I don't know," said Naomi. "I don't even know the name of the boarding school where I'm supposed to go. My parents are having a doctor examine me today to find out if I'm still a virgin like they did when I came back from the circus in September.

"My parents want to have you arrested for molesting me because I'm only fifteen. I told them it was my idea that you came to the party pretending you were my cousin. They didn't believe me when I told them that I asked you to make love to me on the beach.

"My father slapped me across the face, calling me a whore! Adam, I have to go now. I can't talk much longer. They're in the other room consulting an attorney. I hear someone coming.

"Goodbye, Adam. I'll write to you from boarding school. My parents said that I won't be coming back to Kenosha until I've graduated from high school," sobbed Naomi. "Adam, I love you, and I'll never forget you!"

"Naomi, I love you too. Please wait for me even if it takes ten years before I see you again," blurted Adam.

Adam's face collapsed from worry as he hung up the phone. He was terrified that he'd never see Naomi again and that her parents might have him arrested.

"What happened?" asked his mother, noticing that he was depressed by the conversation.

"Naomi and I left the Halloween Party and went down to the beach at Pennoyer Park. We were together there for a couple of hours."

"Did you have sex with her?" asked Gertrude, pacing the kitchen floor.

"Yes, we had sex," he confessed.

"Adam, how could you do it! You know that her parents didn't approve of you dating Naomi. Your father and I thought we could trust you with the car on your birthday. I can't believe that you did such a horrible thing!"

"I don't want to talk about it," said Adam. "I've got to study for a quiz and prepare for confession tomorrow."

"What about Naomi? Do her parents know that you two were together on the beach?"

"Yes, they want to send the police to arrest me for having sex with her."

"Oh my God!" shouted Gertrude. "I'm calling your father at the Alano Club! It's all his fault. I found an unused condom in your pocket when I went to wash your clown suit this morning. I was wondering why your costume was so gritty with sand."

"Naomi told her parents that it was her fault to get me off the hook," said Adam, his fists clenched.

"Oh my God," she screamed. "It's your father's fault. He shouldn't have told you to use condoms like he did when Karl was involved with that Mexican girl. Don't you know premarital sex is a mortal sin?"

"And so is adultery," said Adam, glowering at his mother. "When Dad got drunk, he was ranting and raging that you had a love affair with Father Fortmann and wanted to renew your relationship with him by going to New York with Marie."

"That bastard was screwing Ellie for years behind my back. He deliberately tried to turn you and Karl against me with his false accusations.

"I can't change the past. Your father wasn't a heavy drinker until he came back from the war. Alcoholism has twisted his perceptions of reality," she said, pausing. "I'm so pleased you're going to confession tomorrow so you won't die with mortal sins on your soul."

"Everything's a mortal sin!" shouted Adam, leaving the kitchen and returning to the dining room table. He sat down and opened his Latin text and read, *amo, amare, amavi, amatus. I love, to love, I have loved, having loved.*

"What's Mom so mad about?" asked Marie, sitting across from him, copying sentences from the story of *Little Red Riding Hood.*

"She's mad about me for going out with Naomi after the Halloween Dance on Friday night."

"Father Fortmann was mean to Mom. She was angry with him when we were in New York. I liked him because he bought me ice cream cones. Adam, what does having sex mean?"

"I don't want to talk about it," said Adam. "I've got a quiz tomorrow."

"OK, I won't bother you," she said.

A few minutes later the telephone rang again. Adam turned his head toward the kitchen, fearful that the police might be calling his parents. He could hear his mother talking on the phone.

"I'm so glad you called, Rachel...I'm also very angry with Adam for taking Naomi down to the beach...No, don't tell me she lied to you too...I can't believe they'd do such a thing...You mean your nephew, Benjamin?..I thought he was studying Hebrew in Israel...How awful...I swear they've become compulsive liars...No, I don't blame you for wanting to send her back to California...Is that right. I found Adam's clown suit covered with sand in the laundry room...He's just as much to blame as Naomi. It takes two to tango...Oh, I feel so relieved...Of course you've got to put your foot down...I'll tell Adam ...OK...Thanks for the call. Good night, Rachel."

"Adam, I want to talk to you," shouted Gertrude, hanging up the receiver.

"I'm busy studying for tomorrow's quiz," he said, rising from the chair.

"Rachel Rosenberg told me that Naomi had her period a week ago on Monday," said his mother, sighing with relief. "Thank God she's not pregnant."

"I don't want to talk about it," said Adam.

"Their attorney advised them not to press charges against you because you both agreed to have sex even though you're under age. Naomi swore that she lured you down to the beach and that it was all her fault."

"It's my fault," said Adam, disturbed by Naomi taking the entire blame.

"Where are you going? I'm still talking to you, young

man," said his mother, putting her hands on her hips.

After leaving the kitchen, Adam hurried through the dining room and living room to the vacant porch.

"Where you go in such a hurry?" asked Grandma, coming out of her bedroom with her rosary.

Adam stood on the porch admiring his painting of Naomi, especially her blue eyes and long blonde hair flowing down her shoulders. He turned away from the canvas and scowled at Grandma, coming onto the porch in her pink nightgown.

"Dio Mio! You got such a long face! What happened to you and that Jew girl?"

"Naomi's parents are going to send her to boarding school in California."

"You mean next summer. I don't know about that kind of school. I only go to class in Italy until the fifth grade."

"Her parents are driving her to O'Hare this Friday. She won't be coming back to Kenosha until she graduates."

"Dio Mio! That's almost three years she's gonna be gone. Don't tell me you try to run away with her to a-the circus again."

"No, Grandma. Her parents are angry because they found out that I met her at the Halloween Party and took her down to the beach."

"You mean you go down there with her with nobody to watch you?"

"We made love on the beach," confessed Adam.

"Dio Mio! Do you want to ruin your life? You're only

16 years old. Why do you do such a thing!"

"I'm in love with Naomi, and I want to marry her. I made a big mistake by taking her to the beach."

"Dio Mio! Where's your head?" In nomine Patris et Filii, et Spiritus Sancti. Amen."

"Grandma, I feel terrible. It's my fault they're sending her back to California."

While Adam was talking with his grandmother on the porch, Gertrude poked her head through the door from the living room.

"Maybe your girlfriend's pregnant?" asked Grandma.

"Adam's lucky this time. Her mother told me on the phone that Naomi's not pregnant because she had her period last week."

"How do you know that?" asked Grandma.

"Because Rachel Rosenberg has kept track of her daughter's monthly periods on the calendar ever since she started menstruating at twelve-years old," said Gertrude.

"Dio Mio, that's what you do when you first got married," said Grandma. "You mark a-the calendar."

"It's because I used the rhythm method of birth control recommended by my priest at confession. After getting pregnant with two sons, I decided to try something safer," said Gertrude.

Adam knew all about his mother using a diaphragm since she talked about it openly. He kept silent about Naomi's plan to investigate birth control, feeling depressed because their future together had come to an abrupt halt.

401

"Adam's going to confession tomorrow," said Gertrude

"Dio Mio! You tell the priest everything so that God forgives you and Naomi."

"I'm going to go for a walk in the orchard," said Adam, disturbed about going to confession. He was tormented as he strolled, pausing beneath the willow tree where he had kissed Naomi during the summer.

When he finally returned to the house, everyone had gone to bed, including Karl. Adam didn't even notice him coming home from football practice. He was alone in the dining room separating the venial sins from the mortal sins in his notebook.

Adam tossed and turned most of the night unable to sleep, tormented by his conscience. He got up early to help his grandmother with the chores.

After breakfast he caught the school bus. The driver stopped to pick up the Wilson sisters on Cooper Road before continuing on to St. Mary's.

"We were wondering how the party went last Friday night. You didn't say anything about it yesterday because you were depressed," said Marlene.

"I called your house on Saturday," said Annette. "Your mother answered the phone. She told me you were at the Farmers' Market with your grandmother."

"I called on Sunday," said Marlene. "This time your mom said you were in the garden getting the vegetables ready for Monday's market."

"How did your date go with Naomi?" asked Annette,

closing her copy of Steinbeck's *The Grapes of Wrath.*

"Naomi and I had a great time at the party. We were both dressed in clown suits," he said, explaining to them how he was pretending to be her cousin Benjamin.

He then told them her mother found out that he wasn't Benjamin and decided to send Naomi back to California to boarding school for the next three years, which depressed him because he might never see her again.

"No wonder you're sad. You must really love Naomi," said Annette.

"I shouldn't have taken her down to the beach. That was my biggest mistake," said Adam. "Her mother found sand on her clown costume."

"Oh my," said Marlene. "I hope you didn't have sex?"

"I did, but she's not pregnant. She had her period a week before the party," said Adam. "Please keep this a secret."

"We won't say a word," promised Annette. "Naomi lives next door to Jennifer, and she's a terrible gossip. You know how fast rumors spread at St. Mary's."

"I have lunch with guys who live near Naomi. They knew all about me and Naomi running away to join the circus because Jennifer told them everything."

"I'll guarantee you they'll know about Naomi being sent to California again," said Marlene, her brow furrowed.

49

"What bothers me is that even Joseph wanted to put her away until the Angel of the Lord appeared to him in a dream."

Adam attended mass on Tuesday morning along with the entire student body and faculty. All eyes were on him for remaining in the pew instead of going to communion, which caused murmuring after mass.

As the day progressed rumors circulated in the building that Adam had been to the Halloween Party at St. Catherine's and had left early with Naomi.

Adam found it difficult to concentrate on his classes during the morning due to gossip and whispering. He thought he would be able to relax during lunch, not expecting to be teased by his friends.

"We heard that you got Naomi pregnant last summer and were keeping it a secret," said Ralph. "Everybody thinks she put your baby up for adoption when she went to live with her aunt in California."

"Naomi wasn't pregnant. She was sent to California because her parents didn't want us to go steady," said Adam, feeling angry.

"What did you do after you left the Halloween Party?" asked Steve. "Did you get her pregnant again?"

"What the hell are you talking about? Naomi's not

pregnant." said Adam.

"How do we know you're telling the truth?" asked Fred.

"You lied to us about joining the circus with her. You said that you were taking a course at the university in southern Illinois."

"You didn't say it was intercourse," snickered John. "You came here a week late and kept everything a secret, but now the cat's out of the bag."

"Jennifer told us everything on the bus," said Ralph.

"How many times did you fuck Naomi when you were with the circus?" asked Steve.

"We slept in separate wagons. I stayed with the clowns, and she had to sleep with the trapeze artists. The manager didn't allow unmarried couples to fool around," said Adam.

"Don't tell me you didn't sneak away with her now and then to get some pussy?" said John.

"It's none of your damn business. We planned to get married in Nashville," said Adam.

"Married?" laughed Steve. "You're only sixteen!"

"You guys are disgusting," said Adam.

"Jennifer said that Naomi invited you to the Halloween Party to tell you that she's pregnant again. Of course, I didn't believe in the gossip," said Ralph.

"For Christ's sake! You guys are crazy!" yelled Adam, standing up with his fists clenched...

"Why are you so angry? We all know that pregnant girls go to California to have babies," said Fred. "Jennifer says Naomi's being sent back there this weekend."

"Maybe Naomi had an Immaculate Conception like the Virgin Mary," laughed Joe. "What bothers me is that even Joseph wanted to put her away until the Angel of the Lord appeared to him in a dream."

"For Chirst sake, who told you about Naomi leaving for California again?" shouted Adam.

"Who in the fuck do you think? I live right next door to Jennifer in Allendale," said Ralph.

"What's going on here?" shouted Sister Georgia, rising from her desk, where she was cutting out a picture of a turkey for the bulletin board.

"Adam, come over here. I need your help putting a few things up for me," said the nun.

"Do you put your cock up for her too?" asked Steve.

"She wants you to stay after school so you can put it up for her when no one's around," snickered John.

"You never told us what happened to Camille. I heard you guys were swimming naked in her pool before she took you home drunk. We read in the paper that she crashed her Chrysler and ended up in the hospital with a miscarriage," said Ralph.

"Everybody says you were fucking her," said Joe.

"You really get around, don't you, Adam?" said Ralph, standing up at his desk. "You need to learn self control."

"You guys are crazy," blurted Adam, crumpling up his lunch bag and hurling it into the wastebasket. He turned around and charged Ralph, hitting him in the stomach.

"What the fuck's the matter with you?" asked Ralph,

backing away as Adam pushed over his desk and charged out of the room.

"I'm going to beat the shit out of that asshole," shouted Ralph, chasing after him.

"Ralph, calm down," shouted John, grabbing his arms from behind and restraining him.

"Stop that fighting!" screamed Sister Georgia, standing at her desk, shaking her finger at them.

"Jesus Christ, do you want to get expelled," said Joe.

"You boys are cursing and using filthy language," said Sister Georgia. "If you don't stop, you'll each get six demerits."

After leaving the building, Adam headed toward A&P to buy a pack of cigarettes. His hand was shaking as he lit the cigarette and hurried past Zarletti's Cleaners and Dober's Bakery.

While walking around the block, he reviewed his long list of sins, written down the night before. Adam crushed out the cigarette on the sidewalk before returning to his afternoon class.

A secretary from the office informed the sophomores that she would escort them to church where they were to line up for confession. Upon finishing, they were to return to their afternoon classes.

Once inside the church, Adam knelt down, gazing at the crucifix of Christ hanging on the cross. He was wondering if God was punishing him for rebelling against His will by being in love with Naomi. It seemed as if every time he went out with her something went wrong. They always ended up being separated. Maybe God didn't want them to be together.

After waiting for an hour, Adam was the last one in line to enter the confessional. He noticed that his classmates never confessed their sins more than five minutes. Those who stayed longer were targets for gossip among the students and faculty.

He decided to go into Father Smith's confessional, but the priest stepped out from behind the curtain.

"Why, Adam, you're still here," said the priest. "I'm sorry I'm unable to hear your confession. I have to meet with a woman getting a divorce at the rectory. She's very disturbed over the whole procedure."

"Maybe I can stop by at the rectory after school," said Adam, feeling tense.

"I'll hear your confession," insisted a bald-headed priest stepping out of the nearby confessional and putting his hand on his shoulder.

Adam was terrified because Father Bernard had a reputation of holding students hostage for long periods of time by asking them detailed questions.

In spite of his voice quivering, Adam entered the dark confessional and knelt down on the padded kneeler behind the curtain.

"Since you're the last one in the church, you can take your time," said the priest. "Is there some reason you were last to confess your sins today?"

"I haven't been to confession for a long time," said Adam. "I usually go to Father Smith."

"Just relax. You don't have to be afraid of me. I understand you're new here at St. Mary's. I heard that you live out in the county on a farm. Our students from town go to confession regularly since they've been going to Catholic school since kindergarten."

"This is my first year in a Catholic school," said Adam, feeling tense. "I'm a sophomore."

"Living on a farm is no excuse not to come into town regularly to go to confession. You may begin your confession now. In nomine Patris et Filii et Spiritus Sancti," said Father Bernard, sitting behind the screen in his chair.

"Bless me father, for I have sinned, my last confession was on Good Friday," said Adam.

"You mean, you haven't been to confession for six months?" gasped the priest. "You need to receive the sacrament of Penance at least once a month. You may call me in advance and arrange for a private confession in the rectory. Now tell me your sins."

"I used the Lord's name in vain, only a few times when I got angry with my mother."

"Tell me why you get angry with her."

"I got angry because she's constantly criticizing my father. I called her a bitch, which was wrong of me. My parents are separated, and I don't see my dad very often."

"The commandment is Honor thy Father and thy

Mother," said the priest. "It means that you must bite your tongue and not criticize her. It must be difficult for your mother living on a farm without your father."

"She's angry because my dad's a recovering alcoholic. He's been going to AA meetings regularly and is trying to straighten out his life. He moved out and got an apartment in town because my mom nags him. I hate her for being so mean to everybody."

Adam also told him about quarreling with the guys during lunch and getting so angry that he hit Ralph and then left in a rage. He admitted that he lost his temper because his friends at school were teasing him.

"You must forgive them or your soul will be stained with sin," said the priest. "Please continue."

"I've had impure thoughts and desires. I know it's wrong to have them, but I can't control myself."

"Yes," said the priest. "I'm listening."

"I...I'm burdened with mortal sins," he said, fearful about revealing them.

"Do you find it difficult to remain chaste when you become sexually excited?" asked the priest.

"Yes...I find it difficult," said Adam, the perspiration forming on his forehead.

"Do you masturbate every day of the week, including Sunday?" asked the priest.

"No, Father, maybe two or three times a week," said Adam, his ears turning red.

"Don't you know that masturbation is a mortal sin?"

410

"Yes, Father, I know it's a sin."

"During Biblical times when young men were caught spilling their seed, they were stoned to death," said the priest. "You must stop this behavior by taking cold showers whenever you're tempted."

"We don't have a shower in our house," said Adam.

"Then take a cold bath to quell your sexual desires, rather than indulge in illicit passions."

"Yes, Father," said Adam, wiping the perspiration from his forehead with a handkerchief and dreading to continue with his confession.

"Do you have a girlfriend?" he asked.

"Yes, Father, I'm in love with a beautiful girl. I want to marry her," said Adam. "I have painted several pictures of her on my canvases because I want to be an artist."

"How old are you?"

"I was sixteen last Friday."

"And how old is the young lady?"

"She's fifteen, but she will be sixteen in December. I gave her a ring and we're going steady."

"Going steady leads to committing mortal sins. Do you think about her when you masturbate?"

"Yes, Father," said Adam. "I think about her all the time because I'm in love with her."

"Do you become aroused when you think about her?"

"Yes, Father. I become very aroused."

"How often did you become aroused when you think about being her?"

"Maybe forty or fifty times, I don't remember exactly," said Adam, thinking about the times he kissed Naomi on the beach, in his back yard, under the circus wagon, and then on the sidewalk every few yards, and recently under the blanket at the beach

"Did you ever have sex with her?"

"The first time we tried to have sex, nothing happened because she was afraid. When we actually had sex the second time, I forgot to put on the condom," said Adam, his voice trembling with fright.

"Don't you know that practicing birth control is a mortal sin?" uttered the priest.

"Yes, I realize it's a sin. We got in trouble because her parents found out we had sex. It wasn't the first time we got into trouble either."

"What kind of trouble are you talking about?" asked the priest. "I want you to be completely honest with me."

Adam explained to the priest that his three attempts to meet with Naomi involved lying and deception. He told him he lied to his family about buying a bus ticket to California where he planned to elope with her. At the time she was staying with her aunt.

Next he informed Father Bernard about deceitfully running away with Naomi by joining the circus. The last incident of deception occurred last Friday at the Halloween Party, where he lied about being Naomi's cousin. After the truth was discovered, her parents decided to send her back to California a second time.

412

"You and your girlfriend have been influenced by Satan, the Father of Lies," said Father Bernard. "You are habitual liars. Why was she being sent back to California?"

"Because her parents found out we had sex on the beach last Friday," said Adam, his voice quivering.

"Is Naomi pregnant?"

"No, Father, she's not pregnant."

`"How do you know that?"

"Because she had her period a week before we went out on the date."

"Then she knows about the rhythm method of birth control, but she encouraged you to commit another mortal sin by planning to use a condom while fornicating."

"I never thought about it that way, Father."

"Is this girl you've been dating Catholic?"

"No, Father, she's Jewish."

"Would she agree to raise your children Catholic if you decided to marry her?"

"I don't know, Father. We never talked about it. She agreed to use birth control so we could have sex in the future."

"Isn't she clever! Doesn't she know using birth control devices is a mortal sin each time the two of you have sex? You must stop dating that Jewish girl or you will end up burning in Hell for all eternity."

"I won't be seeing her again for a long time. Naomi won't be coming back to town until after she graduates."

"Thank God for that. What else is bothering you?"

"Earlier in the summer I was swimming nude in the pond with my friend, Neil," sighed Adam.

"Did you commit sexual acts together?"

"No, Father, we never did any of those things."

"Have you ever had sex with a male?"

"No, Father," said Adam, pausing. "But I was raped in our barn by my cousin, Kevin, when I was ten years old."

"Did you cooperate with him during the rape?"

"No, father, he forced me to do it by holding a knife to my throat. It only happened once in our barn," said Adam, informing him that some weeks later Kevin committed suicide after murdering Father Furstenberg.

"I remember the incidents. It was on the front page of the Kenosha News during the summer of 1951. I also knew Father Furstenberg. He was a friend of mine and a very holy man. It's unfortunate that he was accused falsely of being involved with Kevin before he was murdered."

"That's not true. Father Furstenberg was molesting Kevin ever since he was a little boy. That's why Kevin shot that priest and then killed himself."

"Let's not get into that right now," said Father Bernard. "I'm here to listen to your sins, not slanderous comments about the clergy. Continue with your confession."

Adam was perspiring when he finally told the priest about Neil nearly drowning in the pond and praying to God to spare his life.

"I promised God that I would become a priest if He saved Neil," said Adam.

"You did what?" asked Father Bernard. "You have been stacking up mortal sins for months, and now you tell me that you made a promise to God to become a priest!

"You haven't been living in the state of grace. You are a terrible sinner! If you died tonight you'd be cast into the fires of Hell for all eternity.

"Since you promised God to be a priest, you must keep your promise by practicing celibacy to prepare for the seminary. That means no more sex! You must reject every impure thought so that you don't become aroused and commit mortal sins.

"You are to stop painting pictures of your former girlfriend, Naomi, because she's the source of your evil thoughts, words, and actions. You are not to answer her letters or speak to her ever again on the phone! You must discipline yourself daily to prepare yourself for the priesthood, which means a life dedicated to celibacy.

"From now on I'll be your spiritual director. I want you to come to the rectory for guidance every Friday after school. We have been in this confessional together for an hour. Is there anything else that's bothering you?"

"No, Father," sobbed Adam. "I'm sorry for committing so many mortal sins."

"You must say three rosaries for your penance. In addition you are to recite a rosary every night before you go to bed until you are accepted into the seminary. Now make a good act of contrition."

When Adam finally left the confessional, he felt relieved

that he had told Father Bernard everything. The heavy anchor of fear, guilt, shame, and remorse had been lifted.

While Adam was kneeling in the pew praying the first decade of the rosary, he saw Father Bernard leave the confessional and genuflect. He approached Adam and put his hand on his shoulder.

"You've made a very good confession today. I would recommend that you leave St. Mary's after finishing the semester and go to St. Francis Seminary. I truly believe you will be safe there. We'll talk about this in detail next Friday after school in the rectory."

"Thank you, Father," said Adam, rising from the pew and trembling because the priest still hadn't removed his hand from his shoulder.

"I have to go now. May God bless you, my son. In nomine Patris, et Filii, et Spiritus Sancti. Amen," said Father Bernard, heading toward the sanctuary exit.

50

"I always pray to St. Francis because he called the sun his brother and the moon his sister."

Upon returning to his locker in the deserted hallway Adam filled his backpack with books. Since he had missed the bus, he began to walk down Highway 50 reciting his rosary. He continued praying after turning left and heading south down Cooper Road, startled by a car pulling onto the gravel across from him.

"Would you like a ride home?" asked Giovanni, putting his cigarette out in the ashtray.

"Sure, Dad," said Adam, relieved that it wasn't a police car. He entered the passenger side of the Plymouth and set down his backpack.

"Your mother told me about you going to the Halloween Dance and then down to the beach with Naomi. She was upset when she called me at the Alano Club."

"I shouldn't have gone out with her. It was wrong of me to be deceitful. Dad, I went to confession today and Father Bernard told me that I must keep my promise to God and become a priest."

"That's quite a commitment. It takes several years of training before being ordained," said Giovanni.

"I'm still in love with Naomi, but her parents are sending her to a Jewish boarding school in California until she finishes high school. Father Bernard told me that I

417

shouldn't write or phone her," he sobbed. "I'll probably never see her again."

"If it's God's will, maybe you and Naomi will get back together after you graduate from high school."

"I don't know if I'm doing God's will or not. I'm confused. Father Bernard wants me to go to St. Francis Seminary next semester. I'd rather move in with you and take the city bus to St. Mary's. I can't stand living with Mom on the farm. She's always complaining about you."

"Maybe it would do you good to get away for a semester to see if you really have a vocation to the priesthood and to sort out your feelings. When you decide to come back home, your mom and I might be living together again," said Giovanni, swerving into the driveway. "I've come to help your mother get ready for tomorrow's market at Columbus Park."

"Stop the car. I need to check the mail. Maybe I have a letter from Naomi. If I do, I won't read it. I'll have to tear it up," said Adam, dejected as he left the car.

He paused to watch his father go up the driveway. After checking the empty mail box, he strolled up the rutted driveway, shuffling through the ankle deep maple leaves.

Adam entered the porch and set down his backpack on the wicker love seat. He removed his portrait of Naomi from the easel and carried it up the narrow steps into the attic where he stored it among his other paintings.

Realizing he hadn't finished his third rosary, he went to the orchard where Crispy woke up and started barking beneath a pear tree loaded with ripe fruit.

The dog followed him around the orchard while he recited his prayers to the Blessed Mother, trying to reject his thoughts about Naomi. He felt tense and overwhelmed with guilt and shame.

Adam left the orchard, hurrying toward the sidewalk leading to the kitchen door. He saw his father in the garden picking sweet corn, although his grandma was coming through the gate carrying a half bushel of acorn squash.

"I'll help you with those," said Adam, reaching for the basket and setting it down at the spigot.

"Dio Mio, Adam. Why do you come home from school so late tonight?" asked his grandmother.

"I went to confession and stayed an hour talking with Father Bernard so I missed the bus and started to walk home. Dad stopped and gave me ride," he said, giving his grandma a hug and a kiss on the cheek.

"Deo gratias! I'm so happy you go to confession. I pray for you every day to a-the Blessed Mother. Without the Mother there is no Son."

"I had to say three rosaries for my penance," said Adam.

"You gotta pray to Mary because she makes plants and trees grow."

"I always pray to St. Francis because he called the sun his brother and the moon his sister," said Adam. "Grandma, I've decided to become a priest. I'm going to St. Francis Seminary next semester."

"Dio Mio, what's the matter with you, Adam? Those

419

priests don't keep their vows. Do you remember what that no good priest does to your cousin, Kevin? He was from that place in Milwaukee."

"Of course I remember him. Mrs. Solinsky came to our house with photographs of Kevin, lying naked on Father Furstenberg's bed," said Adam, disturbed by the memory.

"I tried to talk to Father Bernard in confession about what Kevin did to me in the barn when I was ten years old, but he wouldn't listen. He didn't believe that Father Furstenberg was guilty of molesting Kevin."

"That's why your cousin Kevin kills that no good priest in his bedroom with Uncle Pete's gun and then shoots himself," said Grandma.

"I've tried to forgive both of them, but I get really angry when I think about it," said Adam.

"Tell me why you change your mind about marrying Naomi? She's such a pretty girl."

"Father Bernard told me I must break up with her and keep my promise to become a priest because God saved Neil from drowning."

"If that's what he tells you to do, then you gotta keep your promise. But you go study someplace else, not St. Francis Seminary. That's where that no good priest friend of your mother studies."

"You mean Father Fortmann?"

"Dio Mio! The bad priests make lots of trouble for this family," said Grandma.

"You should have heard Dad when he came home drunk

after Mom left on the train with Marie to visit Father Fortmann in New York," said Adam.

"Do you think I'm deaf? Your father said Marie's not his daughter. But Giovanni doesn't tell the truth because Marie looks like him, not that no good priest. She got blue eyes like you. They come from your mother's side of a-the family, those Muellers," said Grandma.

"Did my mom really have a love affair with Father Fortmann?" asked Adam.

"I tell your mother not to go to that priest to confession, but she don't listen to me. She goes there late at night and comes home at three in the morning because she has lots of sins to confess."

"Where is Mom?" said Adam, his brow furrowed.

"She digs the potatoes for the market tomorrow," said Grandma, her brow furrowed.

"I've got to change my clothes," said Adam, heading into the house with Grandma shuffling after him.

His sister was sitting at the kitchen table drawing a picture for her father. "Adam, how do you spell Halloween?" she asked. "I'm making a card for Daddy, because he doesn't live here anymore."

He paused to spell the word, informing her that their father was in the garden picking sweet corn. Marie let out a shriek and darted out of the house with the card.

Adam brought in his backpack from the porch and went to change his clothes. He returned to the kitchen where Grandma was listening to the news.

This is Michael Schroeder from WLIP with the 5:00 pm news on Tuesday evening, October 30, 1956.

Since the presidential election is pending and will take place next Monday, President Eisenhower said, "Our Government's stockpile of farm surpluses climbed to $9 billion this year. The cost of storage alone is a million dollars a day---none of it goes to the farmers...

And this is Adlai Stevenson's speech. *"I want to talk to you about the farmers. They are in danger of being swallowed up by big corporations in alliance with big government...At home we can use the farm surpluses to launch a new food-stamp program for those in need."*

And now for the local news: *On Friday, October 19th numerous people testified at the trial of Mr. Clifford Gascoigne...The jury deliberated for almost two weeks before finding him innocent of the murder of Joyce Jacobsen...*

Some of her body parts were first discovered this past summer by two teenage boys, Adam Montanya and Neil O'Connor, who testified at the trial.

The death-bed confession of Mrs. Martha Jacobsen, witnessed by Mrs. Sophia Montanya and Mrs. Marjorie O'Connor, swayed the jury to acquit Mr. Gascoigne...

"The jury makes Mr. Gascoigne not guilty," sighed Grandma, turning off the radio and then reaching for her milk pails beneath the kitchen sink.

"I heard all of our names on the radio," said Adam, frowning. "Everyone will be talking about us at school tomorrow."

"I don't understand why Martha blames Mr. Gascoigne before she dies in the hospital," said Grandma.

"That might have been her way of getting even with him for taking Joyce away from her," said Adam. "Only God knows the truth about what really happened."

"If you want to know a-the truth, you ask a child or a drunk man," insisted Grandma. "Dio Mio! I go milk the cows now. Adam you go help your father and mother in the garden, then you come help me in the barn."

51

Upon leaving the bus, he was startled by a photographer taking snap shots of him.

On Wednesday, October 31st Adam woke up when his grandmother rattled the milk pails in the kitchen and then thundered down the back steps, followed by the screen door slamming.

He knew that she was heading to the barn to milk the cows. It seemed strange that she didn't bother to knock on his bedroom door to wake him up. Maybe she was still worried about what her friends at Our Lady of Mount Carmel Church would think about her testifying at Clifford Gascoigne's trial.

Adam leapt out of bed and got dressed in his work clothes. He knocked on the bathroom door, asking Karl if he could use the toilet.

"Sure," said Karl, combing his hair at the sink. "I'm ready to leave for school. You'd better hurry up or you'll miss your bus.

"I suppose everybody at Bradford will be asking me questions about the trial. Mom said that your name and Neil's were on the radio last night. You guys may be quoted in tonight's newspaper with Grandma and Mrs. O'Connor," said Karl splashing his face with Old Spice shaving lotion before leaving the bathroom.

"I hope not," said Adam, urinating and flushing the

toilet. He was worried about being questioned at school.

Adam washed his hands and face, darting out of the house. He paused as his brother drove away in the 1936 Nash that he had repaired earlier in the summer. Taking a deep breath, he dashed to the barn to get the oats to feed the chickens. After finishing his chores, he returned to the house to take a bath and get ready for school. Twenty minutes later he stood at the end of the driveway waiting for the bus to arrive.

The driver screeched the breaks and opened the door. All heads turned toward Adam hurrying to the back of the bus. The students were murmuring about his testimony at the trial of Clifford Gascoigne.

A few minutes later the driver turned right at the stop sign onto Cooper Road. After driving past Whittier School, he stopped the bus, waiting for Marlene and Annette to board. The sisters hurried down the aisle and sat together across from Adam.

"How are things going?" asked Marlene, noticing that he was slouched in his seat, staring out the window.

"I went to confession to Father Bernard yesterday and had to walk home because I missed the bus," said Adam.

"We were wondering what happened to you," said Marlene, sitting next to her sister.

"No one ever goes to Father Bernard to confession," said Annette. "We should have warned you. He takes students hostage and keeps them in the confessional for hours. He always invites the freshman boys with peroxided hair to go to confession after school in the rectory."

"He was a good friend of the priest who was murdered by your cousin, Kevin, some years ago," said Marlene.

"You mean Father Furstenberg?" asked Adam. "That bastard should have been put in jail."

"I hate to say this, Adam, but there are lots of rumors spreading around school about you and Naomi," said Marlene. "The guys you eat lunch with were asking me questions after homeroom because they know I ride the bus with you."

"I just ignore them," said Annette. "I never tell them anything about you."

"Look, there's Old Lady Jacobsen's house," shouted Jim, sitting in the front of the bus. He turned his head toward Adam. "That's where you and Neil found Joyce Jacobsen's arm and leg in the basement this summer."

"That's the place all right," said Adam.

"What was it like going into that spooky house?" asked Janet, closing her copy of *Gone with the Wind.*

"It was really disgusting," said Adam.

"Did you see Joyce's severed head?" asked Pete.

"No, the police found it in a barrel in Mr. Gascoigne's basement across the street over there," said Adam, pointing to the bungalow. "Ray Wilson and Fred Jacobsen identified it as Joyce's head in the lab downtown."

"What about all those other skeletons they found in the orchard?" asked Jim.

"If you want to know more about the skeletons, you'll

426

have to ask my friend, Neil. He accidently dug them up while burying a dead horse."

"Would you speak to our *Future Teachers of America Club*, about the trial? We meet after school on Thursday in Bell Hall," said Emma, smiling at Adam.

"I can't make it because I have to help my family with the chores after school."

"We'd like you speak to our *Mission Club* on Friday after school," said George. "We'll be wrapping bandages at Janet's house to send to missionaries in India. They work with people who have leprosy."

After refusing a second invitation to speak, Adam felt like a celebrity. He was surprised that the students on the bus were so interested in the trial since they had never spoken to him before except for a 'Hi' or 'Goodbye.'

Adam was relieved when the county bus came to a halt in front of St. Mary's. Upon leaving the bus, he was startled by a photographer taking multiple snapshots of him. It was Joe from his homeroom.

Adam followed Annette and Marlene toward the entrance, where they were stopped by reporters from the school newspaper and yearbook.

"We'd like to interview you about the Gascoigne trial," said Rita, the red headed editor of the newspaper. "Ralph told me that you and Neil O'Connor were at the trial. I was hoping you could give me his telephone number because he used to shovel snow for Mr. Gascoigne."

"I'd be glad to talk to you during my lunch hour and

give you Neil's number," said Adam.

"Neil's been dating Jennifer for quite a while now. She's Naomi's best friend," said Rita.

"Adam, I'm sorry about what I said to you yesterday during lunch," said Ralph, shaking hands with him. "It wasn't very Christian of me."

"I shouldn't have hit you," said Adam. "I was tense about going to confession."

"Maybe we could do an article about you and Naomi eloping to the circus," interrupted Joe, snapping a picture of Adam standing between Marlene and Annette.

"Ralph's the assistant editor of the newspaper and Joe's our photographer," said Rita. "That would be quite a story. Jennifer took pictures of you two dressed as clowns at the Halloween Party last week at St. Catherine's."

"We want to put them in the yearbook," said Joe, "along with the article about the circus."

"Jennifer took a lot of pictures of the elephants and tigers when the circus was in town for Labor Day weekend," added Ralph. "We can use them for the article."

"We'd better get going before we're late for homeroom," said Marlene, glancing at her watch.

"I've got some information that will surprise you. I'll tell you during lunch time in Bell Hall," said Adam.

"Tell us now," said Rita.

"I don't have time," said Adam, following Marlene and Annette down the steps into the high school.

While Adam was removing books from his backpack at

his locker, a group of students surrounded him asking him questions about the trial. He responded without going into a great deal of detail.

"Yes, the trial was tedious... I was shocked by the lies of the witnesses... Yes, my grandmother was a friend of Martha Gascoigne...Leona Fortunato actually had Joyce's hand in a jar...It's time for homeroom."

During mass that morning Adam prayed to God to help him forgive the guys who were harassing him during lunch the previous day. All eyes were focused upon him as he walked up the aisle to communion. Some of the students were whispering in their pews. After mass he went to his classes, where several of his teachers asked him to speak to the students about the trial for a few minutes.

By the time he went to Bell Hall for lunch, he had a short speech rehearsed for the school newspaper and yearbook reporters.

"How did you feel when you lifted the lids off the barrels in Martha Jacobsen's house and found Joyce's arm and then her leg?" asked Rita.

"It was very shocking because I saw Joyce's name engraved on the lid of the barrel. The letters were made with my wood burning set that I lent to Mrs. Jacobsen."

"In today's newspaper I read that you and Neil had explored Mrs. Jacobsen's basement more than once," said Rita, holding a microphone connected to a tape recorder.

Adam informed the students about finding the pig's head back in 1951, when he first explored Mrs. Jacobsen's

429

house with Neil.

While he was talking, numerous students crowded into Bell Hall to listen to his interview with Rita. Finally Sister Georgia got up from her desk, encouraging Rita and Adam to sit behind it to continue the interview.

Rita asked questions based upon the testimony of the witnesses quoted in the Kenosha News. After nearly forty minutes of answering questions, Adam felt weary from the interrogation.

"Let's wrap up this interview," said Sister Georgia. "You all need to get ready for your afternoon classes. The bell will be ringing in five minutes."

"Wait! I have a few questions to ask Adam before we leave. I'm writing an article about the *Star Crossed Lovers* running away with the circus disguised as clowns," requested Ralph.

"Naomi and I ran away with the circus because we planned to get married at the Parthenon in front of the statue of the goddess of Athena in Nashville, Tennessee. The Greek Temple was built there for the World's Fair at the turn of the century. Our plans never materialized because it wasn't God's will," said Adam.

"We all believe that you and Naomi are truly star crossed lovers," said Ralph. "Adam, do you have a comment about your future with Naomi?"

"The last time I saw Naomi was at the Halloween Party at St. Catherine's in Racine. I'm very sad, and I miss her a lot. I truly love her and even gave her a ring."

"Is it true that Naomi's parents sent her to California to live with her aunt over the summer, and they're sending her there again this Friday?" asked Ralph.

"Yes, it's true. I know that there are rumors that she was pregnant, which was not true when she went to California early in the summer and it's not true now," said Adam, sighing with relief.

"What is the truth about you and Naomi?" asked Ralph.

"The truth is that Naomi is going back to California to attend a Jewish boarding school. Her parents won't let her return to Kenosha until she graduates from high school."

"Do you intend to elope with her again as you did before?" asked Ralph. "There are rumors that you plan to meet her during Christmas vacation and run away with her to Mexico, where you'll be married by a Jesuit priest."

"Those rumors are false! The truth is I will be leaving St. Mary's at the end of the semester. I'm planning to transfer to St. Francis Seminary in January. I'll be going there to study so that I can become a priest," said Adam, hearing the crowd gasping and murmuring.

"What? You must be out of your mind," blurted Ralph, his jaw dropping as the bell rang, signaling that the lunch period was over.

"Maybe so," said Adam, heading toward the door.

The Serenity Prayer

O' Lord grant me the serenity
to accept the things I cannot change;
the courage to change the things I can,
and the wisdom to know the difference.

Reinhold Niebuhr (1892-1971)

Biographical Information

Dominic Cibrario (Nick) was born in Kenosha, Wisconsin, where he was raised on a small farm with his three brothers and sister. He attended local schools and graduated from Saint Joseph High in 1959. After three years of college, he joined the Peace Corps, where he taught school in Nepal. Upon returning to the states he attended a Jesuit Novitiate at Milford, Ohio for two years, finally completing a BA degree in English at UW-LaCrosse. After a year of graduate work at the University of Pennsylvania, he was hired to teach at William Horlick High, eventually obtaining his MS degree from the College of Racine.

Cibrario taught English and Latin. He took a sabbatical in 1976 and returned to Nepal, where he wrote the manuscript for his first novel, *The Pomelo Tree*. After coming back to Wisconsin, he married Geraldine James. They settled down in Racine, where they raised three children.

Upon retiring from teaching in 2000, Nick published *The Garden of Kathmandu Trilogy, Secrets on the Family Farm,* and *Murder in the Mountains.* In addition to writing, he studies Sanskrit, oil painting, and sculpture, exhibiting his work at local museums and galleries. For more information see **www.pomelotree.com**

Bibliography

1. Jewish Rituals: A Brief Introduction for Christians by Rabbi Kerry M. Olitzky and Rabbi Daniel Judson, Jewish Lights Publishing, Woodstock, Vermont, first printing 2005. Kosher pp.17-18

2. The Koren Mesorat Harav Siddur, The Berman Family Edition with commentary based upon the teachings of Rabbi Joseph B. Soloveitchik. Translation of the tefillot by Rabbi Lord Jonatha Sacks, Ou Press, Koren Publishers Jerusalem, First Hebrew/English Edition, 2001

3. Time: The Weekly News Magazine, July 2, 1956, The Presidency: All Up to Ike. p.9 Egypt: Moment of Victory p. 18; Israel: Walking Home p.19; Business Abroad; Stockbroker Stirke in Italy, p. 67; New Pictures; "Safari" and "The Great Locomotive Chase" p.76; Books: Intellectual Thriller---Colin Wilson's "The Outsider," p. 80; State of Business: Summer Strike (Steel) p.66; Bad Roads Are Picking Our Pockets (National Steel): Senator Carlson, pp.30-31.

434

4. Time: The Weekly News Magazine, June 18, 1957; National Affairs: The Presidency: What a Bellyache! Eisenhower's surgery pp 20-22 Religion: Heavyweight Bout...Catholic Priests p.94; Art: Josef Albers' Art Exhibit at Yale p.80; Milestones: Hiram Bingham's Obituary p83

5. The Unpanisads, Penguin Books Ltd. Baltimore, Maryland, 1965, Prayer of St. Francis, p.8 Juan Mascaro

6. Time: The Weekly Newsmagazine, July 19, 1956, The Doubtful Victory: George Walters p.12, Final Vote: p.13, Larbor: The Big Strike (Steel) p.14, Red China: Seductive Words p.25, Tibet: Wave of Rebellion, p.28, People: Gina Lolobrigida p.34,

7. Time: The Weekly News Magazine, July 25, 1955. Cinema: The Censors—"Blackboard Jungle," "Cat on a Hot Tin Roof," "Tea and Sympathy," and "The Shrike," p.87

8. Tibet: Lonely Planet Publications, Melbourne, Oakland, London, Paris---Bradley Mayhew, John Vincent Bellezza, Tony Wheeler, Chris Taylor, copyright 1999.

9. The Fourth Commandment: Remember the Sabbath Day, Francine Klagsbrun, Harmony

Books, New York, Copyright, 2002 pp. 1-248

10. Time: The Weekly News Magazine, July 30, 1956. Foreign News, Diplomacy, Accentuating the Negative, India, The Uncertain Bellwether, pp.15, 16, and 17.

11. Celebration: The Book of Jewish Festival, Consulting Editor, Naomi Black, E.P. Dutton, New York, copyright 1987, pp.1-153

12. In the Jewish Tradition: A Year of Food and Festivities, Judith B. Fellner, Smithmark, copyright 1995, pp.1-128

13. Roman Missal: Alterations And Additions To The Missal, Ordained by the Holy See to Come into Force January 1, 1961, Printed in Belgium, pp.651-732.

14. Time: The Weekly News Magazine, July 30, 1956. People: John Ringling North, p.31, Adolf Hitler's Sister, Paula Wolf, p.31, West Germany, The Undesirables, G.I. crimes, p.20, Medicine, Pins for Polio, p.32.

15. Time: The Weekly News Magazine, October 22, 1956, Religion: Sex & Censors—National Organization for Decent Literature, p.52

16. Time: The Weekly News Magazine, Sept. 10, 1956. Music, One Man Band...Don Elliot,

songs, "Making Whoopee," and "Moonlight in Vermont," p.59

17. **Time: The Weekly News Magazine, Oct. 8, 1956. National Affairs. "Ike on the Farm," p.20, "Adlai on the Farm," p.21

18. Time: The Weekly News Magazine, August 13, 1956, Sport, Willie's Luck p. 50

Made in the USA
Charleston, SC
22 September 2013